Praise for the novels of Candace Camp

"A truly enjoyable read." —*Publishers Weekly* on *Mesmerized*

"Fun...frothy...entertaining."
—*Smart Bitches, Trashy Books* on *His Wicked Charm*

"A smart, fun-filled romp." —*Publishers Weekly* on *Impetuous*

"Alex and Sabrina are a charming pair."
—*BookPage* on *His Sinful Touch*

"Those who have not discovered Camp's Mad Morelands
are in for a treat... Camp is a consummate storyteller whose
well-crafted prose and believable characterization ensure that
this intriguing mystery...will utterly enchant readers."
—*RT Book Reviews* on *His Sinful Touch*

"From its delicious beginning to its satisfying ending,
Camp's delectable [story] offers a double helping of
romance." —*Booklist* on *Mesmerized*

"[A] beautifully written charmer."
—*Publishers Weekly* on *The Marriage Wager*

"A clever mystery adds intrigue to this lively and gently
humorous tale, which simmers with well-handled sexual
tension." —*Library Journal* on *A Dangerous Man*

"Delightful." —*Publishers Weekly* on *The Wedding Challenge*

Also by Candace Camp

A Stonecliffe Novel

An Affair at Stonecliffe

The Mad Morelands

Mesmerized
Beyond Compare
Winterset
An Unexpected Pleasure
His Sinful Touch
His Wicked Charm
Her Scandalous Pursuit
His Improper Lady

The Aincourts

So Wild a Heart
The Hidden Heart
Secrets of the Heart

The Matchmaker Series

The Marriage Wager
The Bridal Quest
The Wedding Challenge
The Courtship Dance

An Independent Woman
A Dangerous Man

The Lost Heirs

A Stolen Heart
Promise Me Tomorrow
No Other Love

Suddenly
Scandalous
Impulse
Indiscreet
Impetuous
Swept Away

CANDACE CAMP

A ROGUE AT STONECLIFFE

CANARY STREET PRESS

CANARY
STREET
PRESS™

Recycling programs
for this product may
not exist in your area.

ISBN-13: 978-1-335-51310-6

A Rogue at Stonecliffe

For questions and comments about the quality of this book, please contact
us at CustomerService@Harlequin.com.

Canary Street Press
22 Adelaide St. West, 41st Floor
Toronto, Ontario M5H 4E3, Canada
CanaryStPress.com

Printed and bound in Barcelona, Spain by CPI Black Print

A special thanks to Alexzandra for being such a wonderful friend to Anastasia, and to Grandma Beth for sharing her love of Regency novels with Alexzandra. We wish nothing but the best for you both, as well as the newest reader in the family—no matter what type of books Norah grows up to like. May life be full of happily-ever-afters for all of you.

CHARACTER LIST

RUTHERFORD FAMILY

Sloane Rutherford—Son of Marcus, nephew of Thomas, cousin of Adam and Gil

Marcus Rutherford—Younger brother of Thomas Rutherford

Noelle Rutherford Thorne—Widow of Adam, mother of Gil, now wife of Carlisle Thorne

Gilbert (Gil) Rutherford—Current Earl of Drewsbury, five-year-old son of Adam and Noelle

Thomas Rutherford/Lord Drewsbury—Deceased, former Earl of Drewsbury

Adam Rutherford—Deceased, son of Thomas and Adeline

LOCKWOOD FAMILY

Annabeth Winfield—Granddaughter of Lady Lockwood, daughter of Martha and Hunter Winfield

Lady Lockwood—Mother of Adeline and Martha, grandmother of Annabeth

Adeline Lockwood Rutherford/Lady Drewsbury—Countess of Drewsbury, widow of Thomas Rutherford, daughter of Lady Lockwood, sister of Martha, aunt of Annabeth

Martha Winfield—Mother of Annabeth, daughter of Lady Lockwood, widow of Hunter Winfield, now wife of Lord Edgerton

Hunter Winfield—Deceased, Martha's first husband, Annabeth's father, friend of Sterling Lockwood

Sterling Lockwood—Deceased, son of Lady Lockwood, brother of Adeline and Martha, uncle of Annabeth

Petunia—Lady Lockwood's pet pug

Lord Edgerton—Martha's current husband, Annabeth's stepfather

OTHER RELATIONS

Nathan Dunbridge—Neighbor of the Rutherfords, close friend of Annabeth Winfield and Carlisle Thorne

Russell Feringham—Longtime friend of Hunter Winfield

Carlisle Thorne—Husband of Noelle, guardian of Gil, son of Horace Thorne, raised by Adeline and Thomas

Judy—Annabeth's maid

Harold Asquith—Sloane's former employer

Parker—Mob boss, Sloane's competitor

Priscilla and Timothy Haverstock—Childhood friends of Annabeth and Sloane

Sprague Haverstock—Deceased, close friend of Sloane, brother of Priscilla and Timothy

PROLOGUE

1810

SLOANE TACKED INTO the wind, then settled back, one hand on the rudder, and savored the moment. The sunlight sparkled on the water, and the ocean breeze cooled the heat of the summer day. The sky was blue, with puffy white clouds drifting by. His father was rusticating here at home, so Sloane didn't have to wonder whether he might even now be gambling away their house or running up his bill at some shop that was still foolish enough to extend Marcus's credit.

But what made it perfect was Annabeth, sitting on the bench across from him. The wind stirred her light brown hair, sending the freed curls dancing around her face, and the light shimmered on the blonder strands that were the result of days spent in the summer sun without her bonnet. A few summer freckles were sprinkled across her cheekbones, which made her mother scold and treat with cucumber poultices. Sloane wanted to kiss them.

But then, everything about Annabeth made Sloane want to kiss her. And it made his heart swell in his chest to know that she loved him—not as much as he loved her, for Sloane was certain no one could love him that much, but still, she loved him without reservation.

"I've loved you from the moment I saw you," he said,

for he could say anything to Annabeth, reveal any weakness, any flaw. She knew them all, had known them for thirteen years, and yet still she loved him.

She laughed now, turning her gaze from the ocean onto him. "You pulled my hair."

"You kicked me in the shin."

"Well, you'd knocked Nathan down. And for no reason."

"Isn't the fact that he is Nathan reason enough?"

Annabeth grimaced at him, but her voice was without heat as she said, "You are unfair to him."

Sloane made a scornful noise. "He's such a little gentleman. His clothes are always right for the occasion; his hair is never mussed; he always says the right thing."

"Most people consider those good things."

"He loves you."

"I love him, too." She said it with such platonic affection that Sloane couldn't claim too much jealousy. "But it's not the way I love you." A sensuous smile touched her lips.

That smile went through him as if she'd stroked him. It took little from her to fill him with desire; looking at her was enough to make heat surge in him. Kissing her was an almost unbearable delight, and when he held her in his arms...well, he wasn't sure what word, what phrase could describe how he felt... It was as if her warmth, her goodness, her beauty poured into him as well, chasing out all the anger and resentment and loneliness.

Annabeth shaded her eyes and looked at the sky. She sighed. "It's getting late. I must get back by teatime, or else Grandmother will quiz me."

Little as he wanted this time to end, Sloane began the

process of turning the boat. "How much longer is your grandmother going to visit?"

Annabeth chuckled. "That's exactly what Papa asked me this morning. Poor man, he's been almost living in his workshop since she arrived. The answer is, no one knows. She will leave whenever she wants to. She arrives with almost no warning and then one day will suddenly declare that she's leaving. I think she enjoys keeping everyone wondering."

"I'm sure she does. Every time I see her, I feel an almost uncontrollable urge to hide beneath a tea table. Apparently I am too bold, my hair too long, and my manner unpolished. Once, she told me that my eyes were too blue." Sloane paused. "I'm not sure what she expected me to do about that."

He didn't mention that Lady Lockwood would also frequently remind him of his father's faults—which he agreed with but would rather not hear discussed—and worse, warn him that he was likely to turn out the same way, a fear that had long lay buried deep within Sloane no matter how much he had shaped himself to be different.

"'The woman is a menace,'" Annabeth quoted. "That's what my father always says. But of course, poor Mama simply cowers before her. She cannot say no or argue. I am the only person who ever disagrees with Grandmother."

"Ah, but she won't beat you down. You are the person she loves—you and that damn silly dog, Petunia."

"I think she loves her children," Annabeth told him, and Sloane snorted. "No, really, she loves Adeline and Mama, and I think she adores Sterling."

"She has an odd way of showing it."

"That's true."

When the small boat drew near the shore, Sloane dropped anchor and waded through the water, carrying Annabeth.

"You don't have to carry me, you know," she told him, though she made no move to leave his arms. "I could tie up my skirts and wade through the water myself."

"While that would be a lovely sight, I'd rather carry you," he told her.

She smiled and snuggled against him. "I would, too."

They reached the beach, and Sloane let her down, her body sliding along his in a way that stirred his senses. She did not step away, and her arms curled around his neck, her face upturned to look into his. He couldn't look away from her. Wouldn't even if he could. He could drown in her clear green eyes, he thought, and have no desire to save himself.

Sloane bent his head and kissed Annabeth. Her mouth opened beneath his, her body pliant against his, and he lost himself in the kiss, lost himself in her. He wanted more, wanted so much more than kisses and caresses, wanted to sink into her, taking her fully and completely. To belong to her and her to him.

"Forever," he murmured as he lifted his mouth from hers and kissed his way down her throat.

His hunger for her lay always just beneath the surface, awakened to roaring by tasting her, touching her. But of course he could not satisfy that hunger. Annabeth would be willing, even eager; in the ways of the heart, she had a bright confidence that he did not. She believed love would overcome all obstacles, heal all wounds, that the world would treat her well, that if she wanted something enough, she could make it happen.

Sloane knew better. And he would not do anything that would dishonor Annabeth or cause her harm. He would wait no matter how much desire drove him.

Annabeth twined her hands through his hair and tugged. That little touch was enough to stir him, but when he lifted his head, she went on tiptoe to kiss him again, her mouth avid on his. Desire throbbed in him, and he slid one hand up to curve around her breast. Through the material of her dress, he could feel her nipple tighten, and she made a little noise that sent his passion soaring.

He lifted his head and pulled back slightly, his breath coming in pants. Sloane looked down into Annabeth's face, her eyes dreamy, her lips soft and red and faintly swollen, and he ached to kiss her again, to pull her down to the ground with him and explore her body.

Instead, he blew out a sharp breath and rested his forehead against hers. "Is it really four years till we can get married?"

With a notable lack of sympathy, she giggled. "I'm ready anytime for a trip to Gretna Green."

"You know I won't do that."

"I know. It's banns and all for you." She patted his chest. "I just like to tease you."

"Minx," he said with affection, smiling at her.

"And yet you want to marry me."

"I do."

"It's actually three years and ten months until I turn twenty-one."

"Ah. Well, that makes all the difference." He took her hand, and they started up the path again.

"But I'm sure Papa will consent to our marriage, so we needn't wait that long."

"I don't know. Your father is a pleasant man, but no father would see me as a good prospective husband. I have to be able to support you first."

"You mean smuggling doesn't pay you enough?"

"What?" he said innocently, sending her a sidelong look.

"You think I don't know? One of the grooms told me—thinking I knew, so don't accost him. Apparently he's in the same business."

Sloane half shrugged. "I go out in the boat sometimes to take the barrels from the ship. There's not enough money in that to live as you ought."

"And it would be rather unfortunate if my husband was sent to jail for smuggling."

"They'd have to catch me, first." He grinned cockily at her. "Anyway, I won't be doing it for long. I'm just building up money for a ship of my own." He shrugged. "Then I can—well, you know my dreams. I've blathered often enough to you about building a shipping business. Having a fleet of ships. Being rich enough to shower you with pearls and diamonds and whatever you want."

Annabeth smiled and squeezed his hand. "I don't need pearls and diamonds. Just you."

Sloane could tell that she wanted to say more, and he could guess what she wanted to say. "No, I'm not going to go begging to my uncle for the money to buy a ship."

"I'm sure the earl would be happy to help you. A loan to you, if you're too proud to take a gift."

"He wants to send me to Oxford. So I can be his solicitor or a clerk."

"Because he knows you're smart, and he wants to help you."

"You always think the best of people." He set his jaw. "But I'm not taking money from Drewsbury."

Annabeth didn't continue; she had doubtless known what his answer would be. They continued along the path, fingers intertwined, stopping now and then for a kiss, until they reached the copse of trees where they had tied Annabeth's horse. Sloane saddled the mare, and for a moment they stood there, not wanting to part.

"I can wait for you in the gardens tomorrow evening, if you can come out there."

"You could attend the party, you know," Annabeth said. "You don't have to lurk about in the garden to see me."

"With Lady Lockwood there? I think not."

"She doesn't dislike you." Annabeth laughed at the look of disbelief Sloane shot her. "Well, not more than any other person."

"I don't blame her for wanting you to marry a better man than I am. But I've no taste for being raked over the coals by her, either."

"Very well, you stubborn man. Of course I'll come. I'll slip away from the dance as soon as Grandmother has started playing whist."

She went on tiptoe to kiss him lightly, and he pulled her in for a deeper, longer kiss. Then he gave her a leg up onto her horse and stood watching her until she was out of sight, feeling, as always, the clutch of emptiness Annabeth left behind.

THERE WAS A man waiting in the entry hall when Sloane reached home. He checked his steps—the day had been too good to be ruined now by one of his father's creditors demanding money—but continued toward him. The chap wouldn't go away; they never did.

"Sloane Rutherford?" the man said.

"Yes." Sloane offered nothing more. He had long ago become adept at stony silence.

"My name is Harold Asquith."

Asquith didn't really look like a creditor—he had the air of a gentleman, not a tradesman or some ruffian they had sent to force the money out of his father. But neither did the man look like any of his father's friends, none of whom would have dressed in such sober clothes or looked so serious. Certainly he was no one Sloane had ever met before. It stirred his curiosity.

"Is there somewhere we can talk privately?" Asquith asked.

Sloane frowned, but his curiosity won out and he led the man down the hall to the small sitting room. He gestured toward one of the chairs as he closed the door behind him, then sat down on the sofa, slouching, legs stretched out and arms crossed in the pose that usually set the back up of any gentleman who wanted to lecture him.

"I understand you've a little business with Sam Redding," Asquith began.

"I don't know what you're talking about."

"Let's speak straightly, Mr. Rutherford. I know you help the local smugglers, so I know you're a man willing to take risks. One happy to make money."

"Do you have a point?"

"I have a proposition for you." Asquith leaned forward a little, his cool expression gaining a little animation. "I can provide you a ship."

"You want me to smuggle for you?" Sloane hadn't

known what to expect from this plain, sober—even a trifle priggish—looking man, but it certainly wasn't this.

"No, though smuggling is, of course, an excellent disguise, as well as profitable. Given your current association with Redding, I presume you have no moral qualms about that." Asquith paused. "What I require is a man with the means to travel unnoticed between here and France. To carry messages, say, or certain people, in and out of France. Even, perhaps, to accomplish a few tasks for me there."

"A spy?"

"In short, yes. Though, I prefer to call them my agents."

"Why would I want to do that?" Sloane asked flatly.

"One might hope you would feel some bit of patriotism, some loyalty to England. To the Crown."

"I don't give a tinker's damn about the Crown. And I'm not really sure that I care about England, either. Spying's a hanging offense."

"If you're caught, yes." Asquith looked at Sloane challengingly.

"If you're thinking to dare me into it, I stopped that sort of game as soon as I was old enough to have any sense."

"The ship would be yours, of course, free and clear. Whatever profits you made, and of course, you would receive compensation from the Foreign Office as well."

Temptation wriggled through Sloane. Money and a ship. A clear path to the wealth he wanted. The ability to support a wife, to give Annabeth the kind of life he wanted to, the opportunity to marry her far sooner than he'd dared to let himself hope.

"Still, money doesn't bring much comfort when you're dead."

"I have heard that a certain girl has caught your eye. That you're eager to marry her. But surely Miss Winfield—"

Sloane shot to his feet and loomed over the man. "Don't speak her name. Do you think I'd make her a smuggler's wife? A spy's widow?"

"No one need know what you do for a living. Smuggling is, after all, kept a secret."

"I sincerely hope you're not that naive, for England's sake, or else Napoleon will be riding down St. James before long. There would be rumors, suspicions. 'How did he suddenly get all that money? And why did he purchase a ship? And of course, he's always been wild. Lord Drewsbury despaired of him.' It would be an ongoing scandal, and Annabeth and her family would be the ones who suffered. Even worse if I was arrested and hanged."

"We can give the excisemen a nod."

Sloane snorted. "It wouldn't exactly be secret then, would it? On the other hand, I could be caught as a spy in France and executed there, and she wouldn't even know what happened. I'd never subject her to that kind of anxiety and unhappiness. Or to the kind of rumors and speculations that would abound after my disappearance. It's unthinkable."

"But if she—"

"Leave Annabeth out of this," Sloane thundered.

Asquith said nothing, his demeanor as calm as if Sloane had asked if he wanted tea. After a moment he said mildly, "That might be a bit difficult."

Sloane stared at the man, an icy tendril suddenly working its way up his spine. "What do you mean?"

"It would be difficult for her and her family to avoid a scandal if her father was arrested."

"Arrested!" Sloane dropped back down in his chair. Now his nerves were tingling all up and down him, the hairs on his arms and neck rising, signaling danger. He strove for a scornful tone. "What are you on about? Mr. Winfield—"

"Mr. Winfield is a spy."

"What?"

"He's working for the French."

Sloane gaped at him. "What?" He stood up again. "You're insane."

"No. He works in the government, you know."

"Yes, but he's not—what would he know?"

"Papers pass through his hands every day. They are inconsequential to most people—but they specify supplies, movements, a number of things very valuable to the enemy. And he is trusted by a more senior official, to whose office he has easy access. He's an affable man who everyone around him is happy to talk to and gossip with."

"But…but…" Sloane shoved his hand through his hair and began to pace. This was utterly inconceivable, but why else would this man be here? "Why? Why would Hunter Winfield spy for the enemy?"

"They say he's always short of money."

"I can't see that he's gained any sudden wealth."

"No, with him, I think it's blackmail."

"What could anyone blackmail him with?" Sloane asked.

"I'm not sure why he agreed in the first instance. It doesn't really matter. The fact is, Paris has whatever document he originally stole for them, and they have used that to make him hand over more information, more important information. The fact is, he's a threat to the nation."

"Annabeth—God, the scandal. Does it have to be revealed? Couldn't you just feed him false information?"

"We have been since we learned of his treachery. But if the French discovered he is a double agent, I would shudder to imagine—"

"Then stop him!" Sloane barked. "Make him resign his position."

"Perhaps we could...if the French no longer had that document to use against him. If some bold soul were to slip into the country and steal it..." Asquith paused, looking at him.

Sloane's eyebrows shot up. "Are you suggesting I do that?"

"I suppose it would depend on how bold you are. How much you wish to save Winfield and his family from scandal..."

"You're blackmailing me. If I get Hunter out of their clutches, then you won't reveal what Winfield did."

"There'd be no reason to."

"You son of a bitch. You're doing the same thing to me that the French did to her father."

Asquith stood up, and for the first time his cool gray eyes glimmered with emotion. "I am an Englishman. An Englishman who will do whatever is necessary to protect my country. It doesn't matter if you revile me, if you hate me. I will do my duty." He paused. "What I want to know is whether you will do the same because of your love for Miss Winfield."

"You know I will," Sloane said. "I will retrieve the document."

"And continue to work for your country?" Asquith added.

"Yes. But on one condition—you will make Hunter Winfield step down from his post."

"Very good, then. I will be in touch."

Sloane watched him leave, fury pouring through his veins. Damn Asquith and his duty. Damn Hunter Winfield for exposing Annabeth to such scandal. His dreams were crumbling before him. It wasn't a shipping empire Sloane really wanted, nor money. It was only Annabeth.

He had known, deep down, that something like this was inevitable. That life would somehow steal her from him. Annabeth was, had always been, beyond his touch. She was a woman who deserved a gentleman and a comfortable life, not the penniless heir of a second son.

There was no way to escape this trap. He had to do this to prevent her from being tainted by her father's treachery, scorned by everyone she knew. In order to do that, he had to become a man whom she could not marry. A rogue. A scoundrel. A criminal. The sort of man everyone had always said that he would turn out to be.

And he could not even tell her why. There was no way to explain it without revealing her beloved father's treachery. She adored Hunter, and it would break her heart to know what he had done. And what was the point of pulling Hunter out of the fire if it meant devastating Annabeth all the same?

A cold, deep sadness filled Sloane until he felt he would drown in it. To save the woman he loved, he would have to give her up.

CHAPTER ONE

1822

SLOANE RUTHERFORD WAS not a man who hesitated. He made his decisions, for good or ill, and he lived with them. But today he sat slouched at the breakfast table, food untouched, turning a note round and round in his hand, unable to make up his mind. Should he go to the wedding or not?

Actually there was no question whether he *should* do it; clearly he should not. The question was whether he *would.* The event itself didn't figure into his thoughts. While he was surprised and faintly pleased by the fact that Noelle had invited him, he held most of his own family in disregard...and they looked on him with even less liking. Estranged wasn't the word for his relationship with the Rutherfords. Shunned would be more like it.

So, no, he had no interest in the wedding itself, no reason to go, and normally he would have tossed the invitation in the ash can. But what drew him almost painfully to attend was precisely the thing that set up an equal ache of reluctance inside his chest: *she* would be there.

"Annabeth?" Marcus said from the doorway.

Sloane glanced up, startled, and scowled at his father.

"So you're reading minds now? One would think you would have done better at the card tables."

"Yes, wouldn't one?" Marcus replied amicably, and strolled across the room. "Sadly, it didn't seem to work that way. And your problem didn't take much intuition. It's written all over your face."

Marcus settled into a chair across from Sloane. Clad in his dressing gown and soft slippers, Marcus looked every inch the indolent aristocrat that he was—his luxurious white mane of hair combed back stylishly, his jaw smooth from his valet's shaving, and his dressing gown made of the richest brocade and cut to fit perfectly. Even if he looked somewhat more worn than his age from years of reckless living, he was still a handsome man.

Sloane wondered if his father might catch the eye of some wealthy widow who would take the man off his hands...but no, Marcus was equally banned from the *ton*—more because of Sloane's history than his own numerous vices.

"What are you doing up so early?" Sloane asked, ignoring Marcus's comments. "You usually don't stir from your room until ten or eleven."

"Unfortunately the only appointment Harriman had available was at the ungodly time of nine. It's quite difficult to get in to see him on such short notice."

"Ah, your tailor. That *would* be enough to pull you out of bed." Sloane's mouth quirked up. Marcus was still a peacock at his age. No doubt the bill the tailor sent Sloane would be enormous, but Sloane didn't mind. He'd far rather spend his money on his father's fashion than on some of Marcus's other habits.

"But I won't complain. I was lucky he was able to make room to see me."

"I expect he's grateful that I pay your bills on time, unlike most of his aristocratic clients," Sloane said dryly.

"And I'll have the entire afternoon to enjoy the prospect of the wedding," Marcus went on.

"A wedding?" Sloane asked skeptically. "You look forward to weddings?"

"Not everyone is as much of a hermit as you are. Some of us find social occasions agreeable."

"I'm not a hermit."

"Mmm, yes. No doubt that's why you spend so much time alone, brooding. Cornwall suits you perfectly." Marcus picked up the cup of tea the footman had just set before him and took a sip, his blue eyes twinkling with amusement. "But this wedding, I must admit, offers rather more entertainment than the usual one."

Sloane made no response. The last topic he wanted to discuss was this wedding.

But his father needed no reply. He went on, "For one thing, there is Noelle, the lovely bride herself, and the potential of gossip over her scandalous past."

"I can't see how running from Thorne is any scandal," Sloane interjected. "Anyone with sense would do so. I find it far stranger that she stopped."

Marcus chuckled. "Yes, he is a dull one, isn't he? But I suspect Noelle livens him up. Still, the wedding offers more excitement than that. Lady Lockwood can always be counted on to cause some sort of contretemps… though hopefully she will not bring her dog. Of course Lord Edgerton will be there. I believe he annoys her ladyship even more than her first son-in-law—who knows what barbs she will cast his way?" He paused, then added, "And just imagine the stir if you show up."

Sloane grunted and slid back from the table, standing. "Which is precisely why I am not going to the wedding."

"Of course not. That's why you haven't tossed out that invitation. Why you were sitting there mooning over it when I came in."

"I wasn't mooning over anything. I was just…" He trailed off his sentence with a grimace.

"You were just contemplating whether facing down your relatives outweighed the prospect of seeing Annabeth Winfield."

"I don't give a tinker's damn about facing my relatives."

"Ah…then it's whether seeing Annabeth is worth the pain."

"Don't be absurd." Sloane's voice held little conviction, and he turned away, walking over to the window. He crossed his arms and gazed out at the street below. A moment passed, and he said in a quiet voice, "It would be foolish to see her."

"No doubt." Marcus let out a sigh. "The foolish things are always the ones you most desire."

"I've done well enough not seeing her for eleven years." Being out of the country most of that time had helped. But even since he returned to England, Sloane had avoided Annabeth—well, maybe there was that one time when he first returned and he'd stood outside Lady Lockwood's house in the dark to get a glimpse of Annabeth coming down the front steps and getting into a carriage. With Nathan. Sloane's lips tightened at the thought.

It had come as something of a shock to see her at Stonecliffe two months ago. He had not realized that she and Lady Lockwood were visiting or he wouldn't have gone there.

But as he had stood in the entryway with Noelle and the others, a door had opened down the hall, and there she had been: her soft brown hair in a little disarray, her face faintly flushed from activity, carrying a basket full of flowers. And in the moment, he couldn't speak, couldn't move, could only stare. She was as lovely as ever. And he was as dumbstruck as ever.

He'd turned and left like someone had shot at him. He wasn't sure whether he even tossed a goodbye to Noelle and Carlisle. And bloody Nathan—of course he'd been there. That moment had disrupted Sloane's carefully nurtured indifference, and even after his heart stopped beating like a madman's and he'd reminded himself that he'd gotten over her years ago, he had not been able to keep his mind from going back to Annabeth time after time. Like a tongue returning to a bad tooth.

Behind him his father said, "Why do you continue like this? Why don't you go to see her, tell her how you feel?"

Sloane snorted. "I'd have to fight my way through the butler and probably Lady Lockwood, too, to talk to her."

"I've never known you to avoid a fight."

"Maybe not. But I can't fight Annabeth. And she's the one who hates me."

"How do you know that?" Marcus persisted. "She's never married in all this time. She has no money, of course, but a sweet, pretty girl like that? She's bound to have had plenty of offers."

"No doubt." Sloane's jaw tightened. "But that doesn't mean she's been pining after me. I broke her heart. I knew I was breaking her heart. And the fact that I broke mine as well wouldn't have made her feel any better or despise me any less."

"Why don't you tell her the truth?" His father's voice turned sharp, his usual affability gone. "Explain what you did. Why you did it. Tell her that bastard Asquith blackmailed you into it."

Sloane whirled, his eyes flashing. "I can't tell her that. The truth would cause her just as much pain now as it would have then. I knew when I did it that I was sacrificing her love for a lifetime. I just thought my lifetime wouldn't last very long."

Letting out a disgusted noise, Sloane started out of the room. Before he'd taken two steps, there was a furious pounding at the front door. Frowning, he turned toward it. The pounding continued, along with someone shouting his name. Sloane reached the entry hall just as the footman opened the door and began an indignant dressing-down of the boy before him.

But the boy on the doorstep paid no attention and shoved his way past the footman, calling again. "Mr. Rutherford!"

"Timmy." Sloane strode toward the door, alarm rising in him. "What is it? What the devil are—"

"It's the docks, sir. Mr. Haskell sent me. You've got to come quick. The new warehouse is on fire."

CHAPTER TWO

SLOANE TORE OUT of the house, not pausing to throw on a jacket. Timmy had the foresight to order the hack to wait, thank God. He jumped in, and the boy followed right behind him. The vehicle rattled off, the driver spurred by Sloane's promise of a double fare if he got to the warehouse quickly.

"What happened?" Sloane turned to the boy.

"I dunno, sir. 'Twas burning when I came to work, and Mr. Haskell sent me right off to tell you."

When Sloane arrived, the warehouse was almost fully ablaze, smoke boiling up from it. The insurance company's firefighters were there, as were several of Sloane's employees, doing their best to keep the fire from spreading to the buildings around it. It was clear that the warehouse itself could not be salvaged. As if to prove the point, the rear of the warehouse collapsed with a great crash. The front was still standing but obviously wouldn't remain that way for long.

Sloane started forward to help the others, but Haskell intercepted him. "Mr. Rutherford. I don't know how it happened. When I got here, it—"

"Who was on guard last night? Where is he?"

Haskell looked blank for an instant, then his face was washed with fear. "Baker! I forgot." He glanced all around them. "I don't know. I haven't seen him." He turned and looked toward the warehouse. "You don't think—"

"He's still inside?" Sloane asked grimly.

"Yes. I didn't think. I should have looked." Haskell turned his frightened gaze to Sloane, but Sloane was already running toward the building. Haskell followed, calling out, "Sir! Wait! It's too dangerous."

Sloane reached the nearest door of the warehouse. The heat was pouring off the place in waves, eating its way through the building. He jerked open the door and went inside. Smoke filled the air, and only yards away the flames were licking along the crates and walls.

Coughing, he pulled out his handkerchief to cover his mouth and nose and moved forward, looking all around. It was difficult to make out anything in the thick smoke. He stumbled across a crate and fell to his knees. And there, just feet away, lying partially behind another crate, were a man's legs.

Sloane scrambled over and grabbed the legs, pulling the man out from behind the crate. It was Baker, the guard. Sloane managed to pull him up to almost a sitting position so that he could get his own arms under the man's shoulders. Sloane was strong but Baker was large and, unconscious as he was, he felt doubly heavy. Sloane struggled to drag him backward while keeping track of the path behind them. He did his best to keep away from the flames, but even so his skin felt as if it were bubbling. Suddenly there was a large crack like the sound of a cannon and the fire surged toward them, running over Sloane's head along the roof and down the wall.

A second crack came, even louder than the first, and a roof beam crashed to the right of them, sparks flying out as it slammed into the ground. Embers rained down over them, burning little holes through Sloane's jacket and shirt to the skin beneath. The building let out another huge groan and crack, and Sloane staggered through the doorway as the walls gave way. With a great crash the building fell down behind them in a cascade of fire.

Haskell ran up to Sloane, Timmy by his side, and among the three of them, they carried Baker away from the roaring fire.

"It's him," Sloane said. "I'm fairly certain he's still breathing." He leaned over Baker, turning his head gently to one side. Blood was congealed on the side of his head and neck. Sloane brushed away soot and ashes. "He's been hit on the head."

"You think something fell on him?" Haskell asked, his tone skeptical.

"I doubt it. The wound's here, just above his ear," Sloane replied grimly. "More like someone bashed his head from the side." He turned to Timmy. "Fetch Dr. Borden. Tell him I sent you." He gave him an address, and Timmy hurried off.

"Come on." Sloane rose to his feet. "We'll discuss this later. They need all the help they can get with this fire."

The next two hours were a battle to keep the fire from engulfing the warehouse's neighbors, but the firefighters were able to keep the damage to the building next door down to one scorched wall.

By the time the fire died down to smoldering embers, Sloane's arms were aching from carrying buckets, and he was covered in soot and ash, his clothes dotted with holes where sparks had hit him. He left several men to keep the embers from flaring up again and pulled his foreman away from the crowd that had gathered to watch the excitement.

"How is Baker?"

"He came to, sir. The doctor cleaned up the wound and wrapped his head. He's got a giant headache, but he seems to still have his sense. I had Timmy see to it that he made it home to have a lie-down."

"Good." Sloane crossed his arms, studying the ruined building. "What was in the warehouse?"

"Silk, tea, hemp. Brandy. We just unloaded a ship yesterday."

"Nice fuel for a fire," Sloane said grimly.

"Yes, sir, I'd say so."

"With our watchman having been hit over the head, I'd say there's little chance it was an accident," Sloane went on. "I presume it was Parker. Apparently he thinks he can intimidate me into letting him take over the ship-yard."

"Has to be." Haskell nodded. "Bloody bastard. First he tipped off customs that the *Marie Claire* was carry-ing smuggled goods. Before that, there were the thefts at the other warehouse. And smashing up the tables at your club and the tavern. Brawling with your men."

"Yes, he's certainly determined to bring my part of the docks under his 'protection.' But the other incidents were minor compared to this. Arson, assaulting Baker… the lad could have died in that fire, unconscious as he was."

"It's worse," Haskell agreed. "And more personal-like, isn't it? Everybody knows you were proud of the new warehouse—I mean, it's your second and the first one you'd built yourself. Do you think he knew you were planning to move your office into it?"

"It wouldn't be hard to learn. Parker meant to offer insult as well as damage. The others I could shrug off.

I just hired extra guards. But this...this is more than a threat."

"He knows if he can bring you in, everyone else on the wharfs will follow. If you can't stop it, they know they haven't a chance in hell of standing up to him."

"Then it's a good thing I don't intend to give in to him, isn't it?" Sloane's smile was a fearsome thing. "We're going to hire even more guards, step up our patrols. Get Cole Agency. I'd like to get more information on this man."

"Nobody at the agency—out on jobs, I guess."

"Keep checking. I want plenty of men here and at the timber yard. Reliable, competent men. And I believe I may start keeping watch on the whole wharf, give the others some protection to keep them from giving in to him."

"Aye, sir. But you be careful. He's got it in for you. Hurting you personally would be the surest way of bringing you down."

"Trust me, I don't intend to be caught unaware."

Sloane spent the ride home sunk in thought, weighing choices and making plans. It was clear he and Parker were heading toward a direct confrontation. It had been inevitable since the moment Parker moved into this area, expanding his operations. The man ran various illegal enterprises from thievery to prostitution to crooked gambling dens, but perhaps his most successful endeavor was providing businesses with "protection" that they hadn't needed until his gang came along.

But Parker had met firm resistance to his operations in Sloane. This was his territory, his businesses, and his regular patrols had kept the entire wharf safe. Sloane wasn't about to let this ruffian turn the area into a dangerous spot, and he certainly wasn't going to give the man any sort of control over his property. Sloane Rutherford might be what others considered a scoundrel, but he sure as hell always took care of his own.

It was in this mood that he entered his house a few minutes later, slamming the door behind him and striding toward the staircase. His father appeared in the doorway of the drawing room, and Marcus's jaw dropped.

"Good Gad, boy," Marcus said, taking in Sloane's grimy face and clothes. "Have you become a chimney sweep?"

Sloane grimaced. "My new warehouse burned down."

"Oh, my."

Sloane started to walk on, then stopped and turned back to his father. "I think you better go back to the estate."

"What? Why? Surely you can't think that *I* had anything to do with that."

"Of course not. The thing is, there's a man who is orchestrating all this—there have been a number of smaller things before today. He's trying to extort money from me. Gain control of the docks. I don't intend to let him."

"But what does that have to do with me? I haven't done anything scandalous or lost money to anyone. I haven't gone gambling even once since we got here. That's two whole weeks."

"Yes, I know," Sloane said, struggling to keep any note of sarcasm from his voice. Given his father's nature, two weeks probably *was* an impressive amount of time. "It's just..."

"I promised you, and I intend to keep that promise.

So I won't be doing anything in the future that he can use against you, either."

"I know," Sloane repeated, even though he had his doubts about how long Marcus would continue his good behavior. "And I appreciate that. But I'm not talking about debts. It's your safety that concerns me."

"My safety?" Marcus goggled at him.

"Yes. Parker has escalated his attacks. I think he chose to destroy the warehouse because he knew I had a certain pride in it. But when he sees that I'm still not giving in to his demands, he'll realize he needs to use a bigger threat as leverage, someone whom I…who is important to me. That's why I want you out of London. Parker won't venture all the way to Cornwall."

"Well." Marcus raised his eyebrows a little. "I'm a bit surprised. Flattered, too, of course, that I would qualify as such."

"You're my father," Sloane ground out. "Surely you know I wouldn't want you hurt."

Marcus's mouth twitched at the corners. "Well, familial ties are not always enough to make one care."

Sloane scowled. "Are you saying that I'm like the earl?"

"Oh, goodness, no, you aren't so straitlaced. Anyway, that's not important." Marcus waved his hand as though to sweep away the topic. "The thing you need to think about is this—we both know there is someone in London who is far more important to you than I or anyone else."

Sloane's chest tightened as he took in the meaning of his father's words. "You mean Annabeth? She's not—that was—" When his father said nothing, just arched one eyebrow, he went on, "How could he know about Annabeth and me?"

Marcus shrugged. "People have long memories when it comes to gossip. And you must realize that what happened between you and Annabeth was spread about all over town."

Sloane simply stared at him for a long moment. He wanted to argue, to deny, but he could not. Was Annabeth in danger?

That settled it.

He was going to the wedding tonight.

CHAPTER THREE

ANNABETH GLANCED OVER at Nathan, standing on the other side of the groom. He smiled at her, and she felt that familiar little clench in her chest. She would never admit it to anyone, but sometimes she wondered if she had made the right decision. Not that it really made any difference—she would never break her promise.

Her gaze went back to Noelle and Carlisle at the altar, their faces shining with love. She knew how they felt; she'd once felt like that. She had come to realize that she probably never would again. But she wasn't going to think about that. She'd become quite good over the years at keeping her past locked up and out of mind. It was just this occasion that had brought back the memories.

That and seeing Sloane a few weeks ago at Stonecliffe. Dear God, what a miserable experience that had been. The shock of walking in and seeing him standing there…the stony expression on his face when he saw her…the way he'd turned around and left without even a word to her.

Annabeth had known he didn't love her. Certainly she no longer loved him; she'd stopped pining for him long ago. But somehow that abrupt, obvious dismissal had hurt. That was why she had thought of him far too often lately.

There was a rustle in the audience, a wave of move-

ment and faint murmurs, that made Annabeth turn to
look. And there in the doorway, as if her thoughts had
conjured him up, stood Sloane Rutherford.

Annabeth quickly turned her head away. What was he
doing here? He had made clear how he felt about his family. No wonder there had been that stir among the guests.

Annabeth was pleased that she managed to keep her
face emotionless, and she looked only at the bridal couple for the rest of the ceremony. She didn't even glance
across at Nathan, who she was sure was fuming.

By the time the vows ended and Noelle and Carlisle
turned to walk back up the aisle, Sloane was no longer
there. Annabeth let out a little sigh of relief. At least he
had kept his presence to a minimum.

Annabeth took Nathan's arm and followed the others
up the aisle, but they had barely made it to the back of
the church before the remainder of the guests were up
and surging toward the doors. Everyone was eager to
get a look at the notorious Sloane Rutherford.

"What the devil is *he* doing here?" Nathan muttered.

"Noelle did invite him," Annabeth said mildly.

"Yes, but no one believed he would *accept.*"

Annabeth glanced around. Standing at the top of the
church steps, she had a clear view now that the guests
were spreading out. "Well, it looks as though he's gone
now."

"Good riddance."

"*There* you are," a woman's voice trumpeted behind
them, and they turned.

"Hello, Grandmother." One would think Annabeth
and Nathan had been crouched behind a hedge, hiding
from her. Nathan probably would have liked to. Annabeth

smiled at the pleasant-looking man beside Lady Lockwood. "Uncle Russell."

Russell Feringham was not actually Annabeth's uncle, but he had been her father's best friend and a neighbor, and she had grown up regarding him as a member of the family. Polite and easygoing, he was one of the older unattached gentlemen whom her grandmother frequently bullied into escorting her to parties or the theater.

"Annabeth, my dear, you look radiant. It isn't nice, you know, to outshine the bride." Russell took her hand and made an elegant bow over it.

"What a bouncer," Annabeth laughed. "Everyone knows Noelle is the most beautiful woman in London."

"Now, now," he went on jovially. "Pardon me if I quibble with that. I daresay young Dunbridge here agrees with me."

"Indeed, sir," Nathan agreed. He turned to Annabeth's grandmother. "You're looking well this evening."

"Nonsense." The old woman thumped her cane on the stone step. "Haven't had a good night's sleep in ages. That cat keeps yowling out there every night and disturbing Petunia. One would think people would keep better control of their pets and not let them wander about waking up all of Mayfair."

"Mmm-hmm." Nathan kept his lips firmly shut.

"Indeed," Mr. Feringham agreed, a twinkle in his eye. "I have often noticed that cats haven't the slightest notion of polite behavior."

Lady Lockwood turned her gimlet gaze on him. "Don't think I don't know you're making a jest of the matter. You ought to be fetching your carriage. I'm too old to be standing about."

"Yes, my lady, there it is now." Feringham offered his arm to her.

"Come along, you two," Lady Lockwood commanded, and handed Annabeth her reticule. "I must have a free hand for my cane."

They started down the steps of the church to Mr. Feringham's elegant carriage. All the way down, Annabeth continued to cast little glances at the street around them. But Sloane was nowhere to be seen. Obviously he was still eager to avoid her.

It was the usual production to get Lady Lockwood into the carriage and comfortably settled. At least they didn't have the dog and her grandmother's bag of "necessities" to manage this time. In the interest of fashion, Lady Lockwood had left most of her nostrums and remedies behind, carrying in her reticule only her hartshorn—in case she might faint for the first time in her life—and her lorgnette—after all, one never knew when one might have to put down some upstart's pretension with a long look through the eyeglasses.

Once Lady Lockwood was settled, Nathan held out his hand to Annabeth. Annabeth took one last look around, even though she knew Sloane was gone, then took Nathan's hand and climbed into the carriage.

LADY DREWSBURY HAD bemoaned the short time she had had to arrange the wedding celebration at the Rutherford town house, but Annabeth could not see that it lacked anything. Flowers wound up through the posts of the staircase banister as far as one could see, and stood in large vases in the entry hall, where Noelle and Carlisle received their guests. The spacious assembly room at the rear of the house, which was rarely used, had been opened up and the furniture removed to turn it into a small ballroom. It was also lavishly decorated with greenery, ribbons, and great masses of flowers—how had Lady Drewsbury and Noelle managed to find so many flowers at this time of year?

"Mother," Lady Drewsbury greeted Lady Lockwood, with a stiff smile and a little wariness in her eyes. She knew better than to compliment her mother on her health, as Nathan had done earlier. "There are chairs all around the ballroom, so you'll be able to sit. Nathan, dear, why don't you show Lady Lockwood to the assembly room?"

"Humph." Lady Lockwood gave her daughter a withering look. "I know where the assembly room is, Adeline. I'm not in my dotage yet. And I have been sitting for the past hour."

"Well, yes, of course, I didn't…um…" Lady Drewsbury stumbled to a stop as Lady Lockwood moved on. With a little sigh of relief, she turned to Annabeth. "Annabeth, my love. And Nathan. Wasn't the ceremony lovely?"

"Hello, Aunt Adeline. Yes, it was very lovely."

Annabeth would never admit it to her own mother—who was clearly jealous of her sister's disposition that earned her friends everywhere she went—but Adeline had long been Annabeth's favorite relative. Indeed, she was a favorite of nearly everyone, as she was sweet-tempered and generous.

Her son, Adam, had been married to Noelle, and after Adam's tragic death, Noelle and their son, Gil, had come to live at the Rutherford estate, Stonecliffe, with Lady Drewsbury. Her grandson was the light of Adeline's life, and she was delighted that Noelle and Carlisle had decided to continue to live at Stonecliffe after their marriage.

"You and Nathan looked perfect up at the altar, too," Adeline went on, with a dimpling smile. "It won't be long until the two of you are there saying your vows. Have you settled on a date yet?"

"No. Grandmother is quite set on keeping our engagement a secret for a time. You know, to let all the stir about this wedding settle first."

"She's hoping Annabeth will see the folly of marrying me and call it off," Nathan explained.

"No, it's…" Annabeth looked at Nathan, his eyebrow cocked in disbelief, and gave up. "Yes, that is it exactly."

"But, darling, you are so perfect for each other," Adeline said.

"Apparently my mortgaged estate is not perfect enough," Nathan said dryly.

"Oh. Money." Her aunt shrugged off that annoying matter. "Love is what matters. And you mustn't let Mother rule your lives." She chuckled at the expression on their faces. "Yes, yes, I know, I'm giving you advice I don't follow myself. But you are stronger than I am. And you have your whole life in front of you."

"It won't do any harm to indulge her for a month or two," Annabeth said. "After a while she's bound to realize that I won't change my mind. And if she does not, well, we'll just go ahead without her blessing. But you know if we do, she will resent Nathan the rest of her days."

"Not that she's exactly fond of me now," Nathan put in with his easygoing smile.

"Oh, no, she quite likes you, dear," Adeline assured him.

"I'd hate to see her with someone she dislikes," Nathan replied. He shrugged. "I know how difficult it will be for Annabeth, living with Lady Lockwood. I've waited for years. I can manage to wait a bit longer."

They moved on to congratulate Noelle and Carlisle. Noelle's face was alight with happiness, and Carlisle looked smug, as if he'd managed to snare a prize before everyone else. As well he might. Noelle was a true beauty, with large blue eyes, golden hair, and skin like a rose petal. But she was also intelligent and resourceful—she had, after all, managed to elude Carlisle, perhaps the most persistent man Annabeth knew, for five years.

Lady Lockwood, having finished with her greetings to the newlyweds, turned to Nathan and gestured imperiously. He let out a groan under his breath and muttered, "I thought she didn't need my help. And where's Feringham slipped off to?"

Annabeth suppressed a smile. "He's had more practice at escorting Grandmother than you."

Nathan, of course, went forward to give Annabeth's grandmother his arm, and they moved at a majestic pace to the ballroom. Annabeth followed more slowly, pausing here and there to talk with an acquaintance. She reached the hall leading to the ballroom and stopped.

There he was.

Sloane Rutherford stood beside the door to the ballroom, leaning his shoulder against the wall, arms crossed, looking disreputable and handsome and seemingly ignoring the low murmurs and the glances that were shot at him. Annabeth's heart was suddenly pounding. She hadn't expected him to be here. The church was one thing, but not *here*, where he would be watched like a hawk, gossip flowing around him in a steady stream.

She should have guessed. Sloane never cared what anyone thought of him. He straightened, his lazy expression suddenly sharper, and he started toward her. Annabeth was aware of an urgent desire to flee. She couldn't speak to him, not now, in front of all these people. But for exactly the same reason, she could not flee; she refused to create more gossip by running away.

He stopped a polite distance from her. "Annabeth."

His voice was the same low, slightly husky tone that turned everything he said to her into something seductive. He looked much the same—the bright blue eyes, the midnight-dark hair thick and a little bit too long and shaggy to be fashionable, the chiseled jaw and cheekbones. There had always been a wildness to his good looks, and the new small scar on his chin and the addition of fine lines beside his eyes only added to that impression.

"Mr. Rutherford." She lifted her chin a little, her voice cool and formal.

"So I'm Mr. Rutherford now." His lips almost curved into a smile.

"What else would you be?"

"Nothing, I suppose." He cleared his throat. "I see Dunbridge is hanging about you, as usual. I was surprised to find you hadn't married him."

Sloane dares to talk to me about marrying? Anger lent steel to her voice, and she said pointedly, "It appears I am more steadfast in love than some, even when it is wholly undeserved."

"Ah, a direct hit." His tone was lightly amused, but

his eyes darkened, and Annabeth felt a certain satisfaction at seeing that she had at least nettled him.

"Fortunately I got over that weakness," she added, lifting her chin and narrowing her eyes.

His eyes sharpened. "You *are* engaged. To Dunbridge?"

"Yes. We haven't announced it yet, but…"

"Good Gad, Anna, you could surely do better than Dunbridge."

"Don't. Don't you dare say a word about Nathan. He is a good man—faithful, loyal, kind."

"Mmm. Just like any good hound."

"That's quite an improvement over a snake," Annabeth shot back.

Sloane's eyes widened, then he let out a short laugh. "I'd forgotten your temper. You never let it show to anyone but me."

"Because no one else angered me like you. Sloane, why are you here? What are you—"

"Rutherford." Nathan's voice was hard as he came up beside Sloane. "Annabeth, are you all right?"

"Yes, of course." Annabeth was acutely aware of the hush around them, the eyes riveted to the three of them.

Nathan turned to Sloane, his usually warm eyes snapping with anger. "How do you have the gall to show up here?"

"Oh, I have the gall to do far worse things than this," Sloane drawled in that lazy combination of amusement and contempt he always adopted around Nathan and Carlisle.

"I'm sure you do," Nathan responded. "But I will not have you disturbing Annabeth."

"Disturbing? Was I disturbing you, Anna?" His voice

caressed the shortened name only Sloane ever used with her, the name that spoke of familiarity and affection, even intimacy.

She narrowed her eyes at him. "No. Mr. Rutherford no longer has the power to disturb me." She turned to Nathan. "Please, don't make a scene. Everyone is watching us."

"No." Nathan lowered his voice. "*I* have no interest in stirring up scandal." He shot Sloane a venomous look.

"I would expect nothing else from you," Sloane told Nathan. He gave Annabeth a slight acquiescent bow of the head. "I will be perfectly respectable, I promise." He turned back to Nathan. "Though I must say, Dunbridge, you seem much more upset than is warranted for an undesirable guest at a wedding." He smiled in a patently false way guaranteed to be irritating. "One would almost think that you didn't trust your fiancée."

Nathan raised his eyebrows a fraction, then returned an equally insincere smile. "I trust Annabeth implicitly. It's you I don't trust."

"At least some of your instincts are close to the mark, then," Sloane said.

"Mr. Rutherford. I am so glad you came." The new bride swept in to join the tense trio before Annabeth could think of a cutting response. Noelle held the hand of a young boy. "Gil is very eager to say hello to you."

Sloane turned to her, his face softening a little. "Thank you, Mrs. Thorne. I was honored to be invited." His gaze went down to the boy who was impatiently tugging his hand from his mother's. "Hello, Lord Drewsbury."

Gil giggled and held out his hand to Sloane. "I remember you. You're my cousin. Mama says you're the only one I have."

"I suppose I am." Sloane squatted down beside him and shook the boy's hand. "And you are *my* only cousin as well. I guess that means we should stick together, eh?"

Gil beamed and nodded enthusiastically. "Do you want to see my new horse? It's upstairs."

Sloane's lips curled up in amusement, and he put on an awed face. "In your room! I envy you. I was never allowed to keep my pony in the house."

This reply sent Gil into a merry laugh. "No, silly. Not my pony. Thunder's at Stonecliffe. My, um…my wooden one. A…*cheval à bascule*. How do you say it?" He turned toward his mother.

But Sloane replied before Noelle could respond. "Your rocking horse? Oh, yes, I should very much like to see that."

"You can talk French?" Gil's eyes rounded.

"Some. And not in a long while. I'm afraid my skill is not up to yours."

Gil turned toward the others and said graciously, "You can come, too."

"I think Annabeth and Nathan will stay here with me," Noelle said easily.

Sloane gave Noelle a knowing look, but he was smiling and, taking the boy's hand, he walked away.

"I wasn't going to start a brawl at your wedding, Noelle," Nathan protested.

"Yes, well, I'm not as sure about Mr. Rutherford," Noelle said. "Besides, Gil is still rather enamored of the idea that he has a cousin." She looped her arm through Annabeth's. "And I haven't had a chance to have a good coze with Annabeth yet."

"That, I take it, is my cue to leave," Nathan said with

a smile. "Ladies." He sketched a little bow toward them and walked away.

Annabeth smiled at Nathan, but her eyes went to the staircase beyond them. Sloane was climbing the steps, Gil's hand in his, his head bent a little toward the boy. Gil was chattering away to him, now and then pausing to jump up a step instead of climb it. As he jumped, Sloane swooped Gil up to set him down several steps farther along. She could hear the boy's merry laughter even above the noise of the crowd.

A pain pierced Annabeth's chest, and she turned back quickly to face Noelle, pasting a smile on her face. "Thank you for that distraction."

Noelle studied her, a small frown creasing her forehead. "Are you all right?"

"Yes, I'm fine. Really. Sloane killed my love for him long ago. Seeing him doesn't hurt me anymore." Annabeth wasn't sure what seeing him aroused in her— Anger? Alarm? Nostalgia?—but it was not the pain that had sliced through her when he left her twelve years ago.

"Are you sure?" Noelle looked at her a little anxiously. "I didn't want to upset you by inviting him. I just—well, it seemed the right thing after he helped us protect Gil. And, frankly, I didn't think he would actually come."

"No doubt that's why he did," Annabeth replied dryly. "Don't worry about me. I hope he didn't put a damper on your enjoyment."

Noelle's face lit up. "Nothing could hinder my enjoyment. I am over the moon. I must sound like a rapturous fool, but today is perfect."

"Which is exactly how it should be," Annabeth told her. "You looked beautiful standing at the altar."

"It will be you standing there before long."

"Yes. Lady Drewsbury said the same to me." Annabeth smiled, knowing it did not shine with the brightness that radiated from her friend.

A small frown creased Noelle's forehead, and she looked at Annabeth searchingly. "Annabeth…is there anything wrong?" She steered Annabeth away from the other guests and into a small sitting room, closing the door behind her. "Are you and Nathan—I mean, are you having regrets? Did seeing Sloane—"

"No," Annabeth said firmly, shaking her head. "Sloane has nothing to do with it. Nathan and I are fine. There's nothing wrong. I, um, I suppose I am disheartened that my grandmother wants us to wait still."

Noelle crossed her arms, her face skeptical. "I don't think this is about your grandmother. You know, a vow you made when you thought Nathan was dying shouldn't rule the rest of your life. You were worried and distraught and not thinking clearly."

Noelle's words could hardly begin to describe Annabeth's feelings during those frantic hours by Nathan's bedside, tears streaming down her face, fearing each breath would be his last. They didn't touch on the awful guilt she had felt for refusing to marry him when she could have made the last few years of his life happy. The prayers tumbling from her mouth, the promises to do anything if only God would let Nathan live. The joy that had swept over her when he at last opened his eyes and murmured her name. She had felt so sure when she had held his hand to her face, laughing and crying and telling him to propose to her this one last time.

"No," she told Noelle, though Annabeth wasn't sure exactly what she was denying. "It woke me up. I realized how I was wasting his life and mine."

"If you don't love him—"

"But I do!" Annabeth insisted. "I do love Nathan. I've loved him for years and years."

"But do you love him the right way?"

"Is there a wrong way to love someone?" Annabeth turned away, rubbing her arms; she felt suddenly cold. "If you're asking if I love Nathan as I did Sloane, no, I don't love him in that wild, all-consuming way. I was so young and brimming with emotions then. I still believed that life would turn out exactly as I wanted, that anything was possible if your love was great enough. It was stunning and exhilarating at the time. And awful afterward."

"Great love doesn't have to be painful."

"Perhaps not, but I think it happens only once. As they say, it's the love of your life…and you can't expect to get another one just because that great love was a mistake. But I could still have a happy life. Even if it's not exactly the same, I love Nathan so much—I think I didn't realize how very dear he is to me until I almost lost him. He's a wonderful man, kind and thoughtful, smart and funny. Everything about him is just so…right. No one could possibly be a better husband or a better father."

"Yes, he will be a wonderful husband and father," Noelle agreed.

"In the past, when I turned down Nathan's proposals, I thought that he would find someone else, that my refusal would set him free to love another. But it didn't. All I ever did was cause him pain. Now he is so happy that it makes me smile just to look at him. And he will continue to be happy. I will be a good wife to him. We can have a good marriage."

"As long as you are happy, too. That's all I want for you."

"I am happy." Annabeth put a little more iron into her voice. "I will be."

CHAPTER FOUR

ANNABETH RETURNED TO the ballroom, her mind still on her conversation with Noelle. She looked around the room. There was no sign of Sloane, thank goodness. No doubt he'd left after visiting with Noelle's son. A smile touched her lips as she remembered Sloane crouching down to talk to Gil, answering him with all the gravity he would use with an adult. More, probably.

Annabeth's eyes fell on Lady Lockwood. Her grandmother and Russell Feringham were talking to Annabeth's mother, Martha, and Lord Edgerton. Annabeth could barely stand to talk to her mother's husband, but she couldn't avoid her all night just because of Edgerton. Pasting a smile on her face, Annabeth started toward them, but at that moment, Nathan joined her.

"I hope that smile is for me," he said lightly.

"Of course," she said with a twinge of guilt. But one didn't have to stand about thinking about one's fiancé all the time, surely. Noelle was wrong. "I really do love you."

Nathan looked somewhat taken aback but said only, "Um...as I do you."

Annabeth realized that her statement had come out oddly, and she hurried to say, "I was just talking to Noelle about what a good man you are. How kind and thoughtful."

"Kind and thoughtful." He heaved a dramatic sigh. "Alas. I would have hoped it was dashing and charming."

Annabeth laughed. "Well, dashing and charming are a given."

He grinned back at her. "What about handsome?"

"It goes without saying." It was so easy talking to Nathan. "Best of all, you are the man who is going to ask me to dance so I won't have to chat with Edgerton."

"Ah." Nathan glanced over at the small knot of people.

"I know I must seem terrible, but I know that Edgerton will lecture me all over again about going to clear out the rental house with only my maid along. And that will make Uncle Russell alarmed, and he will tell me *again* that I shouldn't overtax myself and he'd be glad to do the job for me."

"As would I. You are loved by many people."

"I know. And I appreciate that, I really do. But I enjoy going through Papa's old trunks. I like being at the house and remembering when we lived there, before Papa died and we had to lease it out."

Their home in London was held in trust for Annabeth, an arrangement set up by her grandfather. After her father died deeply in debt, she and her mother had been left so short of money that they had been forced to move in with her grandmother. The trustees then leased the place to provide Annabeth at least some small amount of income. However, the trust would end when she married, and she and Nathan planned to move into the house after the wedding.

"Still, perhaps I should go with you," Nathan said.

"That's very sweet of you, but I am the only one who can decide what to keep or throw away. And it would bore you." The truth was, Annabeth enjoyed being alone in the house, on her own, with no one to fuss or tell her what to do. "Besides, you'd have to be around my maid the whole time."

"Judy." Nathan scowled. "There's something wrong with that woman. She does not act like a normal maid. Some of the things she says…"

"Grandmother says she's too 'saucy.' But I think she actually rather likes Judy."

"Peas in a pod. Judy watches me like she thinks I'm about to pocket one of Lady Lockwood's figurines. Come to think of it, maybe your grandmother told her to do just that."

"You just don't like her because she doesn't make eyes at you like all the other maids."

"Not true," Nathan protested. "Do they really?"

Annabeth laughed. "Come on. They're starting up the quadrille."

They took their place in the dance, and Annabeth was able to push away all bothersome thoughts. She danced with Nathan again later in the evening. Nor did she lack for partners the rest of the time. She might be thoroughly on the shelf, but she was pretty and pleasant and a safe partner whom a gentleman could take out on the dance floor without being subjected to marriage-minded lasses and their mothers.

Later, flushed from exertion, she strolled out onto the small terrace behind the house to get a breath of air. She stood for a moment, relishing the cool air and the silence, and the rare chance in the city to be utterly alone.

Something moved in the shadows at the edge of the terrace. Annabeth turned, unalarmed. Somehow she knew it was him. "Sloane. What are you doing here?"

"Waiting for you to come outside."

"That seems a bit haphazard. How could you know I'd come onto the terrace?"

"I know you."

SHE WAS BEAUTIFUL here on the terrace, washed by the faint light from the ballroom. She was beautiful anywhere. Sloane knew that most would say that Noelle was the foremost beauty in the church today, but when Sloane stepped inside and saw Annabeth standing at the altar, it had struck him like a blow to the chest, and he had no eyes for the bride or anyone else. At the end of the ceremony, it had taken a force of will to turn around and leave the church without going to her.

"You always dance until you're hot and breathless," he said as he strolled toward her. "Then you want to escape the stuffy ballroom. Revel a bit in the quiet and solitude." Sloane stopped a few feet away. It would be dangerous to get too close. "Remember those dances at the Assembly Hall? How we'd meet on the terrace to escape all the eyes? So we could talk and—"

"I am well aware of what we did," Annabeth interrupted sharply.

Of course she remembered. The heat, the urgency, the stolen kisses, hanging on to their control by the thinnest of threads. Sloane shoved his hands into his pockets to keep himself from reaching out to touch her.

He took a step forward. Inside the ballroom, a waltz started. Annabeth looked away, but not before Sloane could see the way her face changed, remembered pleasure and regret mingling in her eyes. It was an old song, and they had danced to it often.

"Remember how you taught me to waltz?" He moved closer. "You would hum this song."

Annabeth still kept her gaze away from him, but she nodded slightly.

He pulled his hands from his pockets—those were clearly not restraint enough; perhaps with Annabeth, he required manacles—and held them out to her. "Dance with me, Anna? Just once. For old times' sake."

She looked up at him then. Unshed tears glimmered in her eyes, making his heart squeeze within his chest. She put her hand in his, and he swept her into the waltz. They circled the terrace, alone in the hushed night, moving as if in a world apart, a moment filled with sweetness and regret and the beauty of a time long gone. It would never return, but for now, this was enough to fill the emptiness.

All too soon, the music wound to a halt. They turned one last time and stopped. They were only inches apart; Sloane could feel the heat of Annabeth's body, see nothing but her. The scent of perfume filled his nostrils, sweet and intoxicating. He lowered his head toward hers, leaning in, and she began to stretch her body upward toward him.

Annabeth drew in a sharp little breath and whirled away, putting several feet between them. "What do you want from me? Why are you here, Sloane? Why do you keep popping up everywhere I go like some overgrown jack-in-the-box?"

She was right, of course. She always had been—ever the more cautious, reasonable one. Looking before she leaped. He had let his head overrule his heart only once. He forced himself to stay where he was, though everything in him told him to follow her and sweep her back in his arms.

"I beg your pardon," Sloane said stiffly. "That was

wrong of me." If only his body would agree. "I came here because I think you could be in danger."

Annabeth's jaw dropped. "In danger? Of what? If you're going to tell me that I shouldn't marry Nathan, I—"

"No." He brushed the idea aside. "You're in no danger from Nathan…except perhaps being bored to death."

"Sloane…" Annabeth crossed her arms, her eyes narrowing.

"I'm saying that someone might hurt you. Kidnap you. You're in danger. You and Lady Lockwood need to leave for a while, at least the next fortnight. You could go to Bath, say. Lady Lockwood would like that."

"I have no interest in going to Bath."

"Another place then. It doesn't matter where. This city is dangerous. You have to leave London."

"I don't have to do anything, least of all something you demand. I'll do as I please."

"So you plan to expose yourself to danger just because I don't want you to? Damn it, Annabeth, I can't protect you well enough here in the city."

"Protect me? You gave up any right to protect me long ago when you ran away."

"I didn't run away."

"Very well. When you *walked* away after you jilted me."

Sloane clamped his teeth together to hold back the rage that threatened to roar out of him. None of this was her fault. Even when it tore his heart out of his chest, it had never been her fault. He pushed down on the pointless, distracting emotions inside him; perhaps his layers of insulation were not as thick as he had thought.

His voice was calm as he began again. "It is my responsibility to make sure you come to no harm because it is *my* enemy who threatens you. There is a man who is trying to take over the docks, and I stand in his way. He has attacked my businesses in many small ways, and today he went so far as to burn down one of my warehouses. One of my employees was inside and could have burned to death. He's growing worse with each attack he throws against me. I will stop him, I promise you. But it may take me some time. And that is why I want you out of the city. I've already told my father to go back to Cornwall."

Annabeth frowned. "He sounds like a terrible man. But I still don't understand. Why would he try to do anything to *me*?"

"Because you are the one person I would do anything to keep from harm," he shot back.

Annabeth stared at him, the air between them suddenly charged with emotion. Sloane took a step forward, reaching instinctively for her, but she backed away from him. Her hands clenched into fists at her side. "What are you playing at, Sloane? Why are you pretending that I mean something to you? That you care what happens to me?"

"Of course I care about you. I've always cared about you." His temper was rising again. "How could you think—"

"If you had loved me, you wouldn't have left me!"

"I had to leave you! I had no choice!" He realized that he was slipping into dangerous territory. "I could not make you a smuggler's wife. It would have ruined you, damaged your family, made your life miserable. I wanted you to have a better life than I could provide for you."

"*You* decided. *You* thought it was best. You thought

only of yourself and what you wanted. You never asked me what *I* wanted."

"And what was that? For me to stay at home, being the Rutherfords' poor relation, beholden to my uncle for my education, for everything I had, an ordinary drone working for a family that pitied me? *That* was what you wanted?"

"What I wanted was *you*!" Her words vibrated between them, and for an instant neither of them could move or speak. Then she shook her head and stepped back, saying in a calmer voice, "I was young and very foolish. I didn't heed anyone's warnings. But I learned my lesson where you are concerned. The love I held for you died long ago, and whatever you are trying to do, I want no part of it. Just…stay away from me, Sloane. I don't ever want to see you again."

She whirled and rushed back into the house.

CHAPTER FIVE

ANNABETH BREATHED A sigh of relief when Feringham's carriage pulled up in front of Lady Lockwood's home. The rest of the evening had been excruciating—but at least she had developed a headache that convinced her grandmother to leave the party early.

As usual, it seemed to take a millennium for her grandmother to disembark from the carriage, complaining the entire time. Annabeth waited on the grassy strip beside the road while Russell helped Lady Lockwood down.

She saw a figure slip out of the shadows and down the steps to the servants' and tradesmen's door in the half basement. Annabeth could not see the woman's face because she wore a cloak with the hood pulled over her head. She wondered which of the serving girls was sneaking back into the house after a romantic tryst.

Russell saw Lady Lockwood and Annabeth to the front door then hurried back to his carriage, relief in every line of his face and form. Inside the hall, there was another lengthy process as the footman sought to help Lady Lockwood out of her cloak without getting hit by the woman's cane as she untied the garment and shoved it off. His endeavor was made even more torturous by the appearance of Petunia, Lady Lockwood's smushed-faced and poorly tempered dog, who felt the need to add her own screeches to Lady Lockwood's imperious and contradictory commands.

At the other end of the hall, the cloaked woman Annabeth had seen a moment before walked in from the serving area. She stopped when she saw Annabeth and her grandmother at the front door. The woman hesitated for a moment, then shrugged off the cloak and balled it up, sticking it behind an ornate chest.

Annabeth hid a smile. It was her maid, Judy, who had been out when she shouldn't be, which was no surprise when one thought about it. Judy was bold enough, and even in her drab servant's dress and overly large mobcap, she was pretty. She had a fox-shaped face and soft, fair skin, and her eyes were large and golden brown.

Judy walked toward them as if she had been in the hall, waiting for Annabeth's arrival. The footman, finally in possession of Lady Lockwood's cloak, retreated in relief. At that moment, the knocker on the front door pounded, startling them all.

"Who could that be at this hour?" Lady Lockwood demanded.

"I haven't the faintest idea," Annabeth said, though the first ridiculous thought that had flown into her head was that it was Sloane.

Judy swung open the door to reveal a man on the front stoop. She frowned. "Oh. It's you."

"Nathan?" Annabeth said in surprise. "What are you doing here?" She realized how rude her phrasing must sound. She should be happy to see her fiancé. Not… whatever she was feeling.

"A very good question," Lady Lockwood said over the barks that Petunia was emitting at enough volume to make her entire tiny body shake. "Arriving at all hours.

I must point out that we just saw you, Dunbridge. And you're keeping me from my bed."

"It's all right, Grandmother," Annabeth said. "You can go on to bed. I believe we've known Nathan long enough that you can trust him."

"I suppose I can." Lady Lockwood narrowed her eyes at Nathan. "As long as you two don't go gallivanting off alone."

"You have my word, Lady Lockwood," Nathan assured her solemnly. "There will be no gallivanting of any kind."

"I'll stay with them, ma'am." Judy crossed her arms over her chest, resembling a guard more than a maid.

Lady Lockwood nodded at this reassurance and stalked up the stairs, with Petunia following and playing a merry game of tug with Lady Lockwood's skirts that trailed behind her.

"Sorry," Nathan said to Annabeth. "I didn't mean to cause such a stir." He smiled in a way that warmed his eyes. It would be a very nice smile to grow old with, Annabeth reassured herself internally.

"Yuh might try not popping into people's houses at all hours of the night then, sir," Judy said. "It's not appropriate."

Nathan's mouth dropped open, and he quickly snapped it shut.

"It's fine, Judy," Annabeth said. "Why don't you take a seat down the hall? You can still see us from there, so we won't be alone."

"As yuh wish, miss." She gave a curt nod to Nathan and walked a few yards away.

"You see?" Nathan said in a hushed tone, casting a

long look down the hall. "She behaves quite strangely for a maid."

"I don't know if you're one to talk about other people behaving strangely," Annabeth pointed out with a smile. "What are you doing calling on me so late?"

"I just noticed that, um, you left your fan behind, and I thought I would return it." Nathan pulled the fan from his coat pocket and handed it to Annabeth a little sheepishly.

Annabeth thought she heard a snort of derision from Judy, who was still watching them like a hawk. Nathan glared at the maid. Annabeth also turned to look and saw Judy busying herself with straightening a candle-holder on a hall table.

"I also noticed that you seemed upset this evening," Nathan went on. "I know you said you had a headache, but I was worried that perhaps something else was wrong."

"Of course not." Annabeth's chest immediately clutched with guilt. She hated that her fight with Sloane had ruined Nathan's evening, too. But she couldn't explain the situation to him without it seeming more important than it was. "I really did just have a bad headache. That's probably why I was so forgetful as to leave this." She held up the fan.

Nathan looked unconvinced, but at that moment Judy gave a loud exaggerated yawn. Nathan rolled his eyes, but he said, "I should let you sleep then. Good night, Annabeth."

"Good night, Nathan." Annabeth managed to keep the smile pasted on until he left. Turning, she trudged up the stairs to her room, Judy following in her wake.

"Yuh look tired, miss," the maid said as she closed the door behind her.

"Not tired, really. I'm more…I don't know…angry or resentful or…it's just…he's so maddening! Why did he have to show up today?"

Judy looked puzzled as she came forward and began to undo the long line of fastenings down the back of Annabeth's dress. "Mr. Dunbridge, miss? It *is* a bit cheeky, coming over this late, but…"

"No, Sloane Rutherford," Annabeth said in a disgusted voice, dropping her fan onto the dressing table. She peeled the long gloves from her arms and tossed them down as well.

"Sloane Rutherford?" Judy's fingers stilled on her buttons, then quickly began again.

"Yes. Do you know him?" Annabeth asked.

"I, ah, well, it's none of me business, I know, but… um…some of the others… I'm sorry, miss, but, well I can't keep from 'earing…"

"About Sloane and me," Annabeth finished for her.

"I'm sorry, miss."

"You needn't apologize. Everyone knows that he jilted me and ran off to be a smuggler. It doesn't say much for one, does it, when your fiancé chooses a life of crime and spying over marriage to you?" Annabeth let out a little sigh and finished undressing. Pulling on her nightgown, she sat back down in front of the dressing table to unpin her hair.

Judy efficiently took over removing the hairpins. "I don't understand. I thought that 'is family had tossed 'im out. Why was 'e at the wedding?"

"He had an excuse. He told me I was 'in danger,' that I should go to Bath with Grandmother," Annabeth scoffed. "He said some person could hurt me to get at him. That is nonsense. We haven't been anything to each other for over a decade."

"Who is trying to get to 'im?"

"I don't know. Someone who wants to 'take over the docks.' I don't even know what that means. It sounded criminal. Everyone says Sloane's still a smuggler and engaged in all sorts of wicked activities, but I thought that now that he had money, he would have stopped doing illegal things." She grimaced. "Foolish of me, I know. Obviously I never saw him as he really was."

Judy paused and looked at Annabeth in the mirror. "Maybe 'e's right, miss. Yuh know, there *was* that break-in at that other 'ouse of yours the other day."

Two days earlier, when Annabeth and her maid had arrived at the rental house where they were working, they had been shocked to find that the place had been ransacked.

"But that wasn't dangerous. No one was hurt or threatened—the house was empty. It was a terrible mess, but that's all."

"Did yuh tell Mr. Rutherford about it?"

"No. He's the last person I'd tell." When Judy continued to look worried, Annabeth rose to her feet, alarmed. "You aren't going to tell my grandmother, are you? They all worry so about me. Ever since Sloane left, everyone has been so…careful about me. They act as if I were fragile, as if I might fall apart at any moment. They do it out of love, I know, but sometimes I feel as though I can scarcely breathe. I cannot talk freely to anyone but Noelle because they will worry and fuss."

"Yuh can talk to me, miss," Judy assured her, and Annabeth smiled faintly.

"Yes, I know. It's been nice going over to the rental house—being able to say what I want. Do what I like. If we tell my grandmother about the break-in, she'll insist I stay home."

"I'd not give yuh up to Lady Lockwood. I just thought, well, that Mr. Rutherford sounds like the kind of gent that could take care of that sort of thing."

"No doubt he could." Annabeth grimaced. "Maybe that's the reason for his little scene on the terrace tonight. He thought he could use it to worm his way back into my life—though I can't imagine why he would want to be in my life. But I won't allow it. Sloane means nothing but trouble, and I've done fine by myself all these years. I don't need him."

"'Course not," Judy said stoutly. "It's just...well, maybe 'e isn't scheming up something. Maybe 'e is worried about yuh. Maybe 'e still cares and is sorry."

Annabeth snorted derisively. "Sloane is never sorry about anything. Least of all leaving me. He did exactly what he wanted to do."

"Maybe 'e 'ad a reason, maybe—"

"Why, Judy." A smile quirked up a corner of Annabeth's mouth. "I had no idea you were such a romantic."

"Ah, miss, now don't go saying that." Judy grinned back at her. "Yuh'll spoil me reputation. It's 'ard-'earted, I am."

"Oh, yes, I can see that."

The subject of Sloane and danger was dropped as Judy tidied up the room for the night and turned down the bed. But as she left the room, Judy turned. "I could sleep on a cot in here tonight, miss. Just in case 'e's right."

Annabeth smiled. "Thank you, Judy, but I'm sure that won't be necessary. I'm perfectly safe."

CHAPTER SIX

THE NEXT DAY Annabeth's mind kept going back to Sloane and their conversation. She thought of all the things she should have said to him—the witty, acerbic comments that would have put him in his place, the angry words she should have told him when he left and which had, apparently, been stewing somewhere deep inside her all the years since. Despite her anger, she could not keep from also remembering their time together—the kisses and embraces, the thrill of seeing him, laughing with him, their dreams for the future, the certainty that their love would last a lifetime.

Finally, to stop her pointless, recirculating thoughts, she decided to take a book back to the circulating library and look for something new to read. She took her maid with her, as her grandmother insisted for propriety. Judy followed a few steps behind her, carrying the book.

Annabeth stopped and turned to her. "I hope you aren't planning to walk behind me all the way like an exceptionally boring parade."

"Ah, but it would be unseemly, miss, walking alongside yuh like a friend," Judy said in a tone somewhere between bantering and bitter.

"But you are also my friend. Aren't you?"

"'Course I am." Judy smiled. "But this'll please Lady Lockwood, and I'm in her black books right now."

Annabeth started to ask why, but she was interrupted by an old, rather battered carriage rattling down the street and stopping behind them. Annabeth glanced over curiously to see which of her grandmother's friends had come to call on her for gossip and tea. To her surprise, the door of the vehicle flew open, and two men erupted from it.

Judy jumped in front of Annabeth, shouting, "Back in the house!"

The maid flung the book she held at the larger man, hitting him in the groin. He let out a cry of pain, but before he'd even fallen to his knees, Judy had whipped out a knife from somewhere on her person. She faced the other man in a fighting stance. He pulled out a knife from beneath his jacket—did *everyone* besides Annabeth carry a knife while going about their daily business? The smaller man moved forward warily, keeping his eyes on Judy.

"Run!" she shouted to Annabeth.

Annabeth had been unable to move in the first few seconds—too astounded at the sight of Judy's wickedly sharp knife as much as at the men's sudden attack. But she snapped out of it now, saying, "And leave you out here alone? Not likely."

Annabeth ran around Judy and snatched up the fallen book. The man who had been hit by it was now struggling to his feet, and he started toward Judy to help his knife-wielding colleague. Clearly he considered Annabeth no threat. She swung the book with all her strength, bringing it down on the side of his head. He howled with pain and threw a punch at Annabeth, but she ducked, and his fist sailed over her head.

In the flurry of the first moments, their struggle had

been silent, but now Annabeth thought to scream for help. The man she had hit charged her. She fought him off as best she could, kicking and hitting and screaming. They staggered across the sidewalk, grappling.

Behind them, Judy and her opponent were dodging and feinting, circling each other slowly.

"Put that knife down, girlie. I don't wanna hurt you," Judy's opponent told her, panting for breath.

"Well, I *do* want to hurt you," Judy replied, sounding not at all like herself.

Her foot lashed out suddenly and slammed into his knee, and he stumbled, favoring his injured leg and shifting his weight to his other side. Judy jumped on his back, wrapped her legs around his waist and one arm around his neck, and sank her knife into his shoulder. He screamed and grabbed the wrist that held her knife, wrenching it away, and they whirled around and around in sort of a macabre dance, until finally they toppled over onto the ground. They rolled across the sidewalk and into the gutter, startling the horses and making them dance nervously.

Annabeth's attacker threw her back into the carriage. She hit the side of the open door and tumbled onto the floor of the vehicle. In the distance she heard a man shout. *Nathan?* Annabeth struggled back out of the carriage and saw Nathan running toward them. She called to him, but by then the two men had managed to overcome Judy and were dragging her limp body to the carriage. Annabeth jumped forward to block their way, and the larger one picked her up again and tossed her into the carriage once more, throwing Judy in atop her.

She heard the desperation in Nathan's voice as he called Annabeth's name again, and she knew he was still too far away to reach them. The two men jumped in as the driver yelled to his team. The open door swung crazily as they started off.

Nathan reached them and grabbed the edge of the door, holding on as the horses picked up speed. The smaller man kicked Nathan in the chest, knocking him back onto the street, where he hit the ground and rolled.

"Nathan!" Annabeth struggled to get up.

"Shut your mouth!" One of the men hit her in the side of the face and she fell back, knocking her head against the wall. She sank into darkness as the carriage thundered away.

SLOANE SAT AT his desk, a ledger open before him, his brow knotted in thought. He had had far too much trouble concentrating on business today. His mind kept straying to thoughts of Annabeth. The present and the past. The real and the imagined. What he might have said. What she might have done.

It was idiotic of course. He had put a guard on her house, which was all he could do. She didn't want him in her life. He would be a fool to try to be in it. With a sigh, he shoved those thoughts back down inside him and returned to his books.

The number of men he had been forced to hire to adequately patrol the docks was severely reducing his profit. The distillery was safe; he didn't think Parker would send someone to Scotland to attack it. The gambling clubs and the taverns were much weaker spots. He needed men there, too.

Rapid footsteps pounded up the metal stairs outside his office. *What the devil had happened now?* Just as he began to rise from his chair, the door burst open and

Nathan Dunbridge charged in. Sloane stared at him in astonishment.

"What the hell have you done with her, you bastard?" Nathan yelled, and launched himself over Sloane's desk, sending Sloane, chair, and Nathan all toppling onto the floor.

Nathan was atop him, and he got in a good jab to Sloane's jaw before Sloane could disentangle himself from the chair and punch his attacker in the kidney. Nathan flinched, shifting his weight, and Sloane shoved him aside and stood up.

"What the devil is the matter with you?"

"I'll kill you," was Nathan's only reply as he scrambled to his feet. "I'll kill you if you hurt her!"

He lunged at Sloane again, but Sloane was ready this time and he shifted back, grabbed Nathan's lapels, and used the man's momentum to fling him away. Nathan fell into a chair, knocking over a standing lamp as he went, and the glass globe shattered on the floor.

By this time, several of Sloane's employees had crowded into the room, and two of them grabbed Nathan by the arms, holding him still.

"What you want us to do with 'im?" one asked.

"I should probably tell you to toss him in the Thames," Sloane replied, pulling out a handkerchief and dabbing at the blood trickling down from his lip. "But I won't." He narrowed his eyes at Nathan, icy anger coating his voice. "I'm going to overlook that display because Annabeth loves you for some misbegotten reason. But you attack me again, and it'll be the last thing you ever do."

Nathan set his jaw and straightened, calmer now, though his eyes still blazed with fury. He tried to pull his arms from the holds of the men, and at Sloane's brief nod, they released him.

"What have you done with her? I won't bring you up before a magistrate or set the Bow Street Runners on you if you will just give her back to me."

Fear crawled up Sloane's spine, displacing anger. "Give who back?"

"As if you didn't know," Nathan snapped. "Annabeth, of course. I don't know what maggot got into your brain that you would think that kidnapping her would—"

"Annabeth? Annabeth was kidnapped?" Sloane took a long step forward and seized the lapels of Nathan's coat. "Stop your bloody blathering and tell me what happened. Who took her? Where? When?"

"You! Who else would it have been?"

"For God's sake." Sloane shook him. "Tell me who took her, and if you say 'you' again, I'll beat your bloody useless brains in!"

Nathan stared at him, the color draining from his face. "But…if it wasn't you—at least I thought you wouldn't harm her. But who—if it wasn't you who took her, who did?"

"I have a pretty good idea," Sloane said grimly. He released his grip on Nathan and moved over to the coat-rack to pull on his jacket. He jerked his head at his men. "You lot get back to work."

"Who is it?" Nathan asked. "Why would anyone abduct Annabeth?"

"To get at me." Sloane went around Nathan and out the door.

Nathan followed him down the stairs. "I'm coming with you."

"You're not," Sloane replied.

"Don't be an ass. You'll need help."

Sloane cast a sneering look over his shoulder. "You? What could you do to help? Dance with him? Explain the order of precedence? Tell him the proper way to address a duchess? You'd only get in my way."

"I'm not entirely useless, despite what you think. I have brains, for one thing, which is certainly something *you* could benefit from."

Sloane stopped at the bottom of the staircase and turned to face the other man. He sent an all-encompassing look up and down Nathan's trim, well-dressed figure. "Oh, yes, you're clearly someone who will strike terror into a mobsman's heart." He swung around, hurried through the warehouse and out the door.

Nathan followed, saying indignantly, "I can fight. I go to Cribb's parlor to box every week and—"

Sloane snorted. "So do half the young men in the *ton*, and drinking blue ruin while you watch two men fight doesn't make one dangerous."

"I knocked you down, didn't I?" Nathan shot back.

"A lucky punch. You caught me by surprise."

"Yes. And I will take anyone of your sort by surprise."

Sloane's steps hesitated for a moment, but then he walked on.

That didn't stop Nathan. "I was the best shot in my class at Eton."

"Do you have your gun with you?"

"No. I'm not in the habit of carrying my dueling pistols with me to make afternoon calls." Nathan paused. "Though it might be a good idea when calling on Lady Lockwood."

His words startled a bark of laughter from Sloane.

Nathan went on, "You aren't armed, either, I might point out."

"My reputation is a weapon," Sloane said, but he stopped and bent down to pull a knife from an inner sheath of his boot. He reached beneath his jacket and pulled a dagger from a scabbard at the back of his waist. An inner pocket of his jacket produced a small pistol.

Nathan stared at the array of weapons. "Well. I can see there must be many more people than I who'd like to kill you."

Sloane set his lips against another laugh and shoved the weapons back where they belonged. "I can't keep you from following me, but don't get in my way."

Sloane broke into a run.

CHAPTER SEVEN

As THEY RAN, Sloane whistled to one of his men standing watch and gestured to him to follow. The man also let out a sharp whistle and started after them.

"Where are we going?" Nathan asked, keeping pace with Sloane.

"To catch a hackney," Sloane replied. He relented a little and explained, "Parker's headquarters are across the river in Southwark."

As they ran, more whistles sounded among the warehouses, and by the time they hailed a carriage, four men were running after them. Sloane turned to yell to them, "Parker!"

He and Nathan jumped into the hackney, while the other men sought another one.

"I presume those fellows work for you?" Nathan asked, panting from the run.

Sloane nodded. "They guard my warehouses. The rest will remain there, in case this is a feint to draw us away so he can attack."

Nathan gaped at him. "This sounds like a war."

Sloane shrugged. "It's the way men like Parker work. Now, tell me what happened. Exactly."

"I was walking over to call on Annabeth. As I approached, I saw a carriage drive up and two ruffians jumped out. They grabbed Annabeth and her maid and threw them into the carriage."

"And you didn't try to stop them?"

"Of course I did!" Nathan said indignantly. "I was a long way from them. I ran, but I couldn't reach them before they rode off. Of course, I thought it was you."

"Of course." Sloane turned away, staring out the window, tapping his fingers restlessly on his leg. *Why the devil weren't they moving faster?* "I'd like to know where my man was while this was going on."

"Your man? What man?"

"The one I sent there to protect Annabeth. To watch their house and follow her when she went out. It was obvious she wasn't going to pay the slightest heed to what I told her."

"What did you tell her?"

"That she might be in danger, that Parker was trying to bull his way in, and I didn't know what he might do. I didn't really believe he'd go that far, but I wanted to know she was safely out of the way while I dealt with him. Williams is one of my best men. I can't think why he didn't come to her rescue."

"I saw no one else around. Admittedly, I wasn't really looking at anything but Annabeth and her maid struggling with them."

"The maid. I wonder why they took the maid, too."

"If you'd seen the way she was fighting, you wouldn't wonder. They couldn't take Annabeth without subduing her, too. I've never seen anything like it. She fought like a street brawler. It took both of them to knock her out." He winced a little, remembering the moment. "She's an odd duck, but I'm damnably glad she is with Annabeth right now. She clearly will do whatever she can to protect her. We must get her out as well."

"We will." The thought of Annabeth hurt or dying chilled him to the bone. "Parker will tell me where he's taken them. Even if it takes cutting him into very small pieces."

Nathan's eyes widened, his face paling a little.

Sloane smiled grimly. "Still sure you want in on it, Dunbridge?"

Nathan nodded without hesitation. "To save Annabeth, I'd do anything."

Sloane nodded sharply. "Then let's get to it."

He opened the door as the carriage rolled to a stop, and hopped down. Nathan followed, looking around at an obviously old and unused wharf. "There's nothing here."

"His place is this way." Sloane pointed to the east. "We'll walk the rest of the way. A couple of hackneys make too much noise. The longer he remains ignorant of my presence the better."

The hackney with Sloane's men rolled in behind them. Sloane looked back at them and held up three fingers, then turned and started forward.

"Don't you want to wait for them? Give them orders?"

"They know what to do."

"You already planned this?"

"It's one of the plans we discussed. I didn't expect to use it for this, but I knew that at some point, we were going to have to move against Parker."

Sloane sped up, carefully avoiding anything that might make noise, as well as possible traps. Buildings soon loomed ahead, and Sloane slowed to a walk when he reached the abandoned structures. He glanced all around for lookouts and guards, his ears open to the sound of the scuff of a heel, the squeak of a board, a whistled signal. He found none. Parker was apparently too confident in the remoteness of his location.

Sloane stopped in the shadow cast by an abandoned warehouse. In the distance were newer docks, but across a narrow alleyway from them was a brick building where a man stood beside the front door, leaning back against the wall, arms crossed, his gaze turned toward the active wharves, and his wooden baton hanging at his hip.

Sloane turned back. His four men were right behind them, and he gestured toward the guarded door and gave a sharp nod. As his men moved silently past them, Sloane pulled out the small pistol from inside his jacket and tossed it to Nathan. "Here. You better not have lied to me."

In front of them, Sloane's men broke into a run. He took off right behind them, and Nathan joined him. The guard at the door let out a shout and raised his baton, bracing to face his attackers. Sloane's men crossed the alleyway, roaring as they stormed up the steps.

But Sloane veered off, jerking his head at Nathan to follow him. He ran the length of the building and ducked behind it. There, at the rear, was a door. Sloane turned the handle, but it was locked. From another pocket, he whipped out his lock picks and set to work.

"What are you doing?" Nathan whispered.

"More ways to win than a front assault," Sloane whispered back. There was a satisfying click; Sloane turned the handle. He held a finger to his lips for silence, and moved stealthily through the door. Nathan followed, moving more quietly than Sloane would have thought, the door closing on a snick.

Sloane slipped along the wall to an open doorway where light spilled out into the hall. He could hear the muffled sound of the fighting at the front door, and a man's voice inside the room said, "What the hell?"

A chair scraped back, and just as a heavyset, scowling man reached the doorway, Sloane slammed into him, shoving him back into the office and up against the wall, knocking the breath from the man. Behind him, Sloane heard Nathan close the door and turn the lock.

Sloane pinned the man to the wall with an arm braced across his chest, and whipped out a slender sharp knife from his boot. Sloane pressed the point against the man's throat. "Where is she, Parker?"

"Who?" Parker's voice was gruff, but fear showed in the whites of his eyes. "Where's who?"

"I don't have time to waste here. Tell me where Annabeth is or you're a dead man."

"I don't know what you're talking about."

"Are you familiar with a stiletto, Parker?" Sloane's voice was almost conversational, but cold enough to freeze one's blood. "It's a nice little blade I picked up in New Orleans from an Italian. Italian assassins prefer it, I understand. It'll go through almost anything, but right here—" he lightly pressed the knife to the side of Parker's neck "—here, where your head and spine meet, it'll slide in slick as ice and you're dead in an instant. Or maybe just paralyzed for the rest of your life."

"I don't know!" Parker's brow was wet with sweat. "I swear to God. I don't know what you're talking about. I don't know where she is! I don't know *who* she is!"

"I'm losing patience with you." Sloane's nerves were roiling his stomach, a cold fear looming at the back of his mind.

"I'll do whatever you want. I'll pull out of the north side. It's all yours."

"That's good. Now all you have to do is tell me where she is."

"I don't know!" The last remaining shreds of Parker's composure were visibly breaking down. "I don't know who you're talking about!"

"Sloane…" Nathan said in a low voice. Sloane looked over at Nathan and saw his own doubts reflected in the other man's eyes. "I believe him."

Sloane turned back to Parker. "You better be telling me the truth. If I learn you had anything to do with taking her, I'll find you. No matter what you do or where you go, I'll find you. And you're a dead man."

Sloane brought his fist and the hilt of the knife down hard on Parker's head, and the man went limp, sliding to the floor. Sloane swung around and charged out of the room. The hallway was empty, sounds of the fight still echoing down the hall. He burst out the back door and around the side of the building.

He'd been chasing the wrong villain. He'd accomplished nothing. Even in his fury, he had believed Parker wouldn't kill Annabeth or harm her; she was his bargaining tool. There was no assurance like that now. It could be anyone; he had no idea who took her or where she might be or how to find her. Visions of Annabeth hurt and scared filled his mind.

Despair coursed through him, driving out the anger and nerves that had fueled him. He slumped against the wall, cursing.

Sloane had never felt so helpless. He'd been trapped before; he'd been caught; he'd been tossed in jail. But he had always been confident that he would find a way out of it. He would fight; he'd bluff; he'd find a way to slip through the cracks. But now…he had nothing.

No. That wasn't true. He had himself. He had his men and plenty of money. He had this fool beside him, for whatever that was worth—Nathan had held up better than Sloane had expected, little as he liked to admit it. There was always Lady Lockwood, who was never a force to be taken lightly. Sloane had friends in the government—or, at least, former colleagues—men who knew things, and he would have no hesitation in calling in those chips.

He levered away from the wall, willing out the terror of losing Annabeth that had gripped him. He couldn't acknowledge it; he refused to accept the possibility of a world without her. He put two fingers in his mouth and whistled two long blasts. Then he started toward the hackneys, his steps growing ever faster until he was in a trot, then running.

Behind him, his men emerged from the building. Two of Parker's men came out after them and whooped and called taunts from the building's door but did not chase them. Sloane and Nathan reached the waiting carriage and threw themselves inside, too winded to speak for a moment.

"I believed him," Nathan said finally.

Sloane nodded.

"But if he didn't take her…" Nathan's voice trailed off.

"Then how the hell do we find her?" Sloane finished.

Finally Nathan said, "I'm at a loss. I can't even think of where to start. It seems impossible to track down one old coach in this city."

"Yes. We'll go back to Lady Lockwood's house. We'll

question the servants and neighbors to see if we can find some sliver of information. Doubtful, of course, but we have to follow every possibility. If it wasn't my enemy who took her, then it must be a kidnapping for ransom, and Lady Lockwood will receive their demand at some point. We'll proceed from there."

Nathan nodded, and they rode along in silence. After a long moment, he asked, "Would you really have killed him back there?"

"No," Sloane said, and Nathan looked a little relieved. He went on, "You can't get information from a dead man."

"So you're not abstaining from murder because of any moral qualms then." Nathan smirked.

"Didn't you know I'm the bad seed? The twisted branch of the Rutherford family tree?"

"You don't have to convince me," Nathan told him. "I always knew you weren't good enough. Certainly not for Annabeth."

Sloane let out a soft grunt of amusement. Gazing out the window, he said, "You'll soon learn I have no moral qualms when Annabeth's safety is at stake. If Parker had killed her, he would be dead now, you can be assured of that." He turned to look at Nathan. "Wouldn't you kill him for Annabeth?"

Nathan frowned. "Yes, if it would save her. But… I hope I wouldn't be so cold-blooded about it. So heartless."

"Why, Nathan, I thought you knew," Sloane said flippantly. "I have no heart."

Nathan made an irritated noise. "You joke about it, of course. But I've known you since I could walk. You were always angry, always irritating and rude—"

"Careful, you'll turn my head," Sloane interjected.

Nathan ignored him. "But you weren't like this. The Sloane I knew wasn't cold and hardened like you. He wasn't someone who would spy for the enemy or lead a gang of ruffians."

Sloane lifted one shoulder negligently. "Yes, well, that Sloane died long ago."

CHAPTER EIGHT

ANNABETH WAS FIRST aware that she was lying on something hard. Slowly she floated to consciousness. She opened her eyes and saw a wall covered with dingy white, peeling paint. This was extremely odd. She was apparently lying on the floor. She began to sit up, and her head swam. She leaned against the wall, and that seemed to help. Her stomach settled down, and the wooziness in her head turned into a dull ache.

She slowly glanced around her. The room was bare save for a pail in the far corner, and a body was stretched out on the floor a couple of feet away from her. *Judy!* Annabeth crawled across the short distance and looked down at her maid. Judy's cheekbone was reddened and swollen. There were two or three more red marks on her arms, as well as one long, shallow cut.

Those men. Annabeth closed her eyes, remembering woozily drifting in and out of consciousness as someone carried her down the hall. The flickering light of a lantern. A scarred wooden floor and narrow hallway. He had been carrying her slung over his shoulder, and she had felt as if her head might burst from the blood rushing to it. Then he'd turned into a doorway and her head had hit the doorjamb—an accident, she thought, but it had knocked her out anyway.

Just like what happened in the carriage. Her memory

came drifting back—there'd been that carriage driving up and those men and a struggle. She glanced down; there were several reddened marks on her arms as well. But Judy had fought much more than she, and Annabeth remembered how limp Judy's body had been as the men carried her to the carriage.

"Judy," she whispered. If there was anyone lurking out in the hall, she didn't want them to hear anything. "Judy, wake up." She patted the woman's cheek and wished she had a vial of the smelling salts her grandmother always carried with her.

Her thoughts went to Nathan. How badly was he hurt? She gritted her teeth in anger as she remembered the man kicking him in the chest and Nathan falling onto the street. She had to find out how he was.

She continued to say her maid's name and pat her cheek, even shake her a bit, and finally Judy's eyes opened and she looked at Annabeth, her gaze cloudy and vague. "Judy. Wake up. I know you're hurt, but I think we need to be alert and ready to…well, to do something."

"Bleeding hell," Judy murmured, her hands going to her head. Her eyes cleared a bit. "Miss," she said in faint alarm. Under her breath she said another word that Annabeth had never heard before, but she didn't think it was complimentary. Judy groaned, closing her eyes again. "Me 'ead."

"Yes. I'm so very sorry. They hit you. Your cheek is swollen and red. I think you might have a nasty bruise there."

"It's not me cheek. It's the back of me 'ead." She turned her head to the side, and Annabeth looked more closely.

"Ooh. You have a big knot there. But I don't think it's bleeding."

"Bloody bastards." Judy grimaced.

"Do you want to sit up?" Annabeth offered her a hand to pull her up.

"No." Judy sighed and put her hand in Annabeth's. "But I 'ave to."

Annabeth pulled, and Judy pushed herself up with her other hand. Judy looked very pale, but she remained upright. One of her sleeves was half torn off. Her white maid's mobcap had come off in the struggle, and her brown hair hung all around her shoulders. It made Judy look somehow different.

Annabeth felt sure she looked different, too. Her bonnet had been knocked off, and her hair was straggling down here and there. There was dust all over her skirts. Her cheek stung where the man had slapped her. She wondered if her face was going to swell and bruise like Judy's.

The other woman gazed all around the room. "Not much of a spot, is it, miss?"

"No. I'd be very happy to leave it."

"Then I guess we'll 'ave to see what we can do about that."

The two women helped each other to their feet. Judy went over to the door and knelt down to examine the keyhole. She reached up to the crown of her head. "Curse it."

"What is it? Can I help?"

"No," Judy replied, digging through her hair. "Just looking for me picks. Aha!" She fumbled at the neck of her dress and pulled out two little metal rods. "I carry them in me bun, yuh see, and I was afraid I lost them. But they just fell down into me dress. Lucky, that."

Nathan was right, Annabeth thought as she watched Judy work at the lock. Judy was an unusual maid, indeed. "You're awfully good at this."

Judy's grin was almost back to normal. "Aye, I am."

"How do you—were you a thief before you became a maid?"

Judy glanced back at Annabeth over her shoulder. "I might 'ave taken a few things before. But I gave up me old life. Went into respectable work."

"I see."

Judy grinned at Annabeth. "Don't worry. I never took anything from your place."

"I didn't think you had," Annabeth assured her.

There was a clink outside the door as a key fell out of the lock, followed by a click, and Judy turned the handle of the door. She opened it a narrow slit, and Annabeth crowded in to look. It was the tight corridor of rough planks she had remembered seeing as she was carried. And it was empty and silent as a grave.

Carefully Judy opened the door just enough to peer down the hall the other way. "No one." She opened the door more and slipped out into the hall, looking up and down it carefully. Finally she nodded in one direction, whispering, "This way."

She bent to pick up the key lying on the floor.

"Why are you doing that?" Annabeth asked softly.

"Yuh never know when something might be useful. Quietly now." She started down the hall, sticking close to the wall, moving almost silently.

Annabeth followed her, her own half boots making little noise as well. They reached a set of stairs and crept down it. One of the steps creaked, and Judy stepped back, waiting for a moment. When nothing happened, she carefully skirted that spot and continued down the stairs. At the bottom was a similar hallway, and at one end was a door.

They exchanged a look and started toward the door, but the sound of men's voices in a room ahead stopped them. They paused. The voices inside the room rose angrily.

"—the two of them. He's going to kill us. He only wanted the one. Why the hell did you bring the other one, too?"

"It's not my fault! She wouldn't quit."

The women began to back up. The door to the room was open. They'd never get past without the men seeing them. Judy pointed back the way they'd come. On the other side of the stairs, at the end of the hallway, there was an intersecting corridor. They slipped back down the hallway and turned the corner. It was a longer corridor, with only a wall at the end. There were open doorways on the right-hand side, except for one closed at the very end, but no doors on the left.

They ran as fast as they could without making any noise, glancing back now and then to see if they were being pursued. The door at the end was sturdy and locked. It might, of course, only open into another room, where they would be trapped. But the lack of rooms on the left indicated that it was an outer wall of the building, as did the lock on the door. And, really, what other choice did they have?

"Can you pick the lock?" Annabeth whispered. There was a sentence she'd never thought she'd utter.

"Yes, but this might be quicker." Judy reached into

the pocket of her skirt and pulled out the key from their room upstairs. She slid it into the keyhole and twisted. It took some effort and let out a little squeak, but it clicked open.

Judy peeked out, then swung the door open. Across a narrow street was the wall of another building. With a last look behind her, Annabeth followed Judy out, and they closed the door quietly. Judy paused to relock it and slipped the key into her pocket.

"How did you know that key would fit an outside door?" Annabeth whispered in astonishment as they ran down the street away from the house.

Judy shook her head. "I just know 'ow cheeseparing and lazy people are. And incautious. Cheaper and easier to 'ave the same locks and one key to open them all." She gave a little shrug and slowed down as they reached the intersection of another street.

They looked carefully up and down the cross street. It was a narrow lane with a general air of dilapidation, the buildings old and grimy. They were clearly not in Mayfair anymore. Judy turned to the right and walked briskly down the street, avoiding looking straight at anyone.

"Why did you go this way?" Annabeth asked. She was certainly getting an unusual education from her maid. But it was probably more useful, she thought, than the time she'd spent learning to walk like a lady.

Judy shrugged. "We got to get as far away from that building as we can. They'll come looking for us."

"People will remember us. We must look a fright."

Judy looked down at her dress, dusty and torn. "Aye, well. This isn't a place that's shocked by anything. Nor a place where people are likely to gabble...unless they offer some coins."

They continued to walk at a rapid pace, frequently turning onto different streets until Annabeth was completely lost. Hopefully their erratic course would throw off their pursuers as well. Her chest was tight, the palms of her hands sweaty. Judy, on the other hand, looked completely calm and alert, unobtrusively checking the streets and the people around them.

Annabeth wondered what sort of life Judy had lived before this and how she'd come to take a job as a servant. She was obviously quite accustomed to streets like this, which Annabeth, for all her years in London, had never seen.

They finally reached a larger street, and the buildings became interspersed with better ones. Then, in the distance, Annabeth spotted the dome of St. Paul's, and her heart lightened. But it wasn't until Judy hailed a hackney and it stopped for them that she was able to relax and for the first time think about something other than getting away.

"Why did they kidnap us?" Annabeth asked Judy as the hack rolled along.

"I 'ave no idea. It sounded like they were supposed to only grab you. Maybe they were looking for your grandma to pay them money. Or maybe..." She cast a look at Annabeth.

"Or maybe Sloane was right," Annabeth finished, sighing. "I should have listened to him, but it seemed so silly, and I—well, he's someone I cannot trust anymore." She paused, gazing out the window, then said, "Do you think it's the same people who broke into my town house the other day?"

"I don't know, miss. It doesn't seem like it—I mean,

breaking into a 'ouse and messing it up is a far cry from abducting a lady."

"But it's awfully coincidental, don't you think, the two of them happening so close together?"

"Yes." Judy nodded, frowning. "I can't figure it out."

When the hackney rolled to a stop in front of Lady Lockwood's house, Annabeth was so happy that she almost cried. As soon as the vehicle stopped, she jumped down from it and ran up the steps through the front door. Judy was right behind her. The hackney driver roared in protest.

The footman inside the house whirled around at the sound of the front door opening. "Miss Winfield! You're alive."

"Yes, Harris. I am. Will you pay the hackney driver, please?"

He jumped to intercept the coachman, who was charging up the steps. Annabeth and Judy hurried down the hall toward the sound of raised voices.

"Don't just stand there, man, do something!" Lady Lockwood demanded.

"Believe me, I would like to!" Sloane's voice cut through the air.

Annabeth checked her steps for an instant, then went on.

"Please, Lady Lockwood, why don't you sit down?" Nathan coaxed.

"If I had any idea where she is, I would be there right now," Sloane went on. "I have talked—"

"*We* have talked—" Nathan inserted.

"*We* have talked to every blasted servant and resident or passerby, and no one saw anything."

Annabeth and Judy paused at the doorway, their steps

covered up by the angry voices. Lady Lockwood was standing in front of her chair, glaring at Sloane, and he was glaring back. Nathan hovered beside Lady Lockwood, trying to take her arm to ease her down into the chair. Petunia had wisely retreated to the farthest corner of the room under a low table.

"*You're* the one who consorts with ruffians and scoundrels," Lady Lockwood said, pointing her cane at Sloane. "Go ask your friends where my granddaughter is." The old woman's voice wobbled on her words. "Oh, do stop fluttering around me, Nathan. I don't want to sit down." She marked her words with a thump of her cane.

Annabeth stared. She had never seen Sloane looking like this, his jacket and neckcloth rumpled and twisted, his hair sticking up wildly here and there as if he had been running his hands through it, his face stamped with…could that possibly be *fear*?

Annabeth tried to speak, but was drowned out by the loud voices of the others. Judy put two fingers to her mouth and emitted a piercing whistle. Everyone in the room jumped and whirled, suddenly silent.

"Annabeth…" Sloane's face cleared, his whole body sagging in relief, and he took a few steps toward her, then drew up short as Nathan rushed over.

"Annabeth, darling, are you all right?" Nathan pulled her into his arms, holding her tightly. "Thank God, I was beside myself with worry."

Lady Lockwood issued a loud "harrumph" and said, "Really, Dunbridge, contain yourself."

Nathan released Annabeth and stepped back, holding her hand for a moment longer before letting go, his eyes anxiously looking her over. He drew in a breath. "Your face." His hand went to her reddened cheek and hovered. "What happened? Did someone *hit* you?"

"I'm fine, Nathan, really." Her gaze went past him to Sloane. "What are *you* doing here, Sloane?"

"Where else would I be? You were missing."

"Yes. Just where have you been, young lady?" Lady Lockwood scolded.

"I don't know, honestly. They threw us in a carriage and I woke up in this locked room, but we escaped. That's the sum of my knowledge."

Lady Lockwood frowned. "This is most irregular. I don't know what the city is coming to—thieves and kidnappers running all about." She swung and pointed her cane at Judy. "And what were you about, letting her be grabbed like that?"

For the first time, the two men looked over at Judy, who had remained quietly in the doorway.

Sloane stared in shock, then said, "Verity?"

CHAPTER NINE

ANNABETH STARED AT him in confusion. Verity? Truth? What was Sloane talking about?

Judy sighed and came farther into the room. "Yes, Sloane, it's me." There was no trace of her Yorkshire voice.

Nathan's jaw dropped. "Devil take it. Who *are* you?"

The maid turned to Nathan. She put a fist on her hip, her sauciness returning in full force. "Bonjour, monsieur," she said in a French accent. "In Paris, I am Angelique." Her voice changed again. "And in Bahston, Massachusetts, I am Mercy. But in South Carolina, why, I'm just little ole Clara Ann. Right 'ere and now, me name is Judy." She reverted to her familiar Yorkshire accent, then straightened and, in the pristine tone of an English lady, continued, "But my mother named me Verity."

Everyone remained gaping at her in silence for a moment. Nathan snorted. "*That* was certainly a misnomer."

"To *you*, I'm Miss Cole," Judy shot back.

Annabeth's head was whirling. Judy wasn't a thief who'd become a maid. She was…what was she? Annabeth could only stare, unable to come up with any coherent thought. Sloane, however, didn't seem to have that problem. He strode toward the other woman, his eyes flashing.

"So *this* is why your office has been closed. You were spying on Annabeth? What the devil is going on? Who are you working for?"

"You were spying on me?" Annabeth knew it was foolish to feel so betrayed. It wasn't as if Judy were an age-old friend; Annabeth had known her for only a little more than a fortnight.

"No!" Judy turned to Annabeth. "You must believe me. I was *not* spying on you. I was just…"

Sloane took the maid by the arm, his face a study in fury. Anyone else would have stepped back from him, but she just lifted her chin and returned his glare. "Take your hand off me if you want to keep it."

"I want some answers," he said, dropping her arm and stepping back. "After all the time we were together, I think I deserve a little honesty from you."

Together? Annabeth put her hand on her stomach, suddenly sick. Judy and Sloane had been—what? Married? Lovers? Of course, she'd known that Sloane must have been with other women. *Loved* other women. It had been twelve years, after all. But to have it thrust in her face like this was another thing entirely.

"Who are you working for? Why does he want to hurt Annabeth?" Sloane's mouth twisted. "I wouldn't have thought it possible you would agree to do this to an innocent woman."

"I haven't done anything to her except pin up her hair." Judy—no, Verity planted her fists on her hips pugnaciously.

Nathan joined the argument. "We're supposed to believe that you just happened to be pretending to be Annabeth's maid at the very same time someone attacked her?

You were working with those scoundrels, telling them when and where—"

"Oh, yes!" Verity swung on Nathan, her voice dripping scorn. "Of course I was working with the men who punched me in the face and knocked me in the head and cut my arm." She gestured toward the torn and bloodied sleeve of her dress, where a thin red line ran down her arm. "I never did anything to hurt Miss Winfield. *I'm* the one who fought to help her. *I'm* the one who got her away from them while you lot were sitting here, waiting and talking to your neighbors."

"She's right," Annabeth agreed. "She did her best to keep them from kidnapping me, and I'm sure I wouldn't have escaped without her. I cannot believe Judy, um, Verity was in on that plot. Strange as it seems, I think there must be two separate people trying to...do something."

"I never spied on you," Verity told Annabeth again. "And I'm sorry that I had to lie to you."

"Then what the devil *were* you doing?" Sloane asked.

"I was trying to find something." She swung back toward Sloane.

"What were you trying to find? Come on, Verity, this is like pulling teeth."

"I can't say what it was," Verity said with frustration. "It's for our old boss." She sent an obviously significant look at Sloane.

His jaw dropped. "Asq—" He cut the name short. "Are you joking?"

"Do you think I'd joke about him?" Verity retorted.

"I don't understand," Annabeth said. "What were you looking for? Why? Who is your old boss?"

"The man we worked for during the war," Verity responded.

"Verity…" Sloane said warningly.

"What? There's no reason to hide it anymore," Verity shot back. She turned to Annabeth. "He was the spymaster Sloane and I reported to."

"The *spymaster*!" Annabeth stared.

"You mean *you* were a spy for the French, too?" Nathan asked, his voice vaulting up in astonishment.

Verity looked at Nathan with contempt. "Not the *French*, you fool. For England. We were working for the Foreign Office."

"Good God," Lady Lockwood said loudly, and sank down into her chair. Annabeth had forgotten her grandmother was there; it was, she reflected, the longest time she had ever known Lady Lockwood to not participate in a conversation. But her grandmother recovered from her shock quickly and reached out to jab Sloane in the leg with her cane. "What is the matter with you, boy? Why didn't you tell us what you were really up to?"

"It's rather counterproductive to go around telling everyone you're secretly a spy," Sloane replied, moving out of reach of her cane.

Lady Lockwood snorted. "Too proud to explain yourself, you mean."

Annabeth felt as if a knife had been thrust into her chest. *Sloane hadn't told me. He hadn't trusted me enough to tell the truth.* She sank down onto the nearest ottoman. She glanced over at Nathan. He looked as shocked and confused as she felt. At least he didn't feel the pain of it.

"You still haven't said what you're looking for, girl," Lady Lockwood said, clearly feeling back to herself.

"The war's been over for years now, and there wouldn't have been anything to do with it here, anyway. So why were you poking about?"

"I can't talk about it, ma'am." Verity sent another meaningful glance at Sloane. Now his face closed down, remote and hard. Verity went on, "I'm not allowed. It's for the government. I can't tell anyone."

"Just a moment." Annabeth stood up again, her voice filled with suspicion. "I saw that look you two sent each other. You're hiding something, both of you. What is it? Tell me. I deserve to know. *I'm* the one who's been hit and hauled around like a sack of flour and locked up. What is going on?"

"That's what I intend to find out," Sloane said grimly. "Verity, come with me. We're going to have a talk with *him*."

"Wait. I'm coming, too," Annabeth said.

"And I," Nathan declared.

"No. You are not." Sloane bit out the words, his eyes steely. He pointed to Annabeth. "You stay here. And *you*—" he jabbed his finger at Nathan "—you see if you can manage to keep Annabeth safe for a few hours."

All of them burst out in protest, but Sloane ignored them, and, with a gesture to Verity, strode out of the room.

"Arrogant prat," Verity said under her breath, but she turned and strode out the door after him.

SLOANE TROD DOWN the street to hail a hackney. He heard Verity's footsteps behind him, but he couldn't bring himself to say anything to her. He was still ready to explode. Where were all the blasted hacks? Just when one needed one, they disappeared.

"Sloane, for heaven's sake, would you slow down?" Verity said crossly, trotting a few steps to catch up with him. "My legs aren't two miles long, and I've just spent the afternoon fighting and running all about trying to save *your* ladylove."

"She's not my—oh, the devil with it." Sloane stopped and turned to her. "Why didn't you tell me what you were doing?"

"Because I didn't want to upset you!" Verity snapped. "I knew it would bring up all the old memories and the pain." She folded her arms and glared at him. "Although the way you're acting, I don't know why I bothered to try to protect you."

"Neither do I," he shot back. "That's not your style."

Her eyes widened, and she stalked past him, waving her hand to a hackney that had turned the corner.

Sloane blew out a breath. "Wait." He caught up with Verity. "I'm sorry. I shouldn't have said that. I was just striking out, and you were the nearest person. I didn't mean it. You're the only one in the network with a heart."

Verity made a face. "Don't spread that news around. You'll ruin my reputation."

He smiled faintly. Despite the bit of annoyance in her voice, he knew she had forgiven his insult. "I'm not mad at you, really. It's Asquith I'd like to strangle. What the hell is he up to? And why drag Annabeth into it? She never knew about any of it. Not me. Not her father. Nothing."

"I know. But this doesn't have anything to do with Annabeth, really; it's about her father."

"Naturally."

"Asquith wants some paper that belonged to Hunter.

Truly, I haven't been trying to get information out of Annabeth or spy on her. I've just been searching."

"For what? What could matter after all these years?"

"I'll let him explain it to you. It all sounds a trifle vague to me."

The hackney cab she had hailed rolled to a stop beside them, and Sloane gave him the address of Asquith's office. Verity turned in surprise. "We can't go there. I'll send him a message, and he'll meet us at the pub he and I have been using."

Sloane gave her a firm boost into the coach. "Not today. I'm not waiting like a faithful dog for him to show up when he pleases. We're bearding the lion in his den."

Verity shrugged and sat down. Sloane climbed in beside her, and the vehicle rolled away. He was silent for a moment, then said, "I'm surprised you agreed to work for him. As I recall, you two didn't part on the best of terms."

"No, not unless you consider me threatening to slice his throat polite conversation."

Sloane smiled faintly. "So why did you take the job? For that matter, why did he ask you?"

"He didn't. He hired someone else—Richard Forester, and Richard is the one who offered me the job. Forester's not a bad detective, but he knew he couldn't do it as easily as I. Frankly, I think he was intimidated by investigating the aristocracy. And everyone knows I'm the best at disguises."

"That's true. I almost didn't recognize you with that color hair."

"The main thing in being a servant is being unnoticeable—drab clothes, ordinary hair, not looking them in the eye." She pulled a strand of her hair in front of her face to study it. "It'll wash out. Eventually." She sighed and dropped the lock. "I must say, you could have waited and let me clean up a bit. I look like a wreck."

"You look fine," Sloane said in an offhand way.

Verity snorted. "I have dirt all over my dress, one sleeve is nearly torn off, I have blood on my arm, and my hair is unpinned and looks like the rats have been in it." She eyed him critically. "Not that you look much better. Where have you been, wrestling in the mud?"

He shrugged one shoulder. "Trying to find Annabeth. Who kidnapped the two of you?"

She glanced at him in surprise. "I thought it was this Parker chap who ordered it, the one you warned Annabeth about."

"That's what I thought until I questioned him today. He denied it, and you know how persuasive I can be."

"That's one word for it." Verity arched an eyebrow.

"I believed him. Now that I know Asquith's involved, I think it might be about something else entirely."

"Spider didn't say anything about anyone else being after it." Verity used the old code name Asquith had gone by in the network. Sloane understood; it was hard to think of Harold Asquith in any other context than the dark, secretive web he'd spun. "And why would he kidnap Annabeth when he knew I was with her and searching for that paper? He certainly wouldn't have kidnapped me, too."

"Searching for what paper?" Sloane asked.

"It's a confession Hunter Winfield may or may not have written. It could be in a letter or just a piece of paper, which could be hidden anywhere."

"That's definite."

A corner of her mouth quirked up. "Yes, the whole

thing seems very unlikely to me. Richard couldn't explain it because he didn't understand it—that's why he gave me the task. He had me meet his client in person, and that's when I discovered it was Asquith. 'Course, Richard didn't have a clue who Asquith is or what he does, which is another reason he had so much trouble with the instructions. Spider was his usual secretive self, letting out only what he thought absolutely necessary."

"I'd liked to have seen Asquith's face when he saw it was you."

She huffed out a little laugh. "He was none too pleased, I can tell you. At first I thought he wasn't going to give me the job. But I think he realized that I could do it much better than Forester or anyone else. Asquith could be more open and straightforward with me, too—as straightforward as he's capable of being, anyway. I would have liked to back out when I found out it was him. But I couldn't because the whole thing involved Annabeth. I thought you would rather I was there than some stranger."

"Yes." He nodded. "I'm sorry for being harsh before. I understand, and I'm truly glad it was you with Annabeth today. I had no idea where she was or how to find out once I realized it wasn't Parker behind it."

They rode in silence the rest of the way.

CHAPTER TEN

SLOANE AND VERITY strode down the hall toward Asquith's office, ignoring the odd looks that were cast at Verity's appearance as well as the few futile attempts to stop them. Sloane had made his peace with Verity, but he was still bubbling with fury at Asquith.

The door to Asquith's office was open, and they could see the man sitting at his desk, busily writing. He was a very ordinary-looking man in his fifties. There was nothing imposing about him. He was of average height with light brown hair and gray eyes, and neither attractive nor ugly. It wasn't until he fixed his gaze on one that one could see the power in him.

Sloane strode in, closing the door behind them with a thud, and Asquith looked up, startled. His eyes narrowed. "Rutherford. What in blazes do you think you're doing? I meet you where I tell you. You don't come here."

"I just did."

Asquith's gaze went to Verity, and his eyes widened fractionally at the sight of her disarray. "What happened to you?"

"I was abducted and thrown in a locked room with Miss Winfield."

Asquith's eyebrows rose. "What? Why?"

Verity answered with a shrug. "You tell me."

"Hmm," Asquith said thoughtfully, and settled back in his chair. "So...there *is* someone else after it."

"That's all you have to say?" Sloane asked.

"What else should I say?" The other man looked at him. "Miss Cole is obviously unhurt, and I presume Miss Winfield is as well. The only thing to wonder is why and who? The only reason I can think of is because they want what Miss Cole is after. They think she has it or that Miss Winfield has it and they can pry the information out of one or the other."

"Annabeth knows nothing about any secret paper," Sloane snapped. "You are the one who involved her by setting Verity on her. *You* put her in danger."

"I had no intention of putting Miss Winfield in danger, I assure you. If anything, Miss Cole's presence should have made her safer. I presume it was she who got the two of them out of the kidnappers' clutches."

"Damn it, I want you out of Annabeth's life. I only agreed to work for you because you swore the Winfields would be safe."

"My dear boy, I've always kept to that."

"Then what was Verity doing there?"

"I would have assumed she told you," Asquith said mildly.

"She did, and it makes no sense. A supposed confession from Hunter? After all these years? I can't see him writing a confession, and if he did, why didn't he send it to someone? He's long dead, and the war was even longer ago than that. And why would you want a confession, anyway? You already know what he did."

"I didn't believe he would have written a confession, either," Asquith said. "Hunter never seemed to me to be someone who would be overcome with remorse. I also dismissed the rumors that he had committed suicide."

"Suicide!" Sloane let out a sharp laugh. "Him? Not likely."

"Exactly what I thought. That's why we didn't spend a great deal of time searching his house for a confession after he died."

"You had people inside Annabeth's house, searching?" Sloane said in a deadly tone.

"Oh, do sit down, Rutherford, and stop looking like a bomb about to go off." Asquith gestured toward one of the chairs opposite his desk. "You, too, Miss Cole. It's a long story."

"So you're going to tell Sloane more than you chose to tell me?" Verity asked. "Lovely to know you sent me there with inadequate foreknowledge."

"I didn't hide anything of importance to your task," Asquith replied. "But now, after this kidnapping incident, I am beginning to wonder if perhaps there's something to his story."

"Whose story?" Sloane asked, grudgingly sitting down as Asquith had suggested.

"As I said, we found nothing at the time and I rather forgot about it. But a few weeks ago, we succeeded in capturing a French agent."

"After all this time?"

"Yes. Well, he was an Englishman, you see, so he'd continued to live here. I'm sure he'd thought he was safe by now. But I had never stopped looking. I had always believed that the head of the spy ring here was in actuality an Englishman. Someone knew enough about Winfield to put pressure on him and make him turn. He would never have thought to steal information on his own. Someone coerced him."

"I'm familiar with that method," Sloane said bitingly.

"I am well aware that you resent me," Asquith said crisply. "But I do what's best for England, not for any individual's feelings. Sometimes I am required to do difficult things."

Sloane nodded, though he suspected that the things Asquith did weren't all that difficult for him.

"So the head of the French spy network in this country, the one who coerced Winfield into giving him the information, is the agent you caught recently?"

"Unfortunately, no. But this chap was certain that Winfield had left a confession, which I sincerely hope would reveal the name of the head of the French network. That confession is what Verity is looking for."

"But after all this time—if her father had left a confession, Annabeth would know about it, and I am certain she does not."

"Miss Cole has told me the same. Miss Winfield knows nothing about the confession. But that doesn't mean it's not in her possession. Or he might have given it to his wife."

"Annabeth's mother?" Sloane snorted. "Clearly you don't know Martha. No one, even Hunter, would entrust an important document to her. And there's no reason to search Annabeth's home. Hunter never lived at Lady Lockwood's house."

"It's not her house," Verity spoke up. "It's the rental house. The one her father left her."

"You mean the one that her grandfather was sensible enough to leave in trust for her instead of giving it to Hunter."

"Is that the way of it?" Verity asked. "I didn't know. Annabeth just told me she got the rent for it, but since she's marrying, they're going to move into it."

Sloane's jaw clenched but he said nothing.

"She's clearing all the old things out of the attic," Asquith said. "Her father's things, as I understand it. Before that, I hadn't realized anything of Hunter's was still packed away somewhere."

"How the devil did you know she was clearing out the attic of her house?" Sloane asked.

Asquith sent him a look. "My dear chap…"

Sloane shook his head. "That's right. I forgot—you know everything."

"I like to keep informed." Asquith went on, "It was the perfect opportunity—all I had to do was pay a maid to leave Lady Lockwood's and send in 'Judy' with sterling references."

"Why did you go to this other detective, Forester, who has no idea what's behind this? Why didn't you go to Verity immediately? Or me."

Asquith quirked an eyebrow. "I believe you and Miss Cole were rather definitive in your declarations that you would never work for me again. And, frankly, I was a bit skeptical still that the search would turn up anything. It didn't seem worth trying to convince Miss Cole to return.

"But of course, I was delighted when I found out she was working on it instead of Forester. This occurrence today indicates that someone else is looking for the same information." As much excitement as Asquith ever revealed crept into his voice. "Who else would want it except the man at the center of the spy ring? The one whom Hunter's confession could reveal is a traitor? Even if there is no confession, we can catch the spymaster by finding the man who tried to kidnap Miss Winfield today."

"Asquith..." Sloane leaned forward, planting his hands on the other man's desk and fixing his gaze on Asquith's face. "I don't care about the confession. I don't care about the other man. All I care about is Annabeth's safety."

"The only way to make sure she's safe is to find out who attacked her," Asquith pointed out. "That's why I'm sure you will be happy to hunt him down."

"I beg your pardon," Verity snapped. "I can hunt him down. I'm already in this."

Asquith turned his pale gaze on her. "No. You need to guard Miss Winfield now. Rutherford obviously can't do that. Rutherford is clearly the right person to look, and you will report to him."

Sloane's jaw clenched. He had sworn he'd never work for Asquith again, but here he was, just like Verity, being pulled back into the man's web. "I want to talk to this French agent who gave you this information."

"Ah. Well." Asquith sighed. "I'm afraid that's impossible. He died in his cell. Hanged himself."

"That's certainly convenient."

"Not for me," Asquith retorted. "I'm sure I could have discovered more, given time. He may not have wanted to face the scandal or maybe he did it to keep from telling me what I wanted to know." He paused. "Or...maybe the man we're looking for got to him, even in jail."

Sloane sighed. "Very well. I'll do what you want because it's the only way to make sure Annabeth is safe. But I am not going to tell her that her father was a traitor, and neither are you or anyone else. I didn't give her up for her to find that out now."

"Whatever you say," Asquith said agreeably. "Though I'm not sure how you'll explain all this to her."

"I'll figure it out," Sloane said tersely.

CHAPTER ELEVEN

ANNABETH PACED BACK and forth across the room, as she had been doing since Sloane's abrupt departure. Petunia had trotted along with her the first few times, but she grew disinterested when the activity did not result in treats and went back to sleep on her pillow at Lady Lockwood's feet.

"Do sit down, Annabeth," Lady Lockwood said. "You're making me dizzy. Pacing won't make him return any earlier. And neither will looking out the front window every few seconds. Worry does nothing for the passage of time."

"I'm not worried… I'm… I don't know what I am." Annabeth's first feeling—after complete astonishment—had been hurt. Sloane hadn't told her that he was working for the British. All this time he had let her believe the worst. As if she was nobody to him. It didn't matter to him that she had been wounded inside by the rumors that he was working for the French, that she had hurt for him. And when he left her—had what he told her been a lie? Had he not trusted her enough to tell her the truth? Not cared enough to ease her hurt a bit with the real explanation?

Next to all that, the betrayal by her maid was only a minor hurt. Still, Annabeth had liked Judy, trusted her. And Judy hadn't even been real. She'd been Verity, a woman who was using her. It was foolish, she supposed, that she'd let herself believe they had become something like friends.

Nathan's sweet attempts to soothe her were more than she could bear, and so she excused herself to go up and repair the damage done to her this afternoon. Annabeth changed clothes and washed away the dirt and put her hair back in place, then sat for a moment to gather herself together. But the longer she sat, the more she thought, and the more her wounded feelings turned into anger. Sloane and Verity were the ones who had been in the wrong, and then they had just run off without a word of explanation about whatever bizarre thing was going on.

None of it made any sense, and it would be just like Sloane to never return to tell them anything about it. Well, that was not going to happen. Annabeth wasn't as meek and mild as everyone seemed to think; there was a bit of her grandmother in her, after all. If they didn't return, she would hunt Sloane down and make him tell her.

Thankfully, she didn't have to set up a hunting party. Nathan was in the midst of giving her and Lady Lockwood what Annabeth was sure was a highly expurgated account of his and Sloane's search this afternoon when there was the sound of a carriage outside. Annabeth flew to the window and saw Sloane and Verity descending from a hack. Annabeth returned to the sofa and sat beside Nathan, doing her best not to look as if she had been pacing the floor for the better part of two hours.

The butler didn't bother to announce them since Sloane paid no attention to such niceties and just strode into the drawing room. Even though she was furious at him, Annabeth's heart lifted at the sight of him, and the anger in her chest was joined by excitement. How could he still affect her this way when she had long ago ground him out of her heart? Why did that wild black hair and those piercing blue eyes still send a spark sizzling through her?

Verity did not look pleased, which gave Annabeth a small flicker of satisfaction. She dismissed that as an unworthy thought, though, as she took in Verity's cut and swollen lips. The woman had managed to braid her hair and wind it into a poorly held knot at the nape of her neck, but that had served to make the bruising and swelling on her cheek even more noticeable.

Before Annabeth could even think about it, she found herself saying, "You should have that cut seen to. Mrs. Archer has supplies. She's rather good at healing."

Verity looked surprised and smiled a little, though she stopped with a wince. "Thank you. I'll see to it as soon as we're done."

It was so odd to hear those upper-crust tones issuing from Verity's mouth.

Sloane said nothing for a moment, and Lady Lockwood thumped her cane. "Don't just stand there, man, out with it."

"I'm not sure where to begin," Sloane said.

"I'll help you." Annabeth popped to her feet, the anger and hurt she'd been feeling bubbling to the surface, further fueled by irritation at the way her heart had lifted when Sloane stepped into the room. "Why did 'Judy' come to work here?" She stabbed her finger in Verity's direction. "What is she looking for? And don't even think about lying to me again, Sloane."

"I didn't lie to you," he said indignantly. "I didn't know what was going on either."

"But you went running off to find out, refusing to

take me with you. I had a right to hear the story first-hand. I am the one who has strangers poking about in my business, not you. I was the one snatched off the street! I deserve the truth, not some story *you* make up."

"I'm not making anything up." He set his jaw, taking a step toward her.

"The problem is I don't know when you are lying and when you aren't. Clearly you've been doing it for a long time."

"I never—"

"A lie of omission is still a lie. Telling me you're going to do one thing when you're really doing another is a lie. Giving me false reasons is a lie."

Verity cleared her throat and stepped between them. "I am the one to answer those questions. I am here because the man I work for received information that there is an important document here."

"In my grandmother's house?" All the anger in Anna-beth's voice was replaced with astonishment.

"Not necessarily. More likely in the house you and I have been clearing out the last fortnight," Verity explained. "It is something written by your father."

"Ha!" Lady Lockwood interjected. "Hunter Winfield never did anything important in his life. You've been misled."

"Papa was a well-respected man in some circles, Grandmother," Annabeth protested.

Lady Lockwood snorted, but before she could reply, Nathan, ever the one to intercede, asked, "What is it you think he wrote?"

"I can't tell you," Verity replied. At the others' skeptical expressions, she went on, "Truly. I have been expressly forbidden to talk about it. It's government business."

"They're not going to give out secrets about the war," Sloane added. "Even after several years, there are still people and things that must be kept hidden."

"But Papa had nothing to do with any of that," Annabeth said, more puzzled than angry now. "He worked in the government, but nothing to do with foreign affairs or the war. He was important to those of us who loved him—but not to the government."

"He 'worked' in a meaningless job," Lady Lockwood declared. "Something suitable for a gentleman but which didn't take any actual *effort*. Drewsbury got it for him for his wife's sake, to help Adeline's sister."

Annabeth resented her grandmother's attitude, but she couldn't deny the truth of her words. Her father's job had been a sinecure, the sort of thing a gentleman could do without losing status.

"Be that as it may, we cannot reveal the particulars of the document we're searching for," Verity said with finality.

"But why would anything of Hunter's be here?" Lady Lockwood asked.

"It was Miss Winfield's other house we were interested in, ma'am."

"Of course," Annabeth said. "That was why you pretended to be a maid, so you could work at the rental house. But you couldn't have found anything or you wouldn't still be here."

"No, and we've looked through nearly all of it. There's still the trunk we brought back for you to go through at leisure."

"You mean you haven't already searched it?" Annabeth raised an eyebrow, her voice cool. "I would have thought you picked that trunk's lock long ago."

A faint line of red rose on Verity's cheekbones, but she said only, "No, I did not."

"The important thing is finding out who attacked you." Sloane took back control of the conversation. "Whoever did so wanted that document and thought you could give it to him. The best chance we have of finding his identity is to find the document."

"Is there any reason why you believe the individual is a man?" Verity asked.

"It seems likelier than not," Sloane replied simply.

"Not all women are to be trusted." Annabeth shot a look at the woman she'd once thought of as Judy.

"And not all people you might suspect are villains," Verity replied bitingly.

"Man or woman, it doesn't matter," Nathan cut in in exasperation.

"Very well," Annabeth said. "I'll start looking this evening."

"Not you," Sloane said bluntly. "Verity or I can go through that trunk. What you need to do is leave the city. You and Lady Lockwood can go to Bath or Brighton or wherever you choose."

"It's so nice of you to let us have a choice." Annabeth's voice dripped sarcasm.

Sloane ignored her remark. "Take Dunbridge with you. He says he's a good shot, and he can pack a punch."

"I'm not leaving," Annabeth told him firmly.

Sloane's mouth tightened. "Yes, you are. Surely after this afternoon, you realize the sort of danger you're in if you remain in London."

"But now I know the reason for the attack, and I won't

let it happen again. I'll pay more attention to what's going on around me when I leave the house."

"You'll take the carriage," Lady Lockwood declared.

"Yes. When I go out, I'll take the carriage."

"I'll escort you," Nathan said. He looked at Sloane. "And I'll be armed."

"What about inside the house?"

"Inside the house!" Lady Lockwood exclaimed. "What nonsense. We're perfectly safe inside. The doors and windows will be locked, and the house is full of servants. No one would dare. Besides, we have that one." She pointed to Verity. "She can sleep on a cot in Annabeth's room and keep an eye out during the day."

"Just a moment," Verity said. "I'm not really your maid. I won't be living here."

"Yes, you will," Lady Lockwood and Sloane said in chorus.

"Keeping Annabeth safe is our first priority," Sloane told Verity. "You know that. I can't be here to protect her, so that means you will have to."

"But I—" Verity started.

"He put me in charge, and you agreed, Verity," he reminded her.

Verity's eyes snapped, but she subsided, crossing her arms and leaning back against the wall.

"So you see, we'll be perfectly safe." Lady Lockwood turned a scornful look on Sloane. "I am not running off to Bath to vegetate. Lady Bittersham's birthday gala is next week, and we have the opera on Thursday."

Sloane's eyebrows rose. "You'd rather risk your granddaughter's life than miss a party?"

"It's not just *any* party. Lady Bittersham's birthday galas are the event of the off-Season."

Annabeth hid a smile at the expression on Sloane's face. Her grandmother had managed to silence him, at least for the moment.

Sloane turned to Annabeth. "Why will you not listen to sense? You're risking your life."

"Hardly," Annabeth returned crisply. "If this man wants information from me, he isn't going to kill me."

"Killing you is not the only option," Sloane said darkly. "I realize that you don't want to do anything I say, but it's foolish to put yourself in danger just to spite me."

"Oh, there it is. It's all about you, as it always is. You make decisions and it doesn't matter what anyone else says, what anyone else wants." Old anger welled up in Annabeth, past feelings mingling with present ones.

"That's not true. I am trying to protect you."

"I don't need your protection. I don't *want* your protection."

"Then you are doomed to disappointment. I'm not letting someone hurt you."

"Someone *else*, you mean?"

Red skimmed Sloane's cheekbones, and he clenched his jaw, as if forcing his words to stay in his mouth.

Annabeth went on, "I have to remain here so I can search for this document."

"You aren't searching for it. This is government business. It isn't your concern."

"Not my concern?" Her voice rose. "I'd say it is very much my concern. Indeed, I am the person most concerned. It is *my* father who wrote it. *I* am the one who's been kidnapped because of it. *I* am going to help look for it."

"Blast it. I forgot how bloody hardheaded you are," Sloane snapped.

"You shouldn't have. I've always been this way. If you'll remember, I never gave up when I asked you to teach me to sail."

For an instant Sloane's hard eyes softened, and a faint smile touched his face. "Asked me? Badgered me constantly is what I'd call it."

"Then you should realize that I'm not going to give up about this, either."

"Anna…"

"Don't tell me I can't help find that document," she said fiercely. "I am tired of everyone thinking I'm weak and I must be protected. I am perfectly capable."

"I've never thought you were weak. I know how strong you are." Sloane took a step closer to her. "But I cannot help but want you to be safe. This is too dangerous."

Annabeth was suddenly aware of the hush in the room. She glanced around and saw that all eyes were on her and Sloane. Nathan had an odd look on his face, and Verity turned to look at him, raising her brows in a significant way. Annabeth's cheeks flooded with color. She took a quick step back—when had she and Sloane moved closer to each other?—and lifted her chin a little.

She said in a cool voice, "You have no authority over me. I shall look if I want to."

Any trace of warmth was gone from Sloane's face now. "Leave it alone. I don't need your help. You would only get in my way."

"Very well." Annabeth shrugged her shoulders. "If you prefer to work in ignorance, that's quite all right

with me. But obviously I will have to search for it myself now, since I am the one who knows where Papa
might have hidden it."

CHAPTER TWELVE

SLOANE WENT STILL. "What? What do you mean?"

Annabeth tilted her head and said smugly, "I thought you didn't want my help."

Sloane scowled at her. "Blast it, Anna, this isn't a game."

"I'm well aware of that. That's why I wish to help you find it. You are the one who refuses to let me."

"Very well," he ground out, clenching his jaw. "You may help us look for it. Now…how do you know where it is? Did he tell you?"

"No, of course not. And I don't know exactly where it is, but I do know where to look. I think it's quite likely it's in one of his little boxes."

"His boxes?"

"Don't you remember? He was always out in his workroom when we were in the country?"

"Yes, I know he sometimes went off to play with those puzzles and his inventions."

"I remember quite well," Nathan said, shooting a pointed look at Sloane. "He made clever boxes."

"You don't mean those silly things one couldn't open, do you?" Lady Lockwood asked.

"But you could open them, Grandmother. You just had to figure out how. Some were only puzzle boxes and didn't open at all unless you knew the trick. Others were actual boxes, like the one you use for jewelry, but they usually had a secret compartment as well."

"Good Lord," Sloane said softly, his eyes bright with interest.

"How many are there?" Verity's face, too, was lit up. Obviously she was a lover of puzzles as well. Both she and Nathan had drawn closer at the news.

"I've no idea. He made many of them. His joy was in the making of them, not collecting them, so he gave them as gifts."

"How many people might have one?" Verity asked.

"I've no idea." Annabeth shook her head.

"What does it matter?" Nathan frowned. "You can hardly go around asking all of Mr. Winfield's friends and relatives to let you see some box he gave them."

"I wasn't thinking of asking them," Verity replied.

"Why would you, when breaking in is so much more convenient?" Nathan said caustically.

"Sometimes you aren't as dim as you look." Verity smiled at him sweetly.

"I was being sarcastic."

"Doesn't make your statement any less correct."

"It seems unlikely to me that Winfield would have put a secret document in a box he was giving away," Sloane pointed out. "It would be one he kept or at least gave to someone close to him, like a family member, where he could easily retrieve it."

"I have one, of course," Annabeth said, nodding, "and there's one in the trunk that we brought over from the rental house. Grandmother has the jewelry case and a puzzle box. Are there any more?" Annabeth addressed this last to Lady Lockwood, who had an unaccustomed look of guilt in her eyes.

"No. I threw the puzzle box away. Or gave it to someone. I don't remember."

"Did he have other secret hiding spots?" Sloane asked. "Besides boxes?"

"Yes, there were some hidden places in the house where he stored things. But there are more in his workshop. Usually something he was working on. Of course, I might not know the location of all of them since they were secret."

"Will it still be there? You sold your country house, didn't you? Would they have kept the old workshop?"

"I don't know. It's at some distance from the house and rather secluded. The Todds might not have bothered to tear it down. Or they might have decided to store things in it."

"So the house is occupied," Sloane said.

"Well, apparently Miss Cole has no problem with burglary," Nathan said dryly.

"I know," Sloane replied casually, as if such things were ordinary occurrences. "But I dislike creeping about trying to find things in the dark."

"Surely it would have been hidden only in those boxes that Papa was working on at the time he wrote this note. That reduces the number."

"Yes, if we knew when he wrote the thing," Sloane replied.

"Oh, yes, I see. I was thinking of a time close to his death, but of course it was more likely many years ago during the war."

"But wouldn't it have already been opened by whomever he gave it to?" Nathan pointed out. "Perhaps it has already been discovered."

"*If* he gave it away. But I don't know. There may be

some people who were never able to discover how it worked." Annabeth sighed. "Or who may very well have tossed it away."

"I didn't know that it might have some important document in it at the time, did I?" Lady Lockwood frowned.

"No. And I think Grandmother probably wasn't the only one who didn't know the boxes had secret compartments. Papa enjoyed people figuring that part out for themselves."

"That's why it's likeliest that it's in something of his own or perhaps Annabeth's. He wouldn't have put important information into someone else's hands, leaving its discovery to chance," Sloane said. He turned to Annabeth. "I want to see how it works."

Annabeth started to retrieve her treasured box, then stopped. She had no interest in revealing its contents in front of all of them. Instead, she said, "Let's look at Grandmother's jewelry case." She cast a questioning look at Lady Lockwood.

The old woman waved her hand. "If it will absolve me from my sin of throwing one out, I suppose I must allow my things to be rummaged through. Run and fetch it, Annabeth."

She returned a few minutes later, carrying a large jewelry case. She opened the top. "I took out all the jewels, as it's easier to find the latch that way." Inside were two trays to hold jewelry, both of them empty. She held it out to Sloane. "Can you see any way to open another compartment?"

Sloane and Verity examined the case closely, then Sloane shook his head and passed the box back to Annabeth. "No, it's quite well done if there is a hidden drawer there."

"There is. I've opened it before. Papa always let me have a try at his boxes before he gave them away."

Annabeth set the case down on the low table beside her grandmother and knelt in front of it. She closed her eyes for a moment, remembering, then opened the lid, removed the trays, and slid her fingernail into one corner of the box, peeling back the felt lining. Pressing on the wood, she grasped the left back corner and tugged. An inch of wood at the corner swung back, revealing wood beneath it. Annabeth did the same with the right rear corner; she pushed at the middle of the back, between the two opened corners, and there was a click. She pulled, and a tray about an inch deep and six inches long slid out.

"Look, there's a piece of paper in here," Annabeth said to her grandmother, and lifted it from the tray. Behind her Sloane and Verity stiffened, sliding a bit forward, but relaxed at the sight of the small piece of folded paper.

"Well, what does it say, child?" Lady Lockwood said.

"It says…" Annabeth swallowed, tears suddenly shimmering in her eyes. "It says, 'My lady, you have my eternal gratitude for the gift of your beautiful daughter, the love of my life.'"

"Well." Lady Lockwood blinked and looked down at her hands. She cleared her throat. "Hunter was many undesirable things, but he loved your mother." Abruptly Lady Lockwood stood up. "I think that's quite enough for today. With all the goings-on, I missed my afternoon rest." She sent an accusatory look at Sloane and Verity. "And Annabeth is exhausted after her ordeal."

"Lady Lockwood—" Sloane began, but she sent him a look that had stopped many a man in his tracks.

"No. That's enough. You may take up all this nonsense tomorrow. We are about to have a few moments of peace and an early dinner, then go to bed. You, too, Dunbridge." She made a sweeping gesture with her cane. Her gaze fell on Verity. "Not you. You're staying, and you're sleeping in Annabeth's room."

"YOU ARE *NOT* sleeping in my room," Annabeth told Verity later that evening, standing in the doorway of her bedroom, arms crossed. She couldn't help but feel a bit sorry for the other woman—Verity's face had reached the full extent of its swelling and bruising. But Annabeth was not going to just ignore her former maid's treachery.

Verity sighed. "I understand that you are angry with me." She ignored Annabeth's soft snort. "But I could not tell you. I was bound to secrecy. It's not only my life that could be endangered by a slip of the tongue, but the lives of others."

"Yes, like mine. We can see how well your 'secrecy' protected me from harm."

"I didn't—I never expected any attack on you. That was obviously a profound mistake. But it makes it clear that you need to be guarded at all times."

"I will lock my door. The windows are locked, and they're two floors up a sheer brick wall. No one is going to get in to harm me. And I would like to be alone. I think you owe me at least that much."

Verity sighed. "Very well. I can't make you accept my protection. But at least let me come in and help you get ready for bed."

"I can take down and brush my own hair."

"And undo all the hooks and eyes down the back of that dress?"

Annabeth looked at her for a long moment, then stepped back. "Come in, then."

Verity entered after her and closed the door. Annabeth turned her back to her, and Verity began to unfasten the line of hooks and eyes. "You have to admit it was a good thing I was with you this afternoon. I did my best to keep you safe. And I will continue to do so."

Annabeth whipped around to glare at her. "You lied to me. Worse than lying, you pretended to be my friend."

"I *am* your friend," Verity said.

"Just stop." Annabeth turned back around. "You wanted information from me, that's all. You wanted to know about my father. You wanted me to confide in you. I cannot bear to think about the way I told you all about Sloane and…and everything." Humiliation welled in her. "No one likes to be made a fool of."

"Nothing you told me was foolish," Verity said. "I didn't talk to you to get information. I already knew everything I needed to about your father and about you and Sloane. I talked to you because I liked you."

"I liked you, too," Annabeth admitted in a small voice. "It seems I always like people who betray me." She prayed the tears would stay in her eyes instead of spilling over. "I can finish getting undressed by myself."

Verity looked as though she wanted to say something more, but then she went to the door and slipped out so silently it was as if she'd never been there at all.

CHAPTER THIRTEEN

ANNABETH DREAMED ABOUT Sloane that night—the old
Sloane, the one she had loved. They were walking, holding hands, and she was happy. They walked on and
on, never getting anywhere, but then the sweet mood
changed to one of irritation. Sloane refused to stop,
and when she turned to look at him, she realized that
her companion was no longer Sloane, but a man whose
face she could not see. Where had Sloane gone? Fear
gripped her, and she turned around and around, looking
for Sloane, growing ever more frantic. Then something
hit the floor with a thud.

Her eyes flew open. Her heart was racing. She felt
disoriented, caught between her dream and reality. She
heard a soft rustle near the fireplace, and she knew
someone was in her room. She sat up, looking toward
the fireplace, and a dark shape stood and turned.

Annabeth screamed and shot out of bed, groping for a
weapon on the small bedside stand. The dark shadow ran
toward her, saying something in a low guttural whisper.
Her hand fell on a book, and she threw it at the intruder.
Drawing a breath, she screamed again and looked for
something else to throw. There was nothing but a candlestick, so she threw that as well.

The book hit him on the arm, and the candlestick

reached only his ankle, but he let out a loud curse and grabbed at his ankle, then turned and ran out the door.

Anna darted after him, pillow in hand. She had nothing better to throw at him, but she could find better weapons in the corridor. He headed for the stairs, but Verity came flying out of a window seat and launched herself at him.

She wasn't heavy enough to take him down, but he stumbled backward, hit a hall table, and bounced off, landing on his knees. Clasping her hands together, Verity brought them down hard on the back of his neck, and when he scrambled to his feet, she followed and kicked the back of his knees, sending him to the floor again.

With a roar he jumped up and swung at her, but Verity dodged nimbly, and, pulling her encumbering nightgown up to her knees, she kicked the intruder in the stomach. The air went out of him in a whoosh. Bent over and gasping for air, he staggered forward.

From the other end of the hall came a sound like a flock of geese, and a small dog shot into view. Petunia jumped, clamping her teeth on the man's calf. The intruder swung his leg, sending Petunia flying away. The pug hit the floor, but bounced up and returned to the fray. She swarmed around the man's ankles, nipping and growling and yapping. More servants came running into the hall.

"How dare you!" An aristocratic voice rang out. Everyone stopped and swung around to gape at the vision of Lady Lockwood in her nightcap and dressing gown, a candle in one hand and brandishing her cane in the other, as she strode down the hall like an avenging angel.

The intruder had sense enough to break out of his paralysis and run, stumbling over Petunia in the process.

He staggered up and started down the staircase just as Lady Lockwood reached it. She brought her cane down across his back, and he fell, rolling down the steps to the landing. Pulling himself to his feet, he limped down the stairs and out the front door, which stood open. Verity went tearing after him.

"Well! I never!" Lady Lockwood turned, sending an accusing look at the rest of them and slamming the candle on a small console table. "What has this world come to? Kidnapping. Random strangers popping in and out of the house." She bent down and gave the panting pug a reassuring scratch. "There, now, Petunia, don't fret," she said in a kinder tone than Annabeth had ever heard her use with people. "He's gone now."

"And I rather suspect he won't be returning," Annabeth said, stifling a smile.

"I should think not." Her grandmother's sharp gaze fell on Annabeth, taking in her nightgown, loose hair, and bare feet. "Really, Annabeth, you shouldn't be running about dressed like that. Go put on your slippers and dressing gown."

"Yes, ma'am." Annabeth ducked into her room to grab her dressing gown.

When she came back into the corridor, Verity had returned, breathing almost as hard as Petunia, and was receiving a similar lecture about proper attire from Lady Lockwood. Verity gave her a curtsy, murmuring an apology, and started back toward the servants' staircase, but she stopped when she saw Annabeth and said in her maid's voice, "I'm sorry, miss, I couldn't catch 'im. Are yuh all right?"

"Yes, I'm fine."

"Did that man attack you, Annabeth?" Lady Lockwood said.

"No. Not at all. I think he was a thief. I woke up because he was rummaging around in my room. I screamed and threw something at him, and he took off." Annabeth thought it was best not to mention that first move he had made in her direction.

"How did he get in here, anyway?" Lady Lockwood demanded. She sent a sharp look at the butler. "Are we in the habit of leaving our doors unlocked?"

"No, ma'am," Cartwell replied, sounding just as dignified as if he wasn't dressed in his nightcap and nightgown with his white, spindly calves showing below it. "I locked it myself."

"He picked the lock, ma'am, and came in that way," Verity explained.

"I see," Lady Lockwood sniffed. "Well. Then I am going back to my bed. I would like to get at least a few hours' sleep."

She thumped back to her room, talking in a low voice to Petunia.

Annabeth retreated into her bedroom. She picked up the candlestick and now-broken candle that lay beside it and, reinserting the largest piece of candle, she lit it and walked over to the fireplace. The small old trunk stood open. It was the one she had taken from the rental house a few days before.

She was startled by the sound of her door opening, and she turned to see Verity, now in Lady Lockwood–approved attire of a blue flannel wrapper, lugging in a folded cot.

"I don't care what you say. I'm sleeping here tonight," Verity said pugnaciously as she set down the cot and faced Annabeth, arms crossed. "Lady Lockwood ordered it. So if you don't want me in here, I'll make my bed across your doorway in the hall."

Annabeth nodded. Frankly, after tonight's adventure, she would prefer to have Verity sleeping here. Somewhat stiffly, she said, "Thank you for coming to help me. Were you sleeping on that window seat?"

"Trying to." Verity gave her the quick, infectious grin that made it so easy to like her. She came over to stand by Annabeth and gazed down at the trunk, her hands fisted on her hips. "What are you looking at that for?"

"Clearly the intruder was rummaging through it. I wasn't sleeping with papers strewed about the floor. And that—" Annabeth pointed at the glass paperweight "—was probably what made the thud that awakened me."

"Did they take anything?" Verity asked.

Annabeth sifted through the odds and ends and letters, running her fingers over one of her father's small clever wooden boxes. "I don't believe so."

Annabeth reached into the box and pulled out a very poorly knit mitten, misshapen and marked with holes where a stitch had been dropped.

"I can see why he gave up knitting," Verity said with a small smile.

"It was one of my first childish attempts at knitting." Annabeth tightened her fist around it, her eyes dampening at the thought that her father had kept the thing.

"I figured. I was just trying to get a smile out of you. I can tell by the tears that I'm doing a bang-up job."

"Logically I know it's been five years since he died, but sometimes it feels as if it was just yesterday. Whatever my father's faults—and I can admit that he had several—he was a kind and loving father, and I adored him."

"That can make up for a lot." Verity nodded.

"He might have been careless and irresponsible, his head stuck in the clouds, as Lady Lockwood is fond of pointing out, but what I remember was his smile, his tolerance, his sense of fun and curiosity."

"I can't say I have too much firsthand experience with good dads." Verity moved over to her cot and slid a blade under her thin pillow. "But it sounds like he was one."

Annabeth noted the weapon. "You must be a less restless sleeper than I. I'd wake up missing an eye if I did that."

"I doubt I will be getting much sleep at all. As impregnable as Lady Lockwood thinks this house is, Sloane and I assumed there was a chance the intruder might try again."

Annabeth felt the same stab of curiosity, the insistent hunger to know about Sloane and Verity. It was foolish. It made no difference. Yet somehow she couldn't stop herself from saying, "You and Sloane seem to know each other well."

"Yes," Verity said, fondness in her voice. "We worked together a good deal."

"Were you, um, more than—when you said you were together, did you mean—" She stopped, unable to complete her sentence.

"Are you asking if we were ever in a...*romantic* relationship?" Verity asked with a suggestive raise of her eyebrow.

Annabeth blushed and nodded her head. "I'm sorry, that's too personal. I shouldn't—"

"No, we weren't," Verity said. "That's not to say I

didn't think about it once or twice early on—he's a very good-looking man—but he was obviously still in love with you. He talked about you enough. And I have never had much interest in men that are interested in someone else. It's not a good idea, anyway, to get too attached to someone in the network. We were friends and colleagues, that's all. He saved my life once, and another time I broke him out of jail."

"You did?" Annabeth's eyes widened. "How?"

Verity looked up soulfully at an invisible person, clasping her hands together prayerfully beneath her chin. "Oh, sir, please, he's my brother. I can't bear not to see him…one last time." She dabbed artistically at her eye and sniffed. Relaxing, she grinned. "It sounds better in French."

Annabeth couldn't help but laugh. "You're very good at getting people to like you."

"I don't think your man would agree." The idea didn't seem to bother Verity much.

"Sloane's not my—oh. Nathan? To be fair, he probably would like you more if you weren't rude to him."

"Me? Rude?" Verity retorted, sauciness on full display.

"Most people like Nathan."

"He's a very agreeable man," Verity admitted. "Too agreeable, really."

"How can one be too agreeable?" Annabeth asked.

Verity scoffed in response.

"Well, he's certainly not Sloane," Annabeth said. "Which is a good thing."

"Is it?"

Annabeth didn't have an answer.

CHAPTER FOURTEEN

SLOANE ARRIVED AT Lady Lockwood's house the next morning so early that Annabeth was still at breakfast. The butler had tried to announce him, but Sloane had followed on the man's heels in his usual manner, so that he was in the doorway of the dining room before Cartwell could get his name.

"I'm sorry, miss," the butler said, with a disapproving look at Sloane, "but he would not wait in the entry."

"It's all right, Cartwell. You may go." Annabeth rose to face Sloane. "I see that your manners haven't improved over the years."

"Probably not," Sloane agreed. He glanced around. "Have I managed to catch you without all your retinue?"

"Grandmother rarely appears before eleven, and of course Nathan, being a gentleman, calls on us at an appropriate time in the afternoon."

"Ooh—direct shot." Sloane winced and laid a hand against his chest, a glimmer of amusement in his eyes. And for a moment, he looked so much like the boy Annabeth had known that it made her throat tighten.

She turned away to conceal her expression, and went to the teapot on the sideboard. "Would you like a cup of tea?"

There was a moment of hesitation, then he said, "Yes,

thank you. That would be nice." He sat down across the table from her.

"Breakfast?" Annabeth asked, going back to her seat and stretching across the table to set the cup in front of him, carefully avoiding getting too close. The glint in his eye told her he knew exactly what she was doing.

"I'm not going to attack you, you know. You needn't stay three feet away from me."

"Of course not. I know that."

"Then it's yourself you don't trust around me?" He cocked an eyebrow.

"I'm not sure if you're trying to flirt with me or annoy me, but I have no interest in bantering with you," Annabeth said firmly. She looked straight into his eyes. "We are not what we used to be to each other, Sloane. We aren't even friends. We simply have a common goal, and I suggest we stick to achieving that."

He shrugged, his face devoid of expression. "Where is Verity?"

"I've no idea. I have not seen her this morning. Miss Cole and I are not bosom friends."

"Mmm-hmm. I suppose not." He paused, then said, "Don't be too hard on her, Anna. I don't think she ever meant any harm, and she'll be protection for you when I'm not here."

Annabeth started to point out that Verity had failed to keep out an intruder last night, but she stopped. The less Sloane knew about the break-in, the better. He would start haranguing her once again about leaving the city.

"Then let's look at the boxes. I presume that's why you're here." She stood up. "I'll get them."

Annabeth rather wondered where Verity had gone. Annabeth would have preferred not to be alone with

Sloane, but she knew they would work better without Verity or Nathan there. The two of them would only add to the sniping, and Annabeth would worry about whether Nathan might be hurt or jealous.

She returned a few minutes later with her own three boxes from her father. Last night she had opened the secret drawer of the largest box and taken out the pressed flower that was her last remaining memento of Sloane's, as well as all the other odds and ends she kept openly in the chest.

"This is the box that was in the trunk we removed from the rental house," she told him, handing him the small puzzle box. "I've not opened it before. These two are mine."

While Sloane set to work on the sliding pieces of the puzzle box, Annabeth opened the secret compartments of both the others. They were empty, as she already knew they were, and so was the puzzle box when Sloane shifted the various pieces in the correct order.

"Well, I didn't really expect it to be in one of yours, otherwise you would have opened it long ago. Nor really in one that he had left where anyone might take it. The most likely place is one of Hunter's secret storage places in his home."

"Let's go there," Annabeth replied.

"Without a chaperone?" Sloane widened his eyes in mock horror. "Lady Lockwood would protest."

"Then we'd better leave quickly, before she comes down, hadn't we?" Despite her calm tone, Annabeth's heart sped up. She wasn't sure whether it was in panic or excitement.

He grinned and turned to go, reaching out to take her arm in the way he had in the past. His fingers were

warm against her bare skin, the touch at once so familiar and so surprising that she sucked in a breath. Sloane
glanced at her and hastily dropped his hand.

"I must change," Annabeth said, stepping back
abruptly, then hurried up to her room. There, she quickly
changed into a walking dress of light green that comple-
mented her eyes—not that that mattered. It was simply
her favorite. Adding her newest hat and a pelisse of a
slightly darker blue, she went back downstairs.

Outside, Sloane gave her a hand to step up into the
hackney. It was a small vehicle with only a single bench
seat. Sloane took up more space than Annabeth thought
was warranted, but she wasn't about to let him know that
his closeness bothered her. She would be aloof. Cool.
They were no longer anything to one another. She was
not going to let him rattle her or stir her emotions.

Still, she found it a bit annoying that he made no more
effort to talk on the trip than she did. One would think
he might say something. He might explain himself and
his actions, might even apologize for having deceived
her. Not that anything he said would change what she
thought of him. How she felt about him.

However, as soon as they left the carriage and stepped
into what had once been her home, the past all around
her, she could not hold her tongue any longer. "Why did
you not tell me?"

"Not tell you what?" Sloane closed the door behind
them, keeping his eyes on his hand as he turned the key
in the lock.

"You know perfectly well what. Why did you not tell
me that you were working for our government, not the
French? That you weren't a traitor."

"I told you yesterday. It defeated the purpose if I told people," he replied, still not looking at her.

"I thought I was something more to you than just 'people.'" Her voice thickened.

Sloane turned to her then, his blue eyes bright with emotion. "Of course you were more to me. More to me than anyone else. I loved you. You must know that."

"No, I don't know that. I feel as though I never really knew you. If you hid such an important thing from me, what else did you hide? Which of your words were true? What vows did you mean?"

"I didn't lie to you." His eyes burned into hers, and he moved closer.

As it always had, Sloane's gaze went all through Annabeth, dancing along her nerves and flooding her chest, making her forget what she wanted to say. He had always won their arguments because when he looked at her that way, she could think of nothing else.

But not anymore. She ignored the pulse that leaped in her and the breath that quickened—the remembered pain made that easier—and said, "Not telling me is the same as lying. Letting me wonder what I had done, why you turned away from me, examining everything we'd done and said for some clue to the answer—it was cruel."

"I'm sorry. I wouldn't have hurt you for the world..." It was there in his face, the remorse and the pain. He reached out and gently cupped her cheek. For one aching moment, she thought he was about to kiss her, and she yearned to feel it.

Annabeth took a quick, jerky step back. "Yet you did."

Sloane let out a breath and moved back, as if he, too, had been caught in that moment of closeness. His expression settled into its more recent cynical lines, and the hunger and regret were leached from his voice. "It would have been dangerous for you to know. My very existence depended on secrecy. Not just my life, but the lives of others."

"You didn't trust me."

"Of course I trusted you. But no matter how little you said, how well you pretended, you would have looked different, acted differently, because deep down, you would have known the truth. It could have created doubt. Suspicion."

Annabeth felt cold, then hot. "So my heart was sacrificed to create an illusion."

For an instant, heat flashed in his eyes, then it was gone. He gave a little shrug. "I suppose, if you want to look at it that way."

"I don't want to look at it *any* way," Annabeth retorted. "I just want all this over with. I want my life back. So I suggest we find this document as quickly as we can."

She whirled and strode off. She went first to what had been her father's study, where bookshelves that were set into the wall opened when she flipped up a carved decoration and pressed the small button beneath. Inside the wall was an empty cabinet.

"Clever." Sloane ran his finger over the nearly invisible seam that separated the rosette from the rest of the wood.

"I don't think we'll find anything. I went through all the hiding places when we first moved out of the house," Annabeth said, forcing a businesslike tone.

"And what if you didn't know where all of them

were?" Sloane pointed out. "Perhaps your father kept a secret place hidden even from you."

"It's possible," Annabeth said doubtfully. "I suppose we'll have to examine everything with an eye to that." She didn't like the thought. It meant more time being alone here with Sloane.

They went through the rooms, Annabeth showing him her father's various hiding spots. She didn't reveal the space in her own bedroom that had once held the letters Sloane had sent her. Those were long gone, tossed in the fireplace during a bout of tears, but somehow even seeing where they had been seemed too intimate.

It was Sloane who discovered that if he pressed the base of the finial atop one of the staircase's newel-posts, the knob could be twisted off. In the hollow beneath the finial was a small leather pouch. It was the only item they had found, and they smiled at each other in anticipation.

"It's light," Annabeth said as she pulled out the little bag. "I think maybe there's nothing in it." She tugged at the knotted ties that closed the pouch.

"I'll cut it." Sloane reached into his boot and pulled out a thin sharp knife.

"You go around everywhere armed?" she asked.

"Not until recently, after the trouble with Parker started. At least, not *this* well armed. It seemed a good idea to take up my old ways." He reached for the bag.

"Stop. You are always so impatient. I almost have it undone. There." Annabeth reached in and pulled out a small leather notebook. "This is it!" She held it out to him. "Isn't it?"

He snatched the notebook from her fingers and opened it. He frowned. "What the—"

Annabeth hadn't really seen what was on the pages and she moved closer, craning her neck to see over Sloane's arm. Unconsciously, she laid a hand lightly on his back to steady herself, then realized what she had done, how close she was standing to him.

Color flooded her face, and she jumped back. "I—I'm sorry. I—um—"

"Sorry for what?" He turned his head toward her.

Obviously he hadn't even noticed, which somehow made it all the more embarrassing. "Nothing. What does it say?"

He handed the notebook to her. It was curled from years of having been rolled up inside the post, and she had to stretch it out to read the pages. Every page was the same, each having two columns. The one on the left contained a few letters on each line and the column on the right held numbers, and at the end of each was a triangle or circle. Around the margins there were little curlicues, and here and there was a question mark or an exclamation mark.

"What is all that?" Annabeth asked.

"I have no idea. I was hoping you could tell me."

"Well, I can tell you that it's my father's hand. He used to make those little curlicues on his drawings and notes. I don't understand all the numbers and letters."

"Neither do I," Sloane answered, frowning down at the pages. "I suppose they could be a code of some kind. It hardly seems like a—"

"Like what?"

"Like a document. I was expecting something more like a letter." He shrugged and tucked the slender book inside his jacket. "Whatever it is, I think that we have exhausted all possibilities here. We should go back, I suppose."

"Yes. We've been gone longer than I expected. Grandmother will be furious. I told Cartwell where we were going, so she won't be worried."

"But she certainly won't be pleased."

CHAPTER FIFTEEN

NATHAN WAS IN the drawing room with Lady Lockwood when Sloane and Annabeth returned. Annabeth felt suddenly swamped with guilt. *You didn't do anything wrong,* she told herself. But her actions themselves didn't really matter—she knew the emotions that had been swirling inside her just from being in Sloane's presence.

"I was surprised Sloane and Miss Cole weren't here when I arrived," Nathan said. "But I suppose you were all off searching for this mysterious document. Where is Miss Cole, anyway?" He looked past Sloane and Annabeth.

"That impostor went off to see their 'spymaster.' There was a break-in last night," Lady Lockwood answered before Annabeth could stop her. "I would've told you that straight away if you'd asked instead of dancing around the subject and making inane small talk."

"A break-in!" Nathan goggled at her. "What? Someone broke into this house?"

"Nice of you to mention that to me." Sloane glowered.

"I didn't plan on mentioning it to anyone at all." Annabeth frowned. "It was all over in a matter of moments. Grandmother whacked him with her cane."

"That would be enough to send anyone running," Sloane said.

"If only you'd told me that years ago." Lady Lockwood turned a jaundiced eye on him. "I'd have tried it out on you, happily."

Nathan let out a gurgle of laughter. "I'd like to see that."

"Petunia helped. She's a fierce little thing, when it comes down to it." Annabeth smiled.

"My boots are ample evidence of that," Nathan said wryly. He went to Annabeth. "Are you all right? Were you hurt?"

"No," Annabeth began, but Lady Lockwood interrupted with a thump of her cane.

"So, Rutherford, what do you intend to do?"

"Do?" Sloane echoed.

"Yes, of course. About all this." Lady Lockwood waved her hand in a vague gesture. "Thieves and vagabonds popping in and out of the house at will."

Annabeth took pity on Sloane and said, "We don't really know that he was a vagabond, Grandmother. He may very well have a home in London."

"You know what I mean," Lady Lockwood said. "Kidnappers, scoundrels, lurkers, mountebanks, and robbers. People playing masquerade in my own house. It's scandalous."

"There is always Bath, as I have suggested to Annabeth," Sloane told Lady Lockwood.

"I'm not going to Bath," Lady Lockwood said with finality. She sighed. "I can see this is going to take some time. Since you're here, you might as well sit down and have some tea." She waved her hand at the tea cart.

Annabeth was pouring a cup of tea when the butler appeared in the doorway, Russell Feringham beside him. "Mr. Feringham, my lady."

"Uncle Russell! What a nice surprise."

"I heard there was a commotion this past evening, and I wanted to inquire as to your welfare and see if I could be of any service—"

"Humph," Lady Lockwood said. "Be that as it may, it's unfashionably early in the day for a call, isn't it, Feringham? What if what we needed was to sleep in after our ordeal? Not that it would have mattered with these young men calling on Annabeth at the crack of dawn. Everyone knows Sloane has the manners of a house mouse, simply coming and going as he pleases. But one would hope Mr. Dunbridge would be better behaved. Unfortunately he apparently *lives* here."

"Now that we've finished this discussion of proper manners, can we please return to the subject of the break-in?" Sloane raised his eyebrows.

At that moment there was the sound of voices in the entry hall. Lady Lockwood scowled at the open door of the drawing room. "Now what?" As the voices came nearer, she sighed. "It's Martha and Edgerton. Obviously everyone has decided to plague me this morning."

Annabeth's mother rushed in, exclaiming, "Oh, my dear! Are you all right?" She gripped Annabeth's upper arms, gazing deeply into her daughter's eyes. Martha was a more dramatic yet somehow more bland, weaker version of her sister, Lady Drewsbury.

"Yes, Mother, I'm perfectly fine." Annabeth smiled at her reassuringly.

"I suppose everyone is calling on us because you have heard about Annabeth being kidnapped," Lady Lockwood said. "To think running off an intruder early in the wee hours was just the start to a string of interruptions."

Russell gave an incredulous look, popping up from his seat in alarm. "Annabeth, dearest, are you all right?"

"I'm fine," Annabeth hastened to say. "Really, there's no need to worry."

"Of course we're worried!" Martha's hand went to her chest. "I haven't had a moment's peace since I heard about the incidents."

"I don't understand how any of you knew about either one," Annabeth said. "They just happened a few hours ago."

"Well, my maid, of course," Martha replied as if it were obvious.

"My valet got it from the egg man, I believe," Russell offered. "He's a pipeline of news. One never needs to read those gossip sheets." He added, "Though I must say they're entertaining. The editor of *The Onlooker* has a wicked way with words."

"Stop wandering off the subject, Russell…" Lady Lockwood sent him a stern look. "A child in a sweet shop is more attentive than you."

"Edgerton and I were *so* distressed when we heard, weren't we, darling?" Martha turned toward her husband, a tall, conservatively dressed man with white hair and a permanent expression of disapproval.

"Yes, Martha was most upset, naturally," he replied. He nodded to Nathan and to Russell, his mouth tightening as he took in Russell's attire.

Russell Feringham was short and rather pear-shaped, and his hair was thinning on top, but he was always dressed in the latest fashion. Today he was wearing buff-colored breeches and a dark green jacket with eye-catching gold buttons in a double row across his upper chest, a colorful paisley waistcoat showing beneath, and an intricately tied neckcloth.

Lord Edgerton's gaze went on to Sloane, and he

scowled, then came forward to make a formal bow to Annabeth's grandmother. "I'm sure you were quite frightened, my lady."

"Frightened?" Lady Lockwood stiffened. "Of some petty criminal? I should say not."

"Lady Lockwood has never suffered from cowardice, Edgerton," Sloane said. "Though that may not be something easily understood by you."

"Are you calling *me* a coward?" Edgerton's face reddened. "Well, such words carry little weight coming from a traitor to the Crown like you." He swung toward Lady Lockwood. "My lady, what were you thinking letting a scoundrel like this into your home?"

Russell, who until now had been quietly watching the show, said, "Now you've done it."

Edgerton flicked a dismissive look at Russell and turned to Sloane. "Leave this house now. Do you hear me?"

"I suspect the whole house can hear you," Sloane replied mildly.

"Don't you move a step, young man," Lady Lockwood ordered Sloane. "This is my house, and I am not in my dotage. I assure you that my reputation will stand up to a great deal more than one of Annabeth's and Nathan's old friends calling on us. If I say Rutherford is welcome, then he is. Now, sit down, Edgerton, and stop acting like a fool."

Lord Edgerton puffed up, but he clamped his lips shut, and when his wife murmured, "Please, dear," he sat down.

"Now, before everyone arrived, we were discussing Lady Lockwood and Annabeth going to Bath."

"Running away isn't the answer," Annabeth told Sloane. "We should focus on finding what Papa wrote."

Sloane shot Annabeth a harsh look. But right now she didn't care that Sloane and the government wanted secrecy. She just wanted this to be over with.

"Hunter?" Martha said in surprise.

She turned to her mother. "Something Papa wrote was apparently important."

Beside her Edgerton snorted and said, "Hunter Winfield never wrote anything important."

"Somebody seems to think he did," Nathan put in.

"But, my boy," Russell said, looking puzzled. "Hunter was a wonderful man, but he was not a literary sort."

"It's not literary," Annabeth said. "It's a secret—"

CHAPTER SIXTEEN

"ANNABETH IS LOOKING for some messages Mr. Winfield left for her," Sloane interrupted. "Words of comfort. Of wisdom. That sort of thing. Like the ones he left in Lady Lockwood's jewelry box."

"Of course. Like that lovely poem he put in one of the boxes he gave me." Martha smiled reminiscently.

"Yes. Just like that." Annabeth went along with what Sloane put forth. His reasons were plausible and certainly easier to explain than the truth, but she still felt uncomfortable lying.

"Annabeth found a note in a puzzle box when she was cleaning out the attic at her house the other day," Sloane continued. "Mr. Winfield indicated that there would be others to find."

Annabeth sent Sloane a warning look. She didn't need him making up stories she was expected to keep up with her family—though clearly he was an expert at inventing lies. "You remember, Mama, how Papa used to do that—it was a little game he and I played."

"Oh yes, dear. You and he were so clever. I never could make heads nor tails of those things."

"Do you still have any of the boxes? May I look at them?"

"Naturally." Martha beamed. "I have several. Though

I have looked through them all and took out any messages."

"Thank you." Annabeth turned to Russell. "Do you have any?"

"Yes, indeed, child, I have several, and you are quite welcome to look through them. Unfortunately they aren't here. They're at my house in the country."

"Oh. Well…"

"I can get them for you, if you'd like." Russell brightened. "I have to go home for a few days—that tiresome estate manager wants to talk to me again. I'm sure it will be unutterably boring, but, well, of course, one must go. Hopefully it won't be for long."

"Thank you." Annabeth gave him a grateful look. "I would very much appreciate it."

Edgerton made a low noise of disgust. "Enough talk about those silly boxes. The important thing is that we ensure your safety, Annabeth. The answer isn't to run away, as some are inclined to do." He cast a meaning glance at Sloane. "It's clear that you should come live with us."

"Darling, come back home," Martha urged.

"That's not my home," Annabeth said quietly.

"Of course it's not," Lady Lockwood agreed. "This is your home, and it is perfectly safe."

"I think clearly it is not, since she has been attacked here twice," Edgerton retorted. "You must come live with us, Annabeth."

Annabeth bristled, but before she could reply her grandmother declared, "It's not your place, Edgerton, to decree what my granddaughter can or cannot do. Annabeth is *my* charge."

"I'm not *anyone's* charge," Annabeth snapped. "I am thirty years old, well past my majority."

"Oh, no, dear," her mother said in alarm, leaning over to pat Annabeth's arm. "A lady must never mention her age."

Sloane let out a hoot of laughter, and Annabeth had to cover her mouth to stifle her own. Well, at least her mother had managed to reduce the whole argument to the merest frippery.

Lord Edgerton still looked incensed, but before he could speak, Nathan decided to take down the temperature of the room by changing the conversation. "I understand you have a new vehicle, my lord. Everyone at the club was talking about it."

Russell, who was also accustomed to calming conversational waters, chimed in, "I've heard that it's quite dashing, Edgerton. Though I'd never buy a phaeton myself. They're too easy to turn over. I was never much of a driver. It's why I didn't participate in curricle races with Hunter."

"And London was the safer for it," Edgerton snorted.

Russell merely chuckled as he rose to his feet. "Did you drive your phaeton here today? You could show me as we leave."

"I'm sure Edgerton would love to do that," Lady Lockwood said. She turned to her son-in-law. "No doubt you were going to take your leave, anyway, since you wouldn't want to stay longer than the appropriate time for a call, especially one made so early."

There was little Lord Edgerton could do after Lady Lockwood's clear dismissal. "You are correct, of course, ma'am. Martha, we should go."

Martha rose, too, looking disappointed, and Annabeth said, "I'm sure Grandmother didn't mean you had to leave, too, Mama."

"Of course not."

"It's been ages since we talked," Annabeth said. "Do stay."

"That would be nice." Martha turned to her husband. "What do you think, dear?"

"I cannot stay," Edgerton told her, even though he had not been included in the invitation. "I promised to see Hanborough at the club. And I don't want you going home by yourself. Annabeth may come visit you at our home."

"No doubt you're right." Martha's face fell a bit, but then she smiled up at her husband. "You take such good care of me, Edward. I am the luckiest of women."

"You are the world to me." Edgerton lifted Martha's hand to lay a brief kiss on her knuckles.

Lady Lockwood let out a groan. "Sorry," she said when the others turned to look at her. She patted her stomach. "Touch of dyspepsia." After her daughter left, Lady Lockwood added, "Thank heavens Alistair never took such good care of me."

Annabeth giggled at the thought of her mild, sweet grandfather ever telling Lady Lockwood what to do. Indeed, his most common response to any question or concern was, "Go ask your grandmother."

"It makes me so angry when he tells her what to do," Annabeth said crossly. "He acts as if she were a child. Why doesn't she ever stand up to him?"

"That's the way your mother likes to be treated," Lady Lockwood declared. "It's why she married Edgerton as soon as her year of mourning was over. She cannot bear not to have a husband."

Annabeth thought her mother's departure was probably more due to a desire to escape living with Lady Lockwood than anything else, but she knew better than to say such a truth.

"Martha has no responsibility for anything this way, and yet she usually still manages to get what she wants by being biddable. She enjoys being coddled and fussed over, and she simply ignores everything in Edgerton that is unpleasant. If you'll remember, she never stood up to your father, either. She simply paid no attention to his wasteful habits and irresponsibility."

"Yes, but Papa was kind and pleasant and…and fun."

"Doesn't mean he was a good husband. At least Edgerton pays his bills, gives Martha an ample allowance for clothes and fripperies, and doesn't have her worry about bill collectors. He doesn't gamble or drink, and she doesn't have to wonder what he and his wild friends might take it into their heads to do—like racing their curricles all about. Goodness, I was sure Hunter was going to break his neck within a year of their marriage."

"Papa was that wild? I thought he was one of Lord Drewsbury's circle."

"Yes, like my father," Nathan said.

"Oh, no. Hunter usually ran with a different set—your father, Marcus, for one." She nodded in Sloane's direction.

"Yes, I remember," Sloane said. "He and Russell used to come over to drink and play cards with my father."

"But Uncle Russell isn't wild."

"Not anymore," Lady Lockwood admitted. "To be fair, your papa had mostly settled down about the time you were born, too. Gave up his foolish racing. So Russell settled down as well. He always followed Hunter's lead. Hunter was that way—people were drawn to him." There was a bit of wonderment in her voice at the notion of her son-in-law's popularity.

"Not Lord Edgerton, surely."

Lady Lockwood let out a crack of laughter. "I'd say not. Both he and Hunter were courting Martha, you see. Of course, Edgerton disliked Hunter more than Hunter disliked him. That's just their natures."

Lady Lockwood cast her gaze over Sloane and Nathan. "Clearly you two haven't the manners to have left with the others. So sit down and let's decide what we're going to do." When the two men took their seats, she went on, "Now, Rutherford, I hope you've thought of a better plan than slinking off to Bath."

"I'd like to hear this plan, too," Verity said from the doorway. She was dressed in her maid's attire and carried a duster to keep up her disguise with other servants. But she closed the door, laid the duster on a table, and adopted a very un-servant-like pose, arms crossed and chin raised. "Since Sloane seems to be making decisions for all of us."

Sloane cast her a quelling look. "I didn't notice you waiting for any instructions before you ran off this morning."

Verity shrugged. "I had people to talk to."

Nathan cleared his throat. "The plan?"

"Yes." Sloane turned back to the others. "As soon as you can—tomorrow if possible—Annabeth and Lady Lockwood will drive to Stonecliffe."

"Stonecliffe! I told you I'm not going to go anywhere, much less burst in on a couple of newlyweds," Annabeth protested.

"Noelle and Carlisle aren't there. They went to his

estate—which is exactly the sort of insipid place Carlisle would choose for his honeymoon. So there's no one at the house but Lady Drewsbury. It seems a perfect time for Lady Drewsbury's mother and niece to visit."

"Hmm." Lady Lockwood considered it, her eyes brightening. "It would be nice to get out a bit. See the child." Annabeth's grandmother's softer side always came out around young Gil. "And Adeline, of course," she added almost as an afterthought.

"Stonecliffe is the safest house I can think of," Sloane went on. "The servants are all accustomed to being on guard, after the trouble Noelle and Carlisle had there. You can close the gates to the courtyard, leaving only the garden door that needs to be watched. Verity can accompany you for protection, and Nathan can escort you."

"I told you, I am not running," Annabeth said in irritation. "And I don't see how my hiding at Stonecliffe will help you discover Papa's document."

"I didn't say you would *stay* there," Sloane said, a teasing glimmer in his eyes. "Verity is going to cease being a maid and become you."

"What?"

"She'll dress in your clothes, put on your bonnets, and Nathan will pop over to visit her frequently. They'll take strolls in the garden and sit on the terrace or in the courtyard. From a distance she could pass for you, so if the enemy follows us, they will be lulled into thinking Annabeth is staying put at Stonecliffe in Kent. In the meantime we will go search your father's workshop in Sussex."

"Wonderful!" Annabeth's chest swelled with excitement.

"No!" Nathan and Verity exclaimed simultaneously.

"If you think I'm going to sit in some castle in the country twiddling my thumbs while you have all the fun, you're insane," Verity told Sloane.

"You agreed to help however you could," Sloane said in a steely voice. "This is what will help. It doesn't take four people to search a workshop, and Annabeth is the only person who knows where to find what we're looking for. If people think she's at Stonecliffe, they won't be looking for her in Sussex. Besides, you won't be doing nothing. I suspect that Hunter Winfield might have given a box or two to his sister-in-law."

"Lord, yes," Lady Lockwood agreed. "He scattered them everywhere. He was fond of Adeline, and she's the sort of person who would keep them."

"You know you'd like to get your hands on some of those boxes," Sloane told Verity.

"I like puzzles," Verity admitted.

"And you might want to work on this while you're sitting about." He reached inside his jacket and pulled out the small notebook they had found that morning. He handed it to Verity.

"What is that?" Nathan moved to Verity's side to examine the pages. "It's just gibberish. Why is this important?"

Annabeth said, "Because we found it carefully hidden in one of Papa's secret compartments, one even I didn't know about."

Lady Lockwood harrumphed and banged her cane on the floor, waking Petunia and starting her barking. "Don't just stand there, Dunbridge. Give that to me."

Nathan obeyed, but when she saw it, Annabeth's grandmother looked equally puzzled.

"I thought it might be a code of some kind," Sloane

explained after Lady Lockwood handed the small journal back to him. "I don't recognize it, though."

"Neither do I," Verity said. She looked over Sloane's shoulder at the pages, clearly intrigued. "Perhaps there's a key—a book, say. The number could be the page, or the page and a line. The letters could indicate what book."

"That might explain why two or three of the groups are the same letters," Sloane said.

"Or perhaps the key is here already, in invisible ink…" Verity took the journal, went over to a lamp, and took off its chimney to hold a page over the flame. The paper began to turn brown, but no new writing appeared.

"Careful, don't burn it," Nathan told her.

She sent him a scornful look. "Thank you, Mr. Dunbridge. I wouldn't have thought of that." She shut the notebook and stuck it in her pocket. "Still, I don't need to stay at some boring house in the country to work on this."

Nathan shot Verity a withering look. "Miss Cole's state of boredom is not my main concern. Annabeth can't go running about the countryside alone with Rutherford. Her reputation would be in tatters."

"Which is why we will be leaving Stonecliffe *secretly*," Sloane said, as if speaking to a slow-witted person.

Nathan made a derisive noise. "You can't sneak in and out of Stonecliffe without someone noticing."

"I can." Sloane gave a careless shrug.

"I suppose no one anywhere else along the way will notice the two of you either."

"We are going to be staying with the Haverstocks. Just visiting our childhood chums."

"Do Priscilla and Timothy know about our visit?" Annabeth asked.

"No. I just now thought of it. But I'll send a note this evening. There won't be any problem. Sprague was a good friend." A shadow touched his features.

"I'm sorry," Annabeth said, regretting her light tone. The death of the Haverstocks' older brother had doubtless been very painful for Sloane. Aside from Annabeth herself, Sprague had been Sloane's closest friend.

"It happens. People die." Sloane turned to Nathan. "You see? All your fears for Annabeth's reputation are answered."

"I will go with you," Nathan countered.

"And leave poor Miss Cole without protection at Stonecliffe?"

"I feel sure Miss Cole can manage without my protection," Nathan said dryly.

"You have that right," Verity agreed.

Sloane went on, "My curricle only seats two. And it would be rude of me to bring an uninvited guest to the Haverstocks'."

"*I* should be the one—" Nathan began heatedly.

"For pity's sake!" Lady Lockwood exclaimed, slamming her cane on the floor and setting off another round of barking from Petunia. "Stop all this pointless yammering. I agree with Rutherford's plan. He and Annabeth will go hunt for this silly box. You will stay at your house, Nathan—which I must say, you should do more often than you do—and call on us at Stonecliffe frequently. It will be a trial putting up with Miss Cole, I grant you, but one must do what is necessary."

Nathan swung toward Lady Lockwood in astonishment. "Surely you cannot countenance Annabeth traveling with him."

"Under normal circumstances, I am sure that you would be adequate to protect Annabeth," Lady Lockwood said. "But these men are clearly scoundrels. So it will take a scoundrel to defeat them." She pointed her cane at Sloane.

"Just a moment," Annabeth said crisply. "I hate to interrupt this discussion of what I ought to do and where I should go and who will accompany me, but I have to point out that *I* am the one in charge of my own actions."

"Hear, hear," Verity said with a grin.

"I must go to my father's workshop with Sloane." Annabeth went to Nathan, pained by his wounded expression, and took his hand. "Please, understand. I agree with Grandmother. Secrecy and danger are what Sloane has dealt in for years. Clearly you are the better person, the better man, but for this task, Sloane is the man I need."

The crushed look in Nathan's eyes made Annabeth wish she could pull the words back from the air. It made her wish with all her might that they weren't true. Unfortunately, there was no taking them back. And she couldn't pretend they were false.

Hurting Nathan made an answering hurt sweep through Annabeth, roiling her stomach. She could only console herself that once this was over and done with, she would never have to hurt Nathan again. She could forget about Sloane and move on with her life. And she would spend the rest of her years trying to make it up to Nathan.

"Please, trust me. This is what I have to do."

Nathan simply looked at her for a long moment, then

made a small nod of acceptance and squeezed her hand. However, he didn't kiss her hand lightly as he often had done in the past. "Of course, Annabeth. I always trust you."

CHAPTER SEVENTEEN

THEY SET OUT the following morning for Stonecliffe, Annabeth, her grandmother, and Verity riding in Lady Lockwood's large old-fashioned carriage. Nathan chose to ride his horse, politely saying that it would give the ladies more room. Annabeth wasn't sure whether his true reason was to escape Lady Lockwood's complaints, Petunia's attacks on his boots, or Verity's barbs. Probably all three. Annabeth pushed away the guilty voice that told her it was because he couldn't stand to be in such close quarters with his fiancée after her decision.

When they reached Stonecliffe, Adeline greeted Annabeth and Lady Lockwood with her usual blend of delight and trepidation. Gil was unreservedly happy to greet them. He hugged Annabeth, executed a gentlemanly bow to his great-grandmother, followed by a kiss to her cheek when she bent down to him—as tough as Lady Lockwood was, she was enamored with Gil. He regarded Verity seriously for a moment then smiled at her, and took Nathan by the hand and whisked him away to see his new tin soldiers.

If Adeline thought it peculiar to have a woman in a maid's cap and apron sit down with the other ladies, she was kind enough not to say it, and she listened with great interest to their tale. At the end, she said merely, "Well. I think it would be best if you drop the role of maid from the start here, Miss Cole, don't you? I will make it clear that no one is to mention you to anyone outside the house, of course, but the less confusion among the servants the better. Gil will no doubt find it great fun to pretend that you are Annabeth."

While the room was being prepared, Annabeth and Verity went up to Annabeth's room, where Verity put on the clothes Annabeth had been wearing. She and Nathan took a stroll around the grounds with Gil, who, as his grandmother had said, found it a wonderful game and concocted a reason to shout Annabeth's name at Verity whenever they were in the hearing of anyone.

Before dinner, Nathan and Annabeth took a stroll down the long gallery. There was a gravity in his manner, a sense of sadness that made her a trifle uneasy. He stopped at the library and said, "Let's sit down in here. I need to talk to you."

Annabeth's uneasiness turned into alarm. "Nathan, what is it?"

He closed the library door behind them. "I thought about this all the way here. It's— I—" He cleared his throat, then continued in a determined voice, "I have decided to break off our engagement."

Annabeth stared at him, stunned, unable to find any words.

He went on, "I was wrong to ask you to marry me. It was selfish—I knew how vulnerable you were in that moment, that you were scared that I was going to die and so relieved when I didn't."

"I said yes. You didn't make me become engaged to you," Annabeth protested, though she could not deny his words. She had been beside herself with worry, praying as hard as she could that one of her dearest friends wouldn't be taken from her. When he got better, it had seemed like a gift from God.

"But I took advantage of your emotions." Nathan looked away, as if he could not meet her gaze. "I knew you didn't love me, but I told myself that if we were married, I would be such a good husband and father that you would come to love me. I excused it by saying that you would at least be happier than you are living with Lady Lockwood."

"You *will* be a wonderful father and husband." Annabeth took a step toward him, reaching out.

Nathan moved back, shoving his hands into his pockets. "Annabeth, please... Don't make this even harder than it is. In the past, I thought marrying you would be enough." Nathan's sad smile made Annabeth's heart squeeze painfully. "I told myself that somehow I could love you so much that it would make up for what you didn't feel."

"But I *do love* you."

He nodded stiffly. "Just not the way you love him."

Annabeth froze, momentarily taken aback. "Nathan, if this is about choosing to go on this hunt with Sloane instead of you, that was merely a practical decision. I don't love Sloane."

"Call it what you want to call it. When you look at him, there is a look in your eyes that... Well, I wish I saw that when you looked at me, but it's not there. And I can't ignore that."

"Please, don't do this. There is no future for me with Sloane. You and I will be happy once this is all over."

"I won't pretend this doesn't hurt. And there's a part of me, a very selfish part of me, that wants to hold you to your promise, to make you stay with me. But I refuse to give in to that."

Annabeth felt as if she was being torn apart. Nathan had been her friend for as long as she could remember. "Nathan, I can't lose you."

He smiled, though his eyes glittered with moisture. "You won't lose me. Ever. I was your friend before I fell in love with you. I'll always be here."

Annabeth swallowed, willing back the tears that wanted to flow. Protesting only made this more difficult for him. Nathan was being the stalwart gentleman, as he always was, controlling his own emotions, making the way smooth. But she could see the pain in his eyes—pain she had put there, no matter how much he tried to take the blame. Her protests would only make it more difficult for him. So she said only, "I want that."

"I know you have good intentions, Annabeth. But in the long run it will be better this way. For you and for me. I want to find something real. Something irrefutable. I deserve more than half your heart."

"Of course you do. You deserve the best of everything." *And I'm holding him back from that*, Annabeth thought.

"As do you."

"You're a far better man than Sloane."

Nathan gave her a little crooked smile. "Well, that's a rather low bar." He sighed and ran his hand back through his hair. "Look. I'm not telling you Sloane is who you should be with. God knows, I hope you *don't* choose him. But that isn't for me to say. Only you can make that decision." He paused and took a deep breath. "Whoever the right man is for you...all I know is, it isn't me."

She kept her expression as calm as possible. "Will

you walk me to my room? I think I want to turn in for the night."

"Of course." Nathan offered his arm and walked with her up the stairs. "Annabeth," he said as they reached her door. "Please be careful on your journey with Sloane. You are very dear to me." He took her chin between his thumb and fingers and smiled down into her eyes. "And remember—I am ever at your disposal." He gave her a little bow and walked away.

Annabeth watched him go, her heart aching. She went into her room and closed the door behind her. And there she let the tears escape, crying for a love she wished had been different.

CHAPTER EIGHTEEN

HOURS BEFORE DAWN, Sloane slipped through the garden. He stuck close to the shadows of the hedges and avoided the moonlit path. Skirting the terrace, he went around the corner of the house to the trellis. His father had sent him to the earl's home often enough that Sloane knew how to escape Stonecliffe secretly.

He tugged at the trellis on the side of the house to see if it was still sound. It felt sturdy enough, and he could see the breaks in the ivy here and there where old boards had been replaced by new. He began to climb, silent and stealthy as a cat, finding toeholds and handholds in the latticework and the sturdy older vines.

From there it was an easy move to the narrow ledge that ran the length of the house. He stopped at the fourth window along the wall, which he had instructed Annabeth to slightly raise soon after they had arrived at Stonecliffe. He now pulled it upward and slipped inside.

Sloane glanced around the room. Annabeth clearly had not meant to fall asleep. A lamp was still on, turned down low. She was fully dressed and lying on top of her bedcovers. Sloane edged closer.

For a moment he could not resist standing there and looking at her unobserved. Her face was soft and utterly relaxed, her eyelashes casting shadows on her cheeks, her skin warmed to gold by the light. Her lips were slightly open, and he wanted, quite badly, to bend down and kiss her awake.

It would be the worst way to start. The next few days of being with her promised to be torture enough—to hear her voice, to see her smile, to be so close to her in the curricle that their sides almost touched. No matter that there would be layers of clothes between them—it would still send heat curling through him. Hell, just thinking of it already stirred him.

He probably should have taken Verity or even Nathan with them to provide a barrier between himself and Annabeth. The fact that it was true that the curricle seated only two and it would be peculiar to swoop in on the Haverstocks with an extra guest didn't matter. Those were excuses, not reasons. The reason he hadn't wanted the other two along was that he wanted to be alone with Annabeth, to have—even if it was only a pale shadow and only for a few days—the closeness they had once shared.

It was dangerous as hell. He'd been all right these past years when he hadn't seen her; memories could be locked away and love appeared to fade. But seeing her once again—that little dimple in her cheek and the light of laughter in her eyes, the petal-smooth skin and luxuriant hair—had been like a crack in a dam. Through it, memories had come rushing, long-dead feelings had tingled, growing stronger and tearing down the barriers Sloane had carefully constructed.

Though, however much Sloane might want her, there could never be anything more between them. Annabeth was engaged to Nathan, and in any case, she thoroughly disliked him now. Even if Sloane could win her back, he would be wicked to do so, knowing that the ending would be the same. It would still be a tremendous scandal for her to marry a man such as him.

But he could not deny himself of these few days, the chance to spend time with her, to look at her and listen to her and simply enjoy her presence. He would be circumspect, as gentlemanly as Nathan, and make no effort to woo her or dissuade her from marrying Nathan. Whatever pain it might bring him later, it would be worth it.

"Anna," he whispered, and reached down to stroke his thumb across her cheek. "Anna, I'm here. It's time to go."

He held his other hand ready to cover a scream if she was startled upon waking and finding him looming over her. But when her eyes opened, she only smiled at him, her eyes lambent. "Sloane."

He could see when reality overrode the unthinking pleasure in her. Her face stiffened, the light in her eyes turning cool, and she sat up straighter, saying, "I'm sorry, I fell asleep. Is it too late?"

"Four o'clock," he replied. "We've plenty of time."

She stood up and went to the chair to pick up the cloak she had laid across it. She turned toward the window. "Are we going out that way?"

"I am. If you run into anyone, it's no great matter as long as I'm not with you. The servants are going to learn you aren't here soon enough, anyway. The important thing is that they not know you're with me. Close and lock this window behind me."

He went out the window and retraced his earlier steps. Glancing back up at her window, he saw that she had extinguished the faint light in her room, and he returned to the garden as silently and swiftly as he had come.

Standing in the shadows, Sloane watched Annabeth emerge from the house. She wore her cape and she pulled up the hood as she started across the terrace, instinctively going down the side steps, where the shrubbery cast shadows.

She came up beside him. She looked more awake now, and her eyes were bright with excitement and a tinge of something else that he couldn't quite put his finger on. Even though he had been in far more dangerous situations many times, Sloane felt excitement rising in him, too. He couldn't help but remember waiting for her in the garden or slipping away from a party, making their way to some secluded spot, heat and hunger rising, the risk of being caught setting their pulses even higher.

Annabeth had always been up to any adventure; her tomboy nature had been a stone of contention with her mother when they were boisterous kids running through the woods of their countryside estates. And however quiet and demure she might seem, she never lacked for courage, never pulled away in an attack of nerves. She had always put her faith in Sloane, certain he would never bring her harm, sure that they could get out of any tangle. Looking back, he knew that she had been unwise to trust him so. He would never have done anything he thought would put her at risk, it was true, but he had not been as capable as they both believed. Sloane had learned over the years that distrust was a better place to begin.

Once out of sight of the house, they returned to the path, making their way to the bottom of the garden. After a quick look around, Sloane started across the bare stretch of land to the woods beyond, taking Annabeth's hand to guide her. They were almost to the trees before he realized that the gesture was too familiar; it had simply been ingrained in him. But he made no move to drop her hand.

It was dark inside the trees, but he had left a lantern there, and he lit it, shielded so that it threw only a small glow before their feet. Annabeth whispered, "How do you know where to go? It's been years since you visited here."

"There's a bit of a path, and I left marks as I came." He pointed to a small branch broken and hanging. He glanced at her with a little grin. "I think I could have found my way anyway, but I prefer not to leave anything to chance."

"Then you have certainly changed."

"Yes, I suppose I have."

They reached a clearing where a dilapidated cabin stood. A horse was tied to one of its porch posts, patiently waiting.

"We're both going to ride him?" Annabeth asked doubtfully.

"It won't be for long, just to the house where my curricle will be waiting. I had one of my grooms bring it here, and I came on horseback. It would have been more conspicuous to have been leading a riderless horse."

"You think someone followed you?"

"Not that I saw." He shrugged and untied his horse, leading it to the steps. "But—"

"You prefer not to leave anything to chance," she finished.

"Exactly," he replied, flashing a grin at her.

Without having to say anything, Annabeth went to the top of the steps; they had ridden this way often enough in the past. Sloane mounted the horse and reached down to Annabeth. She took his arm and he pulled her up as she jumped, scrambling onto the horse behind him. She rode astride, her arms wrapped around his waist, her body flush behind his.

It was achingly familiar and devastating to his senses. And he would not have given up this moment, this feeling, for any amount of peace.

CHAPTER NINETEEN

EVER SINCE SLOANE had awakened Annabeth, warring emotions had been battling inside her. Excitement about the adventure she was going on with the man she'd once loved mingled with bitter sadness.

Annabeth hated the way things had ended with Nathan. She could no longer tell herself that she would make up for any hurt she'd caused him. That wasn't a possibility now. For all she knew, Nathan would cease to want to have anything to do with her after they caught the person behind the attacks. The thought of him not coming by for tea every day made her ache a little inside.

She knew Nathan was right to call it off—she may have resigned herself to never again feeling what she once had with Sloane, but Nathan didn't deserve that. He deserved so much more than half her love. He should have an equal partner, a woman who loved him as much as he loved her. And now that he had dropped his long-held pursuit of Annabeth, he could find that woman. But she knew that in this moment, Nathan was hurting, and for that, she hurt as well.

It hardly seemed real. A few weeks ago, she had envisioned a rosy but practical future. Instead of living under her grandmother's rule, she would have her own family with someone she cared about and knew would make a great father. A father as sweet and loving as her own had been.

Yet here she was now, not embarking on that imagined future, but sliding into an exciting but dangerous past with a man she should not trust.

Riding this way with Sloane, her body pressed against his back, she was flooded with memories as well as present sensations—the smooth movement of the horse beneath them, the heat of Sloane's body, the very scent and feel of Sloane against her.

It wasn't even dawn, but Annabeth was wide awake, energized by their secret flight and the possibilities that lay in front of them. She supposed she should not feel this excitement in doing such a risky thing; it was scarcely the emotion of a proper lady. But she could not deny the appeal of tackling the unknown, of discovery, and, yes, even the touch of danger.

Nor could she deny that her breath quickened and her nerves danced at being this close to Sloane, at feeling his hard, muscled body against her arms. Instinctively she started to tighten her arms around him and lay her head against his back, but quickly stopped. This was not the past. They were not what they had once been.

They left the trees and rode through a darkened village, then turned onto a faint trail that was one of the ancient tracks that ran through Britain. It was still dark when Sloane left the track and finally stopped in front of a farmhouse. There were no signs of life until a young man emerged from the ramshackle barn and came toward them, pulling off his cap and nodding to Sloane. "Sir. You made good time."

"Yes. It went smoothly." Sloane dismounted and came around to assist Annabeth. She felt a blush rising in her

face as he put his hands at her waist and lifted her down.
She stepped away from him as soon as her feet touched
the ground, but her legs were stiff from the unaccustomed riding, and she stumbled. Sloane wrapped his
hand around her arm to keep her from falling. His hand
lingered for a moment, then fell away, and he turned to
the groom. "Did you have any problems?"

"No, sir. The team's in fine fettle. The bags are inside."

"Good. Feed and rub down Carrot." Sloane stroked
the horse's neck fondly. "Let him rest and ride him home
tomorrow."

"Aye, sir." The man nodded again and led the horse
away.

"Carrot?" Annabeth couldn't keep from laughing.
"The rough and dangerous smuggler-spy named his
horse Carrot?"

Sloane's lips twitched. "Well, he has a grander name,
but that's what the lads call him. He has a fondness for
the vegetable." He turned toward the house. "Come. You
can get a couple hours of sleep at least, and we'll leave
after sunrise for the Haverstocks'."

"It doesn't seem very secret to travel during the day."

"The main thing was to get you out of Stonecliffe in
secret and leave our enemy watching that house, and
we've done that. From now on it's important that we
protect your reputation. If anyone should happen to spot
us together in a curricle, it would be far worse if it was
at night. Besides, we'll make better time in the day and
you need to rest."

"What is this place? Who lives here?" Annabeth
asked as they walked into the house.

"It belongs to someone I know," Sloane replied, picking up the lantern that sat by the door and lighting it.

"That's not really an answer."

"Someone who owes me a favor, or at least believes they do. You wouldn't recognize the name. They're ordinary people, the sort I know." The lantern lit his face oddly, casting shadows that made him impossible to read.

"You talk as though we live in two completely separate worlds," Annabeth protested. "As if I didn't know any 'ordinary' people. You and I grew up together."

"And I left that world a long time ago. Of course you know ordinary people—servants or, say, a girl who sells you a hat in the milliner's shop. Maybe a doctor or solicitor. People on the fringes of your existence. I *live* with them."

"I'm not a snob," Annabeth said, stung.

"I know you are not. You are kind and pleasant to everyone. All I'm saying is that you belong in Mayfair. And I belong on the docks." He turned away before she could respond and strode across the hallway to an open door. "Wright set up a cot for you in one of the bedrooms."

"What happened to the people that live here? Where are they?" Annabeth asked as she entered the small room, which was empty except for a cot and blankets and the baggage she had given Sloane yesterday.

"Don't worry." Sloane's tone was remote, cold. "I'm not going to try to ravish you."

Annabeth lifted an eyebrow. "I didn't think you would." Clearly Sloane was determined to take anything she said the wrong way.

"Yes, well…you shouldn't take such things for granted," he said gruffly.

"You're saying I *should* be afraid you would make unwelcome advances?"

"No, of course not. You know I wouldn't." His jaw tightened, and he looked away, adding in a quiet voice, "But this morning, when I saw you, I wanted to."

Annabeth's pulse quickened. What was she to say to that? She couldn't tell him that in that first instant when she awoke, she had been flooded with joy. Before she remembered who and where they were.

He took a step back, his voice clipped as he said, "I am glad you're marrying Nathan."

"What? That's certainly a change." She should have been glad, she supposed, but somehow his words annoyed her.

As if swallowing a bitter pill, Sloane went on, "I—whatever I say about Nathan, I know that he is a far better man for you than I. You deserve a happy life, and he would do anything to make you happy."

"Whereas you would not." She couldn't keep the sting out of her words.

"I obviously did not," he replied.

"Obviously." Annabeth knew this was the moment to tell him that she was no longer engaged to Nathan. But if she said it right now, it might seem as if she was inviting Sloane to make advances, and she didn't want that. It felt safer to keep that barrier between them, however false it might be.

"Nathan might be as boring as they come—though perhaps Carlisle could win that dubious honor away from him," Sloane went on. "But he will be a good husband." For a second Sloane stopped speaking, and Annabeth thought he was done until he cleared his throat and finished in low tones, "He'll be a good father. The truth is, you belong with him."

Even though it was precisely what Annabeth herself had thought, it set off a spark of anger in her chest to hear Sloane say it. "I am so glad that everyone feels free to decide what's best for me. Apparently you think I am too dim-witted to manage my life myself. So weak of will or sense that I will immediately fall into your arms if you make advances to me. I'm not sure whether it's how high your opinion of yourself is or how low your opinion is of me."

"Neither," he shot back, grinding his teeth.

"Both, more likely. You were always arrogant. You believe you're a better rider than anyone else. A better sailor. Faster. More agile of wit. More handsome." She wasn't about to add that he had had good reason to think such things.

"Blast it, Annabeth." He set down the lantern with a thud. "Why are you always so bloody sweet and biddable with everyone else in the world and so argumentative and hostile with me?"

"Because I don't care for—" She stopped herself just in time. "That is, I don't care for the way you try to control me."

"Me? Control you? I haven't the slightest control over you. I never did. I have no desire to. But I wouldn't mind a pleasant word now and then." He looked away for a long moment, then said, "Lady Lockwood runs your life, and you don't say a word of protest. You just smile and bend like a willow. You never did that when we were younger. You've changed."

The words gave her pause. She thought for a moment,

then said, "Back then, I thought that I didn't need to hide my emotions. That I didn't have to please everyone." She didn't add that she had felt that way because she had been so secure in Sloane's love, so certain of him and their future. When he had broken their engagement, it had been like the earth falling out from beneath her feet, leaving her clinging desperately to what she had left. She wouldn't tell him that dullness had settled over her and she had followed the easiest path ever since.

"You *don't* have to please anyone," he told her. "Least of all me."

"I know. I have no interest in pleasing you." Thinking of the blue evening dress she had packed, Annabeth had a deep suspicion that she was lying.

He frowned at her, then sighed and relaxed. "What are we fighting about?"

"I don't know."

"Well." He hesitated for a moment. "Then. Good night." He started to leave, but at the door, he turned back and said, "There's a lock on the door." He pointed to the key sitting in the keyhole.

"I *told* you. I'm not afraid of you, Sloane," she said tartly.

"No, you wouldn't be." He looked at her for a long moment, then gave her a sardonic smile. "Maybe it's me that's afraid."

Annabeth crossed her arms and watched him leave, saying under her breath, "You're not afraid of the devil."

CHAPTER TWENTY

ANNABETH WAS AWAKENED hours later by a knock on her door. Sunlight was streaming through the small window. She sat up, feeling stiff all over. It had been a long time since she had ridden a horse. Sleeping on the narrow, unpadded cot had not helped.

The knock came again, and she snapped, "Yes, I'm up. Come in."

The door opened and Sloane stuck his head in. "I've got—" He went still, his eyes sweeping down her, and his face softened, a faint smile touching his mouth.

Annabeth was certain that she looked a mess, her hair half tumbled down, dress wrinkled from sleeping in it. But it could have been worse—thank goodness she had been too tired to change into her nightgown.

Sloane cleared his throat. "I have breakfast."

"Tea?" Annabeth asked hopefully.

"Sorry. No tea." He opened the door wider and carried in a wicker hamper. "But I had Wright bring some provisions."

He set the hamper on the floor in front of her and went down on his knee to open it. He pulled out two rolls of bread, an apple, and a hunk of cheese.

"Not very elegant, I'm afraid." He smiled.

"I don't care," Annabeth told him. "I'm starving. Last night I…well, I didn't eat much dinner." She left out that she'd been too upset by her talk with Nathan to get any food down. Sloane would find out eventually that she and Nathan were no longer engaged, but there was no reason she had to tell him now. Things were already intense without adding that complication to their journey. Besides, Sloane had kept more than his fair share of secrets from her.

He handed a roll of bread to her. Their fingers brushed as she took it; his skin was hot, and her own fingers tingled. Annabeth was careful to pluck the cheese from his fingers without touching him. She broke the roll and took a bite, watching him. She was glad to see that Sloane looked no better put together than she, his shirt rumpled, his hair mussed, no jacket, waistcoat, or neck-cloth, and stubble darkening his jaw. The unfortunate thing was that he looked very good that way.

Annabeth's mouth went dry, and she looked away. She wished she'd had a chance to comb and pin her hair before he entered the room. Though, it should not matter for Sloane to see her in such disarray. He'd seen her many times before with her hair every which way—tossed by the wind as they sailed or as her hat flew off when they galloped…or when he sank his fingers into her hair as he kissed her, heedlessly dislodging the pins.

But that was the kind of thing she was *not* going to think about. Annabeth glanced back at Sloane. He was watching her, his own roll in his hand half-eaten, his eyes suddenly heated, as if he had guessed what she had been thinking. Her heart began to beat crazily, memories of his kisses flooding her.

Sloane let out a soft curse and stood up, dropping the rest of the bread back into the basket. He walked over to the small window and looked out, though there was little enough to see through the dirty glass. Annabeth wondered if he, too, had been thinking of the past and the kisses they had shared.

Annabeth cast about for something to say to ease the suddenly charged atmosphere. "You sent a note about our visit to the Haverstocks, then?"

He turned back to her and nodded. "Besides, I have always had an open invitation to visit there. Because of Sprague." Sorrow showed in his face for a moment before he shut it down.

"I'm very sorry about Sprague. I know you two were very close," Annabeth said gently, putting a hand on his arm.

Sloane glanced down at her hand, and Annabeth quickly pulled it back and took a step away. "Um. You've visited with the Haverstocks since you've been home?"

"I've been to their house a few times since I got back. But I thought it better not to damage their reputation by meeting in public. There was too much gossip already because of the way Lord Haverstock drank himself half to death after Sprague… They didn't need to be known as friends to a social pariah as well."

"You wouldn't be a pariah if you'd just told everyone why you were smuggling," Annabeth pointed out.

He shrugged. "I see no reason to justify my actions to the *ton*. I doubt that they would have believed me, anyway. People believe what they want to. And I make an excellent villain."

"There were some of us who would have trusted you."

He cast a sardonic glance at her. "As much as you trusted me when I came to the wedding?"

Annabeth frowned at him. "You're impossible."

"So I've been told." Sloane walked away.

ANNABETH FINISHED HER BREAKFAST, then washed up as best she could with the bucket of water Sloane brought her. She dressed and twisted her hair into a simple knot at the back of her neck.

When she walked out of the house, she saw Sloane waiting beside his curricle. He was clean-shaven and his hair combed, dressed once again in full gentleman's attire. And he looked just as desirable as he had unshaven and unkempt. Annabeth pushed the thought away.

She climbed into the curricle as Sloane strapped in her bag on the back. The seat, she noted, was not wide, and when Sloane sat down beside her, she was far too close to him for comfort. She could feel the heat of his body, and her arm accidentally brushed against his several times.

He had put up the collapsible top of the curricle to help hide her from view of any passerby, but it made the enclosed space seem even more intimate. It was going to be a long day. She pulled her hood forward and sank into silence.

Sloane's team of matched chestnuts was as good as it looked, and the horses pulled up in front of the Haverstocks' door late in the afternoon. Priscilla Haverstock hurried out to greet them, her face wreathed in smiles and her hands extended. "Sloane. Annabeth. We're so glad you're here."

It had been years since Annabeth had seen Priscilla. They had been close when they were young, but Annabeth had fled to Stonecliffe when Sloane left her, and after that she had spent most of her time in London.

Priscilla had changed little. She had the Haverstock coloring of gray eyes and light reddish-brown hair, with a smattering of freckles across her cheeks.

Annabeth had feared that Priscilla might be stiff and remote with her, but she greeted them both with obvious pleasure and whisked them back to the sitting room to join her brother Timothy.

A fire roared in the fireplace, and the room was stiflingly hot, no doubt for Timothy, who sat in a bath chair, a blanket over his lap. He looked so frail that it made Annabeth's heart hurt. He had always been in delicate health, but his health had clearly declined since the last time Annabeth had seen him.

Still, he smiled and shook Sloane's hand, saying, "Glad you came. And Annabeth—how good to see you. You are as beautiful as ever."

"Flatterer." She reached down to take his hand. "It has been far too long since I have come to call."

"Please, please sit down," Priscilla said. "We are eager to hear all the gossip of London."

They sat down to chat, their conversation light and airy, focused on gossip about the *ton* and the people in the area whom Sloane and Annabeth had known in the past.

Annabeth was struck by how different Sloane was here with his friends. The cynical air, the sardonic smile, the biting words—all dropped away. He was more like the old Sloane, the one who had smiled and been kind, letting Sprague's much younger brother tag around after them. The one who had teased her with laughter in his eyes and told her all his hopes and dreams. The one Annabeth had loved.

"I hope you will not mind. I invited the Todds and Mr. Feringham for dinner tonight," Priscilla said. "They all wanted to see you, and I wasn't sure how long you would be here or, um, what you wanted to do."

Annabeth thought Priscilla was too polite to ask outright why Sloane and Annabeth had rushed down to visit them, but she was clearly edging around the topic. Annabeth looked toward Sloane. Let him be the one to lie to their friends.

"We will not impose on your good nature for long," Sloane told Priscilla, smiling. "Annabeth told me how much she wished she could look over her family's old estate. She would like to see if her father's workshop still exists."

Annabeth thought it seemed the flimsiest of excuses, but Priscilla and Timothy showed no disbelief in it. Which only served to heighten the guilt Annabeth felt.

She hastened to add, "Yes, of course. We would enjoy seeing them. The Todds are a lovely couple, and I am very fond of Uncle Russell."

"We had planned to call on Mr. Feringham while we were here anyway," Sloane added. "Annabeth was interested in seeing some of the boxes her father made for him."

Timothy smiled, his eyes lighting up. "Those boxes! Mr. Winfield used to give them to me when I was sick—to occupy my mind while I was unable to do anything. He was such a kind man."

"Yes, he was," Annabeth agreed.

"Do you still have any of them, Timothy?" Sloane asked.

"I saved them all in a trunk. Would you like to see?"

Annabeth nodded, and Priscilla arranged for it to be brought down.

Two footmen carried in the trunk, and Priscilla opened it, revealing stacks of boxes. She removed them one by one, and they passed them around.

"It took me a while to figure out some, but I managed to get all of them in the end," Timothy replied. He showed them the solutions to all the containers, his pale cheeks flushed with pleasure, looking almost like the young boy he had been. It brought tears to Annabeth's eyes to see the trouble her father had gone to in order to help the boy through his illnesses.

But the search revealed no documents. Nerves danced in Annabeth's stomach. What if after the problems this trip had caused—the painful rift with Nathan, the tension with Sloane, her guilt at lying to old friends—they didn't find anything at all?

CHAPTER TWENTY-ONE

In Sloane's opinion, dinner that evening should have been a thoroughly boring event, but Annabeth wore a blue dress with a wide neckline that distracted him so much even keeping tabs on the pedestrian conversation of Russell Feringham was difficult.

Sloane's eyes went back to her again and again throughout dinner as she chatted pleasantly with the Todds and their hosts. All he could think about was kissing her shoulder, then working his way across her collarbone to her neck. He could almost taste her skin; he remembered quite well kissing that tender flesh, so soft and delicate.

He told himself he was far too old and experienced to be so undone by the sight of a woman's bare shoulders, but he found that the only thing age and experience did was make him aware that he could not act on his desire.

Still, he wouldn't choose to be anywhere else. Even the effort of chatting with Feringham was one he would make ten times over to be in Annabeth's presence.

Sloane didn't care much for the man—he had been too close a friend to Annabeth's father for Sloane to like him. But Annabeth was happy to see Feringham, and her happiness shone in her eyes, making her even more beautiful.

Whenever Sloane managed to tear his eyes away from

Annabeth and glance over at Russell, he saw that the other man was watching him, frowning. After dinner, over port, Russell said to him in a low voice, "Don't hurt my girl again."

"I have no intention of hurting Annabeth," Sloane replied.

"You were never a good match for her. Hunter didn't like it."

"I am well aware of Mr. Winfield's opinion of me." That opinion had not been improved by Sloane forcing the man to resign from his government position. And, oddly, the fact that Sloane had saved him from scandal and ruin seemed to make him dislike Sloane even more.

"Obviously he turned out to be right. It took Annabeth years to get over you, but she's happy now and marrying a good man."

"I know." Sloane kept his voice even.

"Then stop insinuating yourself into her life again."

"I'm not. I am here as a friend. That's all. I am not trying to woo her." Sloane stood up and walked away.

He *wasn't* trying to win her over. He had been circumspect and careful. No matter how much he burned for Annabeth inside, he had not kissed her or done anything improper. He'd made sure they had Priscilla for a chaperone. Hell, he had even told Annabeth she should marry Nathan. When this was over, when he was sure she was out of danger, he would be out of her life. He wouldn't see her again. And he wished that didn't feel like doom awaiting him.

HUNTER WINFIELD'S WORKSHOP was difficult to reach in the curricle, so the next morning Sloane and Annabeth borrowed two horses from the Haverstock stable. They rode along a lane that led to the Todds' estate. Since they had just seen the Todds at last night's dinner, when they reached the long driveway up to the house, they would turn and cross a meadow to the woods beyond instead of stopping in for a brief visit.

They were only a few yards from the Todds' driveway, talking and paying little attention to anything around them, when a shot rang out. Annabeth's horse reared, and she tumbled to the ground. Sloane's mount took off running, but he wrestled it under control and turned back.

Annabeth was lying on the ground. Sloane's insides were turning to ice, but by the time he reached her again, Annabeth was struggling to get up. The mare she had been riding was far in the distance, still running.

Sloane jumped off his horse, keeping a tight grip on the reins with one hand, and reached down with the other to help her stand. "Are you all right? Were you shot?"

She shook her head. "Wind…knocked out."

"Come. We need to leave before he reloads." He pulled her to his horse, and just as they moved from that spot, something splatted into the ground a few feet away, followed immediately by a distant bang.

Sloane practically threw Annabeth into the saddle and scrambled onto the horse behind her. The animal needed no urging; he was already running before Sloane got his other foot in the stirrup. He turned his mount toward the copse of trees and raced for it, not stopping until they were within the shelter of the trees. Sloane's arms were locked around Annabeth, his heart pounding like mad, and his breathing was hard and fast. He could feel Annabeth trembling—or perhaps that was him.

He leaned his head against hers. "I thought you were dead. When I saw you lying on the ground, I…" Sloane wrapped his arms even harder around her and pressed a kiss to her hair.

Annabeth tightened her grip on him and nodded. Her cheek was pressed against his chest, and he felt her head move against him as she nodded. Even through his clothes, the touch electrified him. He rubbed his cheek against her hair, then kissed her forehead. The feel of her, the taste of her skin, the sound of her unsteady breathing tore through his defenses, already lowered by the danger. His lips moved farther down, touching her temple, then her cheekbone. When she tilted her head a little, giving him freer access to her face, it almost undid him.

He let out a short, sharp oath. What the hell was he doing? This was madness. Someone had just tried to kill them, and here he was, thinking of nothing but making love to a woman he couldn't have. With an effort of will, he lifted his head and loosened his arms around her.

He turned the horse's head and looked back across the meadow and road. "I can't see anyone." Not surprising since he'd just spent the last few moments paying no attention at all. "Blast, I should have been watching."

"Or he could have gone back the other way," Annabeth said prosaically, and straightened, a movement that rubbed against him in a way that threatened his already weakened control. "Or he could have escaped while we were fleeing."

Sloane remained there for a bit longer, watching, but he could detect no movement.

"Where did the shots come from?" Annabeth asked.

"Over there, I think." He pointed to a stand of gorse beside a low wall. "I couldn't be sure. He was probably a bit out of range. Both the shots fell short."

"Too close for my comfort," Annabeth said.

"Yes." Sloane sat for another moment. "For all we know, he's still there, waiting for us to return. I'm not going back out on the road to see." He turned the horse and started through the stand of trees.

"This isn't the way to the workshop," Annabeth told him.

"I'm taking you back to the Haverstocks'," he said. "Where you should have been from the start."

"No, you're not," Annabeth replied. "The workshop isn't far from here. I was about to turn off when the shots happened. Just go to your left, and I'll be able to find the place."

"Anna...be sensible. They are going to be alarmed when the horse arrives there riderless."

"I am being sensible. We're not going to waste a day with you taking me back to Priscilla's house. And we will explain what happened when we do go back. A few hours of questions might bring some much-needed excitement to a humdrum routine."

"You certainly are being flippant for somebody that was almost killed just now," he rasped. At least the irritation was helping him ignore that firm bottom pressed against him, moving with each step the horse took. "You need to be somewhere safe."

"I need to find whatever it is they want, or they'll continue trying to kill me," she countered.

"Yes, but I can search the workshop alone. You can tell me where the hiding places are."

"It's not as simple as that. With Grandmother's box, I didn't remember how to open it until I looked at it, and then my hands just went to it. Some are hard to explain, and I'm not sure I remember all of his hiding places, but

I know I will remember when I see the room again. You need me, and you know it."

"I need you safe," he said tightly. "How am I supposed to concentrate, worrying that someone's going to come in and shoot you?"

"Then you can patrol the outside while I look through the place."

"You know I'm not going to do that."

"Yes. And I'm not going to let you go by yourself." She gave him a fierce look.

She was right, of course, and there was nothing he could do but grind his teeth and give in. He turned the horse in the direction she'd pointed. They rode for a time in silence, but it was companionable, not angry or awkward. It was the silence of two people who knew each other with such a bone-deep understanding that there was no need to talk, no expectation, no discomfort.

Well, no discomfort for her. Sloane himself was anything but comfortable. He was hot and hungry, every step a temptation, pleasure mingling with frustration in a potent stew. Annabeth was riding sideways on the horse, and his arms were around her, cradling her. Relaxed, she leaned against him a little, warm and soft. Trusting. Her scent teased at his nostrils—a mingling of perfume and flesh that was uniquely Annabeth; he would have known that scent anywhere, for it never failed to set up that low throb deep in his abdomen.

Worst—best—there was that constant movement of her body, flush against him between his legs, unconsciously provocative, so subtle yet so arousing that he had to hold back a groan. They could change positions so she could ride as she had the other night, sitting behind him, with her arms wrapped around him, pressed against his back. Which was worse, to have his arms around her or her arms around him, her hands on him?

The obvious solution, of course, was for him to dismount and lead the horse or walk beside it. But there was no chance he was going to do that. He wasn't about to give up this moment. It had been twelve years; he'd forgotten how sweet she felt in his arms, how enticing and how satisfying. Heaven and hell it might be, but he was going to cherish it.

"There's the brook," Annabeth said, pointing. "Just follow it up and we'll find the path." After a moment she said, "Whoever it was must have followed us."

"Yes. Unless you think our attacker is Feringham or the Haverstocks."

Annabeth chuckled. "I think we can safely exclude them from the suspects."

"They are the only people who know where we intended to go this morning, so the only other explanation is that we were followed here from the Haverstocks'. Which means someone has followed us the entire way. I was sure no one was trailing me. I should have paid more attention."

Being with Annabeth was always highly distracting, but Sloane was disgusted with himself for not spotting a pursuer. He really was out of practice. But he'd better recover his skills, and quickly. Annabeth's life was in danger. The kidnapping and the break-in were alarming, but he had thought it meant they needed Annabeth alive in order to find what they were looking for. But this time they had clearly tried to kill her.

"The fact that they shot at us shows that we are getting close to finding the document, don't you think?" Annabeth asked.

"Or they're simply afraid we'll find it. If they knew for sure where it was, they would have already taken it."

"And what exactly is 'it' again?" she asked, irritation creeping into her tone. "It's a little hard to find something when you don't know what you're looking for."

"I don't know exactly. And if I did, I couldn't tell you." That wasn't much of a lie; they didn't know precisely what was in the document, and he certainly couldn't tell her the truth about her father. "Hell, I don't know if the ruddy thing even exists. I'll be surprised if we find it in your father's workshop."

Sloane hoped that the paper wasn't there. The last thing he wanted was for Annabeth to read the confession of her father's sins. But he didn't know how to keep her from reading it if they found it together. Was he to snatch it out of her hands? Refuse to show it to her? He could imagine how well that would sit with her.

It would be better if the confession was in the Todds' house. Sloane could sneak out and search it in the middle of the night, with no one the wiser. The problem was that he didn't know where to search, and Annabeth would insist on going with him. This whole situation was a bloody stupid mess. Hunter Winfield could muck everything up even from beyond the grave.

"What if it doesn't exist? Or we cannot find it?" Annabeth said. "Whoever is doing this wouldn't know that. What would keep them from continuing to pursue me?"

"I'm hoping whatever we do discover will give us a clue as to who's after you. And then I'll find them."

"How? And what happens then?"

"Trust me. You won't have to worry about them anymore," he replied grimly.

CHAPTER TWENTY-TWO

ANNABETH HAD SOME difficulty locating the workshop. It had been several years since she'd been there, and new shrubs and trees had changed the landscape somewhat. Nor had she ever approached it from this direction. Being in Sloane's embrace made it difficult to concentrate. Her mind kept straying off into thoughts of his body pressed against her back, his arms around her; and that fire that was building low in her abdomen.

Several times she'd had to wrench her mind away from the daydreams and ignore the growing ache between her legs, but she managed to find enough of the larger landmarks to lead them to the workshop.

Larger than a shed, smaller than a barn, it was a cube of a building, built of wood that had weathered over the years into a pale brown. It was hardly noticeable tucked in among the trees. Sloane pulled up in front of the building and dismounted, but Annabeth could only gaze at the workshop, tears filling her eyes.

Sloane turned, arms reaching up to help Annabeth down, but when he saw her face, he said, "Anna...you do not need to do this. We can come back later or I can go in and search by myself, if you'll give me a bit of guidance."

Annabeth swallowed, blinking away her tears, and shook her head. "No. I want to see it. I haven't been in here since Papa died. I should have gone to the workshop and organized things, packed them away. But I could not face being in the same room where he'd died."

"Very well." Sloane grasped her waist, supporting her as she slid off the horse.

"Let me take care of the horse," Sloane said, and led him back to the brook to drink, then tethered him to a tree surrounded by grass.

Annabeth waited for him, reluctant to enter the building alone. No doubt it was cowardly of her, but she didn't want to face the memories and sorrow without Sloane. It shouldn't matter; she shouldn't need him. But she could not deny that she felt safe and secure with him, that the very feel of him gave her comfort and courage.

Why was it that this man was the one who made her feel this way? Why was it that only Sloane drew her, tempted her? Why couldn't it have been Nathan? Someone good and kind and loving instead of a man who had ripped her heart out and left?

Sloane returned, cutting off her thoughts, and they went into the workshop. Dust lay thick on everything. The back window had broken at some point, and rain had blown in, warping the floor beneath the window and sending leaves and twigs across the floor. The familiar table and stools and cabinets were there, but it seemed so empty, so devoid of life that she felt almost no connection to the place.

She looked up at the missing railing near the top of the stairs, mute evidence of her father's death. Annabeth made herself bring her eyes down to the floor beneath the railing, afraid she might see a bloodstain there. But, of course, there wasn't any; a broken neck had killed him. Taking a little breath, she moved forward briskly.

It was fortunate she had on the supple leather riding gloves Priscilla had lent her, for her hands would have quickly been filthy as she looked through the books and instruments on her father's worktable. On the other side of the room, Sloane was opening and closing drawers and doors and sifting through the contents of the bookshelf.

Working his way back to Annabeth, Sloane pulled out each book to see if it concealed a hidden compartment in the wall. He shook them to make sure there was no paper folded and hidden among the pages. In the meantime, Annabeth was busy finding and opening all her father's secret hiding places.

She found a box he had started before his death, and that brought tears to her eyes. She found pieces of various woods. She found screws and nails and wire and string, springs both large and small. There were windup figures like the one Papa had given Timothy, and others that looked to be failures or had simply been abandoned.

There were plans and drawings and a few letters, and each time Annabeth's heart leaped, but upon perusal, they turned out to be quite ordinary correspondence about supplies or exchanges of information or notes from friends.

Her father had not been much of one for writing. She smiled, thinking of her father sitting out here with his portable writing desk, frowning over a piece of paper, quill in hand. Annabeth pulled in a sharp breath that made Sloane turn, saying, "What? What did you find?"

"His desk! Why didn't I think?"

"What desk?" He came closer, glancing around the room.

"He had a portable writing desk, meant for travel, but

he used it for most of his letters. Its sides all folded out, with holders for quills and inks and paper and a surface for writing on. But it could all be folded back up again very neatly, and when it was, it looked like a box. About a foot square, and maybe ten inches tall." She shaped it with her hands. "He had made it himself, and it was beautiful. It was teak, glossy, and elegant. He loved it. He took it with him whenever he traveled, and he brought it out here. He preferred it, really, to his secretaire in the house. *That* is where this mysterious document would be." She smiled triumphantly.

Sloane let out a laugh and picked her up. Annabeth threw her arms around his neck, still grinning, as he spun her around. But when he set her back down on her feet, she was suddenly, intensely aware of her body sliding down his. Both laughter and triumph vanished; indeed, all thoughts seemed to flee as she looked up at Sloane.

There was nothing in that moment but Sloane's body only inches from hers and the heat in his eyes as he gazed down into her face. Nothing but the feelings and the hunger that blossomed up in her. Her hands were still on his chest, and she slid them up as she moved toward him.

"Anna…" he breathed, and he lowered his head to meet hers.

Her arms curled around his neck as he hovered, his lips almost touching hers for what felt like an eternity. Then he was kissing her, his mouth slow and heated on hers, and she clung to him as the only steady thing in the onslaught of desire. All the hunger that had been building inside her throughout the ride—the past few days, to be honest—welled up in her, sweeping away restraint and logic.

Sloane's hand roamed her body as he kissed her again and again. His breathing was ragged, his body burning, and his desire pushed hers higher. She let out a little moan as his lips left hers to make their way down her neck, and she dug her hands into the front of his jacket as if to hold him there.

But it was clear he wasn't going anywhere. He lifted her from the ground, his arm beneath her buttocks, and she instinctively wrapped her legs around him. He walked blindly forward until he reached the table and set her down on it. She kept her legs tight around him, pressing him against that insistent ache that mingled pleasure and frustration.

She wanted to be closer to him, wanted to feel his skin beneath her hands, and she slid her hands under his jacket. Still kissing her, Sloane fumbled at the buttons on her bodice. His fingers slipped beneath the material, gliding over the soft skin of her breast, and he groaned softly, a shudder running through him.

"Lady Priscilla? Miss Winfield?" a woman's voice called from outside. "Mr. Rutherford?"

Annabeth and Sloane sprang apart and whirled to face the door.

CHAPTER TWENTY-THREE

THE VOICE CAME AGAIN, closer to the building. "Is anyone there?"

Sloane let out an oath and strode to the other side of the room and stood, looking out the window. Annabeth hurried toward the door, rebuttoning her dress with fingers that trembled. She suspected that her hair was disheveled, but maybe that could be passed off as a result of her work in here. But God only knew what was in her face; her cheeks were blazing. Still, she was probably in better shape to face the public than Sloane.

She pressed her palms against her cheeks and drew in a breath before she opened the door. "Mrs. Todd. How nice to see you."

"Miss Winfield. I was rather worried." She gestured behind her to where a groom stood, holding the head of the horse Annabeth had been riding this morning. "One of the grooms found this mare wandering about, and he thought it was Lady Priscilla's. I was worried that she might have met with an accident. It occurred to me that perhaps you and she were here. Is everything all right?"

"Yes. I'm terribly sorry. Please come in." Annabeth stepped back to let the other woman enter. "I borrowed Priscilla's horse. I'm afraid it threw me."

Mrs. Todd drew in a little gasp. "Oh, my. Were you hurt?"

"Nothing but my pride," Annabeth replied with a smile. "Fortunately Mr. Rutherford was with me."

"Ah, yes, I see."

Sloane turned and gave her a polite bow. "Mrs. Todd. It's good to see you again."

"Mr. Rutherford." The older woman looked over at Sloane, curiosity clear in her eyes.

"I should take care of your horse. Pray excuse me," he said abruptly, and strode out of the workshop.

Before Mrs. Todd could ask questions about Sloane and Annabeth being alone in this secluded place, Annabeth said, "I hope you do not mind our coming here. I know I should have asked your permission, but I didn't think about it yesterday, and we were out riding nearby. I thought you would not mind."

"No, of course you're quite welcome to visit it." The older woman looked around doubtfully at the dirty room, made even messier by their search.

"I have many happy memories of this place," Annabeth said by way of explanation. "My father loved it. I'm so glad you didn't tear it down."

"It seemed a bit of a waste. Mr. Todd thought we might be able to use it for something one day." Mrs. Todd gave it another skeptical look.

"There are one or two things I might want to take with me. Would that be all right?"

"Yes, dear." This wish, too, seemed something Mrs. Todd had trouble envisioning. "Well… I should let you get back to work. Perhaps you'd like to come up to the house for tea."

"That's a lovely thought. Thank you for the invitation. But as you can see, we aren't suitable for calling on anyone." Annabeth swept her hand down her front, indicating the dusty state of her clothes. With horror, she saw that she had not buttoned one of her buttons. Her cheeks colored, but she managed to continue to smile at her visitor, if somewhat stiffly.

"Of course. I hope to see you again soon."

Annabeth kept smiling, walking with Mrs. Todd to the door and watching as the lady started down the path toward the house, the groom trailing along behind her. Annabeth let out a sigh of relief and sagged against the doorjamb.

If Mrs. Todd didn't yet think something scandalous had been going on here, she was bound to come to that conclusion when she thought it over. She would spread the gossip all around. Well, at least Annabeth wouldn't be here to hear it. The Haverstocks and Uncle Russell were the only ones who knew them, and Annabeth was certain that neither Priscilla nor Russell would spread any harmful rumor.

But the real problem wasn't what Mrs. Todd thought of her or what gossip she spread. It was what Annabeth had done. She let out a groan and sat down on a low step of the staircase, bracing her elbows on her knees and sinking her head into her hands.

How could she have acted that way? After all the denials of love that she had made to Sloane, after all the harsh words and bitterness, she had just fallen into his arms like a hussy. What would he think of her—that she was a liar, a hypocrite, a wanton woman? And he believed she was still engaged to marry Nathan; she hadn't told him differently. He would think she had broken her vow to Nathan as well.

It didn't matter what Sloane thought of her, she told herself. He'd participated in their mad behavior, too.

The real question was what was *she* to think of herself? She didn't love Sloane. Love didn't last for years, unrequited, and she couldn't have fallen in love with him after he came back into her life. Their relationship since then had been antagonistic.

Her passion had been nothing but physical desire. But that didn't say anything good about her. She could tell herself that the desire she had felt for him twelve years ago, unfulfilled, had simply been reawakened. She could say that the fear and drama of the shooting had put her into an excited state and heightened her senses, turning what she'd felt on the ride with him into something stronger.

But none of that made her feel better. None of it quelled the rising fear that she was about to throw herself into an all-too-familiar fire, that she might give Sloane her body *and* her heart and be devastated all over again. She had to regain control of herself, distance herself from him.

The door opened, and Sloane stepped inside. His jaw was set, his face expressionless, and he didn't look at her. "I apologize for my behavior. I was wrong to kiss you. I—" He shot her a single blazing glance. "I don't regret a moment of that. I couldn't ever regret that. But I broke my word to you. I told you I would not bother you, and I didn't keep my promise. And for that I am sincerely sorry. It won't happen again. I know that I promised that before, but I will be more careful this time. I will stay in control."

"I accept your apology." Annabeth wanted to cry, which was beyond foolish. She should be relieved. Glad. "I was equally wrong. I suggest that we both put that behind us and deal with the matter at hand."

"I agree." He paused. "This box…the folded-up writing desk. Do you know where it is?"

"No. I haven't thought of it in years. I certainly don't have it. Nor, I think, would Uncle Russell. I think it would have to be with my mother. I don't think she would have thrown it away. It was very dear to Papa."

"Could it still be here?" Sloane looked up the stairs. "We haven't looked up there."

"It could." She turned to look at the stairs, filled with reluctance to go where her father had fallen to his death.

"I'll do it," Sloane said, and started up the stairs.

"No, I have to go. I won't be a coward."

He stepped aside to let her climb the stairs in front of him. She stuck to the inside wall, not looking at the damaged railing. But she could not help but see the gaping hole out of the corner of her eye. The riser wobbled a bit as she climbed past the gap in the banister, and Sloane reached out to steady her.

That was how her father had died, she thought, a loose board on a step that made him stumble and go crashing to the ground. She pushed back the sorrow that rose in her chest and continued up the stairs.

The small loft held only a few furnishings—a cabinet, a comfortable chair, a table and lamp, and her father's telescope on its stand in front of the round window. She knew of no hiding places in this part of the building, and it didn't take long to look through the room. The portable desk was not here.

Sloane turned and started back down the stairs. Annabeth went over to the window and stood looking out, her hand resting lightly on the telescope, remembering her father.

"Annabeth…" Sloane's voice was odd—low but with a note of urgency in it.

She turned and saw him standing a few steps down at the place where her father had fallen. "What?"

"Come here."

Normally she would have bristled at his peremptory command, but there was something so peculiar about his expression that she went to join him.

"This board was unsteady because it's missing some nails," Sloane began. "I think your father stumbled on it and fell against the railing."

"Yes." Her voice was slightly questioning. That seemed pretty obvious.

He pointed to the ends of the banister, where it had broken off. "This railing isn't splintered and jagged. It was sawn through. I think your father was meant to fall."

CHAPTER TWENTY-FOUR

"SOMEONE KILLED HIM?" Annabeth stared at Sloane, eyes wide. Her face went pale, and she started to crumple.

Sloane grabbed her, pulling her to him, before she could topple down the stairs. He wanted to continue holding her like that, but he carefully lowered her to a step. He sat down beside Annabeth and curled his arm around her—only to hold her up, he told himself. "I'm sorry. I shouldn't have blurted it out like that."

The truth was Sloane had been too stunned himself to even think of holding back the words. Hunter had been murdered. Why had that never occurred to him? Why had he never questioned the story that Annabeth's father had accidentally fallen?

The war had been long over by the time Winfield died, and Annabeth's father would have been useless to the French after Sloane took away the damning paper they'd used to force him to spy for them. Sloane had been out of the country when it happened, but even so, it didn't excuse his not looking into it after he returned to England. The reason he hadn't was doubtless because he'd done his best not to think about Annabeth and her father.

"But why?" Annabeth turned her head to look at him. "He had no enemies. He was a good, sweet man. Why would anyone have wanted to kill my father?"

Sloane knew exactly why. If, as Asquith had suggested, Winfield was going to confess, obviously the traitor he named in that confession would not have wanted it revealed. Winfield's death would have ensured that he stay quiet. But Sloane couldn't tell Annabeth that.

He said carefully, "It seems to me that the person who caused your father's death might very well be the same person who is after you."

"After all this time? How could the two be connected?"

"Someone murdered your father, and now someone is pursuing you, even trying to kill you. It seems unlikely, doesn't it, that these are two different men with different motives? You ask, why would anyone want to kill your father? Well, why would anyone want to kill *you*? Yet here we are. Someone arranged your father's 'accident,' and someone tried to shoot you today."

"All because of this document you've been talking about? What *is* this thing we're looking for?" Annabeth narrowed her eyes at him. "And don't say you can't tell me. I deserve to know why someone is trying to kill me."

"I don't know exactly what is in this document," Sloane hedged. "I'm not even sure that it exists." That much was true; even Asquith had doubts that there actually was a confession.

"Why would anyone be so eager to get it if it doesn't exist?"

"Obviously someone must believe that it does."

"But it's been several years since my father died. Why would this person have waited so long to look for it?"

"I'm not sure why they started this search now. Asquith—that's the man I used to work for—was told that your father had written a letter and that someone was trying to find it. That is when he started looking for it. Suppose your father knew something that would ruin a person, we'll call him Lord X, and your father was going to reveal it. Lord X killed your father to keep him from revealing his secret. He searched your father's workshop and maybe your home, but he couldn't find the letter. So he decided that it either did not exist or that it was hidden away somewhere where it would never be found. He thought he was safe."

"But when I started looking through my father's things in the town house, he was afraid I might find it."

Sloane nodded. "Or perhaps it was because my old boss heard about this information your father had and he set Verity to looking for it, and Lord X caught wind of that."

"Then why didn't he try to kill Verity?"

"Verity is not easy to kill." Sloane shrugged. "And, remember, he did kidnap both of you. There's nothing to say he won't try to do in Verity as well. However, you seem the likeliest target because you're the likeliest person to find it. You know where your father hid things. Maybe your father could have even told you specifically where he'd put it. So our villain tried to kidnap you to make you tell him. When that wasn't successful, he decided that he would have to kill you, too, to keep you from finding the letter."

"But why would my father have known anything about this person? Lord X. Why would he have written a letter and to whom? I loved Papa very much, but in the eyes of the world, he was not an important person."

"That doesn't mean he didn't know something that was important." Sloane was again on dangerous territory. It twisted a knife of guilt in him to lie to her, but neither could he bear to ruin her father's memory. A partial truth would have to do. "Asquith believes that there was a man in England working for the French, the head of their spy ring. He thinks your father wrote a letter that would expose that traitor."

Annabeth stared at him in astonishment. "You think my father found out someone was a spy? How could he have possibly known that?"

"Mr. Winfield had a great many friends."

Annabeth nodded. "Yes, he was very well-liked. But most of his friends were quite ordinary and not at all powerful."

"It's not always a high-ranking person who is important. And information that seems ordinary can be dangerous."

Annabeth nodded. She looked at the railing, at the empty space that had killed her father. "Oh, Sloane…" Her eyes filled with tears and she buried her face in his shoulder. "I cannot bear it. To think that Papa was murdered. That someone could hate him so."

Sloane wrapped his arms around her and held her close as she cried out her pain. It was almost unbearably sweet to shelter her, to have her turn to him in her need. At the same time, he knew that he had no right to do so.

He wanted her. He wanted her in every way he could think of. In this way, to comfort her, and in a fierce way, to protect her and harm anyone who hurt her. And he wanted her in the way he had only a short time ago, his body surging with lust, aching to bury himself inside her, to know that she ached for him, too.

But that could never happen.

Annabeth's sobs stilled, and for a long moment, she just rested her head against his shoulder. Then she sat up, taking out her handkerchief to wipe the tears from her face. She turned to him. "If you are right, it means that if we find the letter Papa wrote, it will reveal who killed him."

"I think it will."

"Then I am going to find that letter." Annabeth's gaze turned steely. "I am going to find this man. And he is going to pay for what he did."

CHAPTER TWENTY-FIVE

THERE WAS NOTHING else that could be found in the work-shop, and they left soon afterward, taking a longer route through the woods to the Haverstocks' house so they would not be exposed on the open road. Annabeth went upstairs, leaving it to Sloane to explain to Priscilla and Timothy what had happened with their horse that after-noon.

Annabeth took her meal on a tray in her room. She had no idea how much of the truth Sloane would tell the Haverstocks, but she simply could not face other people and keep up any sort of pretense.

There was a knock at the door. She hoped it was not Priscilla coming up to see how she was. But it was Sloane who stood outside, and she relaxed. She gestured him inside and closed the door. At the moment, she had no concern about propriety. She sat down again in the chair by the window, and Sloane moved a delicate chair from the vanity closer and perched on it tentatively.

"I won't ask how you are. I know you're grieving."

She nodded. "I thought I had cried all my tears for Papa long ago, but this brought it all back. And worse, knowing that someone killed him. It's always seemed so unfair that his life was cut short but knowing that it was purposeful...that someone robbed him of many more years. Robbed all of us. He was a wonderful father—the kind of father Nathan would have been. Fair and kind."

There was a moment of silence, then Sloane said carefully, "That Nathan would have been? What do you mean?"

Annabeth sighed. "Nathan broke our engagement. It appears I have a bit of trouble holding on to a fiancé."

Sloane stared at her. "But why? I know the man's in love with you. Always has been. Was it because you came here with me?"

"No, he says it wasn't that. He just…realized it was a mistake. For both of us. And he's right. I think I am not suited for marriage. I doubt I'll ever feel as I should for a husband."

"Because I ruined it for you. I wounded you so much you won't let yourself fall in love again?" Sloane asked in a low voice.

"No. Yes." She shook her head. "I don't know. It's been years, and I've gone past all that. But I, well, I think perhaps I had only a certain amount of love in me, and I loved you so fiercely, so madly, that I burned it all out. I felt too much, too hard, too long. All of it—the love and anger and pain. I simply have not felt that deeply since." Annabeth knew she lied—the desire that had surged in her this afternoon when he kissed her had been as strong and fierce as any she had felt when she was young. It seemed only Sloane could bring up that hunger, just as he could get her anger to flash or her laughter to bubble out. But she was not about to admit that to him.

"Anna, I'm so sorry." He took her hand between his. "If I could change what happened, what I did, I would."

"I know." She straightened and pulled her hand back.

"It's not important now. What's important is finding the man who killed my father."

Sloane accepted her retreat without protest, and leaned back. "I'll find him. I promise you."

"*We'll* find him," she corrected, sensing what he was about to say.

"Anna, I need to take you back to Stonecliffe. You are in obvious danger, and I have failed to protect you. I thought I could get you away without anyone noticing. I was sure I would see if someone followed us. But I didn't. I thought I could fight off anyone who threatened to kidnap you or hurt you, but I cannot protect you from a sharpshooter firing from a distance."

"What makes you think I'll be safe at Stonecliffe?" Annabeth countered. "Someone could shoot me while I'm strolling through the garden there. Am I supposed to spend the rest of my life cowering indoors? I am in danger wherever I go, whatever we do. The only way to make sure I'm safe is to find the person who's doing this and stop them."

"I will," Sloane said grimly. "I'll do whatever it takes."

"You'll have a better chance of finding him with me than you will without me."

"We have already looked through all the places you know. You told me that there's nothing in the Todds' house. Feringham brought us his boxes last night, and there was nothing in them."

"I believe Papa's writing desk is where he would have most likely put it. He might not even have intended to hide it. He may have been writing this document when he was killed, and it was simply in his desk, unfinished this entire time. I don't know what happened to the portable desk, but it's likeliest to be at my mother's house—

as are the puzzle boxes he gave her, which we have not yet examined."

"I can look through the desk and the other boxes."

"If she'll let you." Annabeth raised an eyebrow. "You are not exactly well-liked by Lord Edgerton. You'd be lucky if he lets you in the door."

"Anna...you'll be the death of me."

"No, I won't. And *you* won't be the death of *me*, either. Given that I could be shot anywhere I am, don't you think I am safer with you than at Stonecliffe without you?"

"You'll have Verity there. You'll have Nathan."

"I think it's asking a bit much of Nathan to guard me after he's just broken off our engagement. And I don't want Verity. I want you." That hadn't come out right. "I mean, I trust you more than Verity."

He sighed, and Annabeth knew she'd won. "Very well. We'll go to London tomorrow."

"What did you tell Priscilla and Timothy about this afternoon?"

"The truth—somewhat. I said someone shot at you, and your horse threw you. I suspected Mrs. Todd would tell them about finding your horse loose, so they needed to know something of what happened. And I had to have a good enough reason for our leaving here without doing any of the things Priscilla planned. Besides, I wanted them to be on guard should someone come around here asking about us. They know that something is going on, but I didn't tell them what."

"We're leaving tomorrow?"

"Early tomorrow, before dawn. Even if this sharpshooter is awake and watching the house, the light won't be good enough for him to aim well. We'll take the toll road, which will hopefully have so many travelers that he won't risk firing at you."

Sloane took his leave, and Annabeth packed, glad to have something to do. She was tired from the day's activities, but her thoughts kept her restless. Even knowing that she would be arising before dawn, she found it difficult to sleep. Her mind was too busy with thoughts of her father and his death; despite the evidence, it was hard to believe that he'd been murdered. Who could have done it? And why? What could Papa have known that was that dangerous to someone?

Whenever she managed to pull her mind from that endless circle, she plunged into thoughts about Sloane. She could not help but worry that he must be upset with her for not telling him that she was no longer engaged.

But it was foolish for her to feel guilty for concealing the news. Sloane had no reason to expect anything from her, no rights over her. Anyway, maybe he had been grateful to have a reason he shouldn't kiss her. He might very well not want his passion to get him entangled with her again.

Clearly he had felt passion. There was no mistaking the heat of his kisses. But that didn't mean he wanted a relationship. Of course, she did not want that either...did she? It stirred a fire deep inside her to remember their kisses this afternoon. If they had not been interrupted by Mrs. Todd, Annabeth suspected she would have lain down with Sloane, all thoughts of propriety or reason or past hurts flown from her mind.

But that was desire, not love, and surely it was possible to have one without the other. After all, that was the way it had been with Nathan, although in the opposite way. She had loved Nathan, and she had wanted to, *tried* to, feel that uprush of hunger that came so easily when Sloane kissed her, but it had never happened.

It was so easy to feel passion for Sloane—just one look from those wicked blue eyes started the heat inside her. That lazy, knowing smile, the shaggy black hair that invited one's fingers to smooth it, the hard body and supple hands. Good heavens, it was enough to make her ache just thinking about him.

But she could not act on that passion. She must hide her desire from all but herself. It was the only way to keep herself safe. Because loving him was disastrous. Loving Sloane was pain and heartbreak, however alive it might make her feel at the time.

CHAPTER TWENTY-SIX

ANNABETH WAS AWAKENED by Sloane's tap on her door. She jumped out of bed and dressed quickly in the clothes she had laid out on the chair. Her baggage had been carried down to the curricle the evening before, so she had only to quietly slip down the stairs to the front door, where Sloane stood waiting for her. It felt faintly illicit, sneaking out of the house like this in the middle of the night, with no farewells. She couldn't help but think of a woman running away with her lover.

But of course it wasn't like that at all. Sloane greeted her with a nod instead of an embrace, and they left the house and went to the vehicle without even a word exchanged. Annabeth couldn't deny a little feeling of disappointment.

There was a half-moon, making the road somewhat visible, but they proceeded at a walk along the lane. The night was hushed all around them, the only noise the sound of the horses' hooves or a metallic jingle in the harness connections. Now and then there was a rustle in the bushes or trees, and each time Sloane looked sharply in that direction.

He maintained his intense alertness even after the sky lightened, his eyes constantly roaming over the landscape. He relaxed a little when they reached the toll road to London, but he kept up his continual surveillance of the road.

"After we're in London, we'll use carriage hack," Sloane said. "No walking about or riding in an open vehicle like this."

"Do you really think he will try it again? It seems much more difficult to hide and shoot at one in the city. Are you absolutely sure it was a purposeful attack and not just an accident?" At Sloane's skeptical glance, Annabeth sighed and said, "Yes, I know—you don't believe in coincidences."

"Right. We were quite visible on the road—a hunter couldn't have mistaken us for an animal."

"But we don't know who was the target," Annabeth pointed out. "It could have hit either one of us. Perhaps that enemy of yours tracked you down."

"Parker?" Sloane let out a little chuckle. "I cannot imagine him or one of his men following us into the country. They are city men entirely. They've had ample opportunities to slip in a knife up close. No need to be a marksman. It's you this person is after, however little you want to believe it."

"But surely this man knows you would continue looking for the letter without me."

"Yes. He'd have sealed his fate if he had killed you." His voice hardened, and Annabeth thought that no one could have seen the look on Sloane's face now and not felt a quiver of fear. "But I don't know that he realizes that." After a moment, he said, "I think you should stay with your mother instead of at Lady Lockwood's."

"I don't want to stay with them. And I'd need more clothes."

"I'll take you home first so you can pack a trunk," he

replied. "I know you dislike Edgerton, but Lady Lockwood's house is the first place anyone would look for you. You wouldn't have Verity to protect you because she's at Stonecliffe."

"Or Grandmother and Petunia," Annabeth said, a smile curving her mouth, and Sloane sent her an amused glance. "But there will be servants there, and everyone will be on the lookout. The servants at Lord Edgerton's wouldn't be half as alert, and Lord Edgerton doesn't strike me as much of a brawler. Besides, if they didn't find me at Grandmother's, my mother's house would be the next logical place to look."

He sighed and was silent for a long moment, then said, "The safest place is my house."

The air was suddenly charged. Sloane kept his gaze firmly on the road ahead. Annabeth's voice seemed to stop working—which was just as well, for her mind seemed to have stopped working also.

Finally she said, "Your house? Sloane, that would be... My reputation would... It was one thing going to the Haverstocks' together, but this would be irredeemable."

"No one will know," he told her. "As far as anyone in London is aware, you have gone to Stonecliffe with your grandmother. It will be dark by the time we arrive. You'll put up your hood, and we'll go quickly inside. There's a small bit of greenery in front with a hedge that shields it. Two steps from the curricle, and you will be out of sight even during the day."

"But your servants will know. They're bound to."

"They won't," he said flatly. "You forget my checkered past. I am a man who relies on secrecy. No one comes into my personal suite of rooms upstairs without my permission or that of my butler. My butler is the only servant who resides there, and I would trust him with my life. Indeed, I have. A maid and a cook come in daily, but I have given them this time off while I'm gone, and I shan't reinstate them while you are there. I sent my father to Cornwall."

It wasn't the servants. It wasn't his father. It wasn't even the fear of scandal. No, what tightened her throat and zinged through her nerves was the same thing that started heat deep in her abdomen: the thought of being alone with Sloane. Indeed, it would have been better if there were a slew of servants or his father, anyone to make it not the two of them alone.

"I have no designs on your virtue, if that is what worries you," Sloane added caustically.

"I didn't think you had." She wasn't afraid of Sloane or his powers of seduction. What she feared was inside herself—the flame that burned in her when she was with Sloane, the hunger that had driven her into his arms yesterday, the dizzying freedom to do whatever she wanted. She should go to her mother's, as he'd suggested. She should remove herself from temptation. "Very well. Then we shall go to your house…*after* we stop at my grandmother's house so I can pack some clothes." Annabeth's tone made it clear that any arguments from Sloane about her reputation should they be seen together would fall on deaf ears.

The rest of the ride to London was awkward. All Annabeth could think about was the night ahead. She wondered why she had agreed. Was it because she wanted to prove that she could resist Sloane? Or because she wanted to give in to the temptation?

Sloane was equally quiet, and though one could

never see unease on his face, the way his eyes avoided hers spoke volumes.

They reached London in the evening dusk, and by the time Annabeth had finished at Lady Lockwood's, it was dark. "Here we are." Sloane stopped his team in front of his house.

Annabeth didn't know what she had expected of the place, but it was not this narrow brown brick building in an ordinary part of the city. It was not large, and there was no ostentation about it, nothing that spoke of great wealth or an aristocratic name. She certainly did not expect the hedge of holly that ran decoratively across the front or the window boxes that hung at both levels, so stuffed with plants that they spilled over the edges.

Though the houses were not uniform in style, all of them were set a few feet back from the street, providing small patches of grass or gardens in front of the houses. A black wrought-iron fence separated the house from the street, but the gate stood open, a short walkway leading to the front stoop.

It was indeed a sheltered place, as Sloane had told her, for the walkway was shielded on one side by a tree just inside the gate, and on the other side, a hedge bordered the boundary between the neighbor's house and Sloane's.

Annabeth pulled her hood forward to conceal as much of her face as possible, and Sloane whisked her up the path and through the front door. "I must go down to tell Antoine we are here and then take the curricle round to the mews. Feel free to roam about the house as you like. Pick out a room to stay in, perhaps."

"Where do you want me to sleep?" Annabeth asked.

His eyes glinted, and she realized the underlying innuendo of her question.

"That is— I mean—"

He smiled faintly. "I know what you mean. Choose whichever one you like."

Sloane turned and headed toward the servants' stairs in the back. Annabeth stood for a moment, looking around her. It felt odd being in Sloane's house, as if she were in some forbidden place…which, she supposed, she was. But it wasn't the social solecism she was thinking of.

It was that this house belonged to Sloane's world in which she had no part. It was all new to her, with none of the memories there had been in her parents' homes or the Haverstocks'. This was the part of Sloane that was a stranger to her, the man who had risked his life, who had built a business and made a fortune.

Annabeth walked through the house, looking into the drawing room and dining room, the office in the rear of the house. She felt a little guilty at snooping, but Sloane had told her she was free to do so. These were the furnishings he had bought himself, the art he had chosen, and yet there was a certain unlived-in feeling to it. Annabeth wondered how much time he spent here.

Annabeth climbed the stairs to the next floor. She stopped at each room along the hall, looking in. The first one she took to be the one Marcus must use when he was here, for there were a few possessions scattered here and there. The one next to it looked as if it had never been occupied, bare of all but a basic bed, chair, and dresser.

She moved on. This clearly was a sitting room, uncluttered, with comfortable chairs by the fireplace. There was a door on the interior wall. Going over, she opened it and saw another bedchamber.

This obviously was his bedroom—a jacket thrown

carelessly across a chair, his brushes scattered across the dresser, along with a set of cuff links, a book open on the seat of a chair. The smell of his shaving soap still clung to the air, mingling with the scent that was uniquely Sloane.

"I've put the curricle away," he said behind her.

Annabeth jumped and turned to him, her face flushing. Why had he had to catch her here, as if she were spying on him, as if she were thinking what it would be like to be in that luxurious bed? Which, of course, she was, but she hated for him to realize that.

"I was, ah, just wandering about," she said, with a vague motion toward the room.

He smiled. "I'm glad. I like to see you here." He shifted. "That is to say, you are welcome here, anywhere in the house."

If she hadn't felt so stiff and embarrassed herself, Annabeth would have smiled. It was so rare to see Sloane looking unsure. The black walnut bed frame and its incredibly soft-looking mattress seemed to fill the room, and she suspected that it was as much on Sloane's mind as it was on hers, for his eyes went toward it and quickly away. The line of his cheekbones was tinged with red, too, though she thought it was probably not embarrassment that brought his blood up.

"Well," she said as if summing something up, and looked toward the door leading into the hall. "Uh, I… I suppose I've toured it all."

Annabeth started toward the door, and Sloane stepped aside politely, then followed her out of the room. "Have you chosen where you would like to stay?"

"Any of the rooms will suit. They are all quite nice. I thought the one by the stairs might be your father's."

"Yes. That's where Marcus usually stays." He gestured across the hall to the opposite door. "This is the most comfortable chamber. It's at the rear of the house and you don't have the street noise. And it's the closest to mine. I mean, if there was any danger or…anything, I could hear you cry out."

"Yes, of course. That sounds the best." She could hardly say that being right across the hall from him would only add to the illicit sort of thoughts she kept having.

"Well… I'll leave you then. Perhaps you'd like to wash off the dust of the road and rest. I can send up a pitcher of water."

"Thank you, yes. That would be nice."

"I'll be downstairs. Antoine is putting together some sort of dinner for us."

Annabeth nodded and went into her chamber. She emerged later, feeling much refreshed from the wash and change of clothes, but she hadn't rested. Even though she was tired, she was also too much on edge to nap.

The meal Antoine had arranged for them was simple—cold meats, cheese, and bread—but it was delicious, and Annabeth was too hungry to care if it hadn't been. When they had satisfied their hunger, they lingered over a coffee and slice of cake.

"Your house isn't what I expected," Annabeth said.

"No?" Sloane lifted his brows. "You thought something more garish?"

"No." She smiled. "Not that. But something bolder, I suppose. Noelle described your home in the country—a haunted-looking castle, I believe is what she said."

"Yes." He smiled. "It appealed to my sense of the dramatic. But there's nothing around there for miles.

Here…" He shrugged. "I find it's better not to proclaim my presence. It's close to my business yet still a pleasant area, and it's not easy to break into. Only one door, few windows. The drainpipe is far from the windows, and there's no trellis nor a tree large enough and close enough to climb. The hedge across the front of the house covers the bottom of the windows downstairs, making it difficult to pry open the locks, and upstairs, the large and overgrown flower boxes create a nice obstruction to the windows. The attic windows don't open and are too small for anyone to get through other than a child."

Annabeth stared at him. "*That* is why you have the plants?"

"Well, I do like for them to be attractive as well. But I've made something of a habit out of avoiding possible dangers."

She shook her head. "I feel as if I hardly know you sometimes. You were never cautious."

"A few scars taught me to be more circumspect. Boldness is all well and good until you get a knife in the side."

Annabeth sucked in her breath. "Sloane, no…"

He shrugged. "It hit a rib. I lost a little blood."

"How often did that sort of thing happen?"

"It happened more often at first. I learned to check my back and trust no one and to scout any rendezvous beforehand."

"It sounds terrible."

"It had its moments. I won't deny that it was exciting. I liked outwitting the enemy. The time I spent in America was less enjoyable. I came to know the enemy there, and I liked many of them. Just foolish people who wanted to revive the glory of France…from a safe dis-

tance. That's when I left Asquith's employ and found
my excitement in making money."

"And you were a success."

"Mmm. I suppose." He toyed with a spoon. "Sometimes I wonder what I've built it all for."

"A family? A legacy for your children?"

"I've no inclination toward marriage." His smile held
no humor. "Or children."

"But you used to talk about those things. You said
you wanted a home for your family."

"I was young," he replied. "I outgrew those notions."

"But surely—"

His eyes flashed. "That was with *you*, Anna." He
leaned forward. "I wanted that with you. I wanted you
in my house. I wanted you in my bed."

Her breath caught in her throat, and she stared into
his eyes, dark and heated. The air was electric with possibility, and for a moment, Annabeth was sure he was
going to pull her up and kiss her. She went taut, waiting, knowing that she would welcome his kiss. Yearned
for his touch.

He shoved back his chair and stood up. "The devil."
He strode to the end of the room and stood for a long
moment, arms crossed, seemingly studying the array of
china in the cabinet before him.

Anna simply sat. She didn't know what to do. What
she ought to do. She wanted to follow him, to lay her
hand upon his taut arm and tell him—what? That her insides were quivering just from his gaze? That his words
stirred a fire deep in her abdomen? That she wished they
were young again and could do everything differently?

He took a breath, visibly relaxing his shoulders. "I beg
your pardon, Annabeth. I shouldn't have said that. It was

long ago and well gone." He turned, his face composed. "I am not good company tonight. You should go upstairs and get some sleep. It's been a long day."

She stood up, wanting to refuse to do what he said and knowing how foolish that would be. Had he made one gesture toward her, moved one step nearer, Annabeth thought she would go to him and toss all good sense aside. But Sloane remained still, and she was too wise. Turning, Annabeth left. She climbed the stairs to her room, alert for his call or the sound of his steps following her, but he did not follow her.

And that, she thought as she closed her door behind her, was a relief. A reprieve from having to make a decision whether to go the way of temptation or stay on the side of sanity and safety.

She could not deny that she wanted Sloane. If she could sleep with him without giving him her heart, she thought she would do it in an instant. But she knew, deep down, that that would be impossible.

Indeed, she was already feeling far more for him than was wise. If she was honest with herself, she knew that part of the reason she argued so hard to continue the investigation with Sloane was not just that she was determined to find her father's killer, but that she simply wanted to continue to be in Sloane's company.

Every morning she woke up anticipating seeing him. On the few occasions when he smiled at her in the way he used to—the familiar boyish grin, full of life and fun—her heart lifted inside her chest. Wherever he was, whoever they were with, her eyes always sought him out first. The world seemed brighter, lighter, more filled with possibilities. It was so easy to laugh with him, to talk to him; with Sloane she had never felt constraints. With Sloane everything felt *right*.

But all those things were just fool's gold and would vanish along with Sloane when this whole ordeal was through. There was no holding on to him, none of the certainty that Annabeth had once felt. Sloane would leave, and she would go back to her life. Safe and secure, surrounded by the people she knew. Bobbing along like a toy boat while life streamed on around her.

Looking back, she could see how she had done that for the last twelve years, moving along as others wanted her to, bending not breaking, arranging her life in small ways, never stepping outside the parameters, never taking charge. Going where her grandmother chose, smoothing the sharp edges Lady Lockwood presented. Accepting Nathan's proposal because she was so over-joyed and grateful that he had not died.

Had she always been like that? It would be easy to blame the crushing blow of Sloane's leaving. But that, she thought, had only revealed her hesitancy and depen-dence. What had she done when he broke their engage-ment? She'd run away to her aunt at Stonecliffe.

She hadn't stood her ground, hadn't refused, hadn't demanded anything from him. Yes, she'd been too stunned by his words to think what to say, but she could have confronted him later. She could have gone to his house and argued with him. She could have insisted that he tell her the truth. But in her pride and her hurt, she hadn't done any of that. Instead she had fled.

Well, she wasn't going to run away any longer. She was tired of letting others make decisions for her. What-ever happened with Sloane, good or bad, she was going to face it this time.

CHAPTER TWENTY-SEVEN

AT BREAKFAST THE next morning, Sloane announced that he was going to visit Mr. Asquith. "I need to find out what else he might know."

"I'm going with you," Annabeth replied.

"No. The less you know about Asquith, the better, trust me. More importantly, the less he knows about you, the better."

Annabeth stared at him. "What do you mean? I thought you worked for this man."

"That doesn't mean I *like* him. He will use anyone and anything if he thinks it will benefit England. He's a *spymaster*, Anna. He doesn't have a heart. There's a reason he was called 'Spider.' He pulls anyone he can into his web. If there is any way that he thinks he can use you, he will not hesitate to do so."

"What use could he possibly make of me?" Annabeth said. "I'm of no importance."

"You are to some people," Sloane snapped. He looked away quickly and continued in a milder voice, "There are a number of people who could be persuaded by a threat to you—don't you think Lady Lockwood would do whatever it took to keep you from harm? Or your mother?"

"And you?" As soon as the question was out of her mouth, Annabeth wished she could take it back. It was pathetic, really, hungering for some indication that Sloane cared for her.

"Yes, me." He looked at her, his eyes filled with emotion—was that regret? Sorrow? She wished she knew, wished she could look into his mind and know what he thought, what he felt. "Surely you know I would do anything for you."

Except stay with me. But Annabeth kept the thought to herself. "Then take me with you to see the man you work for."

Sloane sighed. "Very well. But be careful what you say to him."

"You speak as if he were the enemy."

"He's not that. But neither is he your friend."

THE MAN WHOSE office they entered later that morning did not look like the formidable person Sloane had warned Annabeth about. He was neither tall nor short, portly nor thin, and his clothing was perfectly correct and just as perfectly dull. He looked, not dangerous, but very ordinary, the sort of man whom one would not recognize a day after one met him. It was, she supposed, a useful appearance for a spy.

His head snapped up when Sloane opened his door, and his lips tightened. "I told you not to come here."

"I'm not interested in spy games," Sloane said, shutting the door behind him. "I told you that. However, if you'd prefer not to hear what we've learned..." He turned toward the door.

"Stop posturing, Rutherford, and sit down." The man turned his sharp gaze on Annabeth. "And you are Miss Winfield, I presume."

"I am." She took a seat. Sloane leaned against a wall, arms crossed.

Asquith looked over at him, raising his brows. "And Miss Winfield is aware of..."

"She knows about your search for her father's letter. Though she has no idea of its contents, and, indeed, no knowledge of its existence until Miss Cole and I brought it up. Lady Lockwood, I must tell you, was less than pleased to find that you had planted a spy in her household."

"I do beg your pardon, Miss Winfield," Asquith said. "Miss Cole was not there to spy on you. We were trying to find it without bringing you into the matter. I hope that your grandmother was not greatly inconvenienced."

"Only if you consider having her house broken into an inconvenience," Annabeth replied calmly.

"Broken into?" Asquith turned to Sloane in surprise. "You said nothing of a break-in."

"It hadn't happened when I spoke to you."

"My goodness. That is distressing." He frowned. "I was under the impression, Miss Winfield, that you had departed London for refuge in the country," Asquith said to her.

"We did depart London, though not for that purpose. We went to look for this letter you think Papa wrote," Annabeth said crisply. "It would help a good deal if I knew what this letter is supposed to say. How am I to know it when I see it?"

"Sloane will know. Better, I think, to let him handle the matter. Where is Miss Cole in all this?"

"She's staying in the country to throw our enemy off the scent." Sloane abandoned his relaxed pose and moved closer to the other man. "Not that it did much good, as Miss Winfield was shot at and nearly killed."

"Indeed?" Asquith's eyebrows rose slightly. Annabeth wondered if his appearance was ever anything but unruffled. "I think perhaps you should join Miss Cole in the country, Miss Winfield, and let Rutherford continue the search."

"I am the one who can find it," Annabeth told him.

Sloane updated the other man on their search, then said, "What is going on here, Asquith? What aren't you telling us?"

"My dear boy…why would I conceal anything from you?"

"Because that is *your* nature," Sloane retorted. "This whole thing has been suspect from the start. Why did you hire an outsider to investigate this? Why did you turn to someone who knows nothing about any of it, to whom you can't even reveal all the facts? I know you, and you don't act illogically. Why didn't you go to Verity immediately? Or to me, for that matter?"

"As I said before, both of you told me you were through with the business. I assumed you wouldn't want to take on this job."

Sloane snorted. "That's never stopped you before. You know we were the logical choices. You know we are the best. The most familiar with it."

Asquith said carefully, "Sometimes it is better to have someone not so familiar. An outsider can take a fresher look on an internal matter."

Sloane straightened. "What are you saying? Are you suggesting that you suspect someone within the organization? That there is a traitor within?"

Asquith shrugged. "There are some things that indicate someone inside may have betrayed us. I have to look at every possibility. You remember that time in Lyon, when you were caught and put in jail? Or that 'cargo' you were supposed to unload but they opened fire on your ship and you barely got away. And there were others, weren't there, where it seemed that the French knew where you were going to be and what your plans were?"

"Yes, of course. But spying is the kind of business where nothing is certain. There are often missteps." Sloane frowned. "Even so, if you thought there was a traitor among your men, why wouldn't you have hired the very best person to sniff out the treachery? Someone who knows the business inside out and everyone who was involved? That would be Verity."

Asquith shifted in his seat and glanced away, for the first time looking uncomfortable. "Well, there were reasons—"

Sloane's jaw dropped. "Are you saying you think Verity is the traitor from inside? That's ridiculous."

"No, of course I don't think it's Verity. But, whatever my personal feelings in the matter, I have to be objective. I must look at all the possibilities. We can't discount her just because she's a woman. A woman can be as much a villain as a man. And I cannot ignore the fact that Verity was involved in most of those failed missions."

"Verity was one of the people at risk many of those times. When I was arrested, she was the one who got me out of jail. Why would she have done that if she was responsible for my being there?"

"That could be an excellent way to gain your trust. Sometimes that can be more important in the long run than capturing you at that moment. Especially since you seem to be pretty adept at getting yourself out of such situations, anyway."

"That's absurd. You might as well suspect me."

Asquith made no reply, simply continued to look at him.

"Oh. Of course. You suspect me as well," Sloane said in disgusted tones.

Asquith shrugged. "Not really. But, as I said, one has to consider—"

"All the possibilities," Sloane finished for him. "Very well. Who else do you suspect of being the traitor in your little web? Surely Verity and I are not the only ones."

"No, of course not. But there is no one in particular whom I suspect. Without any evidence, I cannot narrow it down. I have to look at everyone."

"Then give me all their names."

"Rutherford!" Asquith looked shocked. "I can't do that. That would put the integrity of the whole operation at risk. You know that one of my most basic rules was to keep everyone's identities secret. You knew only the people who actively participated with you, like Miss Cole—and you wouldn't have known her real name if the two of you hadn't shared that information with each other, as you were ordered *not* to."

"I don't give a damn about your ring's 'integrity,'" Sloane shot back. "The war is long over. There's no reason to continue to keep the names secret. We are running out of options. We have only some of Lady Edgerton's possessions to look through, and the longer we look, the more unlikely it seems that we shall find any letter Mr. Winfield left. Either the thing has long since been lost or thrown away or it never existed to begin with."

"Is there nowhere else? Are you sure you've examined everything?"

"Yes, I'm sure. But the person who is trying to harm Annabeth doesn't know that we have little hope of finding out who he is. You may have only a failed mission, but Miss Winfield's very life is at stake. I have to find out who that traitor was by any means I can. I want those names." Sloane looked at him levelly, his face hard as stone.

Asquith sighed. "Very well. I will write down a list of names and send it to you. Though I don't think it will do you much good. I've sifted through all of them for weeks, trying to find the man."

Annabeth stayed silent for the rest of the meeting. Once they'd made their departure and were walking back to their waiting carriage, Annabeth said, "Do *you* think Verity could actually be the traitor?"

Sloane shrugged. "It's hard for me to believe. She's saved my life, and I got her out of a tough spot or two as well. But Asquith is right. There were a number of missions that went awry—an agent whom I was supposed to give passage from France was shot on the beach, or the time the French caught me at the rendezvous point where I was to meet Verity. But, as I said, she was the one who got me out of the jail and back to safety. I cannot really believe it was her. However, we cannot go on faith alone. We have to suspect everyone."

"I know she lied to me, and despite how betrayed I felt at first, I still like her. I still trust her. And we know she's been at Stonecliffe, so she couldn't have shot at us at my father's workshop."

"No. I think it's more likely one of the others if it's anyone in the old group at all. Asquith sees enemies in every shadow. It could just as easily be no one connected to the network. But it gives me a place to start."

"Then you really think we're not going to find Papa's letter?"

"I think the chances are getting slim. We've only whatever boxes your mother has left and the portable writing desk. But there is the same problem with all of them—if one of them had contained such a letter, it seems unlikely that it wouldn't have been found in the years since."

"Yes." Annabeth sighed. "If Russell had come across something like that, he would have carried out Father's wishes. He would have shown it to the authorities. Mother would as well—or at least have told my Grandmother. It seems rather hopeless, doesn't it?"

"No. I'll still find him. It may take a little longer, but I won't stop until I do."

"Do you really think that Mr. Asquith will give you that list? He didn't seem very cooperative."

Sloane let out a little huff of laughter. "Oh, he'll send it. Much as he may want to keep everything secret, he wants to catch whoever betrayed him even more. It's not just treason, but a personal insult to him." He shrugged. "Besides, he knows I'll get the names from him…one way or another."

Annabeth looked at him. There had been no bravado in Sloane's words, only a flat practicality that was actually more frightening. Sometimes Sloane seemed much the same—the flash of a smile, a certain mischief in his eyes, the heat of his kisses, or the tenderness of his embrace when she had broken down in tears.

But more often, like now, she was reminded that he was not the same man she had known. There was something hard and cold in Sloane now, a shuttered quality. Once, his emotions had lain just beneath the surface, strong and easily read. But that was far from the case in the present. Annabeth was certain he had kept things from her, and he refused to tell her anything of his life the past twelve years. He seemed to have a close bond with Verity yet he was cold enough to also consider her a suspect. Lies slid off his tongue, as smooth as honey, and he could cut a man in two with a look. And yet… there was no one Annabeth trusted more, no one she could depend on more. No one she wanted more.

Sloane was not the boy she had loved. But she had the uneasy feeling that she was falling in love with the man he'd become.

CHAPTER TWENTY-EIGHT

NOW THAT THINGS felt slightly more settled—at least Asquith had relented and promised to send him that list of names—Sloane was finding it harder and harder to ignore the tension that had been brewing inside him ever since he had suggested that Annabeth stay with him at his house. It had been a ridiculous, foolish idea. How much more temptation could he really take before he did something he could not take back? But even now, Sloane knew that if he had it to do over, he would do exactly the same thing. He wanted Annabeth with him even more than he feared his dwindling control over his emotions.

After Sloane had instructed the driver to take them to Lord and Lady Edgerton's, Annabeth leaned closer to him, her soft perfume filling his head with libidinous thoughts.

Damn, but it was hard to not yield to the impulse to kiss her, to woo her, to hold her in his arms. It had been difficult enough when she was young and naive, but somehow it was even more difficult to act the gentleman with the woman.

She was even more lovely than she had been then, her form more enticingly rounded, her face refined to sharper beauty. And there was a sense of experience that was written on her features now. He worried that much of that experience had been pain—and surely the lion's share had been inflicted by him. But it made him want even more to protect her so she would never have to know such pain again. He shouldn't even allow the thought of himself as her protector. He was more likely to be her downfall.

Or perhaps time had not changed her so much and instead he had forgotten exactly how she looked back then, his memory attempting to assuage his pain? He had carried a miniature of her—admittedly stolen from her father's study, but that had seemed very minor compared to all his other sins—but he had not needed the reminder of her to call up her image in his mind. He could remember each line and curve of her face, the full underlip and the dimple that sprang up at one corner of her mouth.

Finally, taking pity on himself, he had stored the little painting away at the bottom of his trunk, and over the years he had thought of her less, ached for her less. He had ceased wishing that he had not done what he had to do. He had covered up that tender spot with steel, worn away his boyish emotions with reality.

Sloane wished to God he had not entangled his life with Annabeth's again, but he knew he would not have given up this time with her for anything. It was hellish wanting her all the time, but it was a hell he relished. He was, in short, a fool.

WHEN THEY ARRIVED at Annabeth's mother's home, they found that Martha was not there. It was Lord Edgerton who greeted them.

"Welcome," he said, though the glance he shot at Sloane was anything but friendly. "Please, sit down.

It's not often that you call on us, Annabeth. It's so good to see you."

"Thank you." Annabeth tried to think of some polite way of saying that they wanted to talk to her mother and not him.

Sloane was not so careful of the niceties. "Miss Winfield was hoping to ask her mother a few questions. Do you know when Lady Edgerton will return?"

"She's out shopping, so…" Edgerton gave them a thin smile and a shrug of the shoulders. "Is there anything I could help you with? I believe I can say without contradiction that my wife shares everything with me."

"Mother had said she would show me the boxes that my father gave her."

"Those boxes again?" His tone was a mixture of condescension and amusement. "Why this sudden interest in a few little boxes? I suspect that Martha has thrown them away."

"I certainly hope not," Annabeth said. "She said that she had some of them. In particular, I am looking for Papa's traveling writing desk."

"They're important." Sloane looked at Annabeth a little questioningly, and she nodded. Her stepfather was correct in saying that her mother shared everything with him; Lord Edgerton would know anything they told Martha soon enough.

"We've been to Mr. Winfield's workshop," Sloane went on. "The place where he died."

"That seems a bit morbid, but what does it have to do with these boxes?"

"My father was murdered," Annabeth said bluntly, annoyed at the man's supercilious attitude.

"What?" Edgerton's eyebrows shot up, and he stiffened in his chair. "Murdered? What nonsense. He died in a fall. It was an accident. Everyone knows that."

"That is what everyone *assumed*," Sloane stated. "No one actually saw him fall."

"That doesn't mean that he was murdered," Edgerton protested. "I cannot imagine why you are spreading such nonsense."

"We are not spreading it. You are the only person we have told. And it isn't nonsense or idle conjecture. We looked at the staircase from which he fell. A board had been purposely loosened, nails taken out, so that it would unbalance Winfield and cause him to grab the banister for support. But the railing had been neatly sawn through on either side so that he would fall when he leaned against it."

"Sawn through?" Lord Edgerton pushed up out of his chair. "You're mistaken. I am certain that you are wrong."

"I'm not," Sloane returned flatly. "I know sabotage when I see it. Someone intended him to fall."

"But someone would have seen that it had been sawn."

"His distraught valet, who discovered him lying on the floor? His grieving widow or daughter? I doubt anyone really looked at the railing."

Edgerton frowned. "I suppose…but it seems so unlikely. Why would anyone murder Winfield?"

"That's why we want to look at the boxes."

"You think they have something to do with his death?" Edgerton's frown deepened. "I don't see how…" He shook his head as if to clear his thoughts, then turned to Annabeth. "Don't tell your mother this."

"She has a right to know," Annabeth protested.

"She wouldn't *want* to know," Edgerton shot back. "It will only bring up bad memories for Martha. Reopen the wound. She shouldn't have to go through that all over again." He held his stepdaughter in a steely gaze. "Let her be. In fact, none of this needs to be brought up at all."

"Papa was murdered," Annabeth snapped. "He deserves to have justice done."

"That's scarcely any use to him now," Edgerton retorted. "It's in the past. It's done. You will set tongues clacking for no reason. No one will benefit. You should not keep on with this 'investigation' of yours."

"There are other things at stake that are more important than a bit of scandal or bringing up bad memories," Sloane said, stepping in between Edgerton and Annabeth, as if to shield her. "I have a duty to discover what happened."

"Duty!" Edgerton spat. "What would *you* know about duty? You've been nothing but a disgrace to your family."

"You have no right to speak to Sloane that way," Annabeth said, moving around Sloane to face Edgerton once again. "You have no idea what he's done, the dangers he's faced—receiving no credit for it, only contumely from people like you who haven't any knowledge of the facts."

"Annabeth…" Sloane murmured, amusement quirking up the corners of his mouth. "There's no need for you to defend me, no matter how well you play the role. I don't care what people like this man think of me."

They were interrupted at that moment by the sound of Lady Edgerton's voice in the foyer. "Are they here? How delightful."

Annabeth's mother sailed into the room. "Annabeth,

dearest, what a pleasant surprise. I thought you went to Stonecliffe with Mother."

"I did." Annabeth saw no reason to tell her she had immediately left. Even worse would be to say where she was staying now. "I've been visiting friends."

"I wish I had known you were stopping by. We could have gone shopping together." Martha proceeded to launch into a description of her morning at the modiste's.

Annabeth smiled and responded, then eased into her reason for being here. "You said you had some of Papa's boxes that I could look at." She wasn't going to tell her mother about Papa's murder here and now, with Edgerton looking on. She would do it later, when the two of them were alone.

"Yes, of course. I had a maid find them in the attic and bring them down." Lady Edgerton stood up and went to use the bellpull.

"I've been trying to think of other friends of Papa's who might have some boxes." Annabeth doubted that her father had left them anything important, but it might be useful to talk to his other acquaintances. "Do you remember anyone who used to visit Papa?"

"Oh, well, he had many friends, but fewer of them came to visit him in the country. We were there more and more toward the end. And most of his set were not the rural sort." She let out a little rueful laugh. "Nor was I. Of course, dear Russell was frequently at the house. They used to call on each other a good deal." She nodded at Sloane. "Once or twice your father came to see us. When things weren't…pleasant for him in the city."

Sloane grimaced. "When he was rolled up, you mean."

"Really, Rutherford…" Lord Edgerton objected.

But Martha only smiled. "Exactly. It seemed as if one or the other of those men was always in that state. Hunter, too." She sighed. "He was never very lucky in his investments."

Edgerton made a little noise deep in his throat but said nothing.

"Oh, and you came once or twice," she said to her husband. "Do you remember?"

"Lord Edgerton visited Papa?" Annabeth looked at the man in astonishment. "I thought—I wasn't aware that you were friends with him, sir."

Edgerton shifted in his seat. "Mr. Winfield and I were merely acquaintances. However, there was a matter of an inheritance that I needed to see him about."

"Yes." Martha nodded. "It was one of his distant relatives, a great-aunt, I believe. What was her name?"

"Mary," Edgerton said shortly. "It was nothing, really."

"Yes, Mary. I didn't remember her, actually, but it was most providential. Poor Hunter had invested heavily in that gold mine that failed, you see, so that inheritance was quite helpful at the time. Sad, of course, but…"

"I don't remember that," Annabeth said.

"It was long ago, during the war, and you were quite young. Hunter wouldn't have mentioned it to you."

"My lady." Sloane leaned forward, saying in a gentle tone, "Do you remember anyone in particular who called on Mr. Winfield toward the end? Was there anyone there with you when his accident occurred?"

"No. I was all alone. It was most distressing. Annabeth was visiting Adeline. But Russell came as soon as I sent him a note, and he was a great comfort to me. Then Mother arrived, so she took care of everything."

"Naturally," Edgerton commented dryly.

A maid entered the room, carrying three boxes, and set them in front of Annabeth.

"There you go, dear, just take those with you."

"Thank you. But do you remember that writing desk of Papa's, the one that folded up?"

"The traveling desk? Hunter was very fond of it."

"Do you still have it?" Annabeth's throat tightened. What if it had been discarded? "Could I see it?"

"I'm sorry, darling, but I don't have it any longer. I gave it to Simpson, poor man. He was so fond of your father."

"Papa's valet?"

"Yes. Simpson always carried it when they traveled so it wouldn't get nicked or scratched. I had no use for it, and Simpson was so distressed by Hunter's death."

"Yes, I remember. Do you know who he's working for now?"

"I don't think he's a valet anymore. Hunter left him a little inheritance, and I believe he moved to the country. I'm not sure where. His sister's, perhaps?"

Edgerton, who had obviously had enough of talk about Hunter and his death, changed the subject with no subtlety. "Martha, dear, did you remember Lady Ambrose's dinner this evening?"

"Yes." Martha grimaced. "I do hate these dinners with people in the Home Office. It's always about political things, which quite puts me to sleep. And I have so much trouble choosing the proper dress to wear. It's difficult to find something that blends in with the others but isn't dull."

Edgerton smiled fondly. "Yes. But one has to keep

up one's alliances, you know. And you always succeed in wearing exactly the proper gown."

"Thank you, darling." Martha beamed at her husband. "But I believe I shall take a little nap before we go, just to fend off doing it tonight during the soup course."

"We should be going as well," Sloane said, and Annabeth rose, too, eager to get away where they could discuss what they'd just learned.

Outside, Sloane started toward his carriage, but Annabeth tugged at his arm and he stopped, immediately scanning the area around them. "What's wrong? Did you see someone?"

"No. Nothing like that. But I think I can discover where Simpson is." Annabeth turned toward the steps going down to the half basement where the servants lived. "Mother's maid, Frances, is still with her, and I suspect she will know."

Annabeth was proved right, and a few minutes later, they left the house with the name of Simpson's village in hand.

"The Lake District," Sloane grumbled as their carriage rattled off down the street. "That's a three-day trip. You'd have thought he would have stayed close to home."

"Simpson can't help that his only living family is a sister who married and moved there. Of course, Frances didn't seem to approve of it either. I always thought she had a bit of a *tendre* for Simpson."

"I don't like the idea of you traveling in an open curricle for three days each way. I can protect you from a close attack, but I can't stop a bullet. And apparently, whoever is pursuing is clever enough that I didn't catch him following us," Sloane said in disgust.

"If you're about to suggest again that I go hide at

Stonecliffe, you needn't even start. Simpson is not going to allow some stranger to look through my father's things."

"I'm not a stranger. He's bound to know of me."

"Anything he heard about you would not have been good," Annabeth pointed out. "You need my help."

"Are you sure the paper will be there?"

"Of course not. I didn't even know it existed until you started looking for it. But it seems the likeliest possibility. I don't think these boxes are going to be of any help." She had already opened one of them and found nothing and was now investigating another. As Annabeth worked, she said in a thoughtful voice, "Sloane… did it seem odd to you—what my mother said about Lord Edgerton visiting Papa? My grandmother said they were bitter enemies. I've certainly never heard him say a kind word about my father."

"It sounded as if it was just business. An inheritance."

"I suppose. But couldn't it have been handled by mail? Why would he come to visit them?"

"To see your mother, perhaps?"

Annabeth's eyes flashed. "My mother was *not* carrying on an affair with him."

"I didn't say that. Of course she didn't return the feeling. I'm talking about Edgerton. Sometimes, you would give anything just to see a person even though you know that it's hopeless."

Annabeth stared at him, suddenly tongue-tied. Did he mean that was how he had felt about her? Heaven knows, she had often enough ached to see Sloane, even knowing the pain it would bring her. He turned his head away.

She cleared her throat. "Perhaps you are right. But if so, that is more proof of how much Edgerton wanted to marry her. I can't help but think—what if Papa's murder wasn't anything to do with this letter we're chasing? What if it was because of jealousy?"

Sloane turned to look at her, his eyes soaring upward. "You're accusing your stepfather of murder?"

Annabeth grimaced. "I don't know. Grandmother said Edgerton had always been in love with Mother. Then, as soon after Papa's death as propriety allowed, he married her. And he was so intent on us not telling Mother that it was murder. He wanted to keep it a secret from everyone, in fact. Doesn't that indicate a guilty mind?"

"Or one who doesn't want scandalous rumors of the sort you're espousing all over the *ton*," Sloane answered. "If Edgerton killed Mr. Winfield so he could marry his wife, then there must be an entirely separate enemy trying to harm you. I don't like coincidences."

"Or maybe it's not two different men."

"Why would Edgerton be after the letter your father wrote? Why would he try to have you kidnapped and shot? That would scarcely endear him to your mother."

"Not if she didn't know it was him," Annabeth retorted. "Neither you nor I know what's in this letter. Maybe it has nothing to do with what the Foreign Office assumes it does. Papa could have written it because he found out Lord Edgerton was plotting to kill him. I suspect Edgerton would very much want to find *that* letter."

CHAPTER TWENTY-NINE

SLOANE THOUGHT ABOUT Annabeth's theory the rest of the way to his house. It was hard to imagine the stiff and cold Lord Edgerton committing a crime of passion. But the crime had been done in a very calculated, removed way. Perhaps it was worth looking into.

When they arrived at his house, he pushed the hows and whys out of his mind and carefully surveyed the street before he got out of the vehicle. Whatever they had learned today was not enough to keep Annabeth safe, not yet. He glanced up and down the street again. Seeing nothing, he turned to Annabeth and said, "You may—"

Out of the corner of his eye he saw the flash of a movement, and he turned just as the driver of the hack jumped down at him. Sloane threw up his arms, catching the man by his shoulders, and they crashed into the open door of the carriage. The force of the collision knocked them back, and they hit the pavement. Sloane heard Annabeth scream his name and willed her to stay in the carriage. *Don't come out. Don't come out.*

They wrestled on the ground. Sloane's attacker was heavier than he was and difficult to push off, and Sloane's blows were hampered by their position.

Then Annabeth was there above them, holding aloft one of her father's boxes. She swung it down with all her force into his opponent's back. The driver let out a roar and turned toward Annabeth. Sloane shoved the man off him and scrambled to his feet. "Damn it, Anna! Run!"

The other man rose to his feet as well, pulling a knife from his belt. He charged at Sloane, who quickly twisted aside. The knife sliced through his waistcoat, and Sloane could feel the cool metal as it grazed his stomach. He caught his opponent's arm and slammed the man into the side of the hack.

They grappled, Sloane holding off his adversary's knife arm but unable to free his other arm from the man's clutch. That was when Sloane caught sight of another man running toward them. Coming to his aid, was Sloane's first thought. Then he saw the knife glittering in the second attacker's hand.

Annabeth, who, naturally, had not done as he said, let out a blood-curdling shriek and threw the wooden box at the second man. It hit him in the chest, hard enough that he stopped, startled, and swiveled toward Annabeth. It gave Sloane time to pivot, grasp his opponent by his jacket, and fling him into his accomplice.

Both the men stumbled back. Sloane reached into his jacket and pulled out his gun. His attackers went still, eyeing the weapon.

"I believe I have the advantage," Sloane said. As the two men glanced from him to each other and back again, he went on, "Of course, a ball through the chest would kill only one of you. So it's fortunate that I also have this." With his left hand he pulled a knife from his belt and smiled fiercely. "Which one of you wants to die right now? And which one wants to die more slowly?"

The two men bolted off down the street. Sloane let out a long breath and leaned against the side of the carriage. "The hack driver." He cursed. "I never thought of that. I'm getting old."

"Yes, you're clearly ancient," Annabeth said. She managed to keep her words nonchalant, but her voice was shaky.

She came toward him. "I was so sca— Sloane! You're bleeding."

He had lifted his jacket to put the gun back in his inner pocket, and now he glanced down. "Damn. I quite liked this waistcoat."

Annabeth gave him a withering look. "I hope you didn't like this jacket as much—there's another cut here on the sleeve."

"Blast."

"Not to mention the bloodstain," Annabeth went on dryly. "Honestly, Sloane, how can you be so cavalier about it? You've been stabbed. You need to see a doctor."

"Not stabbed. Just cut."

"Oh, well, that's all right then." She shook her head and went off, muttering, to pick up the box she had been wielding.

"I would never have guessed that your father's boxes would come in so handy," Sloane said, retrieving the other boxes from the hack.

Inside the house, Sloane said, "I think a bit of whiskey would be in order. Would you like something?"

"A little sherry might be nice."

As he poured their drinks in the study, Sloane grumbled, "Why didn't you run when I told you to?"

"Did you really think I would run away and let you fight off two men?" Annabeth took the glass of sherry he handed her. "Do you not remember that time with the bees?"

"The bees?" Sloane stared, then began to laugh. "You came in swinging that shawl of yours all around like a madwoman." He sighed and took a drink. "No. I suppose I expected you to do exactly what you did. But, if you will remember, you ended up with almost as many stings as I. And this is more serious than bees. Those men want to harm you."

"I'm not sure they were after me. It was *you* they attacked."

"They were trying to get me out of the way so they could get to you."

"If that were true, why didn't that second man grab me while you were occupied with the first attacker? Instead, he went to help his colleague."

"Then they were hoping to remove me from the situation permanently, but again, it was in order to get to you."

"Perhaps." Annabeth frowned down at her glass. "But if your fellow Asquith is correct and this has something to do with that traitor, then I would think you are far more dangerous to them than I. After all, you know something about that time and those people. You are far more likely to figure everything out, even without Papa's letter. And you're more likely to track down the man who killed my father."

"Well, hopefully I can keep us both safe," Sloane replied lightly, and shrugged, wincing a little at the movement.

"It's clear you're hurt." Annabeth set down her glass of sherry. "Since you're too stubborn to see a doctor, I hope you will at least let me patch up your little 'cuts.'"

"You needn't. I can manage, I'm sure." Just the thought of her touching his skin nearly took his breath away.

Annabeth planted her fists on her hips, her eyes narrowed. "Do you really think I'm that useless? That I could not clean a wound? Or is it that you think I'm so delicate I'll faint?"

"No. Neither. I don't think you're useless at all. But it's just, well…you know…"

She stared at him. "No, I don't know. What are—oh! You don't want to take your shirt off in front of me?"

Sloane felt a faint flush rise in his cheeks. God help him, now he was blushing like a shy virgin. "No. I mean, well, yes, but it's not—" He broke off with a glare. "Oh, bloody hell, come along then."

Sloane strode out of the room. Annabeth followed him as he went up the stairs to his bedroom. "There are bandages in there." He pointed to a small cabinet. "Rags are over there by the shaving stand."

He started to pull off his jacket, but Annabeth moved quickly to slide the coat down his injured arm and off. His gut tightened. "You needn't."

"Oh, stop being stoic. Your arm hurts. I saw you wince." She stepped back, examining the ripped sleeve, then folded and put it on the chair.

"It was just that the dried blood on the jacket pulled a bit at the wound." Sloane began on the buttons of his waistcoat. Annabeth was watching him, and Sloane found it damnably disturbing to undress in front of her. It was even more disturbing when she moved closer and slid the waistcoat from him as she had the jacket. *And he had thought the jacket was difficult.* This was closer, more intimate, her fingers sliding down his arm, with only his shirt between his skin and hers.

He fumbled at his neckcloth, his fingers clumsy. He could only hope she wouldn't look down and see the reaction of his body. He turned away as he untangled the long narrow cloth, pretending that he did so in order to toss the neckcloth on the chair with the other things. Sloane remained with his back turned as he untucked his shirt. The shirt was long enough it covered the tell-tale bulge in his breeches.

The unfortunate thing was, it also covered his wounds. Sloane tugged open the ties at the top of his shirt, which opened only halfway down, then reached for its hem and began to pull it up over his head, hesitating at the twinge of pain in his arm.

"Oh, for goodness' sake, Sloane. Let me help you," Annabeth said impatiently. "You are the most contrary man alive. Just stop. Let me dampen that cloth so it doesn't pull." She went to the washstand and returned with a wet rag that she laid over the wound on his arm, holding it there.

She was so close, he could smell the faint scent of her perfume, could feel the warmth of her body. Her hair was tousled, and he ached to smooth the wayward strands back across her head.

Annabeth gently lifted the now-softened material off his arm, then did the same task on the cut across his stomach. Putting the damp cloth aside, she took hold of the hem of his shirt and pushed it up. "Bend over, or I can't pull it off you."

He didn't want her to. And he wanted it more than anything. He bent as she requested, and she slid the shirt from his arms, then tossed it aside.

"Oh, Sloane." Annabeth slid her fingers gently across his arm. "This slice is so long." She smoothed her finger across his stomach. "Are you certain we shouldn't call a doctor?"

Sloane drew in a sharp breath and steeled himself against her touch. "It's not that deep." His voice was tight. Perhaps Annabeth would assume it was from the physical pain.

"If this *had* been deeper...well, it doesn't bear thinking of." She looked up at him, concern in her eyes.

Once, he would have grinned and kissed away her worry. All he could do now was look away. "It's a bit cold." In fact, he was filled with heat. But he needed her to hurry up.

"Yes, of course." She wet the cloth again and returned to gently wash his arm. "You're right. This isn't very deep, thank heavens. It won't need stitching." She wrapped a strip of bandage around his arm and tied it.

Sloane thought he had passed that test pretty well. But the next one was an utter failure. As she stroked the wet cloth across his stomach, his skin and the muscles underneath jumped at her touch. If there was any pain, it was swamped by pleasure. He clenched his teeth, managing not to let out a groan, but he could not stop the deep pulse of hunger in him. It was a relief when she stopped, but he ached to feel it again.

Annabeth looked up at him, and there was a soft, dreamy look in her eyes that nearly destroyed all his good intentions. But she let out a little sigh and moved away to get the bandage. Annabeth wrapped it around his abdomen, standing so close there was only a sliver of air between them as she reached around him to grasp the end of the bandage. For an instant he was in her embrace.

Annabeth tied the bandage and took a step back. Her eyes roamed his chest. "There's another scar." She slid her finger down a small scar high on his chest. "What happened?"

"That was a ball from a musket."

"And this?" She trailed a finger down a longer scar on his side.

"A knife in an alley in New Orleans. I let down my guard there. I was thinking only of espionage, and I didn't think of thieves."

"And here?" She touched his other arm.

"I don't remember."

She walked slowly around him. "There are so many of them." She came to a stop in front of him, looking up into his face. "Sloane…"

"But I survived all of them." He tried to keep his voice light, but looking down into those luminous green eyes, it was difficult to. He swallowed.

She laid her hand on his chest, her palm spread. Sloane felt as if it burned into him. He laid his hand over hers, keeping it there.

"Was it worth it?"

"Was what worth it?" He was having difficulty thinking. The only things in his head at the moment were Annabeth and the need that churned inside him.

"The ship—the reason you went with Asquith. The reason you left me."

"No. No ship would have been worth that. You haunted my thoughts, my dreams. I loved you beyond reason. I wanted you with everything I had in me."

"Then why—"

He shook his head. "Please… I had to, Anna. I just—I had to."

"Do you want me still?"

"You know I do. You had to have known that when I kissed you. But I can't—"

"No." She laid her finger against his lips. "Don't tell

me what you can't do, what I can't do, what rule we must follow." Sliding her hand from beneath his, she glided both hands across his chest. "You were the only man I ever felt desire for. The only one I will ever feel desire for, I'm beginning to think," she added wryly.

His heart was hammering, his head struggling to keep a hold on reason, every part of him aching. "Anna, please…" He wasn't even sure anymore what he was pleading for.

"You could have died today. I could have died. And I would never know." She pressed her lips gently against his chest, and it was like a bolt of lightning through him. She raised her head and looked up at him again, her eyes filled with the same passion that thrummed through him. "I want to know, Sloane. I thought I would have you for the rest of my life, and I know that's all gone now. But I want to know what it would have been like. How it would have felt. What I would have had."

For a moment he stood still, locked in her gaze. Then he bent to kiss her.

CHAPTER THIRTY

A TINY VOICE of reason in the back of Annabeth's mind was sounding an alarm: this way was dangerous, this path led to heartbreak. But Annabeth pushed it away, lost in the sensations that flooded her. This was what she had yearned for all these years—to be in Sloane's arms, to feel his hard body pressed against hers, to drown in the pleasure of his kiss. She wanted him. She had always wanted him. And she was going to have this moment, this bond with him, and if this was all she had for the rest of her life, so be it. A memory of joy was far better than the bitterness she had lived with for the past twelve years.

She poured herself into Sloane's kiss and wrapped her arms around him, pressing up into his body as if she could become part of him. He lifted her up into him until her feet no longer touched the ground, and she wrapped her legs instinctively around him. A groan sounded deep in his throat and he turned, setting her on the dresser, sweeping away the objects atop it and sending them tumbling to the floor.

Flush against him in that intimate way, Annabeth felt the swell of his desire, the persistent pulse that stirred her even through the barrier of their clothes. His mouth left hers to kiss her neck, and his hand slid up her body and cupped her breast. The touch startled her a little—

but not as much as the flood of moisture between her legs. The ache between them grew with every kiss and caress, and her legs squeezed around him. Her whole being was yearning, urging, seeking satisfaction.

That brought another low sound from him, and he raised his head, gazing into her eyes. His voice was hoarse as he said, "Annabeth, are you certain? This is a gift that should belong to your future husband."

"This is a gift that belongs to *me*," she retorted fiercely. "And I'll choose who I give it to." She sank her hands into his hair, holding his eyes steady. "This is the time, and you are the man. Make love to me, Sloane." She leaned forward and took his mouth in a deep, hungry kiss.

His fingers sank into the material of her dress as his body leaned into her, and when he raised his head again, his breath was coming fast and hard and his eyes were dark with desire. "It seems to me that this is unfair. You have on altogether too much clothing."

He reached behind her and grappled with the hooks that fastened her dress, undoing them with a speed that she thought probably sent several of them flying. Sloane slipped his fingers into the shoulders of the frock and pulled it down slowly, his eyes fastened on her. He drank in the sight of her for a long moment before he untied the ribbon that closed her chemise and slid it up and off her body.

"God, you are beautiful," he murmured. He cupped her breasts in his hands, stroking his thumb around and across her nipples.

Annabeth drew in a sharp breath at the sensations that ran through her. He looked up at her in question, his hands stilling. "Too much?"

"No, don't stop. It's just new. I didn't know how... how delightful it would feel."

A slow, sensual smile curved his lips, and he said, "Oh, I can do better than that, my love."

Sloane leaned down and circled her nipple with his tongue, drawing another breath of surprise from her. Then he fastened his mouth on the hard bud, his lips and tongue sending desire rocketing through her. A moan escaped Annabeth's lips and she clenched her fingers in his hair. His lips moved to her other nipple, still caressing the dampened flesh with his hand. She felt entirely undone, flung into some other universe of pleasure.

He pulled away. His face was flushed and his lips a soft deep red that made her long to kiss them. So she did and was rewarded with his growling murmur of her name. Sloane pulled her from her perch and set her down on her feet. His eyes never leaving her, he pulled off the remainder of his clothes.

Annabeth's eyes widened as she took in his naked form, but it was eagerness she felt, not alarm. Hastily she stripped off her dress and petticoat. Undoing her half boots took more effort, but Sloane scooped her up and set her on the bed, and held her leg, unfastening them for her. Just the feel of his fingers wrapped around her calf, so large and strong, was enticing, but then he slipped his hands up her leg to slide her stocking down. And the glide of his skin over hers awakened nerves she didn't even know she had.

The heat low in her abdomen flamed higher. He undid the ties of her underpants and pulled them off, and when he stood there, his eyes roaming over her naked body, his face heavy with desire, Annabeth thought the fire inside would consume her.

She would have thought that being naked before him would embarrass her, but instead it spiked her passion to see his eyes caress her, the desire in his face etching deeper. She wasn't sure why, but she lifted her arms above her head and stretched under his gaze. And the sound he uttered now was definitely a growl.

Sloane lay down on the bed beside her, propped up on his elbow, and slid his hand down her body, gliding over her breasts and stomach and legs. His fingers skimmed back up the inside of her thigh, separating her legs. And then his hand was there, in that most intimate of places, astonishing her even as it spurred her desire to greater and greater heights. Apparently unsurprised by the thick wetness there, he let his fingers roam over the slick, tender flesh.

Annabeth tried to hold back a long moan of pleasure, but she could not. His touch aroused her beyond anything she had ever imagined. He stroked and caressed, sliding one of his fingers inside her, then another, and Annabeth moved beneath him, pressing against his hand, driven by a need she could not express.

Sloane bent to take her breast in his mouth even as his hand continued its exploration, and she was swamped by pleasure. Passion built in her, spiraling ever upward until she felt as if she was on the edge, desperate for satisfaction. She cried out as that passion exploded within her, sweeping through her in waves of pleasure—though pleasure seemed too mild a word for it.

"Sloane…" She looked up at him, feeling dazed and limp with release.

His eyes were hot with unspent desire, his mouth curved in a satisfaction that bordered on smugness. He bent to press a gentle kiss on her forehead. "My sweet girl."

Sloane pulled back and turned as if to leave the bed, and Annabeth grabbed his wrist. "Wait. What are you doing? There's more, isn't there?" No matter how wonderful that sweeping tide of passion had been, there was still an ache of emptiness inside her, a lingering feeling that there had not been a completion.

"Yes, there's more. But this way your reputation is—"

"Oh, no, you don't." Annabeth moved swiftly, straddling him to anchor him in place where he sat. "Don't you dare talk about ruining my reputation. Or tell me what I ought to do. You agreed."

"Anna, please…"

She knelt across him, and his member prodded tantalizingly at her, surging in a way that told her how far Sloane was from satisfaction. "No, you please. Don't you want me? Is the thought of being inside me so abhorrent?"

He closed his eyes wearily as the surge of his flesh against her made clear what the thought of being in her did to him. "No, you know it's not. Are you trying to drive me mad?"

"No, I'm trying to get you to take me." She slipped her hand down and ran her fingertips along the length of his shaft, and he jerked, letting out an oath. "I want all of it, Sloane. All of you."

"You're torturing me here," he ground out. "I am trying to be the better man."

"I don't want the better man," she retorted, trailing her fingers back up him to the tip. "I want you."

With a growl, he lashed his arm around her and pulled her down to the bed, covering her with his body. Almost angrily he kissed her, but as Anna stroked her hand across his back, curving down over his hip, all trace of anger had turned to desire, hungry and insistent. Sloane made his way down her body, caressing and kissing.

Nudging her thighs apart with his knee, he moved between her legs. She could feel his erection prodding against her most tender, intimate skin, and she pressed upward, seeking satisfaction. Her action brought a low noise from him that stirred her even more.

She wanted more. She wanted everything. Slowly he pressed into her, his flesh separating hers, pushing deeper, until at last there was a burst of pain. She drew in a sharp breath, and he went still. He looked into her eyes questioningly, his breath hard and ragged.

"Don't stop," she said, her fingers pressing into his shoulders. "I want—" Her breath hitched as he eased farther inside her, filling her. "Yes. That. I want that."

He began to move within her. Desire spiraled in her, all her senses aroused—the sound of Sloane's ragged breath, the feel of his hot skin beneath her hands, the hunger in his eyes—all magnified the pleasure created by the slow, deep strokes. He filled and fulfilled her in a way she had never dreamed of, and once again that knot of yearning grew in her, the restless, hungry reaching for something more.

The overwhelming passion exploded in her once again, sweeping through her so that she cried out, but this time Sloane followed her into that bright burst of pleasure, joining with her in a soul-shattering moment of union.

CHAPTER THIRTY-ONE

ANNABETH OPENED HER EYES. She lay surrounded by heat, Sloane's arms still around her. She smiled to herself. It didn't feel strange at all to awaken here beside him. Indeed, she felt as if she had finally come home.

She turned toward him, and at the movement his arms tightened around her for an instant. Then he opened his eyes and gave her a drowsy smile. "Annabeth."

Sloane's voice was lazy and smooth, his vivid blue gaze soft, and he looked as boneless and contented as a cat stretched out in a patch of sunlight. He stroked his hand down her arm. "You are…completely perfect."

Annabeth laughed. "I'll remind you of that next time you argue with me."

"Argue with you?" He grinned and took her hand, raising it to kiss her knuckles. "Never."

She cupped his cheek in her hand and stretched over to kiss him. Her kiss was warm and deep, and she felt a familiar warmth stir in her. When she broke their kiss, Sloane reached up and sank his fingers into her hair. For a long moment he just looked at her, and then sighed.

"We should not…"

"Hush." Annabeth put her forefinger across his lips, silencing him. "You never argue with me, remember?"

His eyes heated, and he rolled over, pulling her under him. "I remember." He kissed her.

Their lovemaking was slow and deliberate this time, a matter of teasing and exploring, of long kisses and slow caresses, building gradually into a storm of passion as fierce as the night before.

Annabeth had thought nothing could equal the force that had swept her the first time, but amazingly, her anticipation of what was to come made it stronger, not weaker. And when they crashed into that wild and blissful abyss of pleasure, she felt even more tightly joined to Sloane.

He was hers. Forever. Whatever else might happen, this was the only man she wanted, the only man she could love.

ANNABETH FELT AS if she could simply float in this haze of pleasure forever, cocooned in Sloane's house, while the rest of the world passed on. But they could not, of course. They must travel to the Lake District to find her father's valet and examine the writing desk.

So after a rather late breakfast, they set off once more in Sloane's curricle. But their trip this time was entirely different. As if by some unspoken agreement, they did not discuss the right or wrong of their lovemaking or ponder what would happen once the present problem was resolved. And though Sloane kept a sharp eye out for possible followers, they did not even talk a great deal about their hunt for the man who had killed Annabeth's father.

The ride was filled with laughter and teasing, and the nights were filled with passion. It seemed like a time cut out from reality, sheltered and secluded, where there was no one but the two of them. Annabeth found herself wishing that their journey could take more time.

It did not, of course. They soon reached the village where Simpson lived and stopped at the small inn. The next morning they asked for directions to his house, and walked to it. Annabeth felt a curious reluctance to talk to the man. It would mean that after the return trip to London, they would once again have to live in the real world.

A girl answered the door and looked astonished when they asked for the valet, but she led them down the hall to a tidy parlor.

"Uncle Alfred, there's someone here to see you," the girl said, adding artlessly, "Fine folks, they are."

Annabeth's gaze went past her to the neatly dressed, bespectacled man sitting by the window, carefully plying a needle through fabric. He looked up at his niece's words, removing his spectacles. "Miss Annabeth!"

"Hello, Simpson. I hope we are not interrupting."

"No, no." The small man set aside the material and hurried over to them. "I do a bit of work for a tailor now and then, just to pass the time." He gave her a little bow. "This is such an honor, miss." He turned toward the girl. "Some tea for our visitors, Jessie, and some biscuits as well."

His cheeks were pink with pleasure, and his eyes sparkled as he ushered Annabeth and Sloane toward the grouping of chairs in front of the fireplace. "Please, sit down, miss."

"You remember Mr. Rutherford," Annabeth said, not quite a question.

The valet looked at Sloane with less delight than he'd shown at the sight of Annabeth, but he bowed politely. "Yes, of course. Mr. Rutherford. Please, sit down."

Simpson remained hovering about them as they took

their seats, until Annabeth said, "Please, you must sit down, too."

"I...well...it's just so very odd," he told her, and perched on the edge of a chair. "Sitting down in your presence, I mean."

"But you're not a servant anymore," Annabeth pointed out.

"No, miss, I'm not. God bless your father for remembering me in his will."

They spent the next few minutes inquiring about the valet's health and that of everyone in Annabeth's family and establishing that they all were living happily. Eventually the pleasantries dwindled, and Annabeth said, "We came here to talk to you about Papa."

"Ah. Mr. Winfield." Simpson smiled sadly. "Such a dear, good man. It was a pleasure, it was, working for him." In his emotion, his voice slipped into more of an accent. "There's no one else, miss, who would have taken on a sixteen-year-old boy from the village to be his valet. But he was so kind. He knew the straits we were in after the accident."

"The accident?"

"My pa, you see, was hit in the road one night and died. And there we were, with no money and about to be turned out. Mr. Winfield heard about it and he came with his lady, and he gave my mam a bit of money to tide us over. What other quality folks would have done that? I ask you. I remember, he looked at me and asked if I'd like a job as his valet. You could have knocked me down with a feather. A valet, mind you. I hadn't been in service at all, not even a pot boy." Tears glittered in Simpson's eyes. "He told me later that he could tell I was a lad that wanted to better himself. But I knew it was only his generosity."

Annabeth felt tears welling in her own eyes at the man's story. "Papa was kind. But I know that he valued you highly. He relied on you."

"I only wish I had gone out there earlier with his tea. Maybe I could have kept him from falling."

"You were the one who discovered him?" Sloane asked.

Simpson nodded. "I've never felt so sick in my life. I walked in with the hamper, and there he was, lying on the floor. I dropped the hamper and ran over there, but... I could see I couldn't help him."

"He fell from the stairs?" Sloane asked. "Did you go up to look at the railing?"

"No." Simpson frowned. "It was clear what had happened. I ran back to the house as fast as I could to get help—to bring him home, you see. No one could have saved him by then." He sighed. "I should have taken Mr. Winfield some luncheon, but he had a late breakfast. He said he didn't want anything until tea."

"Did you notice anything different about the place? Anything odd or disarranged?"

The valet stared at Sloane. "No, sir. I mean, I didn't really pay attention to anything but Mr. Winfield. That was just the way his workshop looked."

"Papa always had things all over the place," Annabeth agreed.

"I tried to tidy it up some, once or twice, but he wouldn't have it." The valet smiled fondly.

"Did you see anyone around that day?" Sloane asked.

"Around the workshop?" The valet frowned. "No. Nobody ever went there except Mr. Winfield."

"How did Mr. Winfield seem? Around that time, I mean. Was he different? Worried, perhaps? Or upset?"

"Why are you asking these questions?" Simpson stiffened. "If you're trying to say that Mr. Winfield did himself in, I can tell you he did not!" Simpson turned to Annabeth. "Miss, don't listen to anyone who tells you it was suicide. It's not true. He would never have hurt you and his lady that much."

"No, I'm sure not," Annabeth said soothingly. "I know that Papa didn't throw himself off those stairs."

"Good." He nodded sharply and shot a look of dislike at Sloane. "Because it's not true."

"We know," Sloane said peaceably. "We're just trying to answer a few questions that have arisen."

Simpson looked again at Annabeth. "It's you, miss, that wants to know?"

"Yes, I want to know. I wasn't there, you remember, and I was so unhappy that I didn't ask anyone about what happened that day. I am trying to get a clearer picture of that time."

He nodded. "Very well, miss. Mr. Winfield had been in London, and he came home a week or so before the accident. He seemed…a bit worried, maybe. Or downcast. But it was probably just that he was tired from the trip."

"Did anyone come to visit Papa after he returned from the city? Did he have an argument with anyone?"

"No. He rode over to see Mr. Feringham one day, of course, but no one came to call. As for an argument, your papa never had an argument with anyone." He shot a glare at Sloane. "Except you, sir. I heard you yelling at him in his office once. You said—well, I didn't hear any words, really, just a bit at the end. Something about if he kept on with it, you'd kill him."

"What?" Annabeth sucked in her breath sharply and glanced at Sloane.

Sloane sighed and shoved his hands back through his hair. "Yes, I probably said something like that. But that was long before Mr. Winfield died."

"That's true," Simpson agreed grudgingly. "It was back when, well, you know, when Mr. Rutherford..."

"When he left." Annabeth supplied the words.

"Yes, miss. You had gone to visit Lady Drewsbury, I believe."

"I see." Annabeth could well imagine that her father and Sloane had exchanged angry words then. "Thank you for answering our questions. I know it must be difficult to remember that time."

"It is indeed." He shook his head. "Mr. Winfield was such a good man."

"My mother told me that she had given you Papa's traveling desk."

He nodded. "It was very good of her."

"I wonder if we might see it. I'm looking for something my father wrote, and it occurred to me that it could be in that box."

"Oh. Of course, miss. If you'll excuse me, I'll get it for you." He left the room and returned a few minutes later carrying a foot-long rectangular box made of mahogany, with an elegant, engraved pattern across the top.

Annabeth's throat tightened; she could not see it without thinking of her father. Simpson set the box on the padded ottoman in front of Annabeth's chair, and she leaned forward to open it. There were no tricks to this box. It simply folded out flat on all sides to reveal a writing area with compartments for pencils, ink, and quills.

There was indeed paper lying inside it, and she picked

up the top sheet of foolscap. Her father's signature was across the bottom, and her heart sped up as she looked at the page. The second paragraph seemed to jump out at her: *In the course of an evening of drinking, I drove my curricle in a race with a companion. Intent on winning, I did not slow my pace through the village of Billingscote, and I did not see a man step into the road. My vehicle struck him, killing him. As it was late at night, no one saw the accident, and in a moment of cowardice, I returned home and kept silent about what I had done.*

Annabeth pulled in a sharp breath, blood draining from her face.

CHAPTER THIRTY-TWO

"ANNABETH? WHAT IS IT?" Sloane snatched the paper from her hand and ran his eyes over it.

He looked sharply at the valet. "Have you read this?"

Simpson flushed, his face stamped with embarrassment. "No, sir. I can't—I'm just a country lad with no schooling, you see. I cannot read."

"This is—this is what we're searching for, isn't it," Annabeth said, her voice little above a whisper.

"Do you want the traveling desk back?" Simpson was obviously doing his best to keep his voice even, but dismay was written on his face.

"No." Dazed and battling back tears, Annabeth struggled to present a normal front. "No, Papa would have wanted you to have his desk. But I would appreciate it if you would let me have this page."

"Of course, miss, of course," he agreed eagerly, folding the box back together.

"Thank you." She took the valet's hand between hers. "Thank you so much."

"Of course, miss," he replied. "Anything for Mr. Winfield's daughter."

Annabeth did not speak as they walked back to the inn, nor did Sloane, a heavy silence hanging between them. Annabeth's mind whirled with thought, shock and pain filling her. Sloane escorted her into the private room at the inn where they had taken breakfast, but she could not sit down. She paced around the room, rubbing her arms as if they were cold.

"Anna…" Sloane began finally.

As if his word had pulled open some door in her, Annabeth burst out, "How could he have done that? He was always so good, so kind. I can't understand it."

"I'm sorry, Anna. I know how much it must hurt you."

She turned to him, her eyes welling with tears. "I cannot bear to think of it. That Papa could have done such a thing!"

"He was young, and young men often do foolish, reckless things."

"He drove away! He didn't stop. He just left that man there in the road. Poor Simpson! To think that he adored Papa so, when all that time Papa had killed Simpson's father. And all this time, he's held Papa's confession, not knowing what it said. Never knowing the truth. Oh, Sloane!"

She burst into tears and Sloane quickly gathered her in his arms. He held her close as she sobbed, stroking her back and murmuring soft words of comfort. Finally her tears dwindled to a stop. For a moment she stood there, drawing strength from his solid warmth, then pulled back with a sigh.

"I knew Papa was…not a strong character. That he was impulsive and foolish with money—one could hardly live with Grandmother without hearing his weaknesses and failures. But I thought it was more than made up for by all his good qualities. The man I saw was the father who always had time for me and answered my questions and built me a dollhouse with a little dumbwaiter that actually moved. We'd make up stories about the people that lived in that dollhouse."

"Your father was all those things as well," Sloane told her. "And he provided for the man's family as best he could, hiring the man's son."

"You're standing up for him now?"

"No. But I hate for this to tarnish every memory you have of your father. I hate that it hurts you so deeply. I'm sorry that you had to see it."

"Life would be easier if I hadn't, but I'd rather know the truth." Annabeth sighed, finally sitting down as weariness overtook her. Sloane sat across from her, holding her hand until she finally said, "Well, there's nothing else to be found here. We should start back to London."

"I'll have the team harnessed and brought round."

Annabeth spent most of the trip in silence, too tired and disillusioned to speak, her thoughts chaotic, but as the day wore on, her mind began to clear. That evening, sitting in the private room where they ate, she said, "I still don't see how Papa's confession connects to what Mr. Asquith is seeking. How could that terrible wreck have anything to do with the war or France or this spymaster Mr. Asquith wants to expose?"

She looked at Sloane, but he just shook his head. "Annabeth, please, don't dwell on this. You'll only make it worse. Just put it out of your mind."

"How could I possibly do that?" Annabeth replied. "I want to read the rest of that letter. I only glimpsed the beginning. I didn't—I couldn't read on. Not with Simpson there so blissfully unaware of the awfulness contained in that letter."

"Anna…" Sloane looked pained. "There's no need for you to read it all, surely."

"Are you refusing to give it to me?" Annabeth asked, astonished. "Are you hiding something *else* from me?"

"It's just…government secrets…things no one should know about." For once, the imperturbable Sloane was obviously rattled.

She stared. "You're going to tell me I can't see this when I have been running about all over the place trying to find it? You wouldn't have even located that note without me."

"Anna," he said pleadingly. "You don't want to see it. There could be things in there…"

"You said you would not lie to me. Are you going to break that promise already?"

Sloane let out a curse, but reached inside his jacket and pulled out the letter. He held it out to her, his face resigned and his eyes filled with misery. "Here."

The look on Sloane's face was so unhappy, even despairing, that Annabeth almost didn't take the letter. But, surely, what could be worse in this letter than what she had already read?

She took the paper from him, unfolded it, and began to read her father's words:

I committed an unforgivable act during my youth, which I have kept hidden for all this time. That initial sin has caused me to commit other wrongs, for which I am deeply sorry.

In the course of an evening of drinking, I drove my curricle in a race with a companion. Intent on winning, I did not slow my pace through the village of Billingscote, and I did not see a man step into the road. My vehicle struck him, killing him. As it was late at night, no one saw the accident,

*and in a moment of cowardice, I returned home
and kept silent about what I had done.*

*I will not name my competitor in this race, for I
was the one who killed the man, not he, and I bear
full responsibility for what happened.*

*It deepens my shame and regret that this inci-
dent was used to compel me to betray my country
by giving information to the French. I was able to
free myself of this blackmail through the interven-
tion of another, but the knowledge of what I have
done has haunted my thoughts since.*

*I have decided that I can no longer remain silent.
I can only beg my beloved family's forgiveness for
the shame this revelation will undoubtedly cause
them.*

William Hunter Winfield Jr.

Annabeth stared at the paper, unable to move or
speak, a buzz filling her ears. She felt strangely de-
tached, as if she were not really there, as if all around
her, the world was receding from her.

"Annabeth!" Sloane said sharply, rising to go to her.
"Put your head down. Don't faint."

"No," she said, finally finding her voice, though it
hardly felt like her speaking. "I'm not fainting. I just…
can't…" She stood, thrusting the paper at Sloane, and
walked away.

"Anna… I'm sorry." Sloane followed, reaching out
to her.

"No. Don't. I can't—" Annabeth stepped back. She
could not explain how she felt, as if she would shatter
if anyone breached the invisible wall around her. "Papa

was a traitor. He helped the French." She held her hand to her stomach, as if holding in the nausea that roiled within. "How could he? I honestly do not know which was worse, his terrible judgment, cowardice, and weakness on a night when he was deeply in his cups and accidentally took a man's life. Or the deliberate deceit he committed for weeks, months—possibly years—when he knowingly hurt his family and his country. To commit treason—how could he do such a thing?"

"I imagine he thought he was protecting his family from scandal," Sloane said soothingly.

"Protecting himself, you mean."

"Yes, that, too. I'm sorry, Anna. I hoped you wouldn't have to know."

Annabeth froze. "You knew, didn't you?" The guilt on Sloane's face confirmed her guess. "You knew about him from the start."

"Yes." Sloane's voice was flat, resigned. "I knew he was blackmailed by the French into giving them information. But I didn't know how. I didn't know what secret they had of his. I knew nothing of the accident."

"Oh, so there was one thing you didn't hide from me." A fresh hurt slashed through her. "Why did you keep this from me? How could you say you loved me and not tell me the truth?"

"I did it *because* I loved you," he shot back. "I knew how it would hurt you, and I couldn't let it happen. I couldn't allow it to ruin your love for your father. I couldn't let you be scorned and shamed by everyone."

"So you lied to me and I never suspected a thing…" Annabeth frowned. "You certainly had the skills to be a spy."

"Blast it, Annabeth, I didn't have a choice. It was better that you lose your faith in me than have your whole world shattered. I did what I had to do to protect you. You would have hated me either way."

"What do you mean, 'what you had to do'? Become a spy? Leave me?"

"Yes!" he thundered. "Do you think I wanted to leave you? Do you think I wanted to risk my life every day instead of being happy and content by your side? Do you think I enjoyed living a lie? It ripped my heart out to hurt you, to deceive you. But that was the only way to save your bloody stupid father."

Annabeth stared. "What do you mean? How did you save Papa?"

"Asquith knew Winfield was giving the French information, and he was going to reveal it to the world unless I started working for him—unless I began smuggling and spying. I couldn't tell you why I was haring off to become a spy without revealing the threat Asquith held over me—and that was precisely what I was trying to conceal. I knew you would hate me either way, whether I ruined your father in your eyes or broke off our engagement."

"I wouldn't have hated you for telling me the truth," Annabeth protested.

"No?" The corner of his mouth twisted wryly. "How do you feel about me right now?"

"I'm angry because you lied to me, not because you told me the truth."

He shrugged. "I was a boy, Anna. I—deep down I knew that marrying you was only a fantasy. Your family was against it, and they were right. I had no prospects.

It would have taken me years to build up enough money to provide for you."

"I would have waited for you." A lump filled her throat. "You didn't have faith in me."

"I had faith in you. I didn't have faith in happy endings." Sloane sighed and ran his hand back through his hair. "Frankly, I didn't expect to be alive for long—spying is not a healthy occupation—and what difference did it make if I left you then or a few weeks later?"

"It would have made a great deal of difference to me!" Her throat felt raw with unshed tears, but she felt somehow too stunned to cry. "I *loved* you, Sloane. You broke my heart, and you justify it by saying you didn't want to *hurt* me?"

"The scandal, losing faith in your father—it would have shattered your world."

"So instead *you* shattered it." Tears filled her eyes, but she willed them back. She would *not* cry over him again. "You may not have believed we would marry, but I did. I believed in you. And that's the belief you destroyed. I *grieved* over you, Sloane." She thought of the dark nights spent lying awake, crying until she had no more tears. She thought of the lonely years, the constant dull ache of loss. "Every time people whispered about your treachery, every time Nathan cursed your name, it hurt me. I wanted to defend you, but I could not because you hadn't loved me enough to tell me the truth."

"No, it was never because I didn't love you. You were all I wanted in the world. I would have done anything for you."

"You didn't respect me enough to be honest with me. What kind of love is that?"

"It wouldn't have made any difference if I had told

you. I would still have had to leave the country and work for Asquith because that was the price for his secrecy. You would have hated me for spoiling your bond with your father. You'd have lost both me and him."

"I wasn't a child that needed to be shielded from reality. I was a grown woman. I could have borne the knowledge about my father. It would have hurt, it still hurts now, but I'm here. I'm breathing. It hasn't stopped me living. And as wildly angry as I am at him right now, I realize it won't stop me loving Papa either. Even before all this, I knew he had faults, and I lived with them."

"But the gossip would have been unbearable. People staring at you wherever you went, whispering about your family."

"I wouldn't have cared about the scandal. I never wanted the social whirl. I would have faced it just as I faced the scandal of you jilting me. Do you think there weren't whispers about me then? Scandal would have been an easy burden compared to you risking your life."

"No," he said fiercely. "I would not have let that happen even if you had known about your father. I'd have done what Asquith wanted. I couldn't have lived with myself otherwise."

Annabeth snorted. "You may tell yourself that, but it's clear that you thought me incapable of bearing up under such news. You decided, all on your own, what I would feel, what I could accept. Maybe I would have been angry with you. Maybe I would have fallen apart. But I would have had a choice. Instead, you cut me to ribbons and left me bleeding. You took twelve years away from us. Twelve years when we could have been happy. We could have been married. We could have had children. We could have had a life together. And you stole all that from us…because you didn't believe in me the way I believed in you."

Annabeth whipped around and headed toward the door.

"Didn't believe in you!" He strode after her, and she stopped with her hand on the knob, not looking at him. "You're all I believed in. Damn it, Anna, I gave up everything for you. I risked my life. I gave up all hope of love and happiness. I ruined my name. And now you dare to say it means I didn't love you?"

"I didn't want you to do any of that!" She turned, her eyes blazing. "I had no desire for you to give up everything. The last thing I wanted was for you to risk your life. I didn't want you to die for me. I wanted you to live for me. But you never gave me the choice."

She jerked open the door and walked out.

CHAPTER THIRTY-THREE

SLOANE SANK BACK in his chair and called for some brandy. God knew, he needed it tonight. He'd known the last few days wouldn't last, that there was no real future for him and Annabeth, but it didn't make the pain any less. She had been the one to leave him this time. And it felt like hell.

Maybe she was right. Maybe it was worse for the one left behind. At least he had known the reason for his hurt; however bad it had been, it had a purpose. Annabeth had had nothing to hold on to. She'd thought only that he didn't love her. That he had chosen a life of treachery over her. He'd told himself that it would make it easier for her to think he was as bad as he'd always worried he was. But maybe he'd just made everything harder for her. Had he really spent twelve years punishing not just himself, but the only person he'd ever loved?

He set his elbows on the table and sank his head into his hands, fingers pushing back into his hair. Was he wrong not to have told her the truth? He thought of her face this afternoon when she'd read the confession, the way she'd sobbed against his chest. Surely it had not been wrong to want to spare her that pain. What kind of man would he be if he hadn't wanted to protect her?

"Sir?" The barmaid stood at the door, tray in hand.

Sloane raised his head and nodded, gesturing at the

table. She set the tray down carefully, and, with a sideways glance at him, hurried out the door. No doubt she thought him a madman or already in his cups.

He poured a large amount of brandy into the glass, and, shrugging out of his jacket and untying his neckcloth, he settled down to drink.

He did well at the task, apparently, for he awoke the next morning in the same room, his head on his arms on the table. Somewhat gingerly he raised his head. The sun slanting in through the window pierced his eyes, going straight into his brain.

Cursing himself for being as stupid as he had been at nineteen, Sloane pushed himself to his feet and set about repairing his looks somewhat. There was no shaving stand in this dining room, leaving him with a dark stubble all over his jaw. There was at least a mirror over the fireplace, so he was able to retie his neckcloth, and he pulled his jacket back on, regaining some degree of respectability.

Annabeth entered the room and took a look at the table, where the empty bottle lay on its side, and then at him. "Good heavens, Sloane, you look dreadful."

"Mmm. I can assure you that looks are not deceiving."

She sighed and went over to the table to set the bottle upright. "I didn't think—you slept in here? Wasn't there another room?"

"I had registered us as a married couple with one room, so it seemed a trifle…"

"Awkward?" Was that actually a tiny smile that tugged at the corner of her mouth? "Well, I am out of the room now, so you can go upstairs and…" She made a sweeping gesture at his appearance. "I'll order us some break-fast. I'll have coffee brought up for you if you'd like."

After a shave and pouring half a pitcher of water over his head, along with drinking two cups of coffee and changing his clothes, Sloane felt some semblance of nor-mality. He returned downstairs, not looking forward to talking to Annabeth, but knowing there was no way to escape it.

He found her sitting at the table, finishing off the eggs and sausages on her plate. "Glad to see you waited on me to eat."

Annabeth raised an eyebrow. "Frankly, I wasn't sure you would be interested in eating breakfast anyway."

Sloane looked at the poached eggs on his plate. "Per-haps you're right." He sat down, setting the cover back on it. "I would take a cup of whatever it is you're drink-ing."

"Of course." She poured him a cup of tea, leaving it black, as he liked it.

Her movements were stiff. No doubt she felt as awk-ward as he did. This was not going to be a pleasant jour-ney. He wondered if they might be able to make London in only two days instead of three.

Well, he could not put it off any longer. "Annabeth… I… I must apologize to you."

"You must?" she asked.

"I *want* to apologize," he corrected. "Obviously, I can-not give you back the last twelve years or change what I did. It was not that I did not believe in you. The truth is it was myself I didn't believe in. I feared, deep down, that I would never be good enough, never accomplish enough, to marry you. But smuggling, spying—*that* was something I knew I could do. I was nineteen, and even if my father had been around, it would have been useless to ask him what to do. So I did what seemed to me to be the right thing."

"I know." Annabeth toyed with her spoon. "I am sorry that I was so harsh to you last night."

"You said what you felt. What you thought."

"Well…yes." She studied the table for a moment. "But I think perhaps I was cruel, rejecting the deed you did for me. I don't want to belittle the sacrifice you made for me. I think your intentions were good. I don't believe you meant to hurt me so much."

"I didn't," Sloane agreed earnestly. Perhaps it was not all lost between them. "I would never try to hurt you."

"I know." Annabeth nodded and raised her head to look at him. There was a sadness in her eyes that pierced him. "It seems you and I keep hurting each other even though we never mean to. I think that too much has passed between us. That our happiness is inevitably followed by sorrow."

"Ah. I see." Then it was lost after all.

"You have told me that there is no future for us," she went on. "Our past is entangled with pain. I was foolhardy to push you into an affair."

"You didn't need to push." He smiled faintly.

"Maybe not. But I did. I don't regret it. The past few days have been wonderful. But I see now that if we continue, I will only get deeper and deeper, and when this is over and we go back to our normal lives, it will be the same as it was before. I don't want to live through that again. I'm not sure I can."

Sloane wanted to argue. He wanted to tell her that it would not be the same, that they would not part and go back to their old lives. That they would marry and live happily ever after. But of course he could not. He had made the life he had, and he could not plunge Annabeth into that. So he said only, "Very well."

THERE WAS SILENCE in the curricle on their way back. Sloane had nothing to say, and apparently neither did Annabeth. Stiff and awkward at first, the atmosphere gradually softened under the boredom of the ride and the need to be on the alert for their enemy. By the time they reached the inn that night, they were back to normal—or what had passed for normal before he had made the mistake of making love to her.

They could not reach London that night, but Sloane passed through the town where they had stayed before; there was no way he was going to spend the night in the same place they had stayed on the way to the valet's house. The last thing he wanted to think of was the joy of that night. He pulled up at another inn later, and there he got a chamber for each of them. It amazed him how heavy his heart was at the process.

As they waited for their food, Annabeth said, "Tell me exactly what happened with my father."

"Annabeth, why bring this up again?"

"Because I want to know. I don't want to be operating in the dark any longer. If you haven't noticed, I have a large stake in this whole thing, and I want to solve it as soon as we can so I can go back to my life." Her voice wobbled a bit on the last few words, but she kept her chin up and her eyes on him.

"Yes, of course. You're right. What do you want to know?"

"Everything you know about the matter. Start at the beginning."

"As I told you, I knew nothing about the accident in his letter. Nor did Asquith. We were aware there was something that the French had used on your father to get him to take and hand over a document with information they wanted. After that, they used the document he had stolen for them to keep him in line. Asquith approached me and said that I could counteract what Mr. Winfield did if I turned spy for our side. He gave me a ship for smuggling."

"Obviously he was not above blackmail either."

"No. I think England is the only thing he cares about. He views everything through that lens. Information is what he deals in. He gathers it and stores it in case he needs it for the future. He knew how I felt about you—though I guess that was not much of a secret anyway."

"It sounds to me as though his own power matters to him as well."

"You're no doubt right about that. It matters to him that he is important to the government, that those in power regard him as indispensable. I think he enjoys being the head of the spy network as well—moving the pieces around, solving the problems. That's one reason why finding this confession was critical to him. It galled him that he didn't know what secret the French had had over your father to begin with, the one they used to get the incriminating document your father stole. He wants to ferret out the villain he was unable to find all these years, the enemy who damaged Asquith's own network. He wants to be the final victor over that man."

"I don't understand. Why were there two different things the French used to threaten Papa? Why didn't they just use the incident with Papa's curricle?"

Sloane shrugged. "It does seem a bit excessive,

doesn't it? But I think it must have been this—the curricle incident, if revealed, would have been a scandal and the first information Hunter gave them was fairly minor. At the time he might have thought it was a fair trade-off. With the more important information though, he might have balked. What he had done in that curricle race would have been a blot on the family name, but it was an accident that had happened long ago, and he was a gentleman, related to an earl and a friend to many in the nobility. The likelihood that any charges would be brought against him was very slight."

"Yes." Annabeth sighed. "It's reprehensible, but I'm sure you're right."

"But by giving the French that first information, he had made himself a traitor, and treason is a great deal worse than scandal. It wouldn't matter who his family and friends were, and he could hardly claim it had been an accident. He would have been tried."

Annabeth paled. "And the punishment for that is hanging."

Sloane nodded and looked away. Facing death had been easier than facing that look on her face.

After a moment, she said, "Why did they not use it?"

"The threat is what gets the mark to do something. Actually *doing* what they threatened makes it certain that he will not do it. To that extent, the threat of exposure is useless. In any case, I was able to retrieve the incriminating document, and your father left his employment, rendering him of no use to the French."

"That is what Simpson heard you arguing with Papa about, isn't it?"

"Mmm. I was, perhaps, overly dramatic. But I was

not a happy man at that time. We burned the document in his fireplace, and he left the Home Office."

"That is why Father retired to the country for the rest of his life," Annabeth mused. After a moment, she said, "It doesn't seem that Papa's confession will be very useful for Mr. Asquith. It doesn't tell us the identity of the man who blackmailed him."

"No. Your father was remarkably silent about anyone but himself. But if I can discover the identity of the other man involved in the accident, I think that may very well tell us who gave your father up to the French."

"You think the master spy is the man Papa raced? That they are one and the same?"

"He and your father were the only people who knew about the accident. Obviously your father's valet had no idea of it, and surely the dead man's family would have learned of it if anyone in the village had witnessed the accident. So it seems likely that your father's competitor was the man who blackmailed him—or that this man gave this information to the blackmailer, in which case he could identify the spy."

"Yes, I see that. But why would he have done that? Surely he was Papa's friend."

"That sort of tragedy could end a friendship. Besides, he didn't have to be a close friend, just someone your father might race. Another gentleman at the club."

"That leaves a great many people for suspects," Annabeth pointed out.

"Unfortunately, yes," Sloane said grimly. "But some are more likely than others. And too close to home."

"Who do you mean?" She looked at him in confusion, then her face cleared. "Oh. You're thinking about your father."

"Yes." It had been at the back of Sloane's mind since he'd read Winfield's confession. "It would be someone foolish enough, drunk enough, and too fond of gambling to turn down a bet. That's a portrait of Marcus."

"That's absurd," Annabeth said. "It couldn't be your father."

"Why not? It's not as if the man has a strong moral code."

"No. But his faults are weaknesses. I can believe that he could have done as Papa did—impulsively, unintentionally commit a terrible sin. But it simply isn't in him to murder my father in cold blood. Or to be a spy. He's not the kind of man to plot and scheme and keep secrets."

"As I am?" Sloane asked, raising a brow, but his insides relaxed a little. "You're right. Marcus has too loose a mouth to keep that accident a secret for years, especially when he's in his cups. And he hasn't the competence to be a spy."

"Sloane…" Annabeth's face softened and she reached out her hand to him, then stopped and let it fall back in her lap. "I know he was, well, not a good father in many ways, but he wasn't *wicked*. He was weak, like Papa."

"Mr. Winfield was a tower of strength compared to Marcus," Sloane said with a wry twist of his mouth. "Your father stopped the gambling and racing once he had you in his life. My father never could. Whatever his faults, Hunter loved you with every fiber of his being."

"Oh, Sloane, you mustn't think your father doesn't love you. I'm sure he does in his own way."

"No doubt."

"As you love him," she added.

"In my own way?" He smiled faintly.

"You take care of him."

"I pay for him. That's easy enough, and it keeps him from being an embarrassment to me."

"Of course. Because you are so concerned about what people say." She gave Sloane a teasing smile, and it sent a little pang through his heart. It was foolish to want this, to ache for familiarity and ease, to wish that everything had been different. Because, of course, the past could not be changed, no matter how much he wished it.

"Lady Lockwood would be the person to ask the names of the men Mr. Winfield raced against, I suppose," Sloane said, changing the topic.

"Yes, she and Lady Drewsbury."

"And your mother of course."

"No. I can't tell Mother about this. It would devastate her."

Sloane raised an eyebrow, sending Annabeth a pointed look.

A blush rose in her cheeks. "Yes, yes, I realize that I decried you not telling me about my father's treachery. But this is different."

"Isn't it always?" he murmured.

"It is," Annabeth insisted. "I'm not choosing to devastate her in a different way instead. There's nothing in there that she needs to know, and I can promise you that she would rather not know disturbing things. Besides, she tells Lord Edgerton everything, and he's the last person I would want to know that Papa had done something terrible. He already says enough hurtful things about my father."

"As it happens, I agree that we should not tell her. The fewer people who know, the better. Just your grandmother."

"And Nathan," Annabeth said quietly. "I won't keep

it from him. He deserves to know. He stayed at Stone-cliffe to help with our ruse even though our engagement was over. He has been an asset every step of the way."

"Yes," Sloane had to admit. "We will tell Nathan and Verity as well. We seem to have formed some sort of team, so I suppose we must trust them."

"A foreign concept to you, I know." But her dry words were accompanied again by the teasing smile.

He wanted, quite badly, to lean over and kiss the little dimple that formed at the corner of her mouth. But he turned his head and said, "Then after we reach London tomorrow, we'll go on to Stonecliffe."

CHAPTER THIRTY-FOUR

As it turned out, there was no need to travel to Stonecliffe, for when they arrived at Lady Lockwood's home in London late the next afternoon, they found the mistress of the house very much in residence.

"Grandmother!" Annabeth exclaimed in surprise.

"Yes, yes, it is I. Don't stand there in the doorway gawking, girl. Come in and sit down." Lady Lockwood gave a short nod to Sloane. "You, too, Rutherford."

"What are you doing here?" Annabeth asked, bending down to pet Petunia, who had rushed forward to greet her with a great deal of jumping and high-pitched yips.

It was Nathan who answered, rising from his seat on the nearby sofa. "Miss Cole decided to leave Stonecliffe, so there seemed little point in staying."

"Hello, Nathan." Annabeth searched his face anxiously. He seemed somewhat subdued, but showed no other sign of unhappiness. But then, of course, he was always the perfect British gentleman. She went forward, holding out her hand in greeting.

"Annabeth." He took her hand and bowed to her in the exactly proper way for a close acquaintance.

Why, oh why couldn't I have fallen in love with Nathan instead of the man beside me? It would have been so much better for all of us.

"Carlisle and Noelle returned," Lady Lockwood explained. "I didn't want to intrude on the newlyweds."

"Or miss all the excitement," Nathan added with a little grin toward Lady Lockwood.

"Oh, you hush," Lady Lockwood said almost indulgently. Apparently the relationship between her grandmother and Nathan had improved considerably now that he was no longer engaged to her granddaughter. Annabeth wondered if Nathan had broken the news to Lady Lockwood yet.

"Where *is* Verity?"

Nathan shrugged. "I've no idea. She said she was tired of sitting around doing nothing and she was going to talk to some people she knew, see what she could discover."

Sloane frowned. "She was supposed to stay at Stonecliffe. Why didn't you keep her there?"

"Keep her there?" Nathan's eyebrows shot up. "What exactly should I have done? Tied her to a chair?"

"That wouldn't have stopped her anyway," Sloane conceded.

"I did point out that she was directed to remain at Stonecliffe. You can imagine how well that was received."

"Blast the woman. Why didn't she do what she was meant to?" Sloane scowled.

"Sloane…" Annabeth said in a worried tone. "Do you think—are you still thinking it could be Verity behind all this?"

"Verity!" Nathan gaped. "What are you talking about? Behind what exactly?"

"Yes, tell us. What happened?" Lady Lockwood demanded.

"Someone has attacked us twice," Sloane said bluntly.

"And we discovered that Hunter Winfield did not die in an accident. He was murdered."

For a long moment, Annabeth's grandmother and Nathan stared at him, then began to talk at once.

"What the devil—"

"You're joking, surely."

"He's not joking," Annabeth assured them. "Though he certainly could have said it with a little more grace." She shot an irritated look at Sloane. She went on to explain their visit to the workshop and what they had discovered there, as well as the two attempts on their lives, though she glided over the details of those.

There was another lengthy silence as they absorbed the news. Finally Nathan said, "And you think Miss Cole is the one who attacked you? But she was working with you."

"Mr. Asquith thinks there could be a traitor in his own organization, someone working on the inside," Annabeth explained. "He thought it was possible that it could be Miss Cole."

"But that's mad!" Nathan exclaimed. "She was with us. How could she have attacked you in two other places?"

"She could have someone working for her," Sloane pointed out. "Give herself a handy alibi with you and Lady Lockwood."

"I thought she was your friend," Nathan said.

"She is."

"Well, thank God I'm not your friend if this is how you treat them," Nathan said scathingly.

"I don't believe it's Verity," Sloane replied. "But there have been a few things that point to her."

"Such as defending Annabeth from kidnappers and robbers?" Nathan shot back.

"I have to consider all the possibilities," Sloane told him. "Blind trust can be a fatal mistake. When lives are at stake, you cannot rely on your emotions."

"That certainly suits you, then, since we all know you are impervious to emotions."

Sloane smiled thinly. "It's curious, though, how quickly you spring to Verity's defense. You hardly know her. When did you become her champion?"

"I'm not. Miss Cole is an excessively irritating woman, but she's no murderer," Nathan responded.

"You are naive if you think Verity isn't capable of that and more."

"She may be *capable* of murder. That doesn't mean she would try to kill you and Annabeth. It's not in her personality. And if you think she would, then I'd say *you* are the one who hardly knows her."

Lady Lockwood rapped her cane on the floor, drawing attention back to herself. "All this is beside the point. The curious thing is why would anyone have murdered Annabeth's father?"

Annabeth and Sloane exchanged a glance, then she said, "We think it is because of the document we've been searching for. A confession Papa wrote. We think someone murdered him to keep him from sending it to the authorities."

"A confession?" Lady Lockwood said dismissively. "What could Hunter possibly have to confess? We were all well aware of his various follies."

"Not all of them, I'm afraid." Sloane pulled the folded paper from inside his jacket and handed it to Annabeth's grandmother.

"Papa killed a man," Annabeth explained. "It was an accident, of course."

Lady Lockwood, scanning the confession, gasped. "Traitor? That idiotic man. The accident would have been a scandal one could weather, but this…"

"What?" Nathan yelped, and Lady Lockwood handed him the piece of paper to read. "Good Lord!" He read it through a second time, then looked up at Annabeth, his eyes filled with sympathy. "I am so sorry, Annabeth. I know how much this must have hurt you."

"Thank you." Trust Nathan to think of the pain her father had caused, just as her grandmother's first thought was the family name.

"So this is why you and Miss Cole and the government are concerned in the matter," Nathan said to Sloane. "Miss Cole told us this Asquith chap is looking for a traitor among his workers. You thought Mr. Winfield would name him in his confession."

"Miss Cole was certainly chatty while we were away," Sloane said.

"I asked her," Lady Lockwood said, as if that settled the matter.

Nathan gave Sloane a sardonic glance. "Have you ever been interrogated by her ladyship?"

"Point taken."

Ignoring their asides, Annabeth's grandmother went on, "But this paper says nothing that would implicate anyone else in the matter."

"Whoever killed Hunter clearly didn't know that Mr. Winfield's confession named only himself," Sloane said. "And, of course, there was always the possibility that someone could figure out who else was involved, using the information in here, so the French spy wouldn't ever be able to feel entirely safe."

"Well, we cannot let any of this get out," Lady Lockwood said, snatching the letter from Nathan's hand. "What do you plan to do with this paper, Rutherford? I say burn it."

"No, we cannot destroy it since it could be evidence," Sloane replied. "It might help us discover whoever killed Mr. Winfield. Annabeth is still in danger. We have to find the blackguard. I thought we might give it to you, my lady. I believe you mentioned once that you have a safe."

"Excellent idea." Lady Lockwood smiled. "I have a very good safe in the room where all my gold and silver plate is stored, and that room is locked as well."

"Not to mention guarded by a ferocious watchdog," Nathan said.

"I realize you are making a jest, young man." Lady Lockwood shook an admonitory finger at him. "But very little gets by my Petunia."

They all cast a glance at the small pudgy dog slumbering at Lady Lockwood's feet.

"Yes, well," Sloane said. "I am sure it will be quite safe here."

"I thought you would give it to Mr. Asquith," Annabeth said.

"No." Sloane shook his head. "Not yet, at least. If Asquith is right and he does have a turncoat within his group, that person could have access to anything I gave him. I shall tell Asquith that we found it, of course, but I see no reason for him to know about your father's accident. I shall simply tell him that we found the document, but that it was incomplete and did not implicate anyone but your father. If there is a spy in his network, that will either quell his fears of what the document says or it will draw him out." Sloane's sinister smile showed which outcome he preferred. "I'll have someone watching Lady Lockwood's safe."

"And that is your plan of action?" Nathan asked scornfully. "Just sit here and see if someone shows up to steal the confession?"

"Of course not. I'm going to search for Mr. Winfield's opponent in the race. It seems clear that that is the heart of the matter, whether he himself was the traitor in our network or just someone who used the incident as leverage over Annabeth's father."

"What we need, Grandmother, are the names of the men my father used to race against."

"Oh, goodness, several of them were given to racing, and he had a number of friends. My son, Sterling, for one, though he was not as given to either gambling or horses as some of them. Feringham was Hunter's closest friend, of course."

"Uncle Russell?" Annabeth scoffed. "It couldn't be him."

"Why not?" Sloane asked. "We have to consider every possibility."

"He would never have harmed Papa."

"Yes," Nathan agreed. "Hard to see Feringham as a master spy, either."

"His mild demeanor would be a good disguise."

"Lord Edgerton is a more likely candidate," Annabeth said.

"Annabeth, really!" Lady Lockwood exclaimed. "It can't be Edgerton. He's a gentleman. A peer."

"I don't think we can limit our suspects to the lower classes, my lady," Sloane said sardonically.

"We should ask Sloane's father," Nathan said. "He

was one of Mr. Winfield's set, wasn't he? He could name them, I imagine."

"Yes, but he went back to Cornwall."

"No, he's not. He's here."

"What do you mean, he's here?" Sloane frowned.

"I mean, he's *here*. In this house. He, um, got tired so he's catching a few winks on the chaise longue in the sitting room."

Lady Lockwood snorted. "Tired, my left foot. Bosky is more like it. I told Marcus he shouldn't start on brandy in the afternoon."

Nathan looked pained. "I was trying to avoid the embarrassment."

"Embarrassment? Why would I be embarrassed?" Lady Lockwood retorted. "Marcus is the one who can't hold his liquor any better than he can play his cards."

"I believe he meant embarrassment to me, my lady," Sloane said dryly. He nodded to Nathan. "Thank you, but I am long past embarrassment where my father is concerned." The faint flush along his cheekbones belied his words. "In any case, we cannot tell Marcus what Mr. Winfield did."

"Lord, no," Lady Lockwood said. "We'll simply ask him whom Hunter used to race. We don't have to tell Marcus the whole story."

"Tell me what whole story?" Marcus said from the doorway. He was a trifle unsteady on his feet, and there was a red mark on his cheek where he had slept on the fringe of a decorative pillow, but he carried it off with his usual aplomb. Every strand of his white hair was in place, and his attire was in perfect order. "Ah, we have visitors. I thought I heard voices. Why, Sloane, here you are. I thought you were running about the country."

"I returned," Sloane said flatly. "Why are *you* here? You told me you were going home to Cornwall."

"I was, but when I heard that everyone was going to Stonecliffe, I changed course. Much more congenial company."

"Where you could play whist with Lady Lockwood."

"She's the only one who'll play me for pennies," Marcus said in an aggrieved tone, giving his son a dark look.

"And you should be glad," Lady Lockwood commented. "Since you've lost thousands to me."

"True," he said amiably, and turned to greet the others. "Annabeth." Marcus came forward to kiss her cheek. Annabeth did her best not to recoil at the scent of brandy that emanated from him. "Dear girl. You get lovelier every day." He moved on to greet Nathan, then sat down. "Now…what story is this that you aren't going to tell me? If it's as long and confusing as that one Carlisle and Noelle were involved in, I'd just as soon not hear it."

"It's deadly dull," Sloane assured him. "But all we really want from you are the names of Hunter Winfield's friends, that group that used to race each other."

"There were four or five of them," Marcus said. "Never could see the appeal myself. Enjoyed placing the odd crown or two on them, of course."

"Of course," Sloane murmured.

"Well, Jamie Kidlington—he was a terrific whip. He was one of the first members of the Four Horse Club, you know. Though Hunter had given it up long before then. Congrove—he's dead now, poor fellow. That Smythe chap—can't remember his given name. He was an unpleasant fellow. I remember one time Kidlington accused him of cheating. Couldn't prove it, but after that Smythe stopped coming around. Alexander—he was a military sort. Peter Alexander. He came and went, you see, being in the army."

"Anyone else?" Sloane asked when his father stopped.

"Oh, there were some who might get in the spirit every now and then. I did myself, once or twice."

"Lord Edgerton?"

"That stiff-necked paragon?" Marcus laughed. "No, he was never one of us. The only one he ever challenged was Hunter. They raced a few times. But that was all about something else, of course. Edgerton never forgave him for snatching Martha away from him. Let me think—there must have been one or two others. Can't recall them offhand. Oh, and naturally there was Feringham."

"Feringham?" Sloane glanced at Annabeth.

"But Uncle Russell didn't race."

"No, not usually. He was terrible at it, and he knew it. But every once in a while, if he drank enough, Hunter could talk him into it." Marcus paused when the others all glanced at each other. "What's wrong? What did I say?"

"Nothing," Sloane assured him. "Just a—a slight disagreement."

"I see," Marcus said in the tone of one who clearly did not. "Well." He turned to Lady Lockwood hopefully. "A game of whist after tea, my lady?"

"I think that you and I should probably go home," Sloane told him firmly.

Marcus sighed. "Naturally. You know, my boy, if it weren't for your hair, I would think the faeries put a changeling in your crib."

Sloane smiled faintly. "Perhaps you and I could play a game or two this evening, if you'd like."

"Of whist?" Marcus perked up.

"Whatever you like."

Marcus turned to Annabeth. "Well, what a change you've wrought in our boy, my dear. He seems almost congenial."

"I'll return tomorrow," Sloane said to Annabeth. "We can discuss it all then. Make plans." At her frown, he shook his head and said, "No, I won't act without you. I just… I believe we could all use a little rest."

"Tomorrow then."

Sloane and Marcus departed, and after they were gone, Nathan stood up as well. "I should also be going."

"Stay for tea," Lady Lockwood said. "It's almost time."

"No, thank you, my lady. I have some things to do. I will return tomorrow for the discussion, if that is agreeable."

"Of course. You're welcome anytime," Annabeth assured him. She walked with him to the front door. "How are you? Really. Not for Grandmother's ears."

Nathan smiled faintly. "I am fine. I had too much to do trying to maintain peace among Miss Cole, your grandmother, and Marcus to worry about my finer feelings."

"I'm sure that's true," Annabeth said with a smile of her own. "Sorry to inflict all that on you." She paused, then went on, "I'm sorry for all of it. Truly. I never wanted to hurt you."

"I know. And you shouldn't fret. I haven't been brooding. Indeed, in a way it's been almost a relief."

"A relief?" Annabeth's eyebrows shot up.

Nathan chuckled at her expression. "No, not a relief to be parted from you. It's not as though it doesn't hurt, but there's a sort of…freedom, I suppose, in something ending. Miss Cole told me I've just been trying to best Sloane—in more uncomplimentary words, of course. I don't think that's true, but I do think it's time to get on with my life. See what I can make of it instead of holding on to the past."

"Good. I'm glad for that." Annabeth felt as if much of the burden of guilt she'd been carrying fell away. "I want so much for you to be happy."

"And I will be. I'm sure of that. We both will be. But I can't leave until this is finished and I'm sure you're safe. After that, perhaps I shall visit Hubbard—I'm not sure you know him. He's a friend of mine from Oxford. He moved to Italy a few months back, and he's been after me to come stay with him in Florence for a while. I might visit more of the Continent as well." Nathan's eyes began to twinkle. "This is *not*, you understand, inspired by my mother and aunt deciding to set up house at the manor."

"Oh, no. Really? They're both coming? Permanently?"

"One hopes not. Mama is one thing, but Aunt Sylvie's lectures are more than a man should have to bear."

Annabeth laughed. "Then I hope you have a long visit in Italy."

"Thank you. I'm sure I will." Nathan took his hat from the waiting footman and bowed over Annabeth's hand. "Goodbye, Annabeth."

CHAPTER THIRTY-FIVE

ANNABETH SAT IN the rocking chair beside her fireplace, brushing out her hair. She had spent the evening listening to her grandmother's many aggravations during her brief stay at Stonecliffe, not the least of which seemed to be Verity Cole's tendency to ignore Lady Lockwood's strictures. Verity apparently played too lively games with Lady Lockwood's great-grandson, Gil, that all too often involved Petunia joining in the fun, barking and darting about. She did exactly as she wanted to, paid no attention to Lady Lockwood's advice, laughed too much with Marcus Rutherford, and squabbled too much with Nathan. Most irritating of all was that Aunt Adeline seemed to enjoy the woman's company.

Annabeth had made soothing comments and gratefully escaped to her room when Lady Lockwood finally went to bed. Changing into her nightclothes, Annabeth had sat down to brush out her hair, hoping the familiar, rhythmic routine would calm her own nerves. It wasn't that she was afraid; whatever Sloane said, Lady Lockwood's house seemed solid and safe to her, especially with the guards Sloane had planted at the door to the safe and the front entrance.

No, her edginess was due to being alone. She had always enjoyed the time she had spent by herself, reading or writing letters or simply basking in the silence. But now, in the matter of weeks, hardly a fortnight, of being with Sloane, she felt the chill of loneliness. How was it possible to have become so accustomed to his presence, so attuned to him in such a short time?

Yes, she had known him well in the past, but that was twelve years ago, and he was not the same man he had been. He was altogether harder, colder, and more cynical. He'd lived in a world she had no knowledge of; his life no longer touched hers. And yet, somehow, despite all her efforts to the contrary, her mind, her heart, had somehow twined with his as it always had. She had tried to deny it—to him, to the world, to herself—but the truth was, she loved Sloane. She had always loved him. Deep down inside, beneath the anger and pain, there had remained a small, unconquerable ember of love. It had only taken his presence to fan that ember back into a fire.

Annabeth wanted to be with him again, to feel his arms around her, to listen to his voice, to feel his lips on hers. The last two days had been miserable; she'd cried herself to sleep each night. But she had hoped she'd be past the worst of it soon; instead, she felt more unhappy by the hour. It didn't help to know that she was the one who had pushed him away.

More than once the past two days, she had bitterly regretted that decision. With time and reflection, she had accepted that Sloane had hidden the truth from her with the best of intentions. He was right in pointing out that she was doing the very same thing by not telling her mother about her father's misdeeds. But that was not the relationship Annabeth had always wanted to have with the man she loved. She wanted honesty and trust. She wanted him to share everything with her, good and bad, not shield her from unpleasant truths.

Was Sloane capable of such a relationship? Indeed, was Sloane capable of *any* relationship at all? He seemed content with his bachelor status. He was accustomed to being alone and wary of everyone. He'd built walls around himself, as well-guarded as his house. Even in their moments of greatest passion, he had never once spoken of love or marriage. If she had not pulled away from him, would Sloane have eventually pulled away from her?

That was at the core of her dilemma—the future that lay before them. Or, more accurately, their lack of a future. However much she wanted Sloane, however often she ached for him in her heart and in her body, they always seemed to hurt each other. Their love was a fiery thing, something fierce and deep. It might never burn out, but it would never be comfortable. A man like Sloane, so capable of control and so prone to conceal his emotions, so used to isolation, would never be an easy man. And she herself was no longer the adoring girl she had been before, unable or unwilling to see his faults, content to follow wherever he led, and perfectly happy as long as she was enfolded in Sloane's love.

There would be clashes and disappointments, sorrow and pain. How could she trust him completely, knowing of his deceptions? What if one day he simply turned away from her again, leaving her with a broken heart? Annabeth did not think she could bear to live through that sort of pain again.

Sloane seemed adamant about not marrying. Once, she would have been willing to be his mistress, her love for him overcoming all else. But she held herself too highly now to accept such a shadow life. A passionate affair was one thing; living with the knowledge that he did not value her enough to marry her was quite another.

It was better, surely, to make the cut now. The longer they were together, the more it would hurt. She must stick to her decision, must not crumple, not give in to the heat that flashed through her whenever she was with Sloane. This was what was best.

ANNABETH, SLOANE, AND NATHAN were in the drawing room the next afternoon, discussing their suspects, when Verity, once again dressed in her maid's costume, sailed into the room. "Have I missed anything?"

"Where the devil have you been?" Sloane snapped. "You were supposed to stay at Stonecliffe, not go running off after God knows what."

"It was clear nothing was going to happen there," Verity replied, closing the door and coming to sit down with them. "He can verify that." She nodded toward Nathan. "Either no one believed your ruse, Sloane, or they decided they'd have no luck going after Annabeth at Stonecliffe. We strolled around that garden twice a day, and not once did anyone attack us."

"We were both quite disappointed," Nathan agreed. "Perhaps I less so than Verity. I think she would have preferred getting kidnapped again over having to sit through another dinner discussing upcoming debutantes' coming out balls."

"That's not even a contest. Though I did enjoy besting you in our colorful debates."

"Colorful debates? Is that what we are now labeling your browbeatings?" The twinkle in Nathan's eyes stole the edge from his words.

Verity gave Nathan a cool look and went on, "So, have you two managed to come up with anything?"

"We found the confession." Sloane told her everything they had learned the last few days, beginning with the discovery of Hunter Winfield's murder and ending with the contents of the confession.

Verity leaned forward, her eyes bright with interest, as she listened to the tale. "So you think that the other man involved in the curricle wreck is also the turncoat Asquith is looking for?"

"He seems the likeliest suspect," Sloane said.

"Aside from you, of course," Nathan told Verity. He cast a sardonic look at Sloane. "It's a trifle strange that you are giving all this information to someone you suspect is a traitor."

"Me?" Verity raised her eyebrows.

"I never said I thought Verity was the master spy inside the network," Sloane pointed out. "I just said we had to consider every suspect."

"Well, yes, you would have to," Verity agreed calmly.

"And that doesn't bother you?" Nathan asked. "That your friend and colleague mistrusted you?"

Verity shrugged. "I would have done the same in that situation. You can get killed trusting the wrong person in our line of work." Verity turned back to Sloane. "This man who was racing Mr. Winfield—do you have any possibilities?"

"My father gave us the names of a few. One of them is dead. The likeliest one unfortunately has the name of Smythe, with no idea of the first. Marcus is helpful as always in that respect." Sloane shook his head. "Also a military man named Alexander, and a noted whip named Jamie Kidlington. Do any of those names mean anything to you? Have you ever heard of them in connection with Asquith's organization?"

Verity shook her head. "There's a Smith or two, of course, which may or may not be their real name. But not Smythe. I can look into this military fellow. One of my contacts is high up in the army."

"I thought Nathan could look into Kidlington." Sloane turned to the other man. "You can move in the same circles as he. I couldn't get in the door of a gentleman's club."

Nathan looked startled but said, "Yes, of course. I'll be glad to."

"There are a couple of more possibilities—rather more sensitive situations. One is Mr. Winfield's good friend, Russell Feringham."

"It's not him," Annabeth said.

"We have to consider him, Annabeth. Marcus said he did race sometimes when he was in his cups."

"Yes, but you know what he's like. A cold-blooded killer? A master spy?"

"I don't suppose one could be a master spy if one were obvious," Sloane countered. "There are some things that point to him. For one thing, he was at his country home when someone took a shot at you. He knew we were interested in your father's puzzle boxes. He knew you intended to look at your father's workshop. He returned to London after only a few days."

"So did we," Annabeth said.

"That is exactly my point. It's a little odd, isn't it, that he stayed so little time?"

"Grandmother did the same at Stonecliffe."

"Yes, but I think we can be certain she wasn't targeting you," Nathan cut in.

"Uncle Russell couldn't have tried to kill me," Annabeth protested. "He's been so kind to me. He was always there to help us after my father died." Seeing the look on Sloane's face, she said, "And don't tell me that he came over to the house and helped us clear out Papa's things just so he could look for the confession."

"He also wanted to look through your father's things from the town house."

"He offered to *help*. Out of kindness. He's like an uncle to me." Annabeth knew she was probably protesting too much, as if she wanted to convince herself. But it simply could not be Russell who killed her father and tried to kill her.

"He was the only person Mr. Winfield's valet said came to see your father that last week of his life."

"They were *friends*. They always visited each other." Annabeth drew a breath and sat back. "Very well. I understand. We have to consider everyone, just as you said, no matter how unlikely. But we also must consider Lord Edgerton. I think anyone would agree that he is much more the kind of man who would be ruthless. Obviously he was still in love with my mother. He knows important people—when Sloane and I called on Mother the other day, she was not looking forward to a party that evening because she found all those government people dull."

Nathan spoke up. "Annabeth, I think you're letting your dislike of the man color your reasoning. I could believe him killing Mr. Winfield more than Mr. Feringham doing it. But this person tried to kill *you*. Edgerton wouldn't try to shoot his own stepdaughter." Verity snorted, and Nathan turned to her. "I know you don't believe that aristocratic men have any morals, but even if he didn't care about Annabeth, he wouldn't harm her for the very same reason Annabeth suspects him of murdering her father. He loves her mother. He wouldn't do anything that would hurt Lady Edgerton."

Annabeth said, "When we spoke to him the other day, he clearly did not want us to tell Mother about Papa's death or someone shooting at me. He was trying to keep the news from her. Besides, she wouldn't know that he had shot me or ordered it done."

"Much as I hate to say it, I agree with Nathan," Sloane said. "If you were hurt, there's no way he could keep it from Lady Edgerton. And even if she didn't know he was responsible, it would still make her terribly unhappy. I don't think he would do something that would hurt Lady Edgerton that much."

"You can't take him off the list of suspects just because you think he loves his wife," Annabeth protested.

"No, of course, we won't take him off the list. We have to consider him, just as we have to consider Feringham." Sloane turned. "Verity, what have you found out?"

"Nothing," she said in disgust. "We searched all over Stonecliffe—no secrets stashed away there." Verity pulled out a notebook and tossed it onto a table. "And this code in the notebook you found at the rental house defeated me. I worked on it till my eyes crossed, and I couldn't figure it out."

"She even let me have a try at it," Nathan said.

"So I decided to take it yesterday to someone I know is very good at codes. He couldn't come up with anything that made sense. I think it wasn't a code at all, but just what it appears to be—an ordinary notebook. From the pattern, I assume it was a record of something. The numbers could have been money. Purchases? Payments? The letters could have been a sort of code for a product, perhaps. Or maybe the initials of people. The same letters appear often, but the numbers are very different." She shrugged. "I thought the initials might refer to his operatives and the numbers indicate what information he received or what he paid them. They weren't dates. Or maybe it's just a list of clothes or liquor or cigars, who knows? At any rate, it hasn't led me to anything other than a headache."

Annabeth picked up the notebook. Whatever it contained, it had been important enough to her father to hide. She went through the pages slowly. They were all the same, a column of letters and a column of numbers, with a symbol at the end of the line, either a triangle or a circle. If it wasn't a code but a record of something, as Verity now surmised, what would have been so important that Hunter had found it necessary to hide the record? Surely he couldn't have been involved in some other secret than espionage or his racing accident.

Annabeth went still, her mind humming. Going back to the beginning, she ran her finger down the list of initials. "I think—I think maybe this is a record of his bets. And these letters are the people he wagered against."

"Or raced against." Sloane straightened, his eyes intent on hers.

"Yes. Here is a PLA. SQS." She turned the page, once again skimming down the rows. "They're here more than once."

"Peter Alexander. Maybe this Smythe fellow," Sloane said.

"Yes, but here's another one that ends in S—APS. LMC. Could be Congrove."

"Obviously we're going to have to find these men's entire names," Nathan said.

"I know this one—MFBE. Michael Frederick Billingham Edgerton. There's a circle by his name. I think the symbols might stand for whether Papa won or lost—a circle for losing and a triangle for winning. JHK—that must be Jamie Kidlington."

"What's the last name on the list?" Sloane's voice was tight.

Annabeth looked up at him, and her eyes lit with understanding. "The race that made him stop."

"Perhaps."

She thumbed quickly through the pages and stopped on the last set of initials. Her insides turned to ice. "REF. Russell Edward Feringham."

CHAPTER THIRTY-SIX

"WE DON'T KNOW that this means it was Feringham," Sloane told Annabeth as they left the house. After some discussion of the matter, Verity and Nathan had set off to find out what they could about their targets of Alexander and Kidlington while Sloane and Annabeth went to talk to Russell.

"I know. You said it before," Annabeth told him. "But it doesn't look good. There was no win or loss symbol at the end of the line. My father never went back to fill it in."

"It could be that he never followed through with bets with Feringham. They were good friends, and the winner was a foregone conclusion. Everyone agrees that Feringham was a terrible driver."

"Perhaps." She looked at him. "Why are you arguing the other side now? I thought you were sure it was Uncle Russell."

"I hate for you to look so sad," Sloane replied. "Besides, I'm not sure. I, too, find it hard to believe he killed your father or tried to harm you. He should be on the stage if he's played the role of loving friend so well all these years."

"Really, all the clues we have are scarcely hard evidence," Annabeth said, looking a little more cheerful.

She smiled at Sloane. "Thank you for trying to make me feel better."

She laid her hand on top of his, and Sloane could not refrain from turning his hand to clasp hers. Sad or happy, Annabeth was the most beautiful person in the world to him. It had been hell being estranged from her the last couple of days. He'd been lonely and lusting, and far worse than that, a cold pain that was all too familiar had settled in his chest.

He had been careless. Foolish. He'd let down his guard even though he knew full well he shouldn't. The thought of leaving Annabeth after they found her father's killer ripped him in two. How could he go through that again? At least in the past, he'd had the constant danger to distract him. Now he had nothing.

But he didn't have any choice in the matter. Annabeth had given up on him. And she was right. However little Sloane wanted to, it seemed that he always inflicted pain on her. Look at what he was doing right now—setting out to prove that a man who had been a steady, loving, supportive friend all her life had never been what he seemed.

Annabeth left her hand in Sloane's for the rest of the ride.

Dedicated bachelor that he was, Russell had only a flat in the city, but it was a luxurious one, decorated with all the comfort and taste that one would expect from him.

Russell's valet answered the door. Though he looked a little surprised by their appearance on the doorstep, he had no comment or question, just ushered them into the parlor and went to announce their presence.

A few minutes later, Russell came into the room,

smiling. "Well, this is unexpected. But delightful, of course. Dear Annabeth. Mr. Rutherford." He kissed Annabeth's cheek and shook Sloane's hand. His eyes were alight with curiosity, but he went through the social niceties of inquiring after Annabeth's mother and grandmother.

"I confess I was a bit surprised to see that Lady Lockwood had returned to London so soon after she left," Russell commented.

"As did you," Sloane said, watching the man intently.

Russell didn't seem nervous as he replied, "Goodness, yes. I have never understood why poets wax so enthusiastically about the bucolic life. How much entertainment can one get from gazing at trees? I find it deadly dull myself. It was different, of course, in the past, when Hunter was there."

"It was my father we wanted to talk to you about," Annabeth said, her voice tight.

"Indeed? Well, of course, my dear, what did you want to know?"

"We went to see Mr. Winfield's valet."

"Simpson?" Was it Sloane's imagination or had Feringham stiffened a little at the mention of Simpson?

"Yes." He kept his eyes on Russell, looking for any other indicators. "Mr. Winfield had a box that folded out into a desk."

"Oh, yes, it was a lovely thing," Russell said, smiling.

"My mother gave the desk to Simpson after Papa died," Annabeth said. "We went to see—there was a paper inside…" She paused, and now Sloane was certain that there was a look of alarm in Feringham's eyes. "It was about a race."

"Oh, God." Russell sagged back into the chair. "He did confess. I thought, after all this time, that he had not."

"You drove the other curricle," Annabeth said, her voice thick with tears.

"Yes. Yes." Russell nodded. He looked away from her. "Please don't hate me, Annabeth. Hunter and I— we didn't mean to. It was a terrible accident. It scared us witless, and we drove on to my house. We couldn't—we didn't know what to do. I—it wouldn't have been so bad for me. I have no family to embarrass. But you were just a baby, and Hunter couldn't bear to bring such a scandal down on you and your mother. It haunted us, you know. Especially Hunter. He tried to make up for it, taking Simpson on, and he paid for the burial. But he still thought about it, even after all those years. He told me he wanted to make a clean breast of it, but he promised he wouldn't say I was involved."

"He didn't," Annabeth said bitterly. "He didn't reveal who the other man was. We—we suspected. I hoped that it wasn't you."

"It was your reaction that told us," Sloane said, his voice hard. He hated the crushed look on Annabeth's face.

"I wish that it hadn't been me. The thought of it is never far from my mind. Time hasn't dulled the ache it caused. It was worse for Hunter. Years afterward, he'd talk about how Simpson was just a lad when it happened, and I could tell Hunter was thinking of you, Annabeth. The remorse he felt was palpable in those moments. After his death I wondered sometimes if, in fact, it was a mercy that he didn't have to live with that horrible memory anymore. I wondered if I would be better off gone from this earth as well. But I was too much of a coward to do more than think it."

Sloane wondered what Russell was playing at. Was he trying to make them think that Hunter had committed suicide? Or was this what he had been trying to convince himself of—that killing his best friend had been some kind of a noble act?

"Has it all been a lie?" Annabeth burst out. "All these years? Did you just pretend to be concerned about us so you could search for his confession?"

"No!" Russell looked shocked. "Annabeth, no, of course not. I love you. You've been—I've always felt as if you were the daughter I would never have. Surely you must know that."

"I don't know!" Annabeth cried, tears spilling down her face. "How could I? I don't know you at all. How could you do such a thing? Papa was your dearest friend. How could you murder him?"

Russell's jaw dropped, and the blood drained from his face. "Murder him! Hunter? What are you talking about? I could never— Hunter wasn't murdered. He fell." Russell shoved himself to the edge of his chair, leaning toward Sloane, his eyes pleading. "He fell." When Sloane said nothing, Russell's breath came faster, ragged. The shell of his cool, elegant demeanor was cracking.

Was this the moment of confession? When Russell would admit to what he had done and all this could finally be over?

For Annabeth's sake and safety Sloane hoped so. She shouldn't have to endure any more of these awful secrets coming to light. But the treacherous thought that that also meant their time together was over wouldn't stop running through his mind. Clearly Sloane didn't deserve her if he was thinking about himself and what he wanted when she was in so much pain. Annabeth had made the right decision in ending whatever they had been doing.

Russell shook his head forcefully, his eyes darting from Sloane to Annabeth and back. When neither of them said a word, denial receded from Feringham's eyes and reality set in. Russell twisted to the side, his hands coming up to cover his face. It took Sloane a minute to realize that Russell wasn't just shaking from the shock of their accusations. Noiseless sobs racked his body, as if they were torn from deep within his very soul.

"Oh, God. Oh, God. Somebody killed him." His voice was halting and clogged with tears.

Sloane glanced over at Annabeth, who looked as surprised and bewildered as he felt. This was the master spy? The heartless criminal who had murdered his best friend and shot at his goddaughter? Sloane had a sinking feeling that they might have found the man who had been involved in the accident, but he was not the man they sought.

Russell pulled out his handkerchief, wiping the tears from his face. "I beg your pardon." He pulled together the shattered remnants of his cultured manner, as if it provided him strength. "So sorry to, um." He waved his hand vaguely, as if encompassing his bout of grief. "It was a—a shock, you see."

"Uncle Russell…" Annabeth leaned over and put a comforting hand on his.

Russell clutched her hand tightly, saying, "I would never have harmed Hunter in any way. He was…such a bright and wonderful man. I—it was a dreadful secret that we shared, and I shall always, always, regret what happened. But I could not have hurt him."

"You said he told you he intended to confess," Sloane prompted.

Russell nodded. "One evening, not long before he died, when we'd been drinking, Hunter told me that he was so weighed down by his guilt that he felt he must confess. He assured me that he would not mention my name. I believed him, of course, and yet... I could not quite feel easy. And when he fell...no matter how much I grieved for him, I could not squash a sense of relief as well. I hated myself for even thinking about the weight it lifted from my shoulders, knowing that I no longer had to worry that he might reveal my wrongdoing. I shall never, ever forgive myself for feeling anything but sorrow at his passing. I should have been thinking of you and your mother, of all you had lost. I promised myself I would do my best to look after you as Hunter would have wanted. I could never make up for what I felt at those lowest moments, but I hoped I could give you back a little bit of the father you deserved." He tightened his grip on Annabeth's hand, saying earnestly, "Please, my dearest girl, don't hate me."

Annabeth squeezed his hand. "I don't hate you any more than I could hate Papa, despite what happened. And I am so, so happy to hear that you knew nothing about his murder."

"No, of course not." Russell released her hand and sat back, turning his gaze away from them, as if seeing something in the past. "I've missed him so these past few years. So often, I've thought, 'Oh, I must tell Hunter this,' but of course I could not. If I'd only known how short a time I had, I would have visited him more often, talked to him instead of wasting my time on inconsequential nonsense. Regret is a terrible thing. You can never get back the things you didn't do." He sighed, and after a long moment, he turned back to Sloane. "I don't understand. How could it have been murder? Surely Hunter just fell down those steps."

"The railing had been purposely weakened, sawn nearly all the way through," Sloane answered. "It was clearly done so that when he leaned against it, he would fall to the floor below."

"But who—why would anyone want to kill Hunter?"

"We thought it had something to do with that confession, but now we're not so sure." Sloane tried to keep his answer as vague as possible. The less information other people had about what other heinous acts Hunter had done, the better.

"It seems unlikely that he would have even told anyone else about that letter." Russell frowned. "The only person that comes to mind is Martha, but I suspect he didn't even tell her. He so hated to disappoint her, and she would've been so upset. However, I can't imagine what other reason anyone would have for wanting to hurt him," Russell said in a bewildered tone. "Everyone liked—" Suddenly his eyes flashed, and he jumped up. "It was *him*! Edgerton. He was the only person who hated Hunter. He couldn't stand it that Martha preferred Hunter to him."

Sloane looked at Annabeth out of the corner of his eye. Had she been right about her stepfather all along? Perhaps he had subconsciously dismissed the idea because he thought it was only her dislike coloring her thoughts. Certainly there was nothing Sloane would be more likely to kill for than his love of Annabeth. When he'd thought Parker had kidnapped her, he'd nearly murdered the man right then and there.

"Edgerton must have thought that if he got rid of Hunter, Martha would marry him. And he was right. He got what he wanted." Russell whirled to face Sloane. "You must get him. Put him in jail."

Annabeth stood and went to Russell, saying soothingly, "I have wondered the same thing. But we have no proof, only conjecture. They would never arrest him without evidence."

"You'll find it." Russell jabbed his forefinger at Sloane. "I know you can. Hunter said you were a clever bastard."

"He did?"

"Yes. Said you could dig out anything and had no scruples about how you did it."

"Uncle Russell, that's not true," Annabeth protested.

"No. He was right," Sloane said, rising. "I won't stop digging until I find who's doing this to Annabeth. And I can assure you that they will pay. But there are other factors involved here besides jealousy. Did Mr. Winfield ever mention anything else he was involved in?"

"Involved in?" Russell looked puzzled. "I don't know what you mean. A business venture? He didn't mention anything to me."

"You said Hunter was weighed down by guilt those last few weeks. Was there anything else bothering him? Was he anxious? Frightened? Did he mention anyone's name?"

"Well, of course he was afraid of the scandal his confession would cause. But I don't remember him saying anything about anyone else. I mean, beyond some idle gossip about people we knew. That sort of thing."

"Did he express any resentment or anger about any of those people?"

"Um, well, he didn't like you very much, I'm afraid," Russell said with some embarrassment.

Sloane let out a little huff of a laugh. "No, I don't imagine he did." He paused. "Do you remember if Mr. Winfield had any visitors those last few weeks?"

Russell frowned. "I don't remember seeing anyone there. But that was a long time ago. I could have forgotten. And it's not as though I was with Hunter all the time. I don't recall him saying anything about anyone visiting." He looked over at Annabeth. "What is this all about? Who do you suspect besides Edgerton?"

"That's the problem," Sloane said grimly. "We're chasing phantoms."

CHAPTER THIRTY-SEVEN

"I BELIEVE HIM," Annabeth said. She and Sloane were sitting in the carriage. "Don't you?" She laid a hand on his arm so casually it made his heart squeeze.

"Yes. There's no way Russell could keep up such a charade all these years. Just look at what happened today. He crumpled and admitted he'd been in the race before we even asked him."

"Should we go to visit Edgerton, question him?"

"Martha will be there right now, won't she? I'd rather keep your mother out of this if we can."

"You're right." Annabeth chewed at one corner of her mouth. "This is going to ruin her life, isn't it?"

"It isn't something I think we should enter into lightly, no." Sloane frowned. "I'd really like to get some kind of evidence on him first and confront him with it when your mother isn't there."

"That way if he can explain it she doesn't even have to know we accused him." Annabeth sighed. "That would be better, I suppose, but I hate to wait. It terrifies me thinking of her in that house with him."

"Whatever Edgerton may or may not have done, I truly believe he would never hurt your mother. I don't think you should worry about that."

"Even so, I don't want to go home. I cannot face Grandmother right now."

"Of course. Where shall we go? We can't simply walk through the park. You'd be too exposed. My father may be at my house, so that wouldn't do."

"Why don't we go where you work? You have an office, don't you?"

"You want to see the docks?" he asked.

"It'd be a change." She gave him a faint smile.

"Then that's where we'll go." He leaned forward to give the driver directions. Sloane couldn't understand why Annabeth would want to see the place any more than why it warmed him that she did.

They drove to the wharves, then got out and walked. Here, he felt safe. He still had guards in place, just in case Parker decided to renew his attacks, and there was too much bustle, too many people and carts and stacks of crates for anyone to get a good shot. He was careful to keep bales and such barriers between them and the buildings where anyone could hide to shoot at them.

He pointed out his ships. There were two of them in right now, one unloading and the other one being loaded. Many of the workers greeted Sloane, and he stopped to talk to a captain of one of the ships. Annabeth, her hand on his arm, viewed it all with great interest and asked him questions, pointing out various things that caught her eye.

They continued to the row of warehouses, looking in at the stored goods, and finally entered the one that contained his clerks and books. Sloane dashed off a quick note to Asquith telling him that they had found Hunter's confession and that the document didn't reveal anything about the spymaster Asquith sought.

"This way if there is a traitor inside his organization

he will learn of this and know he is not in danger of being caught."

"How does that help Asquith find him?" Annabeth frowned.

"It doesn't. But it should help keep you safe. And really, that's all I care about."

Sloane sealed the note and handed it to a lad who worked in the office. The boy ran off to deliver it, and Annabeth and Sloane went to the upper level, where the back half of the space was taken up with storage, and the front half was his office.

Sloane watched Annabeth as she walked around the room, looking at the utilitarian space. He wondered what she thought of it, but he wasn't about to ask. It suddenly seemed quite bare and plain. She stood for a moment, gazing out the window at his view of the wharves.

"What's in here?" Annabeth turned and went to the open doorway on the side wall. The room beyond the door was smaller and contained even less furniture, only a bed and a washstand. "Oh." Her cheeks turned pink and she turned away.

"Sometimes when I work late, I sleep here instead of going home," he said, uncomfortably aware of the bed, which suddenly seemed to be the focus of the whole office. And, really, what did that say about his life that he'd as soon sleep here as go home? He turned away. He wanted to ask her what she thought of his world, what she thought of him now that she'd seen his world. Instead, he said, "It's hard to believe Edgerton would attack you."

"Yes." Annabeth sighed. "Especially knowing how it would crush my mother. But perhaps he never meant to harm me and just wanted to scare us away so we wouldn't look for the confession any longer."

"That does seem more like him, something calculated to have a certain outcome he desires as opposed to an act of passionate anger."

"Yes, and we are running out of options. It isn't as though I *want* it to be Lord Edgerton. I'd much rather it was not him. However, now that we know that Russell was the other man in the race, that takes those three or four other suspects out of the picture. The only connection is that the accident was used to coerce him into giving the French information."

"Which raises an interesting point," Sloane said thoughtfully. "How did whoever this spy is learn about your father's accident to begin with? Only Winfield and Feringham knew of it."

"It could be that there was someone in the village who saw it."

"But why wouldn't that person have used the knowledge against your father earlier? Why wouldn't he have been getting money from your father for years in return for not telling?"

"Papa was never very flush with money."

"Maybe, but anything's better than nothing. And there's Feringham—he's well off, isn't he? Why not blackmail him as well?"

"We don't know that they weren't blackmailed."

"We can ask him, but I think Feringham would have mentioned that today if he had been."

"The most likely thing is that my father or Russell told someone," Annabeth said. "Maybe let it slip some night when he'd been drinking. Maybe Papa even told this 'master spy' about it."

"Which would indicate it was one of your father's friends."

"Not really. Papa was friends with everyone when he was in his cups. Or the person could have overheard him telling someone or even just talking to Russell about it."

"Edgerton would certainly be the easier choice of villain." Sloane paused, then said quietly, "What if it is him? Would you want him brought to trial? Make your mother face the scandal and the pain?"

Annabeth's eyes filled with tears. "No, of course I don't want her to face that. Oh, Sloane…"

He crossed the room to her, opening his arms, and she folded herself into his embrace. "I hate this so. Learning all this about Papa and Uncle Russell…it's horrid. I wish I'd never heard any of it."

"I know." He held Annabeth close to him, bending his head down to rest against hers. "I'm so sorry, my love." He had tried to protect her from it, and he had failed miserably at every turn. That knowledge burned within him. Sloane tightened his arms around her, murmuring, "My love, my love."

Annabeth pulled back a little, looking up into his face. Her eyes were huge and bright with tears, her mouth soft and inviting. "Kiss me, Sloane."

He went still, her words so much what he wanted to hear that he thought he might have imagined it. "Anna…" He'd never wanted anything as much as he wanted to do as she said, to kiss her until the rest of the world went away, to drown himself in her love. "No. I can't. You're not thinking. This isn't what you want."

"Don't tell me what I want." She went up on her toes and pressed her lips softly against his.

They were warm and soft and tasted like springtime

and sweet cherries and all the good things he'd almost forgot existed when Annabeth hadn't been in his life. Then she opened her mouth to his and the world seemed to spin around him, pulling him down into his endless hunger. He kissed her back, his arms tightening around her, squeezing her to him. Her body was soft and pliant against his, stoking his desire. He slid his hand down her back, curving over her bottom and pressing her against him, wanting her to feel how much he wanted her, aching to satisfy that want. Annabeth made a soft little murmur and moved against him in a primal way that sent his hunger rocketing.

He pulled his mouth from hers in a last desperate attempt to control the situation. "I would be a scoundrel to take advantage of you in your vulnerable state."

She looked at him, a tantalizing little smile forming on her lips. "I've always had a fondness for scoundrels."

Her words were like a spark to tinder. Sloane stood still for a moment longer, in a last futile battle with his body. He knew Annabeth was not for him, knew she was right in saying he always hurt her, knew that this time with her was quickly coming to an end and he would never see her again. But was it so wrong to have this one last moment with her, to take this pleasure and happiness with him into a bleak future without her? Could he not just give in? After all, Annabeth was a woman who knew her own mind.

"Make love to me, Sloane," Annabeth said softly. And he was lost.

CHAPTER THIRTY-EIGHT

SWINGING HER UP into his arms, Sloane carried Annabeth into the adjoining room. She wrapped her arms around his neck, leaning her head on his shoulder. He could feel the soft brush of her breath on his neck, teasing his desire even higher. Sloane shoved the door closed with his foot and set Annabeth down on her feet by the bed.

He ached to let the storm of his passion loose, to rip their clothes off and tumble down onto the bed in a wild cataclysm. But more than that, he wanted to savor making love to Annabeth, to take his time and make the moment last. This was what he would have of her for the rest of his life, and he hungered for her love more than he hungered for the satisfaction.

Slowly he unfastened her clothes and slipped them from her body, tossing her pelisse onto the chair and following it with her dress. His eyes roamed down her, taking in the swell of her breasts beneath the camisole and the dark circle of her nipples that showed through the thin material, the narrowing of her waist and the rounded contour of her hips.

"What about you?" Annabeth murmured, her hands going to the buttons of his waistcoat.

"We'll get to that." He smiled sensually. "But first I must look at you." He brushed his knuckles across her nipple, and it tightened. "You are so beautiful."

"As are you." She returned the smile, but let her hands drop to her sides. It was a small gesture, but one that shook him, a subtle giving herself up to him that betokened love and trust, an untrammeled openness to passion.

Sloane swallowed, pausing for a moment to leash the wild hunger within him. He tugged her down to sit on the bed, then knelt and removed her stockings, sliding them slowly, his fingers stroking her legs. He had done this the first time they made love, and somehow that memory made the pleasure almost bittersweet, knowing this would be the last time.

He removed the remainder of her undergarments, revealing every inch of her in the same slow, delicious way, and she lay back on the bed, linking her arms behind her head, the glow in her eyes conveying that his gaze stirred her as much as the sight of her stirred him.

Sloane pulled off his jacket and tossed it aside, removing the rest of his clothes without taking his eyes from her beauty. Bending over her, he stroked one hand down her body, exploring each dip and curve, running a finger along the hard line of her breastbone and cupping the softness of her breasts. His fingers slipped between her legs, and Annabeth opened to him. Her eyes were hot and hazy, and she moaned a little as he stroked her intimately.

Annabeth moved restlessly beneath his touch, whispering his name. His fingers moved in and out, caressing, pressing, and he could see the tension gathering in her body, building with each touch. "Sloane…" His name was a groan now, urgent and demanding.

He was rock hard, his own need aching for release.

He wanted to be in her, thrusting hard and deep, but he fiercely pushed it back. First, he would have the pleasure of watching desire shatter her beneath his touch.

She let out a cry, arching up against his hand, her body taut, and then she went limp and looked up at him with eyes so full of heat and fulfillment that it took all his discipline not to explode right there.

Annabeth's smile was slow and provocative as she reached out and took his arm. "Come here." She pulled him down onto the bed with her. She pushed him over onto his back, and he went without resistance, his insides humming with anticipation. She swung her leg over him, straddling him. "Now it's my turn."

She gave Sloane a wicked smile that sent heat streaking through him. She ran her hands over his arms and chest, trailing with excruciating softness over every inch of skin. He knew she could feel his hardness pressing against her, prodding at that most sensitive flesh; he knew she realized what she did to him when she shifted position, sliding down to straddle his thighs; and that understanding multiplied his desire.

He loved that she teased him, that her tormenting was done to stoke up the fire within him. He loved that she wanted to touch him, that she enjoyed exploring him, eager to find every sensitive spot that made him leap with desire.

Sloane put his hands on her waist to pull her forward, but she swatted playfully at his arm. "Uh-uh. None of that. It's my time, remember?"

"I remember." His breathing turned even more ragged at the sensual look in her eyes.

"Then you be a good boy and keep your hands up

there." She took his wrists and pulled his arms above his head. "And I will do as I please."

She bent and kissed him, long and slow and hard. Sloane curled his hands around the narrow metal bars of the headboard and held on. Annabeth's lips moved from his own and found his earlobe, nibbling on it, then trailing down to the tender skin of his throat. Her mouth traced across his collarbone, then down his chest, kissing and tasting, and then she settled on his nipple and gently sucked until he groaned.

"Now," he rasped. "I have to have you now."

"Just a second. I want to do this." Her tongue slipped down over his stomach till it reached his navel.

At that, Sloane let out a low growl and flipped Annabeth over onto her back. She laughed in delight as he positioned himself between her legs until her laughter ended in a little sighing moan as he pushed up into her.

He moved slowly at first; if this was his last night with his love, he wanted to draw out each second. But every sound and motion Annabeth made seemed designed to send his control spiraling out of reach. Sloane thought nothing could rival her soft hands barely grazing his skin, light as a feather in a way that made him shiver. That was until they turned harsh and demanding, the raking of fingernails down his back driving him forward until his entire being thrummed tautly. Finally his need was too great and he plunged in and out, hard and fast, the little noises of passion Annabeth made vaulting his desire even higher. He hung on to his last thread of restraint until he felt her tighten around him, her climax rippling through her. Then, at last, he found his own release, the supreme pleasure exploding within him, and he collapsed against her.

ANNABETH WOKE FROM a shallow sleep to see Sloane's face above her. He lay beside her, propped on his elbow, and his finger gently traced the curve of her cheek. The lines of his face were soft, his eyes dark with emotion, and she knew in that moment that he loved her still. She smiled back at him, reaching up to lay her palm against his cheek.

"I love you," she whispered.

His face hardened instantly, and he sat up, turning away from her. "Don't say that."

Annabeth frowned, the sweet peace and joy she had awakened with now draining away. "Why? It's the truth. Sloane…" She laid her hand on his back, and he flinched as if her touch burned him. "What is the matter?" Pain pierced her. Had she been so wrong? "Did this not mean anything to you? Do you not feel as I do?"

"Anna, don't…" His words were almost a groan. "Don't make this any harder."

"Make what harder?" She sat up. "Sloane, just tell me. Do you not love me?"

"Of course I love you." He almost spat out the words.

"Then why are you acting this way? It's not like it used to be. We can be together now."

"We can't." He got out of bed and began to pull on his clothes, in rapid, jerky movements, all the while turned away from her. "You need to get dressed. We must return to your grandmother's. It's getting late. She'll be suspicious."

Annabeth felt suddenly very naked, and she reached for the underthings Sloane had tossed across the bottom of the bed, pulling them on as rapidly as he. "Grandmother is always suspicious. What does it matter? We're adults now. I can marry whomever I wish."

"We're not getting married." He went to the mirror of the washstand to tie on his neckcloth.

"Don't tell me you're still worried about our marriage being a scandal. That's nonsense. I don't care about the *ton*. I don't care if I never go to another party or receive another call. And I'm certainly not going to make my life miserable just because Grandmother doesn't want me to marry you. Trust me, she can handle idle gossip—she is positive that anything said against her is just jealousy."

He fumbled with his tie, and he let out a curse, yanking the long strand of cloth from his neck. He swung around to face her finally. "We can't just will away our past. We can't simply toss out the hurt and the sorrow. It will always be with us. Every time we're together, we cause each other more pain."

Annabeth took a breath and forced calm into her voice. "I wasn't right the other day. I spoke in haste and anger. I hated what my father had done, and I blamed you. It wasn't fair. It wasn't you who caused me the pain and sorrow. It was Papa. It is life that causes the pain, and love is what heals the wounds."

"It was desire that brought us here, not love."

"So now you're claiming you only want me, but you do not love me."

"You know I love you. And it's bloody painful." He shoved his hands back through his hair. "This—" he jabbed his forefinger at the bed "—this does not heal all wounds. It only covers them up for a while, lets you forget, makes you feel as if anything is possible."

"But it *is* possible." She took a step closer, her voice entreating. "Just think, after all that has happened, all these years, here we are again. Together. We are meant to be together."

"Fate has a cruel sense of humor then. Annabeth, none of what you're saying matters. However much I love you, however much I want you, I cannot marry you. I'm not the boy you love. I have lied and broken laws and done things that would make you run from me."

"That's in the past. It doesn't matter if you've changed. I have, too. I'm not trying to marry that boy. I know who you are. And I love you. Now. As you are."

"You've seen my world." He spread his arms out. "How I live. I didn't just do those things in the past. I still step outside the law. Ask your friend Nathan. He's seen me work. I have enemies. From the past, from the present. There are a number of people who would be more than happy to do me harm. They may be unwilling to risk attacking me physically, but they'll know they can destroy me through my wife. You'd be in constant danger. Do you want to spend the rest of your life in that manner? To live always as you have the last few days?"

"I've managed, haven't I?" Annabeth flared. "I think I've proven I'm not weak or cowardly or—"

"It's not about you!" he thundered. "You aren't weak. *I* am. You are my weakness."

"Well, you're right about one thing," Annabeth retorted, grabbing up her pelisse. "You *are* weak. I am willing to do whatever it takes to be with you. But you are too scared to fight for our love."

Annabeth whirled and ran from the room.

CHAPTER THIRTY-NINE

SLOANE CURSED AND started after her. "Annabeth! Stop!"

Of course she didn't listen to him. She was right; she didn't care about danger. And she would do the opposite of anything he suggested at this moment. Sloane gestured to his foreman whom she had just run past. "Wilson. Go after her. Make sure she gets back home safely."

Hopefully Annabeth wouldn't take the man's head off.

Sloane turned around and went back up the stairs to his office. Through his window, he could see Annabeth charging away, Wilson running after her. Then they turned a corner, and Annabeth was gone. Sloane sank into his chair and, bracing his elbows on the desk, dropped his head to his hands.

Well, he'd certainly bollixed that up. He no longer needed to dread never seeing Annabeth again; he'd already ensured that. He'd been a fool to give in to his desire. One last moment with her, indeed. One last pain to inflict was more like it.

If he'd just stepped back from her, if he'd just taken her home, he would have had…what? A few more days of yearning, of dread, of daydreaming like a schoolboy that everything would be all right. No. It was better to have made a clean cut like this. After this it wouldn't matter what he said to her; even if he came crawling to her on hands and knees, she wouldn't have him back. And it was better this way. She was safer this way.

Sloane scrubbed his hands over his face and sat back. He'd get no work done here today. He might as well go home. Perhaps he could waste the rest of the day playing some stupid card game with his father. But Marcus wouldn't be there, of course; he was doubtless over at Lady Lockwood's. It didn't matter; Sloane could just spend the evening drinking brandy and give himself a brain-crushing hangover tomorrow.

Sloane left the office and walked away from the docks, heading home. He walked the rest of the way instead of hiring a hack. There was no need to hurry; nothing awaited him there. Nor did he care whether someone attacked him on the way. At the moment, he'd rather welcome a fight. But no attack came, and he entered the house unscathed and in the same black mood.

"Sloane, my boy," Marcus called from the drawing room. "You're just in time for tea."

God, he really was getting desperate, being glad his father was at home. "What are you doing here? I thought you would be in a fevered low-stakes game of whist at Lady Lockwood's."

"No, that bloody dog of hers chewed right through one of my shoes, so I had to come change."

Even in his present state, Sloane had to smile a little. "One would think that you might have noticed she was chewing on your shoe before she got all the way through."

"I was on a hot streak. Didn't realize what was going on until she sank one of her teeth into my toe." Marcus handed his son a cup of tea and sat back, studying Sloane. "You're home rather early." When Sloane merely shrugged, he peered at him more closely, then groaned. "The devil! You've made a hash of it, haven't you?"

Sloane gave him a sour look and sat down. "Yes. I've made a hash of it. All over again." He shrugged. "It's just as well. Better to make a clean cut than keep hacking away at something impossible."

"I suppose. I try to avoid either of them."

"Trust me, it's easier."

"Mmm-hmm. And you of course always take the easy way." His father smirked in that annoying way of his.

Sloane decided to ignore his words. He didn't have the energy to argue with Marcus. "Annabeth's no longer involved in the case. I won't need to see her again." His lungs froze at the thought, but he ignored that, too. "I'll work from the other end now. It doesn't seem to be one of her father's friends. Unless of course it's Edgerton, but I still find that somewhat unlikely."

"What isn't Edgerton?" Marcus shook his head. "No, never mind. I don't really want to know. I presume you're chasing someone."

"Yes. And when I find him, I'm going to kill the bastard."

"Naturally," Marcus murmured with a sigh, and stood up. "I believe this conversation requires something stronger than tea." He went to a small table and opened the door of the cabinet beneath it. He returned carrying a bottle.

"Why is there a bottle of brandy hidden in a cabinet in the drawing room?" Sloane asked.

"Well, it's a bit of a nuisance, you see, having to pick that lock on your liquor cabinet every time. More convenient in here."

"I don't know why I bother."

"Frankly, my boy, neither do I." Marcus poured a generous dollop of brandy into each of their cups, then took a sip. "Ah, much better. Now…who is it you're going to murder?"

"The man who's been threatening Annabeth."

"I see. That's good."

Sloane shrugged. "Or I'll just turn him over to Asquith, which is probably worse than death, anyway."

"But rather more humane than giving him to Lady Lockwood."

Sloane smiled faintly. "Yes. Death by Petunia. What a fate."

"But I fail to see what chasing him has to do with this 'clean cut' from Annabeth," Marcus said after a moment. "I was under the impression that the two of you were together again. Wedding bells and all that."

"Your impression was wrong," Sloane said flatly.

Marcus heaved a sigh. "What excuse did you find this time?"

"Excuse?" Sloane's eyebrows soared and he leaned forward combatively. "You think I don't want to marry her? That I wouldn't give anything to marry her?"

"Well, yes, since you aren't—speaks for itself, really."

Sloane made a noise of disgust and surged to his feet, beginning to pace. "I can't marry Annabeth. It's obvious to everyone but you and her."

"So the lady didn't reject your proposal."

"No. I didn't propose."

"Mmm. That might be your problem right there."

"Oh, stop making jests."

"One rather has to when someone is doing something as idiotic as you are."

"I'm the only sensible one in this. Annabeth says she

doesn't care about scandal, doesn't care about her name or the *ton* or anything else."

"Neither do you," Marcus pointed out.

"Yes, but she hasn't experienced it yet—she thinks it will be fine. She tells me I'm just scared. *Scared*, mind you. She says she won't miss the parties. Her family will stick by her. Her grandmother will weather the storm."

"She's right about that. Lady Lockwood's more likely to create a storm than be blown over by it. The thing is, don't you think Annabeth should decide what she wants or doesn't want?"

"Of course she should. But I don't want her to wake up in two years and realize what a mistake she's made. She doesn't know, she doesn't understand the sort of life I lead, the kind of man I am now. I bribe officials. I pay constables and magistrates to turn a blind eye. I may not be doing the crimes that occur in and around my taverns, but we all know those crimes go on there. I am disreputable. And I have enemies. They can attack her through me."

"I can see your point." Marcus nodded. "Too bad there isn't someone around clever enough to change things."

Sloane stopped his pacing to glare at his father. "It's too dangerous. Something could happen to her."

"Something can always happen to people. Annabeth could get run over by a carriage tomorrow, whether you stay or go. Love is a risk. Marriage is a risk. You're just too frightened to take it. Annabeth is right."

"I'm afraid of marrying Annabeth? That's ridiculous. You're both mad. I've wanted to be with her since I can remember. I want Annabeth more than anything in the world."

"You think you can't be scared to death of the thing

you love desperately? Just look at me. I don't have to let you stick me away from temptation out in Cornwall. The truth is I'm hiding."

"Love of gambling isn't the same."

"Not to you." Marcus stood up, his face serious in a way that Sloane had never seen. "I know that you think I'm just an old fool who's interested in nothing but clothes and cards. To be fair, I am. But being afraid is something I know about. Not fear of physical danger. No one would accuse you of that. I'm talking about fear in here." He tapped his chest. "Fear of not being good enough. Fear of the hollow space inside you. Fear of people realizing how false your front is."

Sloane stared at him. His heart was thumping wildly, and his feet felt frozen to the floor. Everything in him pushed back against his father's words. He wanted to tell him to stop, but his voice didn't seem to work either.

Marcus went relentlessly on, "You just told me you're afraid that Annabeth will wake up and realize what a mistake she's made. You're afraid to take the risk, to let yourself believe that you can be happy, to accept that a woman like Annabeth can love you. Because what if all that crashes, and you're left with nothing. Worse than nothing."

Sloane turned and strode out of the room.

"Sloane? Wait." His father's worried voice floated after him. "What are you doing?"

He turned back to Marcus. "I need to walk." He strode on to the door, but there he stopped and, without looking at Marcus, said, "And I don't think you're just an old fool."

Sloane left the house.

CHAPTER FORTY

ANNABETH STARTED DOWN the stairs. Lady Lockwood was still in bed, and Verity was already gone, chasing some rumor she'd heard the day before. So there was no one to interfere with Annabeth's plans.

She had calmed down yesterday by the time she reached the house, and after a good night's sleep, her mood had settled into one of quiet determination. She was through with tears and sorrow. She was no longer a young girl who would simply cry her heart out and accept what Sloane had done.

Sloane was behaving in a most irritating way. Annabeth wasn't sure why he was doing it, but she was not about to let him control the course of their relationship. This time she was going to fight for their love. Sloane loved her; she was certain of it. All she had to do was change his mind about marrying her.

But first, she thought, she must let Sloane stew by himself for a while. Let him see how much he enjoyed being alone. She doubted that he would return to her grandmother's house anytime soon—if ever. So this morning, she was going to occupy herself with their investigation.

There was one suspect left among her father's acquaintances, and she was not entirely sure that Sloane would even bother to question Lord Edgerton. Sloane was tied to the theory that her father's murderer was the turncoat in Asquith's spy network, but even though her stepfather had not been the man involved in her father's wreck, there was still the issue of jealousy.

Love, she thought, could be as powerful a motivation as anything—maybe more. Perhaps it didn't seem that way to Sloane because he pushed it away at every turn. Sloane could scarcely ignore the possibility that the murder had been personal if she found some evidence.

There might even be some factor besides love involved. She wasn't sure what that might be, but Annabeth had found it very odd that her mother said Edgerton had brought an inheritance to her father from some relative named Mary. Annabeth couldn't remember any relative, even a distant one, with that name. Sloane hadn't found that important, either, but then Sloane wasn't close to his family.

She had sent her mother a note last night telling her she would visit today. Hopefully Martha would suggest that Edgerton go to the club; she often did that so they could have a bit of mother-daughter time together.

Annabeth thought she could persuade her mother to pull out her father's old family Bible. If this woman was nowhere to be found on the family tree, that would certainly make the story of the inheritance suspicious.

And perhaps she could manage to sneak into Edgerton's office. If the woman really had left the money to her father, Annabeth was certain that the will would be in her stepfather's office. She might be able to find some other sort of evidence there as well. Edgerton was the sort of person who kept meticulous records.

It would be safe enough for her to travel without Sloane. If Mr. Asquith was right about the turncoat being someone inside his organization, the man should have learned about the note Sloane sent Asquith yesterday, realized that he had not been implicated and that there was no reason to try to harm Annabeth anymore. She wasn't going to be foolish, of course. She would take one of the guards Sloane had posted outside the house with her.

Just as she reached the landing of the staircase, there was a knock on the door. Her heart leaped—*Sloane!* She hurried down the steps, but the footman opened the door before she could get there. She saw to her disappointment that it was not Sloane who stood on the front stoop.

"Mr. Asquith."

"Miss Winfield." He swept off his hat and gave her a polite bow. "I am glad to see you. I was hoping we might have a chat."

Annabeth had no interest in chatting with Mr. Asquith. She had had little liking for him to begin with, but after Sloane told her how he had blackmailed Sloane into spying for him, she despised the man. Still, she could hardly get out of talking to him. "Of course."

She gave a little nod to the footman, who took the man's hat, and she led Asquith into the drawing room. She was not, however, going to ask the man if he wished for some tea.

"There's a bit of rain today," he commented.

Annabeth had no interest in chitchatting about the weather. She wanted to leave before Grandmother or any of the others arrived. "Mr. Asquith, I would appreciate it if this was a short conversation. I was about to go out. I have to talk to another suspect."

"Another suspect?" Asquith's brows rose. "Rutherford didn't say he was looking into someone else. Who is it, may I ask?"

"He's not. I am going by myself."

"But isn't that rather dangerous?" Asquith said in alarm. "You shouldn't go alone. I shall go with you."

"No, that's really not—" Annabeth paused. She didn't like the man, but this was the sort of thing he did for a living. Perhaps he would have some idea of what she needed to look for or what the oddity with the inheritance money might mean. "That is…yes, perhaps it would be wise to take you with me. But, first, what was it that you originally came for? Is there something I can do for you?"

"Good. A woman who gets straight to the point." Asquith smiled. "I want you to know how much we appreciate what you've done. You've been of immense help to England."

She wasn't sure how to respond to that, so she gave him one of her grandmother's regal nods.

"Mr. Rutherford told me that you had your father's confession here at the house," Asquith went on. "I would like to see it."

"As I'm sure Mr. Rutherford told you, the confession did not identify anyone else," Annabeth said. She didn't want this man to know about her father's accident. And Grandmother would be incensed.

"Nevertheless, I should like to look at it. I always like to see information for myself."

"You don't trust Sloane's word?" Annabeth raised an eyebrow.

He smiled faintly. "Miss Winfield, I don't trust *anyone's* word. Sloane was always an excellent liar, as no doubt you are aware, and he has a tendency to, um, improvise. As I told you, I believe there is an insider at work here—"

"Surely you can't think Sloane is your turncoat!" Annabeth's cheeks flushed with anger. "He is the one who has risked his life finding that thing for you."

"It seems so, yes. But I have to point out that thrusting himself into the midst of the investigation is a good way to direct its course."

"Wait here," Annabeth said tightly, and left the room. She was not going to let Asquith suspect Sloane of wrongdoing just to protect her father's memory. Her grandmother would simply have to deal with the scandal of her father's accident if Asquith let it out. And, surely, Asquith would keep the information to himself, given his overriding dedication to secrecy.

Annabeth retrieved the key to the strong room from her grandmother's ornate Louis XIV secretary. One of Sloane's guards stood outside the room, and he looked doubtful when Annabeth asked him to move away from the door.

"Um, I don't know, miss…" he began. "Mr. Rutherford said not to let anyone in."

"He didn't mean me. This is my home, and what you're safeguarding belongs to me. If Mr. Rutherford complains, I'll speak to him."

His face brightened. "Yes, miss. Maybe I could go catch a bite of breakfast while you're here."

"Yes, of course." Annabeth unlocked the door and went inside. She didn't spare a glance for the extensive array of gold and silver plateware, but went straight to the safe in the wall and opened it.

When she returned to the drawing room, confession in hand, Mr. Asquith jumped up from his chair, looking as pleased as she supposed the man was capable of.

Asquith glanced at the single sheet of paper in her hand. "Just this? Was there nothing else?"

"Else? What do you mean?" she asked, confused. "Were we supposed to find something besides the confession?"

"I don't know. A note, perhaps? It could have been in code."

Annabeth shook her head. "No. There was nothing else." She paused. "Well, I didn't go through everything in my father's desk."

"His desk? But surely that had been searched."

"No, his portable writing desk. I didn't see anything else but blank paper and ink and such. I suppose there could have been something hidden, though. I didn't look all through it."

"Well," he said briskly. "We'll have to search it more thoroughly, then. But first, the confession." He reached out his hand, but Annabeth took a step back.

"Mr. Asquith…the information in here would be ruinous to my family if it got out."

"My dear Miss Winfield, I am already fully aware that your father was a traitor."

His words stung. Annabeth could feel herself flushing. "It's not just that he was a traitor. There was something else."

"I know all about that race, too, if that's what you mean. His killing that man," Asquith said impatiently, holding out his hand.

"Oh," Annabeth said with blank surprise. How did he know about the race?

Asquith stepped forward, plucked the confession from her hand, and began to read.

Annabeth watched him, frowning. Sloane had told her

that he and Asquith didn't know about the race. She was positive that Sloane hadn't known; his surprise had been too real. But apparently Asquith had known and simply hadn't told him. Sloane had said Asquith collected secrets, knew things about a large number of people. So it probably wasn't surprising that he'd discovered her father's secret.

But how had he done it? Who could have told Asquith about the race? Only the two men involved knew what had happened. Asquith wasn't a friend of her father's; Papa wouldn't have let it slip during an evening of drinking with him. Of course, the French had learned of it somehow and used it against her father, but it seemed implausible that her father or Russell would have let it slip to both the French and English spies.

Asquith nodded and looked up. "Good." His face was stamped with satisfaction. Or perhaps relief. Or both.

In that moment, looking into Asquith's eyes, she knew. It was Asquith. There was no turncoat in his organization. Rather, the turncoat was Asquith himself.

"Well," he said as he folded up the paper. "Now we can go on to question this suspect of yours. Who did you say it was?" He started to slip the folded paper inside his jacket, but Annabeth snatched it from his hands.

"I didn't say." She shoved the paper into her pocket. She wasn't going anywhere with Asquith.

"We can talk to him and then, I think, we should look again at that desk you mentioned," he said affably.

"It's very kind of you, but that is too much to ask. I'm sure you have many other things you need to do." *People to kill, countries to betray.*

"No, no, it's not a problem at all," he assured her.

"It would be my pleasure. Come, get your bonnet and let's go."

He reached out to take her arm, but she slid sideways to avoid him. "No, I've realized I should wait for Sloane. I should talk it over with him."

"Nonsense." Asquith's jaw tightened but he kept his jovial tone. "I promise you, I am better at this sort of thing than Sloane."

"I fear I feel a headache coming on," Annabeth lied. She didn't need any acting skills to look sick. "I should go upstairs and lie down to ward it off."

Asquith's eyes narrowed, and the amiability dropped from his face. She was certain he'd realized she had figured out his secret. In a hard voice, he said, "I insist."

"No. I have changed my mind. I'm staying here."

She turned away, but before she could take two steps, his hand wrapped around her arm like iron and he jerked her to a halt. Annabeth twisted to face him, trying with all her strength to pull her arm from his grasp.

Then she saw the small pistol in his other hand, leveled at her. "You're coming with me."

CHAPTER FORTY-ONE

SLOANE SAT AT his desk, writing. He had arisen far too early to make a call at Lady Lockwood's house, and he should give Annabeth some time to cool down…although he had the feeling that she would probably avoid him like the plague no matter how much time she had. His stomach tightened. Well, that was something he'd brought upon himself, and he'd find some way to deal with it. He was good at getting in where people didn't want him to go.

To pass the time, he had gone to his study to work. He needed to get these business matters out of the way, anyway. But he had worked only an hour when Antoine entered and said in his very un-butler-like way, "There's a man here to see you, boss. Fancy sort like your father."

Sloane's brows went up. "Like my father?"

"Yeah. Says his name is Russell some-English-name-I-can't-pronounce."

"Feringham?" What the devil was he doing here? Sloane felt a momentary quiver of doubt—had he been wrong to believe Feringham yesterday? He slid out the shallow middle drawer of his desk a fraction and casually rested his hand on the pistol inside. "Send him in."

Antoine disappeared, and a few moments later Russell came in the door, his manner tentative. Sloane took his hand off the pistol. If this was a man about to assassinate him, he probably deserved to be shot for being so clueless. "Feringham. Have a seat." He nodded toward the chair in front of his desk.

"This is probably nothing," Feringham began. "I hated to bother you, but… I had a good deal of trouble sleeping last night. I kept thinking about poor Hunter. And, anyway, I remembered this thing he gave me."

Sloane straightened. "What thing?"

"I can't see how it's important. But after you and Annabeth said that someone had killed Hunter, I thought about what you asked. Did I see anyone at Hunter's and was he acting oddly and all that. And I remembered that note."

"What note?"

"It was what Hunter said when he gave it to me that was odd. He said I should keep it, because it was protection. Or it would protect me or something like that. He said I was the person he trusted. I really can't remember his exact words. It was the same time he told me he was going to confess, you see, and that's what I was thinking about."

"Show me the note." Sloane stood up, leaning over the desk. "Did you bring it?"

"Oh, yes." Russell pulled out a small, torn sheet of paper and handed it to Sloane. "It's just a scrap of paper, really. I only kept it because it was the last time I saw him. It makes no sense. It's gibberish."

"It's code. A code I know." Sloane stared down at the paper, stunned. It was a terse command to send information about troop movements in Portugal. It was signed at the bottom, not with a name but with a drawing of an eight-legged creature, a drawing Sloane had seen many times. "Spider." *Asquith's code name.*

It was Asquith who had given instructions to Winfield. Asquith who was the French agent inside his own network. Asquith who had tried to harm Annabeth.

"I'm going to kill him." Sloane charged out of the house without a thought for Russell, standing openmouthed in his study. He hailed the nearest hackney. Asquith would be at his office.

No wonder Asquith had been so eager to find Hunter's confession. No wonder he hadn't wanted to hire Verity to begin with. Asquith must have been even more afraid when Sloane entered the picture. Perhaps Annabeth was right when she suggested the attacks had been on Sloane, not her. Asquith likely believed that without Sloane Annabeth wouldn't be able to find the document. Clearly he didn't know Annabeth. Sloane had no doubt that if he hadn't figured it out just now, she would have kept digging until she got to the bottom of it.

Asquith hadn't needed to have someone follow him and Annabeth to the Haverstocks' estate; he knew that Sloane was going to search Hunter's workshop. He may have believed that Annabeth was safe at Stonecliffe with Verity, and all he had to do to stop Sloane's investigation was lie in wait for him. It was possible, even likely, that Asquith might have searched the workshop before Sloane and Annabeth arrived and had been unable to find anything. Thank God they hadn't told Asquith they were going to question Hunter's valet, or Asquith might have wrested the desk away from Simpson before Sloane and Annabeth reached the man.

Sloane jumped out of the hack as soon as it stopped moving, shoving a payment in the driver's hand without looking, and ran into the building. Asquith's secretary popped up when Sloane strode down the hall toward Asquith's office. "Stop. You can't go in there."

Sloane ignored him, going straight to Asquith's door and turning the handle. It was locked. He swung back around to the secretary. "Do you have the key or shall I break the door?"

"I don't have the key, and it's pointless, anyway. Mr. Asquith is not in his office."

Sloane narrowed his eyes, wondering if the man was lying, and decided that he looked too smug for it not to be the truth. "Where is he?"

"I can't tell you that," the man protested.

"Think not?" Sloane reached over and grabbed the lapels of the secretary's coat, dragging him across the floor until they were eye to eye. The man twisted, trying to break Sloane's grasp, but he was unsuccessful. "You are going to tell me, one way or another," Sloane said in a low, calm voice made all the more frightening by his icy tone. "You might as well tell me now and save yourself some broken bones."

"I—I—he'll kill me."

"No, he won't. I am going to find him, and he won't be coming back here."

"I—he didn't tell me." But when Sloane grabbed the other man's neckcloth and twisted, he squeaked, "But I hailed his hack for him, and I heard him tell the driver Lady Lockwood's address."

Sloane's insides turned to ice. "Annabeth."

He whirled and ran.

CHAPTER FORTY-TWO

ASQUITH GRIPPED ANNABETH'S arm and dragged her toward the entry. Annabeth resisted, but she knew she could not escape him. On the other hand, it was unlikely that he would follow through on his threat to shoot her because he needed her to take him to Simpson. Had she told him about Simpson? Anger and fear were swirling inside her, fogging her memory. She had only mentioned the desk, but perhaps Sloane had said more in the note he'd sent Asquith yesterday. It didn't matter.

Either way Asquith needed her alive long enough to find out the location of the desk. Emboldened by the knowledge he wouldn't shoot, she twisted, launching herself at him and slamming into his chest. She slapped him as hard as she could, digging her nails into his face for good measure.

Fury gave extra force to her blows. "You killed him! You killed my father!" Annabeth hit him again, raking it over his eye so that he jumped back. Even if Asquith won this fight, he wouldn't be able to cover up these scratches. Sloane would figure out what had happened. She knew he would never give up on finding her.

Once he recovered from the surprise of her attack, Asquith tried to restrain her, but the gun in his hand impeded him, and Annabeth continued to hit and kick wildly. Her flailing arm hit his hand, and the gun went flying across the room. Asquith cursed, and Annabeth took advantage of his moment of distraction and jerked away from him. She ran and dove for the gun, but Asquith was on top of her in an instant.

They wrestled for the weapon, but he tore it from her grasp with such force that it sailed off again, slamming into the door frame and bouncing off onto the marble floor of the entry. The pistol went off, shattering a vase on the hall table, and spun to a stop at the stairs.

Asquith scrambled to his feet, yanking Annabeth up with him. One of his arms went around her waist, pinning her arms to her sides. She drew breath to yell, but then she felt a knifepoint against her neck, and she stopped.

"Shut up or I'll slice your throat."

"I can see where Sloane got his weapons-for-accessories sense of style," Annabeth said.

Asquith grunted. "Well, I haven't his appreciation of witty banter, so shut up. Let's go."

He started forward, releasing his hold around her waist and gripping her upper arm so that she was able to walk slowly. All the while he kept the tip of the knife against her neck.

There was a gasp and a quickly cutoff shriek down the hall behind them, and the butler exclaimed, "Miss!"

Annabeth could see a couple of maids now standing at the top of the stairs, looking shocked, and though she could not turn to see them, there must be some in the hallway behind them.

"Stop! Don't come any closer or Miss Winfield is dead," Asquith warned. He pressed the knifepoint against her to demonstrate. Annabeth felt the small sharp prick, and a drop of blood began to roll down her throat. "Get back, all of you, if you want to see her alive again."

The maids disappeared from the stairs, and there was a shuffle of retreating feet in the hall.

"Now. Start walking."

Annabeth did as he said, her steps slow.

"Faster," Asquith said harshly. "Don't try to stall."

"It's a trifle difficult to walk this way," Annabeth shot back.

"Maybe it would speed you up if I ran this knife down your cheek. It would make an unsightly scar."

Annabeth moved a little faster. "Sloane will never let you get away with this."

"Rutherford can—"

The front door slammed open, and Sloane charged in. He stopped dead when he saw Asquith and Annabeth in the entry. His eyes flickered briefly to the stairs and the hallway, taking in the whole scene.

"Well. It certainly appears the pistol came out the victor in the duel with that vase," he said dryly. His gaze went back to Asquith.

"Spare me your quips in the face of danger," Asquith growled. "I know you."

"Then you know what will happen to you if you don't let go of Annabeth." Sloane's voice was as cold and hard as his eyes.

"You don't scare me, Rutherford."

"Mmm. More fool you, I'd say. I'll give you this one chance, *Spider*. Release her and I won't stop you leaving."

Asquith's lip curled. "Get out of my way or I'll cut her throat."

"You do, and you won't make it out of here alive."

"You really think you can take me on, boy?"

"I think you don't want to find out."

"What is all this racket?" A stentorian voice came from above them, punctuated by a wheezing bark, and Lady Lockwood appeared at the top of the stairs. "How is one supposed to sleep with all this banging and shouting going on?"

Asquith turned at the sound, but his knife never wavered from Annabeth's throat. Sloane took advantage of the distraction to turn and run back out of the house.

"There's your brave lad who's 'not going to let me get away with this.' Cut and ran first chance he got." Asquith let out a crack of laughter. "I knew it from the beginning. That's why I got him. I knew he was one of those wild, silly aristocratic boys, full of bravado, knowing nothing."

"You blackmailed him into working for you because you thought he was useless?" Annabeth had no idea what Sloane had planned, but she knew that she must try to slow Asquith down in order to give Sloane time for whatever it was.

"He was a dupe," Asquith said smugly. "Hiring him provided a pretense of carrying out my duties, and I could blame the failures on his incompetence. I could send messages and know they wouldn't get there, lure agents into rendezvousing with him."

"So, in other words, your plan was a failure."

"Nonsense."

"Admit it. You chose the wrong wild aristocratic boy. Sloane turned out to be too good. He delivered the messages and escaped your traps, rescued his fellow agents."

"He never had an inkling of what I was doing."

"No doubt it would surprise him to hear that he was

too honest and trustworthy to see the snake you really were."

"Shut up. Start walking."

Annabeth did as Asquith said, searching for something to distract him. "I don't know what you hope to accomplish. You use the threat of killing me, but you can't actually do that because you need me to take you to Papa's writing desk. Of course, you'll have no use for me afterward and will doubtless kill me, but you have kidnapped me in front of all these witnesses. Everyone will know what you are and what you did, so you will have to leave the country."

"I have a villa in Greece. I have nothing to worry about."

"Except for wondering when Sloane will track you down and what terrible thing he will do to you."

Asquith snorted. "Sloane won't come after me. He just took off and left you here to die."

"Not exactly," Sloane said coolly from behind Asquith. The pistol in his hand was pressed into Asquith's skull. "A wild aristocrat always knows his way around the servants' entrance."

"I'll slice her artery before you can fire," Asquith said. Annabeth felt his hand tremble on the knife and hoped he wouldn't accidentally cut her.

"You think you can?" Sloane asked. "Do you really want to test that? I'm younger than you and faster than you, and I haven't spent the last twelve years sitting in an office. This ball will do very nasty things to your brain."

Asquith broke and ran, shoving Annabeth aside. Sloane reached out a hand to steady her as Asquith scrambled for the door, his expensive shoes slipping across the marble entryway.

"I'm fine," Annabeth reassured Sloane, waving him on. "Go. Catch him."

He gave a terse nod and ran after Asquith, launching himself at the man as he reached for the doorknob. Sloane's left shoulder hit Asquith square in the chest, and Asquith let out a huff of air as they crashed into the door, knocking over the umbrella stand.

Sloane recovered first and drew back his fist, hitting the other man in the face. Asquith's eyes looked hazy for a second, but he quickly shook off the haze and stomped his foot down hard on the top of Sloane's instep. Sloane sent a powerful uppercut to the bottom of his opponent's chin. This time Asquith's eyes fluttered closed, and he slid to the ground, unconscious.

Cartwell and a footman rushed in, twine in hand, and proceeded to tie up Asquith. Another footman scooped up the pistol. Sloane swung around and strode across the entry to Annabeth. He pulled her into a fierce embrace, holding her as if he would never let her go.

"I knew you would come," Annabeth said, her arms wrapped just as tightly around him.

"Always, my love." Sloane kissed the top of her head. "Always."

"Well," Lady Lockwood said from above them, holding a barking Petunia and looking down disapprovingly at the mess. "I hope this means this business is over now. All this breaking in and brawling about is getting rather tiresome. That was my favorite Meissen vase. People nowadays simply have no sense of proper behavior."

CHAPTER FORTY-THREE

SLOANE LEFT THE house with the bound and groggy Asquith. Lady Lockwood decided that her nerves were shattered and retired to her bedroom. The servants swept up the mess in the hall. And Annabeth collapsed on a sofa in the drawing room, her legs suddenly too shaky to stand.

It was only a few minutes before Verity arrived at the house. Bypassing the maids sweeping the entry, she continued into the drawing room. "What happened here?"

"Mr. Asquith tried to kill me, and Sloane stopped him."

It was rather satisfying to see Verity's jaw drop in astonishment. Annabeth went on to explain what had happened, and by the end of the tale, Verity dropped down in a chair as well, stunned. "That twisted, deceitful, murderous blackguard. He was a thoroughly dislikable person, but I thought at least that he was loyal to the Crown. But…this does make some sense, given what I learned this morning."

"What is that?"

"When Sloane and I went to speak with Asquith on our own, he said a French spy had told him about your father's confession. It was what Asquith said set off the search for the document."

"Yes."

"Well, it turns out that spy was caught and interrogated by Asquith several years ago, not recently. No one else questioned the suspect because he died while in Asquith's custody."

"How convenient."

Nathan walked in a few minutes later, and Annabeth went through her explanation again, this time punctuated by furious epithets from Verity, who had taken to pacing the room.

"That's wonderful!" Nathan exclaimed. "It's over now, and you're safe." He went to Annabeth, smiling, and sat down beside her. "I am so very happy for you." He took her hand and squeezed it gently. "Truly. I am."

"I know. You are the kindest of men," Annabeth replied.

"And your friend," he told her, then added, with a little twinkle in his eye, "Though I hope you won't mind if I flirt with you a little now and then, just to annoy Sloane."

Annabeth laughed. "No. I won't mind. If, of course, Sloane is still around."

"He will be," Nathan and Verity said at the same time.

"Did I hear my name?" Sloane strode into the room.

"You did." Annabeth rose, smiling, and went to him. She wanted to wrap her arms around him but managed to restrain herself, only taking his hand.

Nathan said lightly, "We were laying bets on whether Lady Lockwood will praise you for rescuing Annabeth or excoriate you for making a mess in her entryway."

"The day I hear Lady Lockwood praise me is the day I'll know I've lost my mind," Sloane replied. He strolled back to the sofa with Annabeth, not letting go of her hand.

"Where did you take Asquith?" Annabeth asked.

"The proper authorities."

"What does that mean?" Annabeth frowned. "Jail?"

Verity snorted. "You'd have to have somebody higher than a magistrate to take care of Asquith."

"Then what's going to happen to him?" Nathan asked. "Surely the government won't just cover this up."

Sloane shrugged. "They'd certainly prefer this story didn't get out. It would look rather bad to have had a traitor in charge of one's spying operation for fifteen years. I'm sure they would have preferred it to be you, Verity, as Asquith tried to convince us."

"Tried?" Verity cocked an eyebrow. "The way I remember it, you were all quite suspicious of me."

"You'll be pleased to hear that Dunbridge didn't believe you were guilty of any wrongdoing," Sloane told Verity.

"You defended me?" Verity looked over at Nathan, her expression startled. "Why?"

"Because I didn't think you were the sort of person to betray either your country or your friends," Nathan replied. "I could hardly stand by and hear you slandered. Why does that surprise you?"

"Because you're a 'gentleman,'" she answered.

Nathan stared at her for a moment, then shook his head. "Clearly you and I have different ideas of what a gentleman is."

"One of *them*, I mean—an aristocrat. I—well…" Verity paused, a little flustered, her cheeks turning pink. "Thank you." Quickly Verity turned her gaze to Sloane, as though eager to escape the present topic. "So are you saying the Foreign Office is just going to bury the whole thing?"

"They can't let treason go unpunished. I would guess if he confesses to murdering Mr. Winfield, the rest of it won't be spoken of. We haven't any evidence proving Asquith was the murderer, just a traitor. Only a confession from him would seal it. But I think they will be able to get that out of him."

"Why would he confess to murder if he's already been arrested for treason?" Annabeth asked. "Don't they hang murderers, too?"

"Yes, they hang for both offenses, but murder is less of a stain on one's name, and the government can commute a death sentence to a life in prison. If he won't agree to that…" Sloane shrugged.

"He'll have an unfortunate fatal accident in jail," Verity said, completing the thought.

"I see. Did he tell you anything? Why he did all this?" Annabeth asked.

"Greed, I think, was the motivation at the start. As for why he was looking for the confession now, apparently several years ago a former French spy claimed he had it and tried to blackmail Asquith with it, which did not work out well for him."

"That's the spy I learned died suspiciously in his cell while under Asquith's watch," Verity added.

"Yes." Sloane nodded. "But when Asquith searched the man's flat, he couldn't find any confession. Since he felt he'd gotten rid of the problem, he did nothing else."

"Until I started clearing out my father's old things from the town house?" Annabeth asked.

"Then Asquith became worried and decided to send someone to look for the confession," Sloane finished.

"But why did he hire Verity to find it?" Nathan asked. "She would have found out the truth about him."

"He didn't hire me," Verity answered. "He hired a man outside the agency, and I got the job through him. Asquith was furious, I'm sure."

Sloane looked over at Verity. "It was you who was supposed to be kidnapped, not Annabeth. Annabeth threw herself into the fight, though, so they took both of you."

"But why was he trying to kill me?" Annabeth asked. "Clearly I was not the same kind of threat as you or Verity."

"In fact, you were right, Annabeth, about all the attacks being meant for me. Frankly, I think Asquith would have been happy to have me killed even without the issue of the confession. He hates me almost as much as I hate him."

"Because he thought you would be an easy pawn in his scheme, and instead you turned out to be too good at your job," Annabeth said.

"He was concerned that I might realize that he was double-crossing us. Unfortunately, I apparently am not as smart as he thought."

"I didn't realize it either," Verity said. "I suppose Asquith was also the one who betrayed us all those times during the war."

Sloane nodded. "Apparently Winfield was the only one that was aware of the true traitorous nature of Asquith. Hunter even kept an order from Asquith for information about British troops in Portugal. It was written in code." He looked over at Verity.

"Our code?" she asked.

"Yes. And it was signed with a drawing of a spider. Feringham brought me that note this morning. Hunter gave it to Russell not long before he was killed. That's when I realized Asquith was behind this."

"I still don't understand why he would have killed my father. He wasn't involved in spying anymore. You had gotten him out of the whole mess unscathed." Annabeth squeezed Sloane's hand.

"Asquith had continued to keep tabs on him," Sloane said slowly. "Unfortunately, the man who was following Hunter overheard Mr. Winfield tell Russell that he was going to confess. It seems that Asquith mistakenly thought he was naming his spymaster in his confession."

Annabeth's eyes filled with tears. "But he didn't. He didn't incriminate anyone but himself."

Sloane squeezed Annabeth and she let herself melt into him—not caring about Nathan or Verity or impropriety. There was nothing to be said that would make the injustice of it all seem better, but she found some comfort in Sloane's arms.

"Even in his last days, though, Hunter wanted to protect you and Martha and Russell. That's why he gave Feringham that note. He said if there was ever trouble that he could use it as proof if he needed it."

"That's what Asquith was talking about," Annabeth said. "When I gave him the confession, he asked me if there was anything else. I thought it was peculiar, and then he told me that he knew about Papa's racing, and that's when I started to suspect him. How *did* he know about that, anyway?"

"He knew more secrets than you can imagine," Verity said. "He had informers all over the place—barkeeps, tavern maids, servants, in gentlemen's clubs, gambling dens. He paid them or used some secret he knew about them to get them to spy on others. His name was very accurate. He was a spider with a web of secrets all around him."

Silence fell on the room, and they glanced at one another. There seemed nothing else to say.

"Well," Verity said after a moment, rising to her feet. "That's that, then. It's over."

"Yes. I suppose it is." Sloane nodded.

"I, um, I think I will go upstairs and pack then." She paused. "It feels a little odd, leaving here."

Annabeth stood up as well. "I will miss you."

To her surprise, Verity hugged her. "I will miss you, too." She turned around, and her gaze went to Nathan. "Not you, of course. Although it will be a bit lacking, not having someone to peck at."

"Indeed. I shall doubtless miss your barbs as well," Nathan said dryly.

"But perhaps we'll run into each other somewhere." She grinned. "You never know where I might show up."

Verity left the room, and Nathan, after a glance at the two of them, took his leave as well. Annabeth looked at Sloane for a moment. She had so many things she had planned to say to him earlier, before they had both almost been killed. But now they seemed too small, too inadequate to describe the immensity of her feelings.

And then suddenly she was in his arms, kissing him, as his arms pulled tight around her. She knew it said more than her words ever could.

"Anna… Anna…" Sloane planted light kisses all over her face and burrowed his face into her neck. "I was so scared. When I came in and saw you with Asquith's knife at your throat, I thought it was all over, and I'd never even told you…" His mouth took hers again.

She pulled her lips away to kiss his cheek, his jaw, his neck. Her hands dug into his shoulders. "Told me what?"

"How much I love you. How much I want to marry you. How my life would be unbearable if you weren't in it."

"I'll always be in it," she said in a low, fierce voice, stepping back a bit to look into his eyes. "You cannot chase me away no matter how much you try. If you think I would let a little thing like your rejection yesterday keep me from you, you are wrong."

He smiled down at her, smoothing his hand over her hair. "You've turned into a proper little bulldog these last few years."

"What a thing to call the woman you say you love." She grinned back at him, her insides fizzing with happiness.

"I love you in every way you can be. Stubborn, angry, happy, sad—it doesn't matter," Sloane told her. "I was yours the day I met you, and I always have been. I always will be. All those years without you, I was a shell of a man. I volunteered for the most dangerous jobs, took idiotic risks. I didn't care if I was killed. Because without you I was already dead inside."

"Oh, Sloane." Annabeth's eyes filled with tears, and she went up on tiptoe to kiss him. "I was just as miserable. I hated that you weren't with me. I thought about you, dreamed about you. Sometimes I thought I *would* go mad from missing you. I believed that you had lied to me, that you were a traitor—yet still I couldn't stop loving you."

Sloane pulled her close, holding her as if he would never let her go. Finally Annabeth pulled back, her expres-

sion turning quizzical. "What brought about this trans-
formation? I'm very glad, mind you, but yesterday—"

"Yesterday I was a fool. It was my father who made
me realize it."

"Marcus?"

"Yes. Boggles the mind, doesn't it? He told me you
were right. I was scared. A fool who was running away
from the one thing he wanted more than anything else
in all the world. I went for a walk and thought about my
life, and I saw that all the barriers around me, the things
that made it impossible for me to marry you, were walls
that I had thrown up myself. I have no reason to skate
along the edges of the law, no reason to create enemies
for myself."

He stepped back, letting out a long breath. "I have
plenty of money. I'm giving up any smuggling. I'm sell-
ing my clubs and taverns to Parker."

"Parker!"

"Yes. I went to see him last night."

"What? You just walked into his house? You could
have been killed."

Sloane shrugged. "I suppose. But I counted on Parker
being more interested in money than in having me in
the ground. We have an agreement. He gets the clubs
and taverns. I keep my warehouses and my shipping
business—the legal goods. He can take up the protection of the docks—within limits. He agrees not to coerce
other businesses into hiring him. He provides watchmen
and guards for the businesses. And he charges a reasonable fee for it. Breaking any of those rules invalidates
the contract."

"You did all that so you could marry me?"

"I'd do a hell of a lot more than that. Giving up a few

businesses is very little in comparison. I don't need danger. I don't need money. All I need is you. Annabeth, will you marry me?"

Annabeth gazed up at him, her eyes filling with tears. "Yes. Of course, yes." With an impish grin, she added, "And I don't know how you can call yourself a spy if you don't already know that."

"I know." He grinned. "I just wanted to hear you say it."

"You." She gave him a playful push. "Then you know that I would marry you tomorrow."

To her surprise, Sloane shook his head. "No. No elopement. No special license. We'll wait and have the banns. Our wedding will be proper."

"Well…" Annabeth stepped back, her eyes twinkling mischievously. "If you *really* want our wedding to be proper, we should be engaged for a year before we marry."

"No," Sloane retorted. "I said I wanted a proper wedding. I didn't say I was a saint." He paused, then, looking faintly alarmed, he added, "Please tell me I don't have to get your grandmother's permission to marry you."

"I make my own decisions. And I choose you."

Annabeth threw her arms around his neck and kissed him. She was his. And he was hers. Bonded long ago in a cord that could not break.

"It's fate," she murmured.

"It's love," he answered.

* * * * *

ACKNOWLEDGMENTS

MUCH OF WRITING is a solitary job, but the finished book is very much a collaboration and would not be possible without the efforts of many people. I'm beyond grateful to my editor, Lynn Raposo, whose dedication, attention to detail, and insightful guidance made *A Rogue at Stonecliffe* a better book. I also owe a debt of gratitude to the whole team at Canary Street Press—from the copy editors, who catch my mistakes, to the art department for their lovely covers, and, finally, to the marketing department, who help get my books in the hands of each of you lovely readers.

Many thanks to my wonderful agent, Maria Carvainis, for all her support throughout the years, and to Martha Guzman at the Maria Carvainis Agency, who answers all my questions.

And last, but certainly not least, I want to thank Anastasia Hopcus. I could not have written *A Rogue at Stonecliffe* without her. Working with Anastasia on the Stonecliffe series has been an absolute joy.

Keep reading for a sneak peek at the next exciting Stonecliffe novel

A Scandal at Stonecliffe

coming in 2024 from Canary Street Press!

"VERITY…" NATHAN SAID in alarm, taking Verity's arm and steering her toward a secluded corner near the side door of the ballroom. "Why are you pretending to be… whoever it is you're pretending to be?"

"A wealthy widow," she supplied. "Mrs. Billingham."

He cast his gaze down at the neckline of her dress, which skimmed across the top of her full breasts. "That's scarcely what I'd call mourning." He went on in an irritated voice, "And your hair is red." *Well, that was a perfectly idiotic thing to say*, Nathan thought.

"Yes, it is." Verity's voice brimmed with amusement. "Honestly, Nathan, you sound as if the color of my hair offends you."

"No. Of course not." He wasn't about to tell her how far from offended he was by the sight of her hair. "It's just…one never knows what's real with you and what is not."

"Well, my hair is red, and I cannot disguise the color of my eyes, so you see me as I am. Except for the jewels, of course." She touched the diamond studs in her ears. "They are as false as my name."

Nathan gritted his teeth. "What the devil are you doing here in the first place?"

"Stealing a jewel," Verity replied, and slipped out the door.

"Verity! Wait. Come ba— Oh, the devil." Nathan followed her, catching up to her in the corridor. "Have you lost your wits? Someone is going to catch you."

"Well, yes, if you keep nattering on like this," Verity told him.

There were a few people scattered around the hall. As they passed the others, Verity moved closer, her hand slipping into the crook of Nathan's elbow, and raised her fan to send him a laughing look over it.

Those eyes...

"Stop pretending to flirt with me," he snapped.

"Who says I'm pretending?" Verity flashed him a teasing smile.

Nathan felt his heartbeat speed up; it was damned difficult not to react as if that subtle, seductive quirk of her lips was real.

Of course, *she* wasn't wrestling with distraction; she seemed firmly on task. Her fingers dug into Nathan's arm, and she started up the grand staircase.

"What are you doing?" Nathan hissed. "The family's private rooms are upstairs."

Verity touched her fingers to his mouth, stopping his speech. She was wearing lace evening gloves, and the texture of the lace felt odd—and somehow tantalizing—against his lips. He could feel the heat of her skin beneath the lace.

"Shh," she whispered, casting a glance behind them at the three people standing in the entry. "That's why I'm going there. Arden's safe is in his bedroom."

"Verity, really." Nathan tried to protest but let her pull him along. He had to do what he could to keep Verity from getting into trouble. He might be able to talk himself out of it if they were caught, but he actually *was* who he said he was and a well-known member of London Society, whereas Verity was…anything but that. Still, he couldn't deny a little thrill of excitement as they sneaked up the stairs.

The corridor on the floor above was empty, and Verity hurried through it, looking into the darkened rooms as she went. When there was the sound of voices on the stairs behind them, Verity grabbed Nathan's lapels and yanked him to her so hard that they stumbled back against the wall. "Seduce me."

"What?" Nathan's eyebrows shot up.

"Shh!" Verity hissed. "*Pretend*, Nathan. As if you want me in your bed."

Well, that wouldn't be difficult, pressed against her this way. Nathan braced his forearm against the wall and half turned to shield her from the view of whoever was climbing the staircase. He lowered his head, bending toward her and setting his other hand on her waist. "Wonderful," he groused. "Now everyone will say I'm a lecher."

"More acceptable than everyone saying you're a thief."

Verity curled one hand around the back of Nathan's neck, and a frisson shot down his spine like a bolt of lightning. Heaven help him, she smelled good. It wasn't the bold, provocative fragrance he would have expected her to wear, but a light, elusive floral scent that was somehow even more stirring to his senses.

They were so close he could see each individual eyelash, the smooth texture of her skin, the curve of her lips. He had a mad urge to trace that curve with his finger. Her supple body was molded to him all the way down, and he had the embarrassed certainty that Verity could feel his body move in response to her. There was a little glimmer in her eyes that he knew was amusement.

To avoid Verity's gaze, Nathan pressed his cheek to the side of her head. Her hair was soft, a few fine stray hairs tickling his nose. He slid his head down and found that her cheek was as soft and smooth as it looked. He stopped short of her shoulder so that he would appear to be nuzzling her neck. He resisted the temptation to actually press his lips to her skin.

The voices had been growing louder, but now they stopped abruptly. There was the distinct sound of a snicker and someone clearing his throat, followed by a low murmur of voices.

"Are they coming this way?" Nathan whispered.

"Hmm? Oh." Verity shifted so that she could see around his arm. "They're just standing there grinning."

He let out a little huff of exasperation. "How long do we have to keep this up?"

"I know it must be a trial to be this close to me," she told him tartly. "Perhaps I should end the scene by slapping you for making improper advances."

"I'd rather you not." Nathan managed not to add that the only trial was not acting on his impulses. Continuing the pretense but removing himself somewhat from danger, he straightened and cupped her face in his hands, gazing down at her. Her eyes were fascinating, somewhere between amber and whiskey and always alight, whether it was with amusement or anger or curiosity.

"Or maybe we should slip off the other direction and go into a bedroom," Verity suggested.

"Verity." Nathan sighed. "They may have recognized you. Your reputation would be in tatters."

"No. *Mrs. Billingham's* reputation would be in tatters." Her eyes sparkled. "Ah. There they go." An instant later, she added, "We're safe."

Nathan relaxed, realizing only now how taut his entire body had been. He moved away, tugging at his lapels as if he could pull himself back in order if his clothes were straight. "I'd hardly say we're safe."

"Of course you wouldn't." Verity seemed—as usual—irritated with him. She started away. "You needn't stay, you know."

He fell in beside her. "Ah, but then who would you have to play your wicked seducer?"

Verity made a show of rolling her eyes, but the corner of her mouth deepened into a dimple. And her dimple was lethal. "In that case, I suppose I must keep you."

A Scandal at Stonecliffe
by Candace Camp
coming in 2024 from Canary Street Press!

HARLEQUIN
PLUS

Try the best multimedia subscription service for romance readers like you!

Read, Watch and Play.

Experience the easiest way to get the romance content you crave.

Start your **FREE TRIAL** at
www.harlequinplus.com/freetrial.